The Shield

A Novel by
Nachman Kataczinsky

This is a work of fiction. Any references to historical events, real people, real locales, businesses and incidents are the products of the author's imagination or used in a fictitious manner.

First printing: May 2014
Second edition: June 2014

ISBN-13: 978-1499630541
ISBN-10: 1499630549
BISAC: Fiction / Science Fiction / Time Travel

Rank Armor Publishing
www.TheShield.RankArmor.com

To my wife Minda -
You are my inspiration and a great editor.

In memory of my parents who survived the real horrors and in
memory of those who did not.

Chapter 1

Professor Wisotzky was in a difficult position: how do you tell your most gifted student and research assistant that his latest idea was crazy?

"Arye, what you propose is impossible. Your equations are strange and the whole thing is a waste of time. Let's continue with your thesis. It is much more productive."

Arye Kidron was prepared for a skeptical or even hostile response to his presentation and was not discouraged. Yitzhak Wisotzky was a highly respected physicist and professor at the Physics department of the Technion, Israel's most prestigious university. But at 64 years of age he was not as open to new ideas as he might have been thirty years earlier. Arye, on the other hand, was bursting with new concepts and at age 32 was eager to do something new. His doctoral thesis was moderately interesting, but this new idea was a bomb.

"Yitzhak, please take at least some time to check my calculations. Shouldn't take you more than an hour. If you find a serious error, I promise to shut up about this."

"Sure you will, until the next great idea, and anyway, I did go through them already. There are two constants you assume – these are vital to your calculation of quantum vacuum energy. If you are wrong, the whole thing is worthless."

"You're not saying that I am wrong though?" Arye was smiling. He knew his old teacher: If something was seriously wrong with his theory, Yitzhak Wisotzky would say so up front and not have this whole discussion. There was hope yet!

"I'm not saying that you're wrong, but we have no proof that you are right either."

"So, why not set up an experiment and see?"

"Because we don't have the money to do that. It would take your salary for the next ten years."

That was a *very* good sign. The old professor had an estimate of the cost of an experiment that agreed with his own. Maybe they could find the money.

***

"Gadi, it is time to go. You promised to be at the Technion not later than 1600 hours." Lieutenant General Gad Yaari got up from behind his desk, stretched and smiled at his secretary. His compact, lean frame did not show how tired he was; his angular face betrayed some of the exhaustion, but not much. At 52 he was in good physical shape and was used to working around the clock, if necessary, and under a lot of pressure. Not having slept much in the past several nights did not help but was bearable. What was much more difficult to deal with was the task he was given by the government: to protect Israel from a possible nuclear attack. A preventive strike was an option, but one the government really did not like. Lately Gadi was devoting a lot of his time to this problem. He looked forward to some sleep and the hour and a half drive to Haifa would offer that opportunity. Except he had to catch up on some paperwork.

"OK, Liat. Let's go. Please take the stuff I need to work on, especially that combat readiness analysis."

Major Liat Cohen nodded. She had worked as Gadi's assistant since he was the Commanding General of the Southern Command, and that was more than six years ago. She knew him well and anticipated his requests. He never used orders with her, though it was just his style of doing things, and nobody who knew him, even superficially, would ever contemplate not obeying his polite "requests".

In the car Gadi read and signed operational reports and tried to read a long analysis of reserve troop training and operational readiness. He fell asleep in the middle of it. Liat did not wake him until they arrived at the Physics building of the Technion Institute of Technology Mount Carmel campus.

***

"Shalom, Gadi. Good to see you again."

Professor Wisotzky smiled. He had liked Gad Yaari in his student days. Yaari had been interested in physics even though budding electronics engineers like him usually did not mix with theoretical physics. Wisotzky also appreciated Gadi's selflessness, or maybe it should be called patriotism. Gadi had a promising civilian career ahead of him but had decided to re-enlist. The almost national disaster of the latest war convinced him that he was needed by his country. He had also devoted time to convincing others to re-enlist. He was not successful with Arye Kidron, who was immersed too deeply in his strange quantum world.

"Shalom, Professor. Shalom, Arye."

"Hi, Chief," Kidron responded.

"Anything interesting for me to see today?"

The professor nodded at Arye, "It's your show, so go ahead."

Liat looked at her watch. "Please be as brief as possible. The Chief has to leave in about forty minutes."

Arye Kidron gathered his thoughts for a moment. "We started this experiment as a proof of a theory that could lead to a supply of cheap and abundant Zero Point Energy, you know, quantum vacuum energy."

"I didn't think this theory was ever proven," remarked Gad Yaari.

"That was the point of designing an experiment that would prove Arye's newest idea. I have to admit that this one seems less insane than his other endeavors," added Professor Wisotzky with a smile.

"Anyway, a funny thing happened on the way to get energy from vacuum. I'm not sure that our benefactors at the Ministry of Industry and Infrastructure will be happy, but we may yet get there," Arye continued. "As it happens, I hope I found a way to make this project attractive to you. Then we'll classify it as Top Secret and the money guys will never bother us again."

Yaari smiled: "I can't agree unless you show me what it is that I am supposed to hide behind a curtain of military secrecy."

"OK. Here goes."

Arye led them to the far end of the lab. On a simple Formica office desk a rabbit was loudly munching on lettuce, blinking at the visitors through the chicken wire of his cage. Behind the desk was a thick block of wood. Arye placed a two inch translucent cube at each of the four bottom corners of the cage and a similar but opaque cube on top. A pair of wires was attached to the top cube. He withdrew a .22 caliber pistol from a drawer.

"Chief, it is quite predictable what will happen to this rabbit if I shoot it with this gun. Even I can't miss at point blank range. Now watch."

He pushed a button on a box that was connected to the wires from the cube and plugged into a wall outlet. The translucent cubes lit up with a rainbow of colors and disappeared. Yaari thought that the rabbit shimmered for a split second, but that could have been an illusion.

Arye Kidron carefully aimed his gun, though at a distance of one foot it was hardly necessary, and fired it into the rabbit. The animal did not even blink and kept working on his lettuce. The bullet was lodged in the wood directly behind it. Kidron extended the gun to the General. "If you'd like to try it yourself..."

Yaari took the small Beretta and fired the rest of the rounds in the magazine. The rabbit was still chewing.

"Assuming this is not a simple magician's trick, what happened just now?"

Arye pushed the button again. The translucent cubes popped out of thin air and were again at the corners of the cage. Another push of the button, and they disappeared again. Another push and they reappeared.

"Every time I push the button and the cubes disappear, they and the space enclosed by them go slightly out of phase with our space. I am not entirely sure why we can still see the rabbit, but the guy seems to be unaffected by the field. He stays out of phase until a second pulse pushes him back into our reality. As long as he is out of phase he cannot be harmed by anything we do. He can do nothing to us either. You may notice that we even don't hear him munching on the lettuce."

The Chief of General Staff stayed at the lab for much longer than his planned forty minutes. He did not get much sleep that night either, but when he finally went to bed he slept like a rock. He was awakened the next evening by his wife Yael.

"Liat is on the line. She says it's urgent."

Yael never asked why things were urgent and what the callers wanted. After thirty years of marriage she knew that her husband had a burden that only he could carry. There would be no sharing of his professional life.

"Chief, the Prime Minister will see you in two hours."

Chapter 2

Amos Nir woke up suddenly. Even though many years had passed since he had served in the Special Forces, he still had the ability to come up from a deep sleep in an instant. He was in his late fifties, a tall, thin, man with a full head of grey hair and an even temperament. He was relatively new to politics – his youth had been spent in the armed forces. In his early thirties he quit the service and continued his education in history and political science, while working as a manager at a financial firm. By the time he decided that Israeli politics needed to be managed somewhat better, his three children, two sons and a daughter were past their army service and he himself was 46. Amos joined the center-right party and due to his charismatic personality and leadership abilities rose quickly through the organization. It took him close to ten years to become the leader of his party, and two years ago, when the party won an election and formed a coalition government, he became Prime Minister.

The telephone was ringing. The *red* phone. He looked at his bedside clock – three in the morning. Who was calling at this ungodly hour? These days he slept much better and was not as stressed out as he had been only a year ago. The coalition was stable and, except for the usual political squabbling and maneuvering, everything was quiet. It was his third year as Prime Minister and he no longer had to anticipate a nuclear war. Now if it happened they had The Shield.

"Yes, Amos speaking."

"Mr. Prime Minister," said Gad Yaari, "the Shield has been activated. I already told the Defense Minister."

"Come to my house now. I'll call the other members of the Defense Cabinet." Amos Nir hung up the phone and after a short pause called his secretary.

"Moshe, contact the members of the Defense Cabinet and tell them to come to my house now. Some will give you a hard time at three in the morning. Just tell them that I expect them within thirty minutes. If anybody asks questions, tell them that this is the Prime Minister's order."

The secretary knew better than to ask any questions himself. Something important must have happened for the Defense Cabinet to be called to a meeting so early in the morning. It was only the second time in his long service as the Prime Minister's secretary that a P.M. issued an order to the Defense Cabinet. This could not be good.

"Lady and gentlemen," Amos said when everybody was seated at his dining table, "I am sorry to have you come here so early. We have a problem that can't wait. We need to decide very soon what to do. I will let the Chief of General Staff brief you first."

The five members of the Defense Cabinet included the Ministers of Defense, Finance, Foreign Affairs, Industry/Infrastructure and Internal Security. Everyone was equipped by now with a cup of coffee (tea in the case of the Industry Minister) and ready to listen.

"Moshe, please leave us. There will be no minutes taken of this meeting." Moshe Ashkenazi, the PM's secretary, left the room and closed the door behind him.

"Gadi, go ahead."

"All of you know about the David's Shield project. It was completed about eight months ago and tested for the duration of about five seconds. At the time, we judged that such a short activation would go unnoticed. We were right. A little before two forty in the morning our radar picked up a ballistic missile launch from the Tabriz area in Iran. It was traveling in our direction. The Arrow system picked it up about three hundred kilometers northeast of our border with Syria and predicted its point of impact somewhere in the western Galilee, in the Haifa area. At that point in time, an Arrow missile was launched to intercept. Interception occurred about fifty kilometers northeast of the Syrian border, twenty kilometers south of Damascus. The missile was destroyed. The Shield system picked up an increase in gamma emissions and activated. We are now analyzing the radiation data and should know within ten minutes, " He looked at his watch. "No, about now - if the levels are safe. As far as we can tell it is safe but we will know…"

The telephone rang. Amos picked it up, listened and gave the receiver to the general.

"Yaari here."

"Gadi, we are done with the system data analysis. The missile was destroyed far enough away not to pose a danger to our most outlying positions. It did not detonate, but radioactive materials it was carrying were probably dispersed over an area large enough to trigger the Shield. It should be safe to turn the Shield off." The Chief of Military Intelligence paused. He obviously had something else to say. Yaari waited patiently. Zvi Kaplan had an exceptional intuition for the unusual. He could see patterns where others would often miss them.

Finally his voice came back on the line: "There is something you need to know. I don't know the significance yet, but it is very strange. Our optical observers see no fires on the other side. This blast should have ignited at least some brush fires, but we see only empty land. Another strangeness is that Quneitra seems to be intact and occupied by civilians. Nobody on the other side seems to have noticed the activation or the blast. And the Gaza posts report that the area is mostly dark."

"Thanks Zvi. Let me know if you discover anything else." Yaari hung up.

He reported the conversation to the others.

The P.M. looked at each of the five attendees. "Any suggestions or ideas?"

"I have a question," the Finance Minister said. She was a slim, petite woman in her early fifties, good-natured and quick to smile – definite assets for a Finance Minister. She was also one of the best economists in Israel and a successful business woman.

"The way I understand it, the Shield is not really a shield; rather we are out of phase with reality and have to be pushed back by a second activation. Am I correct?"

It was Gad Yaari who answered. "Yes, you are. We can't stay like this indefinitely. Eventually we will run out of food and fuel. Our reserves are good for several months and, for some items only several weeks, so, as regrettable as it may be we have to return to the real world."

"We can gather some intelligence while we are out of phase," the Minister of Defense suggested. "Let's send a reconnaissance mission and take a look at the world. The planes shouldn't be picked up by radar. They're out of phase as well and will remain so until we activate the Shield again." Being a retired general himself, Nitzan Liebler usually made sense in military matters, though he tended to favor the use of excessive force. He was 62, medium height, bald and powerfully built. Having retired from the armed forces he, like many ex-military, went into politics and served as a minister in several coalition governments. He was close to Amos, though he belonged to a different party – what the Prime Minister jokingly called "The crazy friendly right wing".

"I suggest that we send several planes to see what is going on. We will meet here in three hours and decide what to do next. I don't think that we can stay in this strange state for much longer – the world will notice and we'll blow our most effective secret weapon." Amos looked at the others for comments. When none came, he announced the meeting closed, but not before warning everybody to keep quiet about the Shield and the subject of the meeting.

***

Several F15 planes equipped with high resolution cameras left their Israeli base at close to four fifteen in the morning. The sun was shining and it looked like another cloudless June day in the Middle East. One plane went northeast, over Syria and Iraq; the other directly east, over Jordan, and the third south and then southwest over the Sinai Peninsula and Egypt. The pilots were given instructions to turn back within thirty minutes. They would also report by radio if they saw something unusual. This was Zvi Kaplan's idea – he remembered that the radio broadcasts would not be heard by anybody else but the Israeli receivers which were as out of phase as the transmitters in the planes. It was considered vital to turn the Shield off as soon as possible so as not make its existence known to everybody.

***

Sergeant Uri Dayan was tired, and it took him a moment to come back from the peaceful dream he was enjoying. The field phone was chirping. His infantry unit was on constant alert for infiltration and kidnapping attempts from the Gaza strip. After the latest bout of fighting, with Hamas temporarily beaten down, the situation was less tense than it had been in several years, but you could never know. Gaza was lawless and some group of thugs might decide this was a good day to start a fight.

He picked up the field phone: "Uri here."

"Sir, sorry to wake you, but something happened."

"What time is it?" Uri asked.

"Two forty-three," the soldier on the other side responded.

"OK. Go ahead. What's so important?"

"Sergeant, all the lights on the other side of the fence went out. I think I can see something on the horizon, but I'm not sure." The soldier was quiet, waiting for Uri's response.

"You should always identify yourself." Uri responded automatically. He knew the caller for at least ten years of reserve service, but protocol and discipline were important. "Are you sure ALL the lights are out? Can you see any movement?"

"No movement on instruments or plain optics. It is possible that the instruments are on the blink, but we don't see any buildings there either."

"Ok, keep looking. Call me if anything changes."

His phone was chirping again: "Uri here."

Please do not send any reconnaissance missions into our territory. This includes aircraft, ground troops or naval vessels. Any and all such units will be destroyed.

Please give my best regards to Moshe Dayan of the Palmach.

General Wilson looked up at his adjutant: "Is this some kind of joke?"

"Sir, it's certainly not our joke. The message came in on the HQ command frequency in the code our Jerusalem HQ is using."

"Major, please take down my orders."

"Sir!"

"One. Immediately switch to a different code in all our radio communications.

"Two. Send a message to HQ Jerusalem in the emergency code on our alternative frequency. Ask for an explanation of this message.

"I am afraid that we either have a madman or a traitor in Jerusalem or else the Germans have broken our codes."

After the adjutant left Wilson returned to the map. What a ridiculous notion – finish the campaign in a week, especially with the Luftwaffe and the French fighter planes getting more active and dangerous. Time travel! Definitely a madman. He hoped that this person would be found soon so communications with HQ could get back to normal.

***

"Sir." It was the major again.

"Yes. What's new from Jerusalem?"

"We received this message in response to our transmission. As ordered, we transmitted on the secondary frequency and used code Z." Code Z was high security and considered unbreakable – also a nuisance since it took so long to encode and decode messages.

Wilson took the slip of paper and read the message.

To: General Maitland Wilson

From: General Gad Yaari

I am not surprised that you did not believe my first message. I would not have believed it either. I suggest that we meet. This will remove any doubts you may have and will open the way for cooperation between us. If you will come to the village of Alma ash Shab, my adjutant will meet and escort you to a vantage point that will convince you of my truthfulness.

Please respond on this or any other frequency and feel free to use any code you wish.

General Wilson looked at his adjutant: "Major, what do you make of this?"

"Sir, I am not certain, but there may be something to this message." The adjutant looked uncomfortable. "I tried to contact the RAF in Jerusalem, but got no response. As a matter of fact, there is no radio traffic from any of our forces in Palestine. Just before I came here we got a report from an Australian patrol on the Palestinian/Lebanese border in the area of Naqoura. They claim to have observed movement of troops in strange looking tanks. As you know, we have no tanks in this area."

"Very well, major. I need intelligence. Try again contacting the RAF in Palestine. Contact the RAF in Gaza and in Transjordan. Ask them to fly over Palestine - preferably over Jerusalem and Tel-Aviv - and report back as soon as possible. Also send a patrol into Palestine along the Mediterranean coast, from " - he looked at the map - " Naqoura. Report as soon as you have anything".

In the next hour the RAF lost four planes trying to fly over Palestine. Two were lost soon after takeoff from the Gaza aerodrome, and two were shot down when they approached the Jordan River from the direction of Amman. The patrol that left Naqoura was stopped at a checkpoint by strange soldiers and told to turn back. The Australians did not argue – the four menacing tanks, two on each side of the road, the fortifications and the decisive and aggressive, though polite, behavior of the soldiers was very convincing.

***

"Sir, we have information from our patrols."

"Go ahead major," Wilson said impatiently.

"The RAF reports that it lost four planes in an attempt to fly over Palestine. Their Group Captain in Amman is not happy, though he lost no pilots. He has a story of one strange fighter intercepting our planes and shooting them down carefully and deliberately. It seems that the same fighter, or an identical one, took down all the Gaza planes as soon as they were airborne. They seem to have had no chance against him. He came out of nowhere at a crazy speed, flew a couple of circles around them and then, when they did not change course, shot them down.

"The motorized patrol was stopped a couple of miles south of Naqoura. They saw strange heavy tanks as well as fortifications. The patrol was turned back by forces in uniforms close to ours in color but of a different cut. They also carried unknown weapons."

General Wilson did not cherish the idea of asking Cairo for instructions. After all, he was the commander there only a short time ago, but there was no choice. He was stumped by this unusual situation, and Cairo might have additional information.

"Major, please send our exchange with this General Yaari and the intelligence we gathered to General Sir Archibald Wavell in Cairo. Ask him if he has more intelligence on this matter." Wilson was not going to ask General Wavell for orders directly.

The answer he received was short: "At this time we cannot verify your story and have no intelligence to share. Act as you find necessary. Do not forget your main objective."

Cairo was obviously preoccupied with Rommel, in no mood to solve mysteries. Wilson decided to send a message directly to this General Yaari character and see what happened. If things were clarified later, he would think again about the invitation to meet.

From: General Wilson

To: General Yaari

As a show of good will I would appreciate if you would destroy the battery of 75mm cannon that have been pounding my forces for the last two hours. Their coordinates follow.

***

Liat woke up Gad Yaari. It was just after six in the afternoon and he felt rested. Several hours of sleep refreshed him enough to feel human again.

"What's up?" he asked, "and what time is it?"

"It's 18:14. We finally have a request from Wilson. I transferred a copy to the Air force commander and he is waiting for instructions."

"Show me the exchange. I also want a report of what's been happening."

Major Cohen presented Gad with a couple of pages containing the radio exchange with Wilson and Wilson's exchange with Cairo HQ as well as a summary of events up to the moment.

"I must say our historians seem to know a lot and the cryptographers are not bad either."

"Sir, the universities have extensive archives pertaining to WWII, particularly in this region. They knew the military frequencies and some of the codes. The other codes are not very difficult to break if you have powerful computers, or so my husband tells me." Liat's husband was a professor of applied mathematics at Tel-Aviv University and supposedly knew what he was talking about.

"I see that the Air Force has the two Kfir jets above Syria as I requested. Please tell them to do as Wilson asked. Remind them that they are not to be seen. They may be heard though." Gad Yaari smiled.

***

"Sir, we have a report from the Free French."

"Go ahead, Major."

"They report that the 75mm battery is gone. It just went up in flames. No friendly planes were in the area. We received another message from General Yaari. He says that if we let his forces know what we need, they'll take care of it as quickly and efficiently as they did with the artillery battery. He gave us a number of frequencies to use so that field units can request support directly." Wilson nodded in resignation. "Do as he instructed. Give the information to the Free French as well as to the Australians."

***

Thomas Harvey, the U.K. ambassador to Israel, was unhappy. His embassy had lost contact with London in the early morning, and contact could not be restored. Now it was noon, and he was to meet with the Israeli Foreign Minister. Harvey suspected that the time travel story as reported on the radio and in the official ministry communiqué was some kind of an elaborate hoax, but he could not figure out why the Israelis would tell such a tall tale. In any case, the Foreign Minister had a lot of questions to answer! Harvey had served in Israel for three years now and was still not sure whether this was a promotion or if there was someone in the Foreign Office who really did not like him. He wasn't an anti-Semite, he told himself; some of his best friends were Jews. On the other hand, he never really liked Jews either. Objectivity and neutrality were his line.

"Good day, Ambassador," the Foreign Minister said. His tone of voice was cool. Thomas Harvey thought that the minister did not particularly like him.

"Good day, Minister," he responded. "I have a number of questions. The first is why are you jamming our radio and telephone to London?" He let his voice show a trace of indignation. The U.K. was not a superpower but it was not third class either and a small country like Israel should show respect.

"Thomas," the Minister said, "please understand that we are in a state of emergency and I can't answer questions or, as a matter of fact, give you any information whatsoever. You will use your own sources - which I know you have - to verify the situation. The only thing I can say, emphatically, is that the public announcement about our unfortunate time travel incident described the true state of affairs. Tomorrow we will present the information we have to all the ambassadors. I am sure that the invitation is waiting for you at the embassy. I will be glad to see you tomorrow." Then he left.

Thomas Harvey was so stunned that he made no objection. Only on the way back to the embassy did he think of all the things he should have said in response. He also realized that something extraordinary had happened and that he'd have to use every intelligence resource the embassy had to find out what was really going on.

***

The Foreign Minister was in a hurry. The government was meeting in fifteen minutes and he did not want to be late. Traffic in Jerusalem was light. He thought that people were still stunned by the mid-morning announcement and preferred to stay home after work listening to the radio or watching TV, hoping to learn something new.

"Shimon," he addressed his driver, "how are things going with you?"

After several years of spending time together in the car they had a friendly relationship. Shimon, representing public opinion, was a good sounding board for ideas that the Foreign Minister wanted to check out before proposing them to the government.

"Fine," the driver responded. "We were wondering, my wife and I, why we hear so much jamming on the radio. It reminds me of the Soviet Union in its glory days. And speaking of old times, should we expect food shortages soon?"

"Well, as you know we are surrounded by lots of hostiles, the chief being the Nazis, not too far away. I assume we will stop the jamming as soon as we figure out another way of preventing critical information from getting out. As to food: I don't think we will have shortages, but there will be changes. For example, most of our long-range fishing fleet is back in the future, so don't expect to see much canned tuna or any other deep sea fish on the shelves."

The minister was glad to see they were arriving at the government building. These were questions he did not want to contemplate. He had enough problems of his own.

***

Amos Nir looked at the full cabinet. It did not include members of the opposition. They were expected to join after negotiations, but that would take a couple of days, maybe weeks. The elections two years ago had given his party almost forty percent of the seats in the Knesset, so he did not have to pay too high a price for a stable coalition. As of now, his was one of the smallest governments ever – only seventeen ministers, all present today.

"Ladies and Gentlemen, I would like to open this meeting by summarizing the discussion of the previous Defense Cabinet meeting." The previous meeting had been only several hours earlier, but it seemed an eternity.

"We decided to make an immediate public announcement about our strange temporal status. There was really no choice about it. Anybody with a radio would be able to receive broadcasts on the AM band and conclude fairly quickly that those from outside the country were not coming from our time. This is especially true for the segment of our population that speaks several languages – which is most of us. People with satellite TV lost their reception and will soon discover there are no satellites. Our border villages can look out their windows and see changes. Withholding this information would only have damaged our credibility and caused panic. We really need the trust of the people now.

"The government decided to immediately suspend our transmissions on all civilian bands and start jamming all private outgoing radio transmissions to prevent sensitive information from getting to our enemies."

Amos went on for a couple more minutes and finally announced: "We will have the military report now. The Chief of General Staff is a bit busy, so Colonel Gilead will do the honors."

Gilead briefly summarized the events: "Our offer of assistance to the British in Lebanon, which was agreed upon at the last cabinet meeting, was accepted. The intervention against Vichy forces in Syria is going well. We estimate that the French will surrender in a couple of days. They literally don't know what hit them. The orders to our Air Force were to attack with high altitude weapons or if that was impossible, to make low altitude passes at supersonic speeds.

"We used missiles to shoot down six Luftwaffe fighters. This will prevent reports of strange planes in case the pilots survived. We don't think any of the pilots survived. The Vichy air force was nowhere to be seen. General Wilson was smart enough to comply with our request to keep the RAF away. We didn't want interference or them estimating our abilities, and he didn't want to lose more planes."

The P.M. thanked Gilead for his presentation. "I think that now is the time to discuss the issues left open from this morning's Cabinet meeting. Please feel free to raise any questions you find of interest."

In the next hour or so the discussion focused on supply problems. The country needed to be fed and fueled. The reserves of refined fuels were enough for several months, longer with rationing. Natural gas for electricity was cut off and coal was in short supply, only enough for two months. Some of the power stations could be converted fairly quickly to use heavy fuel oil, of which there were more significant stocks. Natural gas supplies could be restored, but that would take some time – the production platforms and pipes were lost in the Event. Food was also available; Israel was self-sufficient in dairy products, eggs, vegetables, some fruits, and almost self-sufficient in grain. Most of the Mediterranean fishing boats were in port during the Event and were still available, though it was thought prudent not to let them sail the open sea in view of possible entanglements with the Royal Navy. The reserves of other foodstuffs would last at least two months. Based on the assumption that they were stuck in this time, the government made several strategic decisions aimed at providing food and energy in the long term and decided to appoint a committee of three ministers to deal with the problems that would inevitably arise.

Several ministers from the left-leaning coalition party argued for an immediate imposition of rationing on food, fuel and electricity. The Finance Minister argued against these draconian measures. She explained that in the absence of a real shortage, rationing would create a black market and stockpiling of goods, which in turn would create real shortages. "Rationing is justified only if and when we have a real supply problem, which we are not likely to have if our plans succeed. If we see that such a problem is about to surface, we will take appropriate action." She smiled her engaging smile and waited for opposing views. None volunteered to argue with the nice lady – she was charming but had no patience for stubborn fools.

People started shuffling their feet and preparing for the meeting to be formally closed.

"We have one other item of business that cannot wait," the P.M. said. The room slowly became quiet again. "I have to remind you that today is Friday, June 20, 1941. The day after tomorrow, on Sunday, June 22, at 3:15 in the morning, Germany will attack the Soviet Union."

"Do you propose that we prevent this attack?" one of the ministers asked.

"No. I don't think we can do that, but there is a consequence of this attack that I would very much like to prevent." Amos Nir looked at each one of the people around the oval conference table. Some of the ministers were already nodding in agreement, a few looked aghast. Only one looked like he did not know what Amos was talking about.

The discussion following his explanation of what he had in mind was tumultuous. At one point it became so loud that one of the guards outside the room opened the door and looked in. The P.M.'s secretary waved to him that everything was OK. Finally the P.M. stopped the discussion and called for a vote. He had a comfortable majority on his side, but only on the condition that he got cabinet approval for any military steps that would likely become necessary. His next move was to make sure that there would be no trouble from the religious parties' ministers due to Foreign Ministry and Government activity on Saturday. It was justified by the fact that such activities would save lives and saving lives overrides the Sabbath. But better to ask first and keep the coalition behind him. He got their agreement later in the day.

***

The Foreign Minister waited for the crowd to calm down. The room was full and some of the attending ambassadors had to sit on improvised benches.

"Ladies and Gentlemen," the minister said quietly – this quiet approach always worked. It worked now. The many conversations stopped and everybody was looking at him.

"I am assuming that everyone here has heard the official announcement. The facts as presented in that announcement are correct." He paused to let the crowd digest the message and quiet down again. "I am also sure that at least some of you have used your own resources to check the situation. I would like to make several announcements and give you additional information. But first, does anybody here have any doubts that we moved in time and that today is" - he looked at his watch - "approximately 4 pm on June 21, 1941?"

The crowd of foreign ambassadors was quiet. Some nodded in confirmation but did not speak.

"I see that the situation is clear. There are some actions to be taken and implications to this condition which, with your permission, I would like to examine more closely." The minister looked at his notes for the first time. "The first thing that comes to mind is that we should do all in our power to keep events as close as possible to our history. I hope that everyone agrees with that."

The French ambassador got up: "Sir, this may be immoral. It is in your power to save many millions of lives. Why not act to do so?"

"And how do you propose we do that?"

"Well, your army could attack the German forces concentrated on the Soviet border and destroy them. This would stop the attack before it began and save many lives."

"A very noble idea, Mr. Ambassador. Do you propose that we magically transport our army to the German-Soviet border in occupied Poland and combat the Germans there? If this is your proposal, I have to disappoint you – we have no means to perform such a feat."

"No, no," the French Ambassador was not amused. "This not at all what I propose. I was thinking more along the lines of using your air force and, if absolutely necessary, non-conventional weapons."

"Mr. Ambassador, I appreciate your good intentions. Let's examine the practical side though. The German forces are spread out over a front several thousand kilometers long. Even though they number close to three million, in effect they form a very narrow ribbon along the Soviet border. Assuming we had such long range aircraft, we could bomb them with pinpoint accuracy but we could not do enough damage in any significant way within the time we have. In fact, as soon as we attack it is reasonable that Germany will assume this to be a Soviet attack and counterattack immediately. We could, of course, use non-conventional weapons, which I am not saying we have. For the sake of the discussion though, let's say we do have them. You suggest than that we drop nuclear bombs on the German army in numbers sufficient to destroy them. Am I correct?"

"Yes, Minister. This is one of the options I urge you to consider," the French Ambassador said.

"Well, say we considered and accepted this idea. The result would be a belt of devastation running through the heart of eastern Poland and parts of the Ukraine and southern Europe, with hundreds of thousands dead. The civilian population will not be excluded from this holocaust. It is also likely that some Soviet forces will be affected – after all nuclear weapons are for mass destruction and not for pinpoint accuracy. And what will happen next? Do you seriously expect Stalin to look to the West, see

Germany defenseless and not pounce? He may decide to wait for a while, but pounce he will. And with nobody to stop him, the Soviet Union will reach the Pyrenees in no time. You think that France will do better under Stalin than it is doing under Hitler? Or maybe you suggest that we also nuke the Soviets? I don't think that this is a viable proposal – Too many innocent people will die, and, despite what some of you may think and have actually said in the past, we are not monsters and will never contemplate mass murder.

"There are also those little side effects that are unpredictable. Let me address one of them: You all know by now that we are jamming every unauthorized radio transmission from our territory. The jamming is dynamic – it starts as soon as our services detect a carrier wave. The reason for this is that we do not want any information about the future leaked to the world outside. Such a leak could be catastrophic. Imagine that someone who wants the Axis to win tells them that the Allies have broken the Enigma codes. This may not let them win the war, but it will cost the allies dearly and will likely prolong the bloodletting. There are more possibilities - too many to mention. I am sure that you will agree with me that even a short transmission falling into the wrong hands may be catastrophic. For this reason the Knesset is now in the process of debating a number of emergency laws which, I am sure, will pass. These are the important points that concern you and your nationals now in Israel:

Any contact with the outside world without the explicit permission of the Government will be punishable by 20 years in prison. This law applies to everyone - there will be no diplomatic immunity. It also applies to the press.

1. All radio transmitters have to be turned over to the Ministry of Communications by noon on Monday, June 23. Possession of a transmitter will be punishable by 20 years imprisonment. Embassies and diplomatic mission are NOT excluded.

2. Under the new emergency laws, the police and security forces can detain anyone suspected of subversive activity for 90 days without trial or an arrest warrant. This applies to everyone, including diplomats.

3. Diplomatic credentials are considered invalid until such time as accreditation is renewed – assuming the current governments of your respective countries choose you as their representatives.

4. Diplomats and other citizens of the Axis countries including Germany and Japan will not be considered enemy aliens. Citizens of countries whose life or freedom may be in danger

from their respective regimes are welcome to apply for political asylum.

"Ladies and Gentlemen, I suggest that you take some time to consider what I just said. You'll have the opportunity to ask questions at the next meeting. Or you can always ask for clarifications through the normal channels." As the assembled ambassadors started filing out of the auditorium, discussing the announcement and the surprising bluntness and assertiveness of the normally mild Israeli Foreign Minister, a guard approached the British ambassador and took him through a side door to the Minister.

***

Lieutenant Shaviv looked at his platoon sergeant. Uri was cleanly shaven and seemed rested. They had nothing to do for the last day and a half. Since The Event there had been no activity along the Gaza border, except a couple of British aircraft trying to get through to Israel north of their outpost.

"Uri," Shaviv said, "we have new orders, and you are getting a new platoon commander."

Sergeant Uri Dayan was surprised. Not by any new orders - Noam Shaviv had predicted that - but the announcement of a new platoon commander. He served with Shaviv for almost ten years and expected them to retire from the service together. "Where are you going?" he asked his long-time friend.

"Not very far. I was promoted to Company Commander. Maybe they will even make me a captain before I am old enough to be put out to pasture."

Actually, Uri Dayan had expected Noam to be promoted a while ago. He suspected that his platoon commander was still a lieutenant because he never accepted an order unconditionally. Independent thinking was encouraged, but Noam Shaviv was beyond independent – he was incapable of accepting an order uncritically. On the other hand, his command benefited from his stubbornness and even the battalion commander admitted that he was a good officer and often was right to argue about the orders he received.

"Well, good luck," Uri said. "Don't forget us."

"Don't worry, I'll come to visit. Your coffee is the best. Even battalion can't match it. Anyway, my replacement is a guy fresh from officer school. He is our age and is also a reservist that decided to become an officer somewhat late in his career. This is going to be his first command.

But he's not inexperienced, having been a sergeant for a while. Treat him well and be sure to educate him.

"Now the new orders: Get the guys ready to move. Pack everything up and be ready in a couple of hours. The new platoon commander will be here by then. The company will move out in the afternoon, and your trucks will be here on time, or so they promised."

"Where?" Uri inquired.

"There was no official announcement, but my guess is that we are going to be part of a force set up to seal the Egyptian border," Noam responded. "Let me know when the new commander arrives. I'll be at the company HQ."

"This is the Sabbath. How come we are going to do something on the Sabbath?" Uri asked. The only exception for Saturday activity would be a war, and he knew nothing about fighting anywhere in Israel. The country was on a permanent war footing, but there had been no actual shooting for a while.

"According to the radio, which you apparently haven't heard, the Government declared a state of emergency and the Knesset is debating instituting emergency laws. They expect the debate to be over in a couple of hours. Even the religious parties are participating, despite the Sabbath. You can assume that it's a more serious situation than just a simple war."

Lieutenant Noam Shaviv shook hands with his ex-sergeant and walked away. Uri Dayan looked after him, with misgivings he could not articulate crowding his mind. He was worried about having to nurse a new, inexperienced officer at a time when trouble could start at any moment. Even more, he had difficulty imagining running the platoon without Noam, in whose shadow he had lived and fought for close to ten years. But there was nothing to do but what he was ordered. At least that part of his army life had not changed.

Chapter 4

Mohammad al Husseini relaxed in his living room's easy chair. It was a nice living room. If you didn't look out the windows you wouldn't be able to tell that it was in Jenin. He had a nice view from his hilltop villa on the outskirts of town and could almost see the Israeli town of Afula in the Galilee, which his people had attacked more than once. Although Jenin was divided between competing (and often violent) militia groups, Mohammad felt safe. He was the local commander of Azz A-Din Al-Qassam – the military arm of the Hamas movement. Since Hamas dominated most of this area, he was, de-facto, the most powerful man in the northern West Bank and did as he pleased. For a while the rival Fatah militia, with the help of the Palestinian Authority, attacked and almost destroyed Hamas' strongholds. It was a close thing, but after a couple of years, with Allah's help, Hamas was on the rise again. This time they were more cautious and did not trust Fatah, or anybody else. Most of their armed force did not show itself unless absolutely necessary. And when they thought it was necessary, their enemies tended to die quickly. In the best tradition of Islam, the families of those killed were subverted to serve Hamas or killed.

The doorbell rang. Mohammad heard his young third wife open the door. After a polite knock at the living room door several men filed in. They sat on the sofa and ottomans. Mohammad gestured to the woman, who, though young and inexperienced, was eager to please and was doing a good job as a servant. She bowed and disappeared into the back of the house.

The men waited quietly until she brought coffee and sweetmeats and placed them on the low table in the middle of the room. After another look at her husband she left, closing the door behind her.

Mohammad al Husseini studied the faces of his underlings. They had known each other for a long time and trusted each other implicitly. This was a group that had sent numerous suicide bombers, initiated shooting attacks, survived years of fighting against Israel and other Palestinian factions, and was still here to plan more. They looked worried, which was no surprise. The Israeli radio had strange news on Friday. No one in the group had heard the news firsthand as they spent most of the day praying in their local mosque, but they heard reports and even today, a day later, the TV kept repeating the amazing story. But at the moment the most worrisome part, as far as Mohammad was concerned, was the announcement that emergency laws were in force. Those were based on the old British laws from 1945-1948 and were harsh and unforgiving – He knew this both from the history courses he took in college and from real life. Habeas Corpus was suspended, so that a suspect was not required to be brought before a judge after arrest and could be held by the security forces indefinitely. Acting against the state became, at least in theory, even more dangerous than usual. As a lawyer, Mohammad al Husseini did not like these laws one bit.

"Allahu Akbar," said Mohammad. Whatever else had changed, God must still be praised.

"Allahu Akbar," the men answered as one.

"I see that you are worried." Mohammad said, smoothing his full beard. "I can't blame you. We lost radio and cell phone contact with our brothers in Gaza. It seems that we also cannot reach our Syrian leadership. I expect an imminent assault by the Jews who will, no doubt, use this situation to their advantage. It is possible that they somehow messed up our communications on purpose and will try to get us. But this is neither here nor there.

"Now to the bright points: We know that the emergency laws have been implemented a couple of times in the past. It never led to serious problems – the Jews are soft and can't repress their enemies brutally or completely. We will benefit from their weakness and be only slightly inconvenienced. The most important fact may not have occurred to you: I think that the Israeli announcement about time travel may be true – they never lie to their own public and are trustworthy in this respect. This means that we are now in 1941 and my great uncle, Hajj Amin al Husseini, the Grand Mufti of Jerusalem, is alive and well in Germany. He has significant influence with Hitler and if we can help the Germans win this war, we will exterminate the Jews just like my great uncle promised our people back in 1939."

"How can we help the Germans?" asked the commander of the northern Jenin district. "We are much weaker than the Israelis, let alone the Allies."

"But we have access to a significant weapon: information. There's enough knowledge in the books at our universities to let the Nazis win this war. And we win with them," Mohammad proclaimed.

"I am assuming you have a plan," the same commander said.

"Yes. And it is devastatingly simple: We smuggle several of our people equipped with books about nuclear technology and 20th century history out of the territories into Egypt, Jordan and, possibly, Lebanon. All we need is for one of them to meet a German agent and give him the books. It should not be difficult – there are plenty of German spies in this area. Some of them are our fellow Arabs and relatives. They'll do the rest. My great uncle has Hitler's promise to exterminate the Jews in Europe and help us to exterminate them in Palestine. With a German victory this promise will be realized."

The assembled commanders looked at Mohammad with awe. This was the thinking of a great man. It would realize their wish: a world without Jews or Israel. They stroked their beards in anticipation of the great events. They also didn't notice the contradiction between their leader's statement of their communications having been nefariously disrupted by the Jews and his trust in the Israeli's announcement of time travel.

The discussion on who to choose for the mission, which routes to take, and other mundane arrangements took a while. In the end, one of the attendees had a proposal: "I suggest that we continue our regular activity. This would be a bad time to stop suicide bombings or rocket attacks. If we do, the Israelis may suspect that we are up to something and start investigating."

"I see that I promoted the right man," Mohammad responded. "It will be up to you. Arrange for several bombings and some rocket attacks. Don't tell me the details. Do it the usual way. Go with Allah's blessing." He chose to ignore the fact that due to the Israeli security service's efficiency and the security fence, the number of suicide bombers successfully getting into Israel was negligible and none of the factions in the West Bank had any rockets – those were all in Gaza. But with Allah's help, anything was possible.

Sulha, the young third wife of the great man, moved away from the living room door, which she had left open a crack, just in time to get out of the way of the dispersing commanders. She jotted down the details and an hour later, left a note in the cracked wall of the neighborhood mosque.

After his commanders left, Mohammad called a number in Ramallah: "I need to meet with the Chairman tomorrow in the afternoon."

"Let me call you back," the voice on the other end responded.

The call came twenty minutes later: "The Chairman will see you tomorrow at three in the afternoon. No weapons, please."

***

Itamar Herz, Managing Director of Israel Aircraft Industries, otherwise known as IAI, felt that he was in a dream. He was chairing a meeting in his large office with the Minister of Defense, several of his department heads, and two managers from Israel Military Industries (IMI). All this was not unusual, except this Saturday, like most Sabbaths, the company was supposed to be closed. The hastily printed calendar on the wall and another on his desk were open to June 21, 1941. He forced his attention back to the proceedings.

"We will need to stay current with operational information from both Eastern and Western Europe," Nitzan Liebler, the Defense Minister, was saying. "We need this capability yesterday. What do we have available now?"

The division heads looked at each other. A spy satellite project manager said: "We have two satellites ready to launch. The plan was to go from Baikonur – it was cheaper than doing it ourselves. If anybody here can give us a rocket, we can launch in two days. That is if the rocket is a Shavit, otherwise we will have to rework the satellite's envelope to fit."

"We have the third stage of a Shavit launcher ready, actually several of them - leftovers from the communication satellite tests last year. We can refuel and have them ready for launch in about 24 hours. We need to get the other two stages from somewhere," Itamar said.

The Military Industries representatives looked at each other. "I'm not a rocket guy, but it seems to me that we can build a Jericho 3 minus the warhead cone and use it to build a complete Shavit. After all, that's what a Shavit launcher is."

"How long will it take to do that?" Nitzan Liebler inquired quietly.

"Probably a couple of weeks," the Military Industries man responded.

"Too long. We need it now." Liebler was getting testy. Israeli Military Industries was a company controlled by the government, as was Israel Aircraft Industries. Since Israel was a small country surrounded by enemies, the government maintained majority control of several strategic companies. This allowed the companies to engage in activities on the open market while giving the government control in matters of national defense.

"We can dismantle a Jericho or two and have the Shavit assembled and ready to launch by Tuesday. A second will probably be ready a day after," the other manager said. "We can restore the Jericho with new rockets in a couple of weeks. We'll need special funding for that though – We have no budget reserves and no way to pay for this stuff."

"Do that immediately. Let my secretary know how much you need. We'll transfer the money from our emergency fund," the Defense Minister was visibly more relaxed. He needed the surveillance ability in place as soon as possible, and having the IAI and IMI cooperate and agree on a way to accomplish it was more than half the job.

"We will need a written order signed by you and the Prime Minister to disable a Jericho," said the first Military Industries manager.

Nitzan Liebler had the quiet serene look that meant he was ready to explode. "May I remind you that we are under emergency regulations? You will receive your signatures, but in the meantime stop wasting time. By the way, will the satellites have any communication relay abilities?"

"The one over Western Europe will not if we launch it as is," the satellite program manager said. "It can transmit high resolution images on request and give us diagnostics data. We can also steer it to a different orbit. We could modify its programming a bit to allow a small text buffer for communications. Just take into account that you will need a small dish antenna pointing at the satellite to talk to it. At the speed it is moving, your window of communication from a mobile station will be about ten seconds. Using burst transmissions will allow the passage of several thousand characters every hour and a half – when the satellite is above the antenna. If you want it, it will take another day to modify the programming and test it. This will also likely decrease the resolution of the images we get, but not very significantly".

"Okay, do the modifications," the defense Minister said.

The meeting dispersed with only Itamar Herz and Nitzan Liebler remaining in the big office.

"Why the urgency with satellites? We can cover the area with spy planes," Itamar asked.

"Our resources are limited and having several jets over Europe at all times is not only wasteful but also dangerous. As you know, it is not inconceivable for a Messerschmitt fighter to reach the operating ceiling of an F-15. And accidents happen. We don't want even a small chance of one of our pilots falling into the hands of the Gestapo or of the Germans seeing our jets. The results would be serious, so we'll take the risk only if absolutely necessary."

The Defense Minister relaxed for the first time since they met today. "I have another project for you. It's not as urgent but the sooner we do it the better. I know that you have an AMOS communications satellite ready to be shipped to Baikonur in Kazakhstan for launch. How about launching it ourselves?"

The Director of the Aircraft Industries was so surprised he was speechless for a moment. "Nitzan, you were the one who killed that project five years ago."

The AMOS is a geosynchronous communications satellite weighing in at about 1400 kilograms and needing much more rocket power than either of the other spy satellites to get it into its high orbit. The smaller satellites weighed about one fifth of the AMOS and orbited much lower. They were light satellites, one providing high resolution imaging for commercial purposes and the other a military version with additional sensors.

"That was in a different time and universe. We don't have Baikonur and cheap launchers anymore. The only things on that site in Kazakhstan are sheep, and they will not help us much. So, what do you say?"

Nitzan Liebler was smiling. His old friend Itamar was obviously still in the process of adjusting to the new reality, but he was resilient and would be on top of the situation soon.

"This is a serious undertaking, as you undoubtedly remember from the proposal we submitted to you when you were the Communications Minister." Itamar smiled, "By the way, the new job fits you better. Anyway, it will be more complicated now. We don't have access to parts that would have been purchased in the U.S. and E.U. Of these, I would assume the most time-consuming to manufacture ourselves will be computer chips for the navigation module. The rockets will not be as efficient as I would like them to be but won't be the bottleneck either." He stopped to think. "If we get the necessary resources, by which I mean money and priority access to one of the microprocessor fabricators, I believe that we can have the first AMOS in Geo-stationary orbit within six to nine months - if we are lucky, more than a year if we are not." He paused. "May I ask why we would need it?"

Nitzan's smile was not amused: "You may, but I will not answer, at least not today. Start the project and let my office know what you need – You'll get it. Oh, and don't be too greedy. I know you. Try not to feed too many side projects from this trough."

***

It was early afternoon and the Prime Minister was longing for his customary nap. Working on Saturday was unusual in itself, but skipping his midday nap was most inconvenient. He looked at his watch again. It was almost one in the afternoon. He dialed his secretary.

"Moshe, please invite the delegation in and ask them what they would like for lunch. Get me the usual."

A group of Knesset members filed into his office. These were the members of the Defense and Foreign Affairs Committee. They needed to be updated on the situation and had agreed to come to the Prime Minister's office instead of having him testify at the committee chambers at the Knesset. The P.M. had asked for this dispensation since his schedule was too busy to accommodate a trip to the parliament building. Amos Nir waited for everyone to get comfortable around the big conference table and for his secretary to finish taking lunch orders.

"I appreciate you coming to see me," he said. "It is a break with tradition and hopefully will not happen again. I have about an hour and a half – It should be enough to answer most of your questions."

"Amos, we know how busy you are at the moment and will take only as much time as we need to clarify a couple of issues," the chairman of the committee and a rival of Amos' for control of their party said. "I have an issue with a foreign policy decision that was made yesterday by the Defense Cabinet," he stated. "Why did you decide to open communications with the British Army in Syria? The Brits are not our friends and never have been. I, and others, think that we do not need them and need not maintain any contacts with them."

"There were a number of reasons," Amos responded patiently. "The cabinet assumed the British command would realize something had happened as soon as they tried to contact their headquarters in Jerusalem, which our historians told us would happen about four hours after the Event. Getting no response, they would investigate. This put a limit on how long we could wait to make contact if we wanted control of the situation, which obviously we prefer. We saw no reason to lie to them or invent anything more bizarre than what really happened. Any lie would come out later and harm our credibility with no real gain for us.

"We also had to take into consideration that the disappearance of British Palestine would deprive the forces fighting in Syria of their reserves and logistic support. This could lead to their defeat, or at best a standoff with the Vichy forces - not something we wanted.

"There were also broader strategic considerations. As you so astutely mentioned, the British aren't our friends. All they needed to do to save lots of Jews was to let them escape from the Nazis into Palestine. Not only didn't they bother, but they actively hunted down any refugees who tried to run their naval cordon. Then in 1948 - of our time-line – they did their best to support the Arabs attacking the Jewish community in Palestine and to prevent the birth of the State of Israel.

"But the situation is different now. We are the superpower here, at least in some respects, and do not need their favors since we can take anything we need by force. We also do not need them as enemies – God knows we have enough of those in this world. Israel can greatly benefit from an agreement of cooperation on a number of issues with the British Empire. The Brits are not stupid, especially Churchill, who has a keen sense of history and knows that the Empire is in danger. Additionally, General Wilson's reports should make them understand that we can cause them serious grief but also be of great assistance. They will not know at this point that we can break them, or the Nazis for that matter, if we choose to, but they will see the advantages of cooperation. We need them to supply us with oil and, maybe, give us access to some of the oil fields they control but at this point in time don't even know exist. We also need them to keep the Royal Navy out of the way as we will start work on our Mediterranean gas fields. Our limited military help should convince them to deal. If they don't see their way to cooperating with us within the next couple of days, they will definitely see the advantages after operation Moses begins.

"Speaking of this operation, we will need the Allies', mostly the Brit's, cooperation to have it go smoothly or we will have to damage them, which may influence the course of the war."

The members of the committee looked at each other. No one could argue against Amos' position, so the chairman went on to their next question: "I have doubts about Operation Moses," he said. "My misgivings are shared by some of the other committee members." He looked around for support from the other eight members of the committee, who nodded encouragement, before continuing. "This whole operation will upset history as we know it, with unpredictable results. I am not sure that we should do it. Possibly when we go back to our own time we will not recognize the world and the changes may not be for the better."

A Knesset member from a left opposition party added: "The basic premise for this operation strikes me as possibly racist and unfair. The other thing I am questioning is your intent to contact the Nazis. I don't know how you can morally justify negotiating with those animals."

The speaker finished and the room was quiet. Apparently the issues he raised troubled others as well.

Amos was surprised by this reaction to something he considered self-evident. The only explanation for this seeming opposition to a good plan was political maneuvering. Everybody was aware of the new coalition negotiations taking place and it was likely that all this posturing was just to ensure a better position in the upcoming national unity government. He relaxed. This was familiar territory and he knew how to deal with politicos, though it was shocking that at this time of emergency some people would continue with their petty political games.

"I will not comment on how racist or unfair operation Moses may be. My personal opinion is that the question is political correctness drivel. The world never treated the Jews fairly. I'd rather leave this to future, or is it past, historians. The more important question is about changing the future. As of now, our scientists are not optimistic about our chances of going back to our own time. But even if we could, we need to ask ourselves if we should.

"History has already been changed by our presence here. We had to shoot down several British planes. How soon do you think they will have their own jets flying, now that they know it's possible? We used missiles to shoot down the Luftwaffe planes we encountered, so they will have no information – the pilots saw nothing and died in the encounters. We did not want to kill the British pilots and so used our jet's cannon to shoot off their tails and give them a chance to escape. These pilots have probably seen something that, we have to assume, will be correctly interpreted by their experts. In our timeline the Germans had operational jets in 1944 and the Brits and Americans were not far behind. Even the least significant aspect of our technology will have unforeseen effects. If we go back now, it is likely that the world we return to will be generations ahead of us in technology and our edge over our enemies will not only be gone but we could be extremely vulnerable. It's my humble opinion - and the consensus of the cabinet - that we should stay here as a superpower rather than go back and risk being destroyed. Here and now we have an advantage which we plan on maintaining. In any case, this is an issue for the Knesset to debate, or even for a referendum."

"Why the squeamishness about killing British pilots?" the chairman asked.

"Since we hope to cooperate with them, sparing their pilots will make it easier. It was a show of both good will and air superiority, just like our help to them in Syria against Vichy. If they don't understand this, we will make it clear soon. We've also assumed that it will be impossible to keep the existence of obvious technologies, such as jets, a secret from our allies, and they are, or will be, our allies. This shouldn't be a problem in the short term – they won't have the technological base to build a jet that will be anything close to even our old ones for many years. We do need to be diligent about keeping the less obvious stuff secret. The Brits, and everybody else, will try to insert spies, which will not be difficult with Operation Moses going. We have some ideas of how to lessen the dangers, but we can't eliminate them entirely."

"How about negotiating with the Nazis?" reminded the chairman.

"As to negotiating with the Nazis: They are disgusting, but in this time-line the bulk of the Holocaust hasn't happened yet and, as crazy as they are, we hope we can bend them to our will. And if they don't bend, we have the power to break them and we will not hesitate using it. As to our planned method of contacting them, we will do it in the most direct and forceful way. We don't plan on negotiating with them in the usual sense of the word. It will be more of a 'do what we tell you or die' kind of negotiation."

There were more questions, mostly clarifications of issues that were presented to the full Knesset earlier in the day. The meeting closed with all the committee members if not explicitly agreeing with the government's policies, at least not opposing them actively.

Amos Nir was satisfied.

***

Thomas Harvey was both flattered and offended. He was the only ambassador to have a private meeting with the Foreign Minister. This put him ahead of everybody else, and he was sure that the U.S. ambassador in particular was annoyed. On the other hand, he was pulled into the meeting somewhat unceremoniously by a Foreign Ministry guard. He decided he was more flattered than offended. These were hectic times for the Israelis; he'll give them some leeway.

"Ambassador, I am glad you could see me on such short notice," the Foreign Minister said when Harvey was led into his office. "We have things to discuss which I hope will benefit both our countries greatly. Of course your country, the British Empire, is not the same as the U.K. you represented, but I hope that you are loyal to the crown that exists in the here and now."

Harvey was perplexed. "Minister, you announced just a couple of minutes ago that all the ambassadorial credentials are null and void. Did I misunderstand you?"

"You did not. I assume that your loyalty does not depend on your credentials?"

"Sir, I am a loyal subject of the Queen, er... King." Harvey said uncertainly.

"In that case, let's get to business. Let me update you on what has been happening in the last day or so." Harvey appreciated this personal briefing. After all, this country was under British rule now, in 1941. He didn't think the Israelis had realized that. The Minister told the ambassador about the events in Syria and the contact that was made with General Wilson.

"Now we come to the interesting part," he continued. "We would like to invite the general for a visit and it would be appropriate for the British embassy to host him for dinner. If you don't wish to host him, we will skip that part, but I think it will be an advantage to everybody if you do so."

Thomas Harvey was at a loss for words. This was not what he had expected. "I will certainly be happy to host General Wilson. I wonder though, aren't you afraid that the embassy will give him information that you're trying to protect?"

"Ambassador, it is a pleasure doing business with you. I always thought that you were perceptive and wise. You are right; we would be very upset if certain information got out. Some of it may also be catastrophic for the British Empire. I have no idea what would happen if your current leaders knew with certainty that they are going to win this war. Will they try to lessen their efforts and direct more of them to preserving the Empire, thus losing the war as a result? Since the future of this world hasn't been set yet, anything is possible." He paused to let Harvey digest this point of view, which certainly the pompous ambassador hadn't considered.

"There are myriad unexpected results to any piece of information that gets out. I suggest that only three or four people attend the dinner with General Wilson - the two of us, the Defense Minister and possibly one of our generals just to keep General Wilson comfortable - you know how the military view us diplomats.

"As you may imagine, our historians have run a number of simulations to try and predict what is safe to reveal to Wilson at this point. They'll discuss that with you as soon as we are done here – assuming you agree to host the dinner?"

"Minister, I tend to agree that such a meeting at the embassy will be most welcome. We will cooperate with you to the extent that it serves the best interest of my country."

"Ambassador, I appreciate your candor in this matter. There should be no problem. In the here and now Israel and Britain are natural allies against a common enemy." The Foreign Minister smiled as he stood and extended his hand, which Thomas Harvey shook.

From the foreign minister's office, the still-dazed ambassador was escorted to a comfortable briefing room. The presentation by the pleasant history professor was fascinating. Harvey had never considered the possibility of alternate courses history might take due to small changes. He directed his attention back from his musings about the complications of alternate history to interrupt what the historian was saying. "But why not share as much technology as possible?"

"It would seem on the face of it that if we expose the British to as much of our technology as possible, it will help them win the war faster and with less casualties. This is an illusion. Consider this: We show them a fighter jet. A likely result will be that they direct some resources to duplicating it. In the absence of all the supporting industries and with their resources already stretched thin, the air superiority balance in the coming years may shift just enough to lose the war or, at best, extend it significantly. The same goes for most of the sophisticated stuff we have.

Our technology, in most instances, is too far advanced for 1941 engineers to be able to replicate. There will be things they will be able to manufacture only 20 years from now – like computer chips. I assure you we ran a number of simulations, using very advanced strategic planning software, and came up with a scenario that allows our allies to benefit almost immediately without disrupting their war effort. This is what we propose…"

After hours listening to the Israeli proposals, Harvey went back to his embassy. He was pleased. Not only was he going to serve his country, but at the same time he had a great opportunity to advance his career. He will be the one to introduce the British Empire to the Israelis and will orchestrate the first encounter. He was sure he would be rewarded by the British. If only his family could know. His wife was back at the embassy of course, but their daughter and both sons were somewhere in the future – independent adults with families of their own who didn't think much of his career. If only they could see him now!

***

After his meeting with Thomas Harvey the Foreign Minister had another meeting, one he had tried to avoid for a couple of days but decided he could avoid no more.

The U.S. ambassador was waiting in a small conference room.

"Hello Dan," the minister greeted the American. "What can I do for you today?"

"Hi, Nathan. I understand and accept your general announcement and the new emergency laws. I also assume that we are going to be exempt from the limitations. Is that correct?"

"My friend, it is not in my power to grant exemptions, and I don't think that the government will do that either, but that would depend on what exactly it is that you want."

The U.S. Ambassador smiled a self assured smile: "As opposed to the other diplomats here, I represent a great power. A great power that was friendly to the State of Israel in its time of need. I am sure that your government will not want to diminish this relationship. I would like the embassy to be free to communicate with the U.S. and do the job we are here to do."

The Foreign Minister lit a cigar – something he never did in his office since smoking in public buildings was prohibited. He needed to think and relax and a cigar did it for him. The American made a slightly disgusted face, but erased the expression almost as soon as it appeared.

"Dan," the Minister began, "we have known each other for what - twelve years now? You know that I always, even before taking my current post, supported the closest possible relationship with the U.S."

The U.S. Ambassador moved as if to interrupt.

"Yes, yes. I know. I opposed your insistence that we make immediate peace with the Palestinians. But you know that there is nobody to make peace with and the State Department was doing its usual thing of sacrificing some of our security and long-term interests for a short term gain with the Arabs. But these are little disagreements. I know that you personally are an honorable man and a supporter of Israel."

"Nathan, it is not just me. The U.S. is a genuine friend."

The Foreign Minister was about to respond truthfully but stopped himself. There was no reason to make Dan McKenzie uncomfortable and possibly an enemy. The Minister assumed that the Ambassador checked a history book or two before initiating this meeting.

In the meantime the Ambassador continued: "We supported the creation of the State of Israel and supported it in later years. In any case, this is in the past. Like I stated, the U.S. is a great power friendly to you and should be treated accordingly." The ambassador sounded almost sure of his position.

"Dan, I can't ignore the lessons of history. If one does, one is bound to repeat past mistakes. In 1948 the U.S. voted for the creation of Israel. That was the only time it supported Israel during our first twenty years. When the war of Independence was raging in 1948 and 1949 the U.S. enforced an arms embargo on the fledgling state, almost costing us our independence. We paid for this embargo in blood. In 1956, when Israel captured the Sinai from Egypt we were forced to retreat – by who else but the U.S. It was only after the Six Day War, in 1967, after years of Soviet support to the Arabs, that the U.S. decided that as part of its global cold war policy it would support Israel. Even after that we were forced to do things that cost us lives to make the U.S. look good to the Arabs."

He wanted to add that the friendship always went only as far as the U.S. political interest, and sometimes the State Department failed to see its own interest in its haste to appease the Arabs at Israel's expense. He did not say that either.

Instead he said as diplomatically as he could: "Don't misunderstand me, I think that for almost half a century the U.S. has been a friend to us. But we are now back in time, when Jews are not a very popular cause in America, and the extermination of six million of us made some waves only after it was done.

The ambassador was quiet for a while: "Nathan, this is neither here nor there. Being a seasoned diplomat, you know that it is legitimate for a country to pursue its own interests as it sees them. The U.S. did what it did not because of hate for Israel but because that was what it judged was in its own interest. I suggest that you leave all the other considerations aside and look just at the fact that I represent a superpower that will not appreciate being treated poorly."

"Ah, here is the crux of our misunderstanding, Dan. First, we are not treating the U.S. poorly. We are treating your embassy like everybody else – no discrimination here at all. Since you were not accredited to us by the administration of President Roosevelt, and since the U.S. hasn't yet recognized us as an independent state, we have no obligations to the embassy. The second misunderstanding on your part is of the position of the U.S. in the world today. No doubt it is a great power, but so are the British, the Soviet Union, Nazi Germany and Imperial Japan." He wanted to add that the only superpower around now is Israel, but decided that this was not necessary.

The ambassador got up. He was disappointed, but not being a fool it took him only a couple of seconds to realize that the minister was right. He sat down again: "The U.S., after it wins the war, will be a real superpower. Do I understand you correctly, that Israel is not going to be friendly to the U.S.?"

"No, this is not what I said. We will be friendly to anybody that will be friendly to us. If the U.S. wants good relations, we will oblige. Of course, like you said, we are entitled to pursue our own policies with our own good in mind. If other countries are unhappy with what we do, it will be their business. This includes the U.S.

"I think that we are getting too far away from the issues at hand. Dan, my friend, consider how you would contact the State Department. I mean the State Department of today – 1941. They don't know you from Adam, and even worse, they never heard about a State of Israel. Even if there were no limitations imposed on your embassy's communications with the outside world, you would have a couple of mundane problems that would preclude you from contacting the U.S.: your experts would have to dig up the old radio frequencies used in 1941 and the old codes. If you don't have them, we could supply all of the information. You know that we would be able to listen in on every word and you wouldn't want us doing this. Would you?"

The American Ambassador thought for a moment: "You are right. I may have been hasty in demanding things we would not be able to use anyway. I appreciate your cooperation and time."

"Don't be too contrite," the Foreign Minister smiled. "We will be establishing relations with the U.S. pretty soon and I hope that you will be willing to help both parties. I would really prefer to see you as the U.S. ambassador here rather than a Nazi sympathizer from the 40's."

The ambassador opened his mouth and closed it again. He knew his history and the Minister's statement was not as outrageous as it sounded.

They shook hands and the ambassador left. He was slightly depressed. Besides not being accredited he also realized that the Minister was correct, at least in part. The U.S. was a great power, but not the only one. Israel had a great advantage in both weapons and technology, and if it managed its assets and policies well it could become very strong indeed. He still did not doubt that his country would become a superpower and dominate the world, together with the Soviets, by 1945. It did not cross his mind that history was being changed – old thought molds and habits tend to persist.

Chapter 5

General Wilson was satisfied with his army's progress. Since the first intervention by the "Israelis" the resistance of the combined Vichy–German force was crumbling. At this point it was not so much the number of these "Israelis" but their effect on the enemy. As a matter of fact, he saw no "Israelis" at all, but whatever troops were resisting his ground assault became a pile of smoking rubble within minutes of asking for help on the radio frequencies assigned by this Yaari character. Neither the Luftwaffe nor the small Vichy air force were to be seen. According to eyewitness reports, at least six Luftwaffe planes exploded in the air for reasons unknown. The invisibility demoralized the enemy, but it also worried Wilson. If these "Israelis" became suddenly unfriendly, he would have no means of dealing with them. He had no doubt that the fate of any RAF squadron would be similar to that of the Luftwaffe fighters if his new allies turned against him. And the Royal Navy fleet assigned to shell the enemy's coastal fortifications would fare no better. How do you fight an enemy you can't see? Especially if he strikes unseen from afar, which all the reports steadily coming in claimed. Wilson knew that no "Israeli" forces crossed the Lebanese border either on the ground or in the air – at least none that anyone saw. So how did they manage to destroy targets so far away from where they supposedly were?

The general was a military man; his success came from an ability to think strategically. He was trying to do that now but could think of only one way to cement the alliance with this new player on the board. The coded message he received earlier confirmed his plans. It seemed that the Prime Minister, who personally read a copy of the report he radioed earlier in the day to the HQ in Cairo and to Downing Street, agreed.

"Major," yelled Wilson, "please come in." They had just moved their HQ to a village several miles west of Damascus. The intercom and field telephone were still being installed. In the meantime, he relied on his loud baritone voice to do the job.

"Sir!" The adjutant was ready to take orders.

"Please send the following message immediately:

From: General Maitland Wilson, commanding Syrian Expeditionary Force

To: General Gad Yaari, Chief of General Staff the Israel Defense Forces

I appreciate your great assistance in our campaign. As I assume you know, we are at the gates of Damascus and expect a formal surrender of the Vichy forces within a day. I would like to meet you and your staff in person in order to better express our gratitude and to discuss future cooperation."

The major saluted and left for the radio room, somewhere in the general mess of the new headquarters.

***

Gad Yaari finished meeting with the full contingent of the General Staff. According to the latest situation reports everything was quiet, even the West Bank seemed to be less restless than usual, probably they were also stunned by the Event. Preparations for Operation Moses were in full swing, as were the other much smaller assignments the Israel Defense Forces had from the government.

Liat Cohen, interrupted his reverie: "Gadi, we have a message from General Wilson." She was smiling.

After reading the short communiqué, the Chief of General Staff thought for a moment before issuing his orders. "Immediately send a copy of this to the Minister of Defense. Let the Commanding General of the Northern Command know that his part starts in about one hour."

***

By now General Wilson was almost used to the efficiency of the Israeli command structure and wasn't much surprised by how quickly he received a response:

From: General Gad Yaari, Chief of General Staff, Israel Defense Forces

To: General Maitland Wilson, Syria Expeditionary Force

It is my pleasure to accept your invitation to a meet. I hope this will lead to greater cooperation between our two countries.

Please come to the town of Naqoura at 21:00 on Sunday, June 22. You will be escorted to Tel-Aviv and dine with myself along with several of our ministers and the British Ambassador to Israel.

If you agree, please radio me and instruct your forces in the area to hold their fire in order to prevent unfortunate incidents.

Wilson looked at his watch. It was late Saturday afternoon. He had plenty of time to get to Naqoura on the Mediterranean shore just north of the Israeli border positions and even to rest before the meeting.

***

On Sunday morning B Company of the 927th Israeli Army infantry battalion was deploying just south of the intersection of the Israeli, Egyptian and Gaza Strip borders. It was a short truck ride from their previous position at the Gaza fence to the north. They had arrived on Saturday and spread out along the section that had been assigned to them. Now they were deploying in an orderly fashion, including infirmaries, kitchens and latrines. Lieutenant Noam Shaviv, the new company commander, had explored his area of the border a couple of hours earlier in a Jeep. The sector was long, much longer than he thought was possible to seal hermetically as his orders called for, with the 270 people he had. Though the company was reinforced by 90 reservists from several "retiree" units, he was still skeptical of his ability to do what he was supposed to do. The retirees were veteran infantry reserve members who were older than 42. They could do the guarding and observation as well as his younger guys.

The ten kilometers he was supposed to seal were only a fraction of the more than 200 kilometer long border with Egypt. He had no idea why his company was assigned such a long section of the border, especially as this was one of the few sections not protected by the sophisticated border fence. The answer arrived in the form of a Combat Engineers captain: "I am here to do your job," the captain joked.

"And how will you do that?" Noam inquired.

"The same way we did it in other places, like Gaza where you came from just now and most of the Egyptian border, only less sophisticated," the captain responded. "We'll put in poles, string wire over them, connect the whole mess to a couple of computers and from that point on your only job will be to catch the poor animals that trigger your alarms. Be merciful to the camels." The Engineer became serious: "It's not going to be a long-lasting structure, nothing like the Gaza, Egyptian or West Bank security fences, but we were told that it needs to last for less than a month.

"With your permission, we'll get to work. I need you to tell me exactly where you want this fence to be located."

They went for a drive along the border, with Noam's platoon commanders accompanying them. He wanted his officers familiarized with the terrain they were responsible for as soon as possible.

***

In the early afternoon of Sunday, June 22, 1941, the Israeli Cabinet was in session again. Most of the ministers looked somewhat frazzled. It had been an exhausting couple of days, even more exhausting than a full scale war would have been. When the country was at war, most of the ministers didn't have much to do. What use was Tourism, or Absorption, or even the Housing Ministers during a war? It was different now.

The head of the General Security Service was reporting: "Generally we have fewer bombings and other terrorist activities than usual. The news of the Event probably had something to do with it, plus the fact that all the terror organizations lost some of their leadership – those that were outside our borders when we activated. I do not expect this lull to last very long. We have reliable information that at least one faction, headed by the Grand Mufti's great nephew, is trying to contact the Germans with modern day information."

"How do you know that?" asked the Foreign Minister.

"You know I won't disclose specific sources. Suffice it to say that it's extremely reliable and that not all Palestinians believe in infinite war. Catching those attempting to transfer the information is a different matter, but we're working on it."

"I remind you that the government decided just an hour ago to change our policies in the territories: no more leniency towards the perpetrators or their controllers. We will use the full power of the emergency laws with no mercy," interrupted the Minister for Internal Security.

After several more questions and clarifications the head of the Security Service was excused.

Amos Nir usually looked quite mild, except when it was necessary to exert his authority. Now he assumed his Prime Ministerial persona. "I would like each one of you to report to the government on your progress to date."

The Infrastructure Minister spoke first. "We are setting up the temporary camps. Contactors have been engaged, and planning is progressing as we speak. I think that we'll be ready to receive the first group in about two weeks. I also started a workgroup on electricity management. We will have to find additional sources of power somewhere. It's not as urgent as housing but will become critical within a year. Same goes for fresh water. The problems we had back in the future are now somewhat mitigated by the fact that the Syrians and the Jordanians are not pumping as much water from the Jordan River and its tributaries as they used to."

When the Defense Minister's turn came, he pulled out a number of diagrams and maps. "Our borders will be sealed within the next couple of days. We are calling up some reserves and preparing for the next phase." He paused. "Now to another issue, though they are connected. All of you are aware of the general outlines of Operation Moses. We're finishing the planning of its first three days. It will be a complicated operation, obviously. We expect the negotiations to be concluded successfully, though the price the other party will pay before they are completely convinced is uncertain."

"As far as I know we have no means of striking the eastern part of Germany, let alone Poland or the Soviet Union. How can we accomplish this without one way trips?" the Finance Minister asked.

"You are correct. The weapon systems we have can't go there and back. We are going to use aerial tankers to refuel our jets, with a couple of escort planes to keep them safe. I've also arranged for spy satellites to let us see what's going on in the areas of interest.

"The extermination phase will begin on Monday, June 23, and last for a day or two. We are still conferring with historians as to the exact position of the targets and will verify them when the satellites start reporting, which should be by tomorrow evening. In any case, we should not expect a 100% success rate. Some of our targets will survive, and we will, probably, strike some unrelated units. This is inevitable in such a complex operation, especially as the targets are intermingled with the rest of the forces in the area."

Next came the Foreign Minister's turn. "We are meeting with the British General tonight at their embassy in Tel-Aviv. Our emissary will be ready tomorrow and I expect that the Brits will provide transportation by Tuesday."

The meeting dispersed after another hour discussing details. Amos relaxed. He anticipated an argument about the means by which the Nazis will be compelled to agree to Israel's demands. It was a relief that he didn't have to argue with his own cabinet members.

***

General Henry Maitland Wilson arrived at Naqoura. The Australians had an HQ in town and he was the guest of a Major John Cummings. The General was deep in thought, sipping the mediocre brandy offered by the Major. Earlier, he had spent a couple of hours in conversation with the young Palmach commander, Moshe Dayan, who was mentioned in the first message from the Israelis, but it seemed that the Palestinian was as uninformed about these strangers as Wilson himself.

The General was trying to anticipate how the Israelis would conduct this first meeting and trying to decide how he should handle himself. It was important to him that he show them none of the wonderment he felt about their military ability. A British "stiff upper lip" seemed to be the best approach. On the other hand, he wanted to appear as friendly as possible. The Empire could not afford alienating these people, whoever they were. The Prime Minister made that clear in his message to Wilson. Churchill also made it clear that he had doubts about the time travel story and asked Wilson to keep his eyes open and report back directly.

Promptly at 21:00 the sentries outside reported a vehicle approaching. General Wilson didn't need the announcement; he could see the vehicle's bright, bluish lights illuminating the drive through the window. These people were not concerned about blackouts, it seemed - either a sign of negligent arrogance or supreme self-confidence. Wilson decided it was self-confidence, supported by power and technology he did not understand.

The vehicle stopping by the front door was big and squat, the engine purring quietly. A uniformed man jumped out a front door. He was obviously an officer - either a lieutenant or a captain. Wilson couldn't tell. The rank insignia would have marked him a captain if he was American or a lieutenant if he was British; who knew what it meant to these people.

Wilson pulled down the blackout curtain and moved away from the window. There was a quiet exchange outside the door. After a knock, the guard sergeant entered the room, saluted stiffly and reported, "Sir, Lieutenant Mosinson of the Israeli Defense Forces asks for permission to see you."

"Very well, Sergeant," Wilson responded.

The soldier who entered gave a crisp but relaxed salute, nothing like the sergeant's. "Lieutenant Abraham Mosinson at your service, sir." Wilson was surprised by the accent, which sounded American. He returned the salute.

"With your permission, sir," the officer said, "please accompany me to the vehicle and I'll take you to your meeting."

"How far are we going?"

"Only a couple of miles, to our border post at Rosh Hanikra and from there to Tel-Aviv," the Lieutenant said.

"I would like my adjutant to accompany me."

"Sorry, sir. My instructions were to bring you alone. I understood that was the agreement." The lieutenant smiled apologetically.

"Indeed it is," said Wilson. He chose to interpret this as a positive sign: the Israelis seemed to say what they meant without equivocation.

The interior of the vehicle was comfortable. It was clearly a military command vehicle, judging by the number of communication sets the General could see in the front. The lieutenant picked up a microphone and said something in a language Wilson did not understand but which sounded like the same language the Palestinian units of his command spoke – Hebrew. The communicator squawked back incomprehensibly.

They arrived at the Israeli position in less than twenty minutes. The young lieutenant jumped out first and, after a short hesitation, opened the door for the British General. He led Wilson to a low building and opened another door for him.

"Would you like to refresh yourself? A drink maybe?"

"I am quite comfortable."

"In that case, General, we can start on our way to Tel-Aviv, to the British embassy."

"How long will it take us to get there?" asked Wilson. "I need to tell my people when, approximately, I will be back. I would also like to arrange some way for them to contact me. After all, a commander should not be out of touch with his forces even if he is absent for a day or two."

"General, it will take us about thirty-five minutes to get to Tel-Aviv and about the same time to get back. The dinner at the embassy shouldn't take longer than a couple of hours. We can have you back here by, say 01:00, 01:30 at the latest, unless you would like to spend the night in Tel-Aviv?"

General Wilson was surprised, but not as stunned as he would have been two days ago. He considered his options. "I prefer to return as soon as possible, but I still need to let my adjutant know when to expect me. I would also like to give my Command a way to contact me."

"Very well," said Mosinson. He picked up the receiver of a sophisticated telephone on the table in a corner of the room, gesturing Wilson to sit in one of the nearby chairs. He said something into the handset and after a minute or so handed it to Wilson. "Your Naqoura HQ is listening on their field set. Please let them know that to contact you at any time during your absence, they can just call us on this line. You will be connected directly. Please meet me outside when you are done."

Wilson took the handset. "Hello," he said. "Is this Naqoura?"

"Yes, sir." The answer was as clear as if the speaker was in the room next door.

"Get Major Alexander on line," Wilson ordered.

The conversation with his adjutant lasted several minutes. Wilson knew his conversation was probably being monitored, but it was a nice touch to leave him alone while he communicated with his subordinates.

Lieutenant Mosinson waited outside near the car that had brought Wilson to the outpost. He put away his cell phone as Wilson exited the building. The embassy was ready and the two ministers were on their way. He and Wilson needed to move.

"General, this way please." They walked behind the low building to where a small helicopter waited.

***

David Rothstein was unhappy. He, along with his wife and two sons, had arrived in Israel two weeks ago, expecting to make the trip back to Boston tomorrow. Now they were stuck here. They had come to Israel for a long overdue visit, which they enjoyed. But they were done visiting and ready to go home. The Dan Tel-Aviv was a very nice hotel, run by the same people as the famous King David hotel in Jerusalem, but now they told him that his credit cards were not acceptable as payment. He had no assets in Israel and the hotel was justified, but what a mess! At least they wouldn't be thrown out on the street. They could stay in their suite, for a while. The bad news was that the hotel was no longer treating them like welcome guests. The management claimed to be cutting staff, so if they wanted clean sheets, available only once a week, they'd have to make the beds themselves. The same went for cleaning the rooms. At least they were still being fed a nice buffet breakfast, though the staff was preoccupied and busy, which made service iffy. And the hotel had given them Israeli shekels to pay for other meals and services they needed. It bothered him that they had to accept this handout and he regretted not having changed more dollars into shekels when it was still possible.

The government circular that was delivered to their rooms on Sunday evening had also upset David. It again explained the time displacement and gave some information on the time period they had been transported to. It stated that tourists would have the option of returning to their countries of origin, assuming those countries would take them. On the other hand, that option would not be open for the foreseeable future, they were informed. After an agitated reaction from David, his wife Rachel pointed out to him that some of the tourists would not want to return - "Dear, do you think that anyone wants to go back to Nazi-occupied

Europe? And do you really want to go back to pre-World War II America? We have no house there and no money to buy another one. We could start from scratch, I suppose, but how easy would that be for Jews like us in this time period? That's assuming the state department is agreeable to admitting us. They didn't issue our passports. The immigration authorities may just send us back to Europe with the rest of the Jewish refugees."

David had to agree with his wife, whom he always considered smarter than himself. Being a history major, she also knew more than he did about this time period.

"Now that you mention it," he mused, trying to lighten the discussion a bit, "I see another reason not to go back even if we could: my hypertension medication will not be invented for another forty years and your cholesterol drug will not be available for another fifty. At least the Israelis have them and, I hope, will not refuse us treatment."

There was another thing in the leaflet that bothered David. He was not very well versed in the history of WWII but the leaflet pointed out that today was the day Nazi Germany attacked the Soviet Union.

"You think my parents will survive again?" he asked Rachel. "I wonder what would happen if I meet them when they are young before I was even born."

"It's not only your parents, David. Most of their – your, our - family was killed in the Holocaust. They're still alive now."

"I'm worried about the boys," Rachel continued. "Since we're stuck here, how long before the Israeli army takes them? They're almost of age." The army was the primary reason they never considered moving to Israel, though their sons liked the idea. Every teenager served here and all were in danger. They had even cut down on their visits in the last couple of years, so the boys wouldn't be tempted to enlist. And now this happens. Josh was almost nineteen, and Jake was seventeen, close to the age Israelis started their service. She thought for a moment. "On the other hand, I'd prefer them serving in a Jewish army to being drafted by the U.S., assuming we join the fight in December of 1941, after Pearl Harbor."

"This whole thing is seriously confusing!" David waved his hands as if trying to push something aside. "I spent more than thirty years of my life working with advanced physics, but now I feel like an idiot."

***

Hans Paulus was even more upset than David, and his family wasn't with him at the Dan to calm him down. Hans was a regional manager for

Siemens, the German industrial giant. He had come to Israel in order to visit the new microprocessor and controller plant being started up near Beer Sheba. It was a joint venture with Israel's Elbit and Intel's Israeli branch. He had planned on going home to Munich on Wednesday. Now, even if he was allowed, it was not an option: Nazi Germany occupied the Republic he knew. And his family was lost somewhere in time.

"What do you mean my credit is no good?" he yelled at the reception clerk. "It was good when I made the reservation, and I am not going away just because you say so." He was furious.

"Sir," said the clerk, "we are doing our best, but the only currency we can accept is Israeli. We're not throwing you out, but we can't provide full hotel services either."

Paulus forced himself to calm down enough to think. He did have a source of credit, assuming they would acknowledge him. "Please call Siemens Israel. I am sure they will solve the payment problem."

"Sir, it doesn't matter. We're emptying the hotel within 30 days," said the clerk. "There is some kind of a government plan to take care of guests after that, but I don't know any details."

***

On the way to the British embassy, Wilson asked the Lieutenant questions about everything he saw. Mosinson was willing to respond, within the limits imposed by his commanders.

The General was especially curious about everything to do with the military. He wanted to know about the vehicle that transported him from Naqoura, and he was even more curious about the helicopter. After several minutes of conversation, looking out the windows onto the brightly lit coastal cities of Israel, Wilson asked: "Lieutenant, how big is the population of Israel?"

"We are near the eight million mark, Sir."

"I noticed that your border post with Lebanon was very well fortified. Were you at war just before you were transported in time?"

"We've been on a war footing ever since the state was established in 1948." Mosinson paused to think. "There were several major wars, with all our Arab neighbors attacking us at once. In the interludes we had an almost-peace – with saboteurs active and Arabs attacking our civilians. When the time displacement occurred, we were at peace, and actually the chances of another war with the Arabs seemed to be diminishing."

Wilson thought for a moment: "I assume that you successfully defended yourselves."

"Well, we defeated all the attacks and acquired some land in the process. Maybe that is the reason they decided to stop those massive attacks."

"Yes, that would explain your military ability. Has Britain been an ally of yours?" Wilson asked.

"Not really, sir. We had diplomatic relations, as evidenced by the embassy you will visit, but as Jews we can rely on no other power to defend us. We had allies in the sense of rendering us diplomatic support, sharing advanced technology, that sort of thing. In our world, for decades, Britain wasn't important enough to count. It did, more or less, what the U.S. asked it to do."

Wilson was taken aback by the last statement: "Young man, what do you mean 'Britain was not important enough'?"

"Sir, I meant no offense. Israel needed to have cutting edge technology to be able to survive. Our government made a decision many years ago that we have to be as self-sufficient as possible. The result was that by the time we were displaced into the here and now we became leaders in a number of technologies, most of them with military use. There was nothing Britain could contribute. As a matter of fact, we were selling advanced equipment to Britain."

"What kind of equipment?"

"Sir, I am not at liberty to disclose that. I can say though that even if I gave you a description it would not be very informative, as even the terminology to describe it doesn't exist yet in your world."

The helicopter was landing on the roof of the British embassy as they finished this exchange. Wilson shook the Lieutenant's hand: "It was a pleasure talking to you, Lieutenant. Will I see you again?"

"Yes, Sir. I will be waiting for you here."

Thomas Harvey was on the roof, shielding his eyes from the dust blown around by the helicopter: "General Wilson, I am Sir Thomas Harvey, Her Majesty's Ambassador to Israel. It is a pleasure to meet you, sir."

"I am pleased to meet you as well, Ambassador."

They shook hands. Wilson paused for a moment: "You said 'Her Majesty'?"

"Yes. It is somewhat confusing. The British government I represent is in the future, and Queen Elizabeth is the Head of State. I hope that the King's government will re-appoint me when the time comes. Please follow me. The rest of the party is waiting for us inside."

Wilson followed the Ambassador into the building, down a short flight of stairs and into an elevator. He was somewhat surprised that the interior of the embassy was pleasantly cool and dry – it was a great improvement over the warm and humid evening outside. It also meant air-conditioning, with which Wilson was familiar mostly through stories. Palestine had progressed indeed.

The room they entered was paneled in dark wood and looked like a dining room at a British club, except it was fairly small and had a glass wall facing the sea. Three men were seated at a dining table. They rose to meet General Wilson and introduced themselves as the Foreign Minister, Defense Minister and Chief of the General Staff of Israel.

"Ah, General Yaari, what a pleasure to finally meet you in person."

"It is my pleasure to meet you, sir. It is amazing to be able to shake your hand. Until now I knew you only from reading history books."

"Gentlemen," interrupted the Ambassador, "may I suggest that we have some drinks and dinner. We can continue our discussion at the table. I am assuming that you still want to return to your headquarters tonight?" he asked Wilson.

"Yes, that would be my preference."

The group exchanged pleasantries while dinner was served. When the wait staff had left them, the Foreign Minister got down to business. "General Wilson, I would like to assure you that the Government of Israel intends to assist Britain in its struggle against the Nazis. We see you as natural allies in this time since it is in our mutual interest that the Germans be beaten."

"I appreciate your declaration of friendship," Wilson said. "Can I count on your assistance with new and advanced military equipment that will give my forces an edge, or, even better, help us defeat Rommel as rapidly as possible?"

Gad Yaari responded: "General, giving you equipment or technology may not be in your best interests. Your country, as advanced as it may seem in this time period, will have no way to either use the equipment efficiently or maintain it without extensive training. Even a seemingly ordinary piece of equipment, like the vehicle that picked you up at

Naqoura, includes technology British scientists will not be able to understand or replicate for many years."

Thomas Harvey nodded his agreement: "As a matter of fact such 'assistance' could be extremely harmful. We can discuss this later, but I completely agree with General Yaari."

The Defense Minister smiled: "We are willing and able to help you though. We can enhance your fighting ability and multiply your forces' effectiveness. These issues will have to be discussed with your government."

"We hope to be friends," the Foreign Minister added. "It did not work out in the time we came from, mostly because of miserable mistakes by British policy makers. I sincerely hope that this time around things will be better." He looked at Thomas Harvey, who picked up his cue:

"General, the Empire, which ceased to exist soon after this war was over, made severe mistakes in its relations with the Jews and the fledgling State of Israel. The Foreign Office had an unreasonable love for and trust in the Arabs, who are doing all they can to curry favor with the Nazis as we speak. I hope, for the sake of Great Britain, that this will not happen now."

Wilson said nothing for a while, concentrating on the excellent steak and good wine. It was not normal British fare, but he had no complaints. The food was very good. "I will report to the Prime Minister," he said finally, "and he will decide how to proceed."

"May I suggest," the Foreign Minister proposed, "that in order to expedite things we send a representative of our government to London as soon as possible. This will make negotiations more efficient."

"I am not a diplomat," Wilson responded, "but it makes sense. I will ask the Prime Minister for instructions."

The conversation that followed touched on Israel's military and industrial abilities but Wilson gained no additional information of any significance.

After the dinner meeting General Wilson was tired and dazed. It seemed to him that the Israelis would be a formidable ally and an even more formidable foe. Although he did not have enough information of the general war situation to be certain, his professional opinion was that their help might be enough for the Empire to defeat the Germans, even without American help, which he knew Churchill sought despite the price. This, he knew, would be welcome news to the Prime Minister. He was quiet on the short flight back to Rosh Hanikra, taking in, again, the sights of the Tel-

Aviv metropolis and the coastal plain, brightly lit as if in defiance of the World War going on around it. He thanked Lieutenant Mosinson and returned to the HQ in Naqoura. It was late, but he had to write his report immediately, while the events were still fresh in his memory.

Chapter 6

SS-Standartenfuhrer (Colonel) Dr. Walter Stachlecker had prepared his speech carefully. He was always a methodical man, a scholar of law. His command, Einsatzgruppe A, included many educated men and he was proud of both his personnel and their assignment. The unit was not large, about a thousand officers and men, but he believed that it was sufficient for the task of exterminating the Jews and other enemies of the Reich in the areas assigned to it.

The Standartenfuhrer climbed onto the hood of his command Volkswagen and looked at his notes. The weather was pleasant, with a light wind. This morning of Monday, June 23, 1941, promised a beautiful day. His whole command was assembled in front of him, with the East Prussian town of Guimbinen as a backdrop. They stood at parade rest, awaiting his words.

"Dear comrades," Stachlecker began after testing the microphone, "we are about to begin our mission for the fatherland. Each of you is expected to do all that is required to rid us of the Jew." Stachlecker paused. A faint, pervasive whine was getting louder, threatening to drown out his speech. It reminded him of something and instinctively he looked up into the sky. Nothing. By the time his gaze was back down to his troops it was too late.

The field was enveloped in fire. It seemed that the ground itself was burning. For all practical purposes Einsatzgruppe A ceased to exist. SS-Standartenfuhrer Dr. Walter Stachlecker was lying on the ground. His right foot was burned, and he could see bones sticking out of the blackened flesh. Otherwise, he thought he was fine, until he blacked out. This could not be said about most of his devoted troops, who died a terrible death, burned alive, shrieking in pain. Some survived badly burned; only a handful escaped unharmed. A couple thousand liters of NAPALM will do that to a tight formation, especially if dropped from a great height and ignited a hundred feet in the air above the target. Not the most humane weapon but one guaranteed to produce the desired result, destroying a large group of fanatics.

***

Hitler was in his office at the Wolfsschanze. He wanted to be as close as possible - while staying at an established command center - to his armies attacking the Soviets. This headquarters, prepared in advance in eastern Prussia, was ideal for his purpose. Its deep bunkers and communications facilities enabled the Fuehrer to observe the attack and intervene, if he so desired. As of now, Monday, June 23, there was no reason to interfere – the Barbarossa plan was working as anticipated.

His secretary knocked on the door; the great man allowed her to enter.

"Mein Fuehrer, the Reichsführer SS wishes to speak with you."

"Let him in," Hitler responded.

The secretary quickly returned with Himmler, who gave the Nazi salute as the door closed behind him.

"Sit," said Hitler, pointing to a chair in front of his huge desk.

"Thank you, mein Fuehrer." Himmler looked serious.

"Heinrich, you look like your dog died today. What's eating you?"

"Mein Fuehrer, I have issued orders to move two battalions of the Shutztaffel from SS division Death-Head to take up the duties of Einsatzgruppen A and B. I just received reports from Guimbinen, which is close to us here, and from Warsaw. It seems that a terrible catastrophe has befallen our Einsatzgruppen A and B. The reports claim that there are less than thirty survivors from both units. Everybody else was burned to death."

"Heinrich, this is a very bad joke," Hitler said, with a grim smile.

"This is no joke, mein Fuehrer. It seems that the attack was directed specifically against the Einsatzgruppen. I also have reports that elements of Einsatzgruppe C and some of D were attacked and annihilated in a similar way."

"How did the Communists discover these units? Why would they attack them? Apparently their love for their Jews is beyond reason. We are pounding them to death, and they hit us just to protect their Jews?"

"Well, I don't know who attacked our units. Why not ask Goering? His Luftwaffe was supposed to give us air cover," Himmler complained. "I was at the Guimbinen site. It looks like somebody took flame throwers to our heroic troops."

"I will deal with Herman later. In the meantime, how much does this delay the execution of the master plan?"

"Mein Fuehrer, the rest of my SS has not been trained for this task but their zeal and numbers will compensate. There will be only a slight delay, maybe a week or so. We can organize locals as planned to do some of the work - They only need a little encouragement. It will not be as efficiently accomplished as it would have been with the troops we lost, but we will spend hardly any additional resources."

"That's not too bad." Hitler smiled. "By then we will be well on the way to finishing off Stalin and I doubt the Communist will have the balls to interfere again."

He was interrupted by another knock on the door. The secretary stuck her head in. "The guard commander has an emergency situation and would like to report to the Reichsführer SS," she said.

"Let him in," said Hitler testily. "Everybody is having emergencies today."

***

Gad Yaari was tense. It was early afternoon of Monday, June 23, 1941. The first reports from the initial phase of Operation Moses were coming in. No losses so far. One of the F15s had had to abort its mission and return to base before reaching its target: They couldn't continue with the targeting computer on the blink. From 20,000 feet in the air you could seriously mess up and hit the wrong target without laser-guided equipment. These things happened, though not often.

Otherwise things were going well. Most of the objectives were achieved either completely or partially. As expected. Not all the Einsatzgruppen were bunched together for a last speech by their commanders. You could only do so much.

According to his computer display, the only units still in the air above Eastern Europe were an aerial tanker and several F15s. The payload to the Wolfsschanze had been delivered. Now the waiting began. Yaari gave orders to prepare for phase two of the operation.

***

The Guard commander explained that the artifact had arrived in what seemed like a regular bomb, except that it dropped from the bright June sky into the middle of the Wolfsschanze parade grounds with no planes in sight. And it did not explode, opening instead like a flower to display a tube inside. When it was clear that the thing was not about to detonate, a brave SS guard opened the tube. Inside was a large rolled-up sheet of film with a message in German.

The guard commander handed the film to Himmler who started reading it with first a surprised and then disgusted expression.

"Himmler, read it aloud."

To: The leadership of Nazi Germany

From: The Great Caliph

We are holding you responsible for the well-being of all Jews under your jurisdiction, including those located in your allied and conquered countries.

You are hereby ordered to immediately stop all persecution of Jews under your control now or in the future. If you continue to act against the Jews, we will kill at least 100 Germans for every Jew you harm.

You will supply the Jews with adequate amounts of food, medicine and clothing to keep them in good health until such time as you will transfer them to us.

We eliminated a large portion of your special troops assigned to exterminate the Jews but as a show of goodwill did not touch the Wehrmacht or German civilians.

You are to confirm the receipt of these orders using the procedure outlined below. If we receive no confirmation within 10 hours, we will destroy a major military target in Germany.

May Allah be with us

Signed: The Great Caliph

Hitler was seriously angry. He sputtered trying to express what he felt. "Whoever had the gall to do this will pay a high price," he yelled. "We will never succumb to demands from the Judeo-Bolsheviks."

His rage exhausted him before he decided what to do with the strange artifact.

"Mein Fuhrer," Himmler said quietly, "I suggest that we wait for Goering. He should be here by evening."

"No." Hitler was calmer now. "We go to Berlin. I want a full analysis of this" - he pointed at the film and the capsule - "by our experts. I will want to hear what options you, the Generals, and Goering propose tomorrow morning."

"This will be past the deadline given by the message." Himmler was uncharacteristically subdued.

"Who cares!" yelled the Fuehrer as he strutted out of the bunker on his way up to the car waiting to take him to the nearby airfield. Himmler had no choice but to follow the great leader.

They were airborne for about five minutes when the co-pilot entered the cabin and saluted. "Mein Fuhrer, we received a voice message. It is still repeating." Hitler made a gesture of acceptance, and the pilot switched on the cabin speakers.

A calm male voice repeated a warning: "The Wolfsschanze will be annihilated in less than a minute. We recommend that everyone close their eyes to preserve vision."

"What is this - another bad joke?" Hitler was looking from the pilot to Himmler.

When the flash came, everyone in the plane wished they had obeyed the instructions to close their eyes. The plane shook with an enormous shock. None of them saw the large, mushroom-shaped cloud rising above Wolfsschanze.

Hitler ordered the pilot to turn around. He must personally see the damage done to his headquarters. "Land on our airstrip," he barked into the intercom. There was no response. After a minute or so, when still nothing happened, he sent his secretary to the cockpit to repeat his order. She came back as the plane was banking into a turn. "The pilots did not hear the order. The intercom is out, as is the radio and some of the instruments in the cockpit," she reported.

They could not land on the airstrip. A huge fire was consuming the surrounding forest. Visibility was limited by smoke, and updrafts made the plane barely controllable. After seeing what he could, Hitler decided to land at the closest place that had an aircraft to take him back to Berlin. They landed in Warsaw, escorted by a fighter plane from the base there since their aircraft hadn't responded to radioed challenges. They had not been shot down only because the Luftwaffe fighter pilot sent to intercept them had correctly recognized the markings as the Fuehrer's personal plane.

On the flight to Berlin Hitler was morose and quiet, except to swear at the Jews and at Goering from time to time. The loss of his devoted and trusted Wolfsschanze guard bothered him not at all. He was annoyed by the fact that the Luftwaffe seemed unable to protect this most important command center. He had ordered Goering to have a Luftwaffe patrol in the skies above Wolfsschanze. Why hadn't they reported anything?

Himmler was hopeful, as he always was when Hitler was angry with Goering, that his position in the leadership was improving.

Another message was waiting when they reached Berlin. This one had been received on the General Staff frequency using the current code.

"You witnessed another show of our good will. The destruction of Wolfsschanze was delayed until after Herr

Hitler's departure. We exterminated a minimum number of German military personnel.

If our orders are not obeyed exactly as given, we will destroy one of your cities."

By now it was close to dawn, an hour before the deadline. Hitler, ever the opportunist, announced to his aides, "We'll start talking to these barbarians in order to gain time. We're bound to learn something that will help us. Promise them whatever they want. They have no way of verifying our promises anyway. Nothing will stop us from solving the Jewish problem." Hitler cheered up at the prospect.

***

At about midnight of the same day the Israeli Chief of General Staff was reporting to the government. "We started the persuasion phase," he said. "A one kiloton tactical device destroyed their headquarters near Rastenburg. This was a target of opportunity we decided to attack. It gave Hitler a good demonstration of what will happen if he doesn't follow our instructions. We will use a seven kiloton bomb, in case the first one did not persuade them. We are also destroying the rail-heads at as many concentration camps as we can reach. This is a list of possible targets for the second bomb and our recommendations." He pulled out a sheaf of papers from his briefcase and gave a page to every member of the cabinet.

It was a list of German cities, with Potsdam at the top and Munich at the bottom.

The Industry and Infrastructure Minister had a question: "I have doubts about the use of a second nuclear weapon. If used once, on Wolfsschanze, it may slip the attention of their scientists. What if they investigate the larger attack we are planning? Will it not advance their research into atomic bombs?"

"It may indeed," responded Amos Nir, "but what choice do we have? We probably could bomb a couple of sensitive targets with conventional bombs, or we could drop an air-fuel bomb on a town. This sort of bomb would cause serious damage, but nowhere as impressive as a nuclear device. It would also have the disadvantage of being easily copied, assuming the Nazis analyze what happened. We don't want to go to war with them – just make them do what we tell them, and do it immediately. To achieve this we must shock the leadership into believing our story or at least convince them to obey us. I think that the risk of this spurring their scientists into a fast development of their own device is real, but acceptable. We will have to deal with this if and when it happens."

***

General Wilson had his reply at about ten in the evening of Monday, June 23, 1941. The radio message from London was short and to the point: "Provide immediate transportation and assist the Palestinian Ambassador with all his needs." – at the Israelis' request their existence was to be kept top secret and all future references were to be to "Palestinians". Since a copy went to Cairo, Wilson was notified by the Cairo RAF wing that, as previously arranged, a Bristol Blenheim was on its way to the Gaza airstrip. It was scheduled to arrive the next morning. The plan was to refuel, pick up the Israeli Ambassador and immediately take off for London, only stopping to refuel at Malta. The Israelis promised an air umbrella for the bomber all the way to Gibraltar with, in their estimate, a safe course directly over Libya and Morocco, potential Italian, French or Luftwaffe interference notwithstanding.

Wilson sent the agreed upon code to the Israelis. Now it was out of his hands. He hoped that this alliance would help Great Britain win the war quickly. In any case, the danger to the home islands had diminished once the Germans attacked the Soviets. If it wasn't for the U boats, Britain would be in great shape. The German submarines were taking a heavy toll on British shipping. Food and oil were hard to get by on the islands, their availability in the other parts of the Empire not being of great help.

Wilson forced himself to go back to the matters at hand. The Vichy Commissioner for Syria had made contact with Wilson's HQ earlier in the day. Wilson was hopeful that surrender would be negotiated soon. There was not much sense in continuing the slaughter of the French forces in Syria. Apparently the Commissioner figured out that to save his troops they either had to retreat or surrender. Any show of resistance left the heroic units dead by means unknown and the rest so demoralized that resistance seemed absolutely futile. The General planned to respond to the negotiation invitation early the next day, Tuesday, June 24.

***

A ministerial committee was negotiating with Hitler. The group was led by the Prime Minister with the Foreign and Defense Ministers at his side. They consulted a variety of advisors - the Chief of General staff, several historians, and a professional police negotiator being the most important. They also had the resources of the Holocaust remembrance organizations at their disposal. The negotiations were less complicated than anyone could have anticipated. In the original history, Hitler consistently approached conflict by trying to bully opponents, making empty promises, and doing as he pleased in secret. This time, events on the ground were known almost immediately, which gave the committee an enormous advantage.

"Let me summarize the situation," Amos Nir said. "As of yesterday night, Monday, June 23, the Nazis promised to take good care of the Jews, like we required of them. Their only condition was that we remove these Jews from Europe immediately. I propose that we explain to them that they have to organize the transportation of Jews by rail to major ports on the Mediterranean and from there by ships to Palestine. We damaged some of the railheads near large concentration camps, but this should not impede their efforts for very long."

"You are assuming they intend to keep the agreement?" wondered the Foreign Minister.

"Not at all. On the contrary, I believe they are preparing to execute their original plans as we speak. According to the history we know, the Nazis stirred up a pogrom in Lutsk, in the Ukraine, on June 25 - tomorrow. This may or may not happen on schedule. We've changed history sufficiently that historical records are now unreliable, becoming more so by the minute. We just have to watch carefully and respond as soon as there is sufficient data to indicate cheating."

The negotiating team was satisfied with the proposed solution, and the experts concurred.

***

Mid-morning, Tuesday, June 24, 1941, found Hitler meeting with his General Staff, Goering and Himmler. With the aid of giant maps on the conference table and on the wall, Field Marshal von Brauchitsch, the Commander in Chief of the German Army, explained the army's advances on the eastern front. Goering was beaming as if the whole success of Barbarossa was his doing – which annoyed Himmler immensely. Undeniably the Luftwaffe had eliminated the Soviet air force very efficiently and was of great help to the Wehrmacht on the ground. On the other hand, he had no explanation for what happened at Wolfsschanze: both the delivery of the message on film and the method by which the base was destroyed remained a mystery.

Hitler was quite satisfied with the army's progress against the Soviet Union and soon dismissed the generals. Only Goering and Himmler remained.

"Send them in," he said into the intercom.

Four people entered the conference room: Professor Dr. Fritz Koenig, Joseph Goebbels, Joachim von Ribbentrop and Alfred Rosenberg. Hitler gestured for them to be seated at the huge table. Koenig looked a bit nervous; he was not accustomed to the presence of The Fuehrer.

"We will begin with Dr. Koenig," Hitler announced. "Please report your findings."

Koenig got up and spread a number of large photographs and diagrams on the table. He was in his late fifties, medium height, medium build and nondescript looks. His appearance was deceptive. Fritz Koenig held doctorates from several universities - including Harvard, Cambridge and Heidelberg - in several disciplines, including physics, chemistry and engineering. He was a veteran Nazi party member, a senior scientific advisor to the SS since 1938 and was highly valued by Himmler.

"I would first like to make a general comment," he began, "on the state of the artifacts. I was given three to examine. One of them looked like some kind of optical device, the other was a transparent film, and the last was a metal structure that resembled a five petal flower about one meter tall and approximately fifteen centimeters in diameter when closed." Koenig went on for several minutes describing and analyzing different parts of the devices.

"Now to the film. This is most interesting. We've been unable to determine what it's made of. It's a polymer, very strong, somewhat elastic, flexible, transparent, extremely tear-resistant and fire resistant. I never saw anything like it and have no idea how it was made. I wish I could meet the people who produced it. If we knew how it was synthesized..." he finished wistfully.

"Are you sure you never saw anything similar to this film?" Goering asked. "What about photographic film, or Plexiglas?"

"Well, it is much stronger than nitrocellulose, which is the material of photo film, and it does not burn, like photo film will. Our chemical analysis showed no resemblance to nitrocellulose or Plexiglas. I have to admit that it showed nothing at all – the material did not dissolve in either acid or alkaline liquids. We tried mass spectroscopy by cutting off a tiny piece of the film and burning it. The results were inconclusive. This film is composed of a bewildering array of elements, some of which we can't identify."

"Are you saying that we could not match or copy this material if we wanted to?" Goebbels asked.

"I regret that is true, Herr Goebbels, at least for now," Koenig carefully responded. "I know of no industrial nation in the world that could make such a material. The same goes for the writing – it is made of microscopic carbon particles imbedded in the film and we don't know how this was done either."

Hitler was thinking and did not say anything for a few minutes. Finally he got up from his chair and started pacing along the long wall of the room in front of the picture windows. "Dr. Koenig, thank you for your time. Continue working on this problem. I want to know who made these things. The Fatherland must have this knowledge as soon as possible."

Koenig left the room, giving the Nazi salute and a "Heil Hitler".

"Now to the other matter," said Hitler. "What is the situation, Himmler?"

Himmler smiled obsequiously: "I have Obersturmbannfuhrer Eichmann waiting outside. He planned the actions and will update us."

Eichmann was called in. He saluted the Fuehrer with a brisk 'Heil Hitler' and smartly clicked his heels.

"You may sit" said Hitler. He didn't like people standing while he was pacing.

"Mein Fuehrer," Eichmann began, "since yesterday SS units have been on the move into the Baltic countries and the Ukraine. We expect to be able to start full scale operations on Friday. In the meantime we moved a number of SS officers ahead of the main force with orders to encourage the locals to start a cleansing on their own. The Wehrmacht is aware of our objectives and is assisting.

"According to the projections I have now, we should be back on the original schedule by the end of July. The total delay caused by the incident with the Einsatzgruppen will be negligible in the long run."

Hitler stopped pacing and took his place at the table. "Eichmann, I commend you on the good job you have done for the Fatherland. My secretary has instructions for you."

Eichmann left.

"Ribbentrop, how are the negotiations going?"

"Mein Fuehrer, I told them, as you instructed, that we will do no harm to the Jews and will treat them well, but only if they remove them immediately. They responded with a detailed set of instructions on how we are supposed to handle the Jews. We are to round them up and transport them to the port of Brindisi in southern Italy. From there we are to ship them to Palestine. They want us to use our own ships, promising that none would be harmed by the British while on this mission. They also claim that British ships will participate in this action."

Himmler smiled. "Well, here we have an opportunity to do just what we planned, with these people none the wiser. Who can blame us if all the Jews die on the way to Italian ports?"

"There is a small problem," responded Ribbentrop. "These people, who we call the "Caliphate" for convenience sake, also warned us that if any Jew dies for whatever reason, they will kill 100 Germans. This includes Jews in territories occupied by us or by our allies. We're to be held responsible for every single one, protecting them under threat of death to our citizens."

Himmler made a dismissive gesture. "And how will they enforce this threat or even know when a Jew is harmed? Besides, nobody knows how many Jews live within our domain and where exactly they are at the moment. The threat is phony - we can disregard it. I hope you agreed to their conditions."

Goering stirred in his seat for the first time since the meeting began. "My people examined the site where Wolfsschanze used to be. Do you know that trees were shattered and burned in a radius of more than five kilometers from the epicenter of the explosion? All the bunkers are either dust or collapsed, including the main Fuehrerbunker which was fifteen meters underground with a roof three meters thick. We estimate that the bomb contained close to two thousand tons of high explosives. Obviously such a bomb could not be delivered by aircraft.

"Himmler, have you taken a look at the Todd Organization? They built the site and could have concealed a huge bomb. There are traitors everywhere, and you seem to be doing very little about them. We can't disregard the possibility that there are bombs concealed in other places ready to explode. The "Caliphate" might have spies all over the place - even here." Goering was at rest again. His dig at Himmler was effective, but it also contained a core of true concern.

"Some of your experts claim that the explosion was in the air above the bunkers," Himmler remarked belligerently. "I have no idea how it was done, but it seems to me that the Luftwaffe did a lousy job protecting the Fuehrer."

Goering was not happy that Himmler knew what the Luftwaffe experts had reported, but he was not surprised. He spied on Himmler, Himmler spied on him. This was a pervasive practice in the Third Reich.

"Stop the bickering!" Hitler was pacing again. "Ribbentrop, I agree that we need an accord with these people. I don't want interference while we're fighting the Soviets. By the way, how do we know it's not the British or the Soviets that are playing this game? Who would want to deliver these millions of Jews to Palestine? It will annoy the British, but they are promising British cooperation. It must be the Bolsheviks hoping to distract us. Goering is right: there's an extensive Bolshevik spy network inside the Fatherland. Himmler, you have to concentrate on exterminating these spies. Start with those in your own organization."

He stopped looking at the blinking intercom light, which meant that the secretary had something important to report. "Go ahead," Hitler said into the machine.

The secretary was apologetic. "Mein Fuehrer, a courier from the General Staff arrived with a message marked important and urgent, for your eyes only."

"I'll see it now," barked Hitler.

From: The Mighty Caliph, may Allah preserve him

To: My Brother, Herr Adolph Hitler the Great

My dear Fuehrer, I admire you greatly. You are the genius leader of the mightiest nation on Earth. The way you deal with the inferior nations is most admirable and a subject of imitation for myself and my subordinates.

Your firm intent of cleansing the world of Jews and Bolsheviks is like a bright star pointing the way for rest of us. We desire to assist you in fulfilling your destiny, ensuring that the Bolsheviks are defeated and that the British and Americans submit to your domination. With this in mind, we take upon ourselves the holy task of exterminating the Jews.

As my brother, the Grand Mufti of Jerusalem, may he bask forever in Allah's blessings, will confirm, we are destined by Allah the Great and Merciful, may He be blessed forever, to exterminate the Jews. The salvation of my people and their future in paradise depends upon our participating in this great endeavor. I therefore demand that you transfer the Jews to us for treatment. We cannot compromise on this issue.

Treat the Jews well and protect them from harm so that they come willingly and our inconvenience is minimized as much as possible. You may intimidate them so they will be willing to come, but do not harm them.

With great admiration,

The Great Caliph

Allahu Akbar

Hitler looked at the attendees, all old comrades of his, and read the message aloud.

Himmler was the first to respond. "This sounds very strange. The Mufti is doing a great job forming whole SS divisions of Muslim volunteers - they can be useful allies - but I can hardly believe that the Arabs suddenly got so powerful."

Hitler looked at Rosenberg: "Well, Alfred, what do you think?"

Rosenberg thought for a moment. "It is not inconceivable that the Arabs got themselves organized and have a Caliph who would want to exterminate the Jews."

"I didn't ask for a strategic evaluation, Alfred. Your specialty is racial purity and our Nordic destiny. How does the Great Caliph, assuming he exists, fit into this?"

Rosenberg was embarrassed, which did not prevent him from assuming a grand pose, difficult to do while sitting. "Every nation has its manifest destiny. As you all know, ours is to rid the world of inferior peoples and to make the Aryan race supreme. The Jews are the leeches of the world, sucking blood and corrupting our nation. It is their destiny to be exterminated. As the Mufti will tell you, the Muslims also have a destiny to purify their land of Jews. Apparently this Caliph is smart enough to realize they must kill them all to solve the problem. It's very clever to use the Jews' fantastic preoccupation with Jerusalem and Palestine to lure them into a trap."

Goebbels waited patiently, and when he was sure Rosenberg was finished, he asked: "It seems to me that our destiny collides with the Muslims' regarding the Jews. Isn't it our destiny to destroy them? I think that our destiny should prevail."

Rosenberg was thinking fast. He had the impression that the Fuehrer liked the Caliph's message, which was even more admiring and flattering than anything Mussolini ever said. If only he could deflect Goebbels' criticism of his analysis, his standing with Hitler would improve.

"Dear Joseph," Rosenberg began, somewhat condescendingly, "you think too literally. There is no conflict of destinies, not even a hint of one. If we hand the Jews over to the Caliph and he implements the Final Solution, both our destinies are fulfilled. We would have purified Europe of Jews, and the Muslims would get their ticket to heaven by exterminating them." He smiled triumphantly.

"Himmler?" asked Hitler.

"I have to admit that Rosenberg makes sense, except that we don't know who this Caliph is and that bothers me. What if he's a British trick to save the Jews?"

"And why would they bother?" inquired Hitler. "They never cared before, and now, with all the problems they are having, with Rommel giving them grief in North Africa and our U boats starving them, they suddenly develop tenderness for the Jews? In any case, the British couldn't have destroyed Wolfsschanze as this Caliph managed to do."

"Mein Fuehrer, you are correct. I can see that a division or two of SS attached to the Afrika Corps would help Rommel kick the British out of Egypt in short order and open a way to Iraqi oil. These divisions, and more, will become available if we stop all actions against the Jews. On the other hand I don't like the idea of the Jewish question being resolved by somebody else – which is what we will have to do if we follow the Caliph's request. Shall we oblige him?" asked Himmler.

"No, don't be silly, dear Heinrich. Go ahead with the plan Eichmann described to us, at least for the next couple of months. In the meantime let's think about moving the rest of the Jews to the port the Caliph designated. It's a good idea to keep those that are not liquidated as happy as possible until they are either moved or, in their turn, liquidated. Present a plan in about two months. The Soviets should be on their knees by then and we can decide what to do next."

***

Avigdor Mizrahi was an experienced diplomat, though he spent the last five years in private business. At 5'6" he was not tall. He was slightly overweight, but otherwise in good physical shape. Starting his career in the seventies as a mechanical engineer, it did not take him very long to decide that he liked the management and negotiating parts of his job best, especially when combined with international travel. When he learned that the foreign ministry was looking for diplomatic service trainees, he applied without hesitation and quickly advanced to the rank of Ambassador. He had represented Israel in several East European countries and for a year had been the ambassador to the court of St. James. His appointment to the U.K. ended when a new government took power in Jerusalem and a political appointee was sent to replace him.

That was it for Avigdor, who resigned from the foreign ministry and went into business. His high tech import/export company was very successful. He was a rich and happy man. His wife, Ruhama, was a pediatrician. A good looking woman, she was his partner and source of strength, supporting him through difficult times in the foreign ministry as well as in business. He, in turn, encouraged her to do what she liked. His job at the Foreign Ministry called for long absences of months at a time, putting a strain on the marriage. Ruhama had accompanied him and did her best to practice her profession in his assigned countries, until their firstborn son was of high school age and they decided that it will be best for him to remain in Israel, with Ruhama. Now all three children were independent. Their son was a career army officer and father of two; the two daughters were also married with families of their own.

Avigdor Mizrahi finished packing two suitcases containing the personal belongings necessary for his upcoming diplomatic mission as the doorbell rang. Ruhama opened the door of their elegant home in the Mevaseret Zion suburb of Jerusalem.

"Lior Kashti," a smiling man said to Ruhama, "to see Ambassador Mizrahi."

They shook hands as Avigdor entered to take the young man into his study. Ruhama did not accompany them – she knew that some things were between her husband and the government.

"I am from the technical section."

"Yes, I know. They warned me that you would be coming. I have an hour before I need to leave and I'm not completely done here, so let's be quick."

Lior got right to business. "This is the 'special'," he said, putting a box on the desk and pulling out a hard-sided leather briefcase. "And this is the work model that goes with it," he said, pulling another one out of the box. The two cases looked identical.

"You will notice, Ambassador, that both briefcases have two combination locks which are very difficult to pick. In addition, they only open if you put your thumb here." He pointed to a spot. "Both are made of titanium. The first case has much less internal space and weighs more. It contains the satellite transceiver, battery, and charger. Operation is simple: you open the case, put your thumb here," he demonstrated, "and the internal lid will open. We will calibrate it to your thumbprint in a moment. Here you have a LCD display and keyboard. This is the on-off switch." He paused. "Is everything clear so far?"

"Go ahead. If I have a question, I will interrupt you. Shy I am not."

"OK. If you have a message, this light will blink. The minimum time between messages is about an hour and a half since the satellite has to be directly overhead." The technician looked at Avigdor, who nodded.

"If you want to send a message, press the 'New Message' button, wait for the display to say 'OK' and type it in. Press the 'Send' button when you are done."

"Wait a minute," interrupted Mizrahi. "How do I know when the satellite is overhead, and what about encryption?"

The technician smiled. "Don't worry about the satellite. The transceiver will send the message automatically at the right time. As to encryption, that happens as you type, the encryption key changing with every transmission as the transceiver gets a new key from the satellite. Anyway, don't worry about security. We tested this system very thoroughly. Never had a leak."

Mizrahi thought for a moment. "So I have to leave this device on all the time in order for it to talk to the satellite. Where is the antenna?"

"The antenna is in the lid. This is the cord for recharging the battery. You can plug it in into any outlet, no matter what voltage. We've provided a number of adaptors that should do the job in England."

Another ten minutes programming the device to reliably recognize Mizrahi's thumbprint and the technician left, giving Avigdor a few moments to say good bye to his wife before a Ministry car stopped outside. "I will do my best to bring you over, as soon as it is safe and possible," he promised.

A Bristol Blenheim was waiting when he arrived at the Gaza aerodrome at eleven in the morning of Tuesday, June 24, 1941. The seat was canvas - not too bad. He had noise canceling earphones and an iPod for entertainment. At 260 miles per hour, or more likely about 200 to conserve fuel, it would take about six and a half hours to reach Malta, about the same time to get to Gibraltar, and again to London. All in all about 24 hours, including refueling stops.

The light bomber was stripped of all armament and non-essential equipment. The pilot, a fresh faced Briton, assured the ambassador they had enough fuel to get to Malta. In case they didn't, the pilot cheerfully explained, the Royal Navy was ready to fish them out. He handed Mizrahi a parachute, which the diplomat donned. He hoped his army service as a paratrooper hadn't been a deciding factor in offering him this job. Despite the passage of many years, he still remembered hating that first step out of a plane high above the ground.

***

Mohammad Husseini spent several hours driving. He made relatively good progress, despite the security checkpoints. At all of the checkpoints but one he was waved through with just a perfunctory inspection of his ID. The checkpoints were manned by combined Israeli–Palestinian teams which today seemed somewhat relaxed. Only at one checkpoint, the first he encountered when exiting Jenin, was he politely asked to exit the car and patted down for weapons. Even that was done superficially; otherwise they would have found the commando knife he always carried in a holster on his leg.

Mohammad arrived in Ramallah with time to spare and began with a visit to his friend and colleague – the Hamas commander of the area. He got a quick update on the local situation and proceeded to the Mukata – the presidential compound. At the entrance he was thoroughly searched and gave his knife and pepper spray to the guards for safe keeping. He was searched two more times, at the entrance to the building and at the guard station inside. Finally he was taken by a guard to the second floor. The guard knocked on the door.

"Come in," a voice sounded from inside.

Mohammed opened the door and entered. It wasn't his first visit, but he still marveled at the setup: the room was big, larger than the corridor with its closely spaced doors implied. A large desk occupied the space in front of a picture window. With the light coming through the large window, the figure behind the desk was not clearly visible. The desk and the chair behind it were elevated on a discreet platform, making a visitor feel small and insignificant.

"My dear friend," the figure behind the desk said, "I am glad to see you."

"As I you, Mr. Chairman," Mohammad responded. "We need to discuss a plan I developed to make us victorious, with Allah's help."

Dr. Ahmad Mazen, Chairman of the Palestinian Authority, rose from behind his desk: "Let's get more comfortable." He moved to the armchairs and coffee table in a corner of the room. A pot of coffee, cookies and sandwiches were spread out on the table. Mazen was a big man with a dominant presence. He was not charismatic, but through clever manipulation of different Palestinian factions he rose to power and intended to hold on to his power. His relations with Israel were as good as could be expected. Just before The Event he had been scheduled to meet with the Israeli Prime Minister for another round of peace talks. As usual, if the negotiations went too far and threatened to become practical, he would order one of the factions, preferably Hamas or one of the smaller groups, to kill some Jews. This would interrupt the talks and return everything to normal. That way he managed to keep talking peace without giving up hope of a final victory.

"What is this plan you want to discuss?" he asked after they were settled with cups of coffee in their hands.

"Mr. Chairman," Mohammad began respectfully, "do you believe the Israeli announcement about this strange time displacement?"

"Well, I have no reason to believe they are lying."

"Okay then, this is my plan." Mohammad went on to describe his plan to contact the Mufti and the Germans.

"Very ingenious, my dear Mohammad. What will happen if one of your couriers is caught and confesses who sent him?"

"We'll not be worse off than before. I will take the normal precaution of the courier not knowing who send him; the worst that can happen is that one of my cell commanders will spend some time in an Israeli jail."

"Yes, I believe we can get away with this. As long as the Palestinian Authority can't be implicated, I will support you. What do you need?"

"Mr. Chairman, our connections inside Israel are not very good. It would be very helpful if we could use some of your people as guides. We will also need up to date intelligence on the movement of Israeli troops and, if it is at all possible, some kind of legitimate ID cards for our operatives that will allow them to pass at least a superficial inspection."

"Let's start with the easy part. When we are done here ask my chief of security in Jenin to arrange for the ID cards. By the time you get back there, he will have orders to supply you with up to date information on troop movements. He will also supply you with guides. Anything else I can do for you?"

"No, sir. I appreciate your help. May Allah be with you always."

"Allahu Akbar" Mazen responded.

Chapter 7

At noon on Wednesday, June 25, 1941, the Reverend John Walker was back at his Jerusalem hotel, mentally exhausted. He had rushed to the American consulate yesterday morning after being informed that the group he was leading on a tour of the Holy Land would have to vacate their rooms in less than thirty days. The consul was very polite but claimed not to be able to help. It was perfectly reasonable, he said, for the hotel to refuse the group accommodations. Walker threatening to move his group into the consulate persuaded the consul to make a couple of calls to Israeli officials and accompany him to the Foreign Ministry.

A harried Foreign Ministry Deputy General Director told them that since the group was not official guests of the state, there was nothing he could do and advised them to try the Finance or Welfare Ministries. They tried both. Everyone was busy; they couldn't even get past reception. The consul, slightly offended, gave up.

The Reverend was ready to explode. Finally – at ten this morning – Walker managed to see a functionary at the Department of Social Security of the Welfare Ministry.

The official was polite. "My dear Reverend," he said in heavily accented English, "it is my pleasure to meet you. How can I be of help?"

"We were told by the hotel management that they expect us to leave within thirty days," Walker responded, with barely contained anger. "We are American citizens and will not accept shabby treatment. I want you to arrange for us to fly back to the United States as soon as possible!" Walker glared at the official, who smiled pleasantly back.

"I completely understand your distress, but I don't know what to say. We are working on long-term solutions and will let you know when we have anything new." The bureaucrat was finished and expected the Reverend to leave.

But Walker couldn't give up. "What do you mean 'long-term'? We have no desire to stay here indefinitely!"

The Israeli official was losing his patience. "Sir, there are no commercial flights from Israel to anywhere. You heard the announcement! There's a war going on in Europe. And even if you did manage to fly safely to the U.S., where would you go, what would you do? No one in the country knows any of you: your homes aren't there.

"Look," he said, seeing Walker's growing panic and sympathizing, "there's no way right now to get you back to where you came from. The only thing to do is to try and take care of your group here, now. In every other place it's 1941.

I can assure you that you will not be thrown out on the street. Your people will be treated well, but we are still working out the details, so please be patient."

Walker walked slowly back to the hotel where he assembled his group in a conference room. They looked good, rested and fresh, unlike their pastor. They did not seem worried; they trusted him.

"We cannot go back to the U.S. as planned," the Reverend announced quietly, "which isn't so bad if you consider the circumstances. Right now there's nowhere else in the world offering the kind of conveniences we take for granted, like being able to consult a doctor who's heard of the medicines we take. The Israeli government has promised to provide us with the services and accommodations we need. So, as long as we're stuck here, think about what we'd find in America now and give thanks."

The group obediently bowed their heads. But it wasn't long before their prayers gave way to a loud discussion. Apparently not everyone felt thankful.

***

Gad Yaari was finishing his report to the negotiating Committee. Unsurprisingly, the Nazis had not heeded the warnings about harming the Jews. According to radio intercepts several 'actions' were planned, the first to take place in Lutsk, Ukraine – just like in the old time-line. Yaari recommended caution, since the Nazis did seem to be complying with some of the demands. Radioed orders seemed to indicate that Jews were not treated as brutally as in the original time-line. The radio intercepts also talked about Eichmann and a bunch of other experts preparing to go to Italy to survey sites for transfer camps in the area designated by the Caliph.

"The German ambassador in Rome was instructed to start negotiating with the Italian government to establish transit camps for Jews on its territory," he reported.

"So do we go ahead as planned if they start killing Jews?" Amos Nir asked.

Mina Katz, a psychologist and experienced hostage negotiator, leaned back in her chair and offered her opinion: "These people are psychopaths. We predicted they'd accept the caliph idea since it fits their warped view of the world. Basically, they bought it. They did not however accept the idea that our Caliph is as dangerous or determined as they are. A strong reaction to their noncompliance is likely to persuade the Nazis that they can't afford to play games. I recommend that we continue according to plan."

Almost everyone in the room had lost family to the Holocaust. All of them, even the few who had no relatives in Europe at this time, had learned in childhood how important it was to never again let Jews be slaughtered. There could be no compromise with the Nazis.

"We need to approve a target then," Amos Nir stated. "The destruction has to be very painful. The way I see it, we have to destroy a large area in order to demonstrate the Caliph's power.

"At the same time, the strategic balance in the war has to be preserved. We're helping the Nazi war effort by making them treat the Jews humanely instead of making a huge investment in the machinery of extermination. We estimate that that alone will prolong the war by another year. After all, tens of thousands of troops can now be sent to fight the Soviets, including construction groups freed to build fortifications instead of concentration camps. Plus huge amounts of ammunition, railway rolling stock, fuel and industrial effort newly made available. Most historians believe the Germans would have won their war against the Soviets, or at least captured Moscow, if they hadn't been diverting so many resources to kill Jews. We must compensate; otherwise we'll have to intervene directly."

The negotiating committee discussed available options for another hour. When a decision was made, the Chief of General Staff gave his orders to the Commanding General of the Air Force.

***

It was almost dark by the time the Bristol Blenheim carrying Avigdor Mizrahi landed in London. He was stiff, tired, and hungry. The cheerfulness of the British pilots annoyed him. A fresh crew had come aboard in Gibraltar who knew nothing about either Mizrahi or his mission. They were the second new crew, with the first exchange having been made in Malta. It seemed that Churchill abided by the Israelis' request to keep the whole affair secret. At the moment Mizrahi didn't care. All he wanted was a hot shower, a meal, a bed.

A car with its lights almost invisible due to the blackout was waiting by the aircraft when they finally stopped taxiing, at a remote corner of the airport. There were no discernible potholes in the landing strip, though Mizrahi knew it had been bombed only a couple of days before.

The driver got out and opened the rear door. The Israeli had the heavy briefcase with him and watched as the rest of his luggage was taken off the bomber and put in the trunk. Nothing more to do but get comfortable in the back of the limousine, where he quickly fell asleep.

It was completely dark when they stopped in front of an open door. The driver ushered him inside and closed the door behind them. When the light came on, Mizrahi was surprised by the size of the entrance hall. The house appeared to be big, well-furnished and comfortable. He looked forward to exploring it sometime, when he wasn't so tired.

***

Several hours earlier, Hitler had been listening to Fritz Todt, the Third Reich's armaments minister: "Mein Fuehrer, I have no idea what happened. According to eyewitnesses from the surrounding villages, at approximately six in the afternoon the sun descended on Wolfsburg. I do not give much credit to peasants' tales, but some of the observers were trained anti-aircraft officers from batteries around the town. I saw them myself - severely burned, some blind. They describe a flash brighter than the sun directly over the Volkswagen plant. We found pieces of the steel structures and machinery, but essentially the plant and town are gone, flattened and burned."

Goering, Himmler and Goebbels listened along with Hitler. Everyone sat quietly, stunned and sobered.

"Mein Fuehrer," continued Todt, "we don't have spare capacity at any other plant to produce vehicles. Volkswagen also made spare parts and assemblies for other manufacturers. I am working on solutions, but as of now we've found no industrial replacement and I'm afraid our war effort will suffer."

"How many people did we lose?" asked Hitler.

"Our best estimate is about seventeen thousand, trained workers and their families. Also some slaves."

The intercom buzzed. "Yes," Hitler said quietly.

"A message from the General staff radio room. Personal and confidential for you, sir."

Hitler had the message brought in and read it. Throwing it on his desk, he told Goebbels to read it aloud.

To: The glorious Fuehrer of victorious Germany

From: The Great Caliph, may Allah cherish and preserve him forever

My dear brother:

I regret the destruction of Wolfsburg. My heart bleeds for all the good Aryans that had to die. If you had followed my instructions, we would not have caused this terrible loss of life and property.

You must stop killing Jews. You already deprived us of more than 300 from Lutsk. No more. You must give them to us unharmed and happy or accept Allah's terrible retribution again.

I extend my friendship to you, dear Fuehrer, and remain,

Your sincere friend and admirer,

The Great and Merciful Caliph, may Allah cherish Him forever

"This was not a pre-positioned bomb, Goering." Hitler sounded hysterical as he paced back and forth. "This was some kind of hellish device that came from the air. Where was the Luftwaffe? Why didn't you do anything to protect Wolfsburg?"

Goering made a dismissive gesture, as if pushing the responsibility away. "I have no idea where this bomb came from – No one at the anti-aircraft batteries saw anything. We debriefed them thoroughly. They claim that there was no aircraft to be seen or heard anywhere in the area."

Goebbels thoughtfully studied the message: "We need to make an announcement. An industrial accident or sabotage - What will it be? Personally, I am for an accident - We don't want to give saboteurs that much credit." The remark seemed to calm everybody down: There was something familiar to discuss and decide, even in this weird situation. An accident it would be. Goebbels had a keen sense for propaganda and the others trusted him in this matter. Silence followed the decision.

Todd was the first to speak: "We can ill afford the loss of another industrial city. Is there a way we could go on killing Jews and not risk retaliation?"

"This Caliph doesn't seem to be rational. He sounds like a religious fanatic that will not stop until he gets what he wants," said Goebbels. "And he has the advantage of having a weapon we can't counter or defend against."

Himmler said: "I suggest we postpone the planned actions. We have a big one planned for tomorrow in Kaunas, Lithuania, plus some smaller ones in other places. The Romanians are also active and I don't know who else. Before we go on, we need to identify who are the spies that give this Caliph information. We can resume our plans as soon as we fix the leaks."

"My dear Heinrich," Hitler's voice was sarcastic and venomous, "are you proposing that we make the Jews safe and happy, just like this maniac proposes?"

"Mein Fuehrer," Goering hesitated for a second, "of course getting rid of the Jews is worth a city or two, but why lose anything at all? If we do as the Caliph asks, we get rid of the Jew infestation with very little effort. They won't be happy for long - they'll be gone. This Caliph seems to be fanatical on the subject of Jews. Why not let him do the work for us. We will have all the resources freed for the war effort and this fanatic will do a good job on the Jews. He certainly seems to have the ability and will for this."

Herman Goering sat very quietly now. He gambled on Hitler's admiration for the First World War ace and commander of the Red Baron's squadron he had been. He needed to draw attention away from the air force's failures guarding against this Caliph. It was unlikely that Hitler would shoot him on the spot. On the other hand, if the Fuehrer was swayed by his argument, he truly became the second most powerful man in Germany and therefore the world. Himmler would never again be a threat or even an irritation.

"You are very audacious, my dear Herman, but there may be some truth to your argument." Goering could breathe again.

It took hours to hammer out a plan of action. The first step was for Goebbels to write a letter to the Great Caliph:

From: The Great Leader of Germany

To: The Great Caliph

My dear friend:

It was absolutely unnecessary for you to destroy a German city. I am in full agreement about the fate of the Jews. They will be transferred to you in as good a condition as possible. I cannot promise that absolutely no Jews will be harmed in the process, especially since my allies are not as well organized and may not respond readily to your demands.

Nevertheless, I will do my best to ensure they follow your instructions. You can be assured that any deviations from your demands will be solely due to their failures, for which you should, of course, hold them responsible.

I trust that no more unfortunate incidents will mar our excellent relationship.

Your partner in this great mission,

The Fuehrer of Great Germany

The letter was approved and immediately radioed on the frequency and code designated by the Caliph. A promising response came while they were still considering the orders and actions to be taken.

From The Great Caliph, may Allah cherish Him forever.

To: The Fuehrer of Great Germany

Dear Brother,

I am certain there will be no more incidents between our great nations. We will be reasonable regarding unintentional accidents. Please emphasize to your allies that their punishment for disobedience will be very severe as they are not pure Aryans and deserve no consideration.

We expect all newspapers and radio stations to immediately instruct the populations in Germany, your conquered territories and the territories of your allies to treat Jews well, promising the usual reprisals if they do not.

Looking forward to putting Jews on ships, with your cooperation, I remain

Your admiring friend,

The Great Caliph may Allah smile on his fortunes forever

***

Amos Nir was hosting a number of Knesset members for a Q&A session. The Prime Minister preferred these discussions to a full debate in parliament. It was easier to quell opposition and explain things to a small group than before the full Knesset.

The attendees were briefed, as he was doing for all the members of parliament, on the first use of nuclear weapons by Israel. Some of them were extremely unhappy and not shy about expressing it. A member who was also the leader of a human rights organization had told him, "Prime Minister, you can't continue with your barbaric policies. We will not be a party to Israel murdering tens of thousands of innocent civilians. This behavior is not fit for civilized people and absolutely unacceptable to us as Jews. Your actions put us on a level with the Nazis, and I cannot possibly condone this!"

Amos looked at the group in front of him. Judging by their reactions, many of them agreed that the bombing of Wolfsburg was "un-Jewish". It was his belief that their attitude was self-defeating, extremely dangerous, and demonstrated a serious defect in their understanding of Jewish values.

"I will respond first to the claim that we killed innocent civilians," Amos Nir began. "This is a fallacy based on the assumption that the German civilian population is neutral in this conflict. I don't think it is. They're enthusiastically making weapons, growing food and generally are doing all they can to support their state and its policies. It is immaterial whether they do this voluntarily or not: as long as the Nazi state is supported by its population, that population is a legitimate target."

He paused to allow some of the group to indicate disagreement.

"Let me ask you a question," Amos continued. "If enemy planes are attacking us, do we limit ourselves to just destroying the aircraft overhead or is it legitimate for us to go after their airfields?"

"Yes, but this is irrelevant," the human rights advocate asserted. "We are talking about civilians here."

"So you agree that we can attack the airfields," Amos continued. "If so, then why not attack the factories that make those planes?"

"That's legitimate," was the response, "but not killing people in their homes."

"So you are saying that we can kill them at work but not at home, or we can kill them as long as they are in uniform, but not if they take it off?"

"Exactly," responded the Knesset member smugly.

"In that case, we can't touch any of the millions of Nazi party members or the Gestapo or any of the other functionaries who are the foundation of this regime - just because they don't wear uniforms. I hope you see that what you are saying amounts to fighting the army but leaving its supporting infrastructure and political leadership in peace. That's a very cruel policy - the war will go on indefinitely with huge numbers of people killed, after they don uniforms, of course.

"And let's not forget that in the current situation such a policy will lead to the extermination of millions of Jews and others who truly *are* innocent."

Amos sensed a change in mood, though his opponent still seemed dubious. "We made this mistake with the Arabs. In my opinion, we would have had peace with them years ago if we had behaved toward them along the lines of our actions towards the Nazis. Our strategy only prolonged the conflict and cost many more lives than it should have. I repeat: we will regard any civilian population helping and abetting our enemy as *being* the enemy - and treat it as such. *No one* is innocent or immune to violence in a war. This was the strategy the Allies used against Germany in this war and it worked."

"You don't know what you're saying!" his opponent cried. "Your statement justifies terrorism – It's just what the Arabs have always said! Are you saying they were right?"

"Certainly! The terrorist were, and still are, attacking our population. This population supports the state by serving in its armed forces, working in its factories and otherwise participating in making it stronger. As far as I'm concerned this is a legitimate application of force. But don't forget that this argument cuts both ways: we are justified to attack the civilians who enable the terrorists to act by sheltering them, providing them with materiel and moral support and allowing them to disappear into their crowds. To give you a simple example: If rockets are fired from a neighborhood against us we are justified to destroy the neighborhood by artillery fire. We have no obligation to hunt down just the perpetrators and keep the civilians safe, just as they have no such obligation. Our only obligation is to the citizens of this state.

"Let me answer the claim about this being un-Jewish behavior. Our holy book says we were commanded to destroy the nation of Amalek as punishment for 'smiting the hindmost, all that were feeble behind' when they attacked us soon after the exodus from Egypt, near Refidim in the Sinai. The Israelites were severely punished for not obeying this command and subsequently King David waged a war of extermination against the Amalekites. Our Torah also states that if a man rises to kill you, you are obligated to rise and kill him first. Is that un-Jewish? You will excuse me if I see killing mortal enemies in defense of our people as *very* Jewish indeed." Amos was gratified to see that all, except one, of his visitors were nodding in agreement.

***

Avigdor Mizrahi woke up late. He had been tired and nobody disturbed him, so he slept until ten in the morning. He felt rested and ready for work, but it seemed that the Prime Minister of Great Britain was not in a hurry to see him.

After a shower and late breakfast, Mizrahi called in the butler and inquired about his schedule for the day. The P.M. could see him at nine in the evening; otherwise his day was free, which was just as well. He needed to hire a secretary and other staff, set up contacts and arrange for living quarters, office space and transportation.

One of the options that had been considered by the Foreign Ministry and historians in Israel was to approach an operative of the Jewish Agency in London for this kind of help. It was decided to postpone contacts with the Agency until later. The Agency was under constant surveillance by the British and other intelligence services and posed a high exposure risk which would severely harm the rescue operations in Nazi-occupied Europe.

The butler assured him that last night's limousine was available for his use, so he decided to take a ride. He told the chauffeur to take him to the nearest synagogue, which seemed to surprise the chauffeur but elicited no other response except a "Yes, Sir."

After a short drive the limo stopped in front of the Bevis Marks synagogue.

"Sir, I will wait around the corner," said the driver apologetically. "There is no parking in the front." Mizrahi nodded and got out of the car.

He tried the front door of the old building and, to his surprise, it was open. Inside, the synagogue reminded him of the old Sephardic one in Amsterdam. After a couple of minutes of looking around a bearded man in his sixties emerged from somewhere in the back.

"Welcome to the Bevis Marks synagogue. I am the caretaker, Shlomo Sassoon."

"My name is Avigdor Mizrahi, from Palestine. I just arrived in London."

"Can I help you in any way?"

"I need you to give the following message to Abraham Herz: 'Your uncle is very sick and requires surgery. Please contact the doctor as soon as possible.' "

Shlomo Sassoon looked at Mizrahi for several minutes before asking "How long has the uncle been ill?"

"Almost two weeks" Answered Mizrahi.

"How soon do you need to do whatever it is you are going to do? That is unless you insist on dealing with Herz."

"As soon as I have a real estate agent and some other contacts."

After more than an hour of conversation, Mizrahi had the contacts he needed. He thanked the older man and departed. He was glad that someone bothered to record the story about the secret codes their father used while conveying messages between Palestine and London and that the story was preserved in the archives. He still had a couple of hours before his meeting with Churchill and decided to use the time to explore London on foot. Realizing he should have done so earlier, he sent the limousine away and walked back to his temporary residence at 10 King Charles Street in Westminster.

Chapter 8

The Ministerial Committee on Absorption and Infrastructure, now known as the Development Committee, was in session. The Absorption Minister chaired the meeting: "I would like to go over our preparations to deal with the five or six million people that will start pouring in fairly soon. My ministry is trying to hire thousands of new employees, but with the current labor market we've had only limited success so far. We have difficulty finding Yiddish-speakers, which we need since that's the most common language of the European Jews. We found some, but not enough. We do have people who are fluent in the other languages. I think we'll manage communications." He looked at his colleagues, "Who is going next?"

The Infrastructure Minister volunteered: "We are well on the way with temporary accommodations. We'll put people up in old army barracks that we are renovating and in mobile homes but mostly in tent cities. We've done most of the surveying and will start earth-moving in a couple of days, with roads and plumbing to follow. I believe that we will be on schedule, assuming the first shipments come in about a month."

"Why not use the available hotel rooms?" asked the Absorption Minister.

The Tourism Minister answered. "The hotels are fairly full right now and there hasn't been any decision what to do with the tourists - We can't just throw them out." He hesitated. "I do have a list of available rooms. I wonder if we should assign them on a first-come basis or use some kind of gradation system for the new immigrants?"

The Absorption Minister was shaking his head: "No, no, no! No systems and no discrimination. It will be strictly first come/first serve. By the way," he looked like a thought just dawned on him, "our immediate problem may not be as big but much more complicated than anticipated.

"Consider the fact that a high percentage of our current population are descendants of holocaust survivors. I am sure that many of them will be delighted to offer hospitality to their lost families. Very few will have houses big enough to house all of their extended family, but some of the close relatives may be housed with families. That's the good news. The bad is more complicated: we still have live survivors – how will they react to meeting themselves and their families? Since many of the newcomers will have family here I am sure that there will be problems with claims of preferential treatment. We need to resolve these problems early, but I am not optimistic that we will be able to do much – human nature is not easily amenable to modification."

He looked at the Education Minister: "We need an intensive education program in order to successfully integrate these people into our society."

The Education Minister nodded, "Don't worry. We'll be ready. The Ministry of Defense has agreed to provide soldiers to serve as instructors of both modern life and Hebrew, just like they did when the state was first established. We are training some of them already. We'll be ready."

The committee kept at its work planning details and coordinating. This was a big job, larger than any previous immigration wave, and no one wanted to repeat past mistakes. The million Jews from the former Soviet Union had been absorbed over several years, a process that hadn't been easy for anyone. Now more than five times that number – almost doubling the current population - was expected to arrive within less than a year. It was not just almost doubling the population, but doubling it with people who, even if highly educated, were almost a century out of date. Where to find jobs for everybody? Where to house them? What about health care? The Israeli leadership was struggling with all these questions. Soon the general public would have to struggle with them as well.

***

"I have no idea why anybody would listen to these rumors." Zalman Gurevich was excited and shouting. "Since before the Germans came we heard of atrocities in the part of Poland they occupied. The Germans have been here for almost a week and we are okay. And still the rumors!"

"What do you mean 'okay'? We are still alive, but this may be a very temporary condition judging by what they did in Poland" Jacob Hirshson, his friend and neighbor, responded. "Didn't they give your grocery store to a Lithuanian already? Don't you have to wear this yellow star on your clothes all the time? Don't you have to step down into the gutter every time a German passes you on the street? Do they pay you for the work you do in the factory every day? Who knows what else they will do to us. It's early days yet. Mark my word, it'll get worse. I'm sorry I gave in to my mother and sister and stayed here. If we'd left on the day the war began, we could have gone to Russia – anything is better than the Nazis."

The two friends were having their nightly discussion in Hirshson's kitchen in Vilnius, the capital of Lithuania. The town had been occupied by Germans on the third day after attacking the Soviet Union and conditions worsened every day. Confusing and conflicting rumors circulated. Some said all the Jews were to be moved into a ghetto; others claimed there was to be deportation to Palestine. One thing was sure: Jews were singled out and separated from the general population.

Zalman was adamant. "I am not going anywhere even if they offer my family passage to Palestine. Why would we go to a land of sand and camels? I have bread here - why should I go search for crumbs? Anyway, the Germans are okay. They were civil enough in the First World War, much better than the crazy Cossacks or the Lithuanians who slaughter us every so often. Besides, they need us to run their factories. As long as we do as we're told, they'll make sure we have food. There's nothing to fear."

As far as Zalman was concerned, this was the end of the discussion. The rumors came from Polish refugees in town, whom he considered Galicianers and therefore untrustworthy. Why listen to their talk of all the calamities that could possibly befall his family?

Jacob did not agree. He believed the refugees' stories of shootings, starvation and crowded ghettos. The dentist that escaped from Warsaw with his family, for instance, had no reason to lie, so Jacob expected the Germans would sooner or later start behaving the same way here. He was an experienced businessman, young and with a degree in engineering. At the moment he had no alternative to living with the Nazis, so he waited. But if the rumor about Palestine was true, he was ready to go at a moment's notice, whatever his mother and sister said. He also realized that the rumors about Palestine might be just a German deception to make the Jews docile and go peacefully to wherever they wanted them to go. It would have been much easier to make a decision if more information were available, and not from the Germans.

***

Nitzan Liebler was slightly worried. His telephone conversation with the Managing Director of Israel Aircraft Industries was informative, but the information was not what he wanted to hear. The Minister of Defense needed a second spy satellite over Western Europe. He wanted it to have the capability to detect submarines in addition to the high resolution imaging. Itamar Herz, the Aircraft Industries Managing Director Nitzan spoke to, was quite adamant about the projected timetable: "Nitzan, there is not much I can do. We don't have enough engineers to make the design changes. I could do it in a week, if you get the Armaments Development Authority to assist us with the magnetic field sensors, but then there's the shortage of machinists and assembly personnel. This is not new. We had manpower problems before the Event. They haven't gotten any better."

"Calm down, Itamar." Liebler understood the problems which, indeed, were not new. "I'll get the Armaments Development Authority to give you all the help you need. There is no instant cure to the manpower issues but since the tourism business is going to be slow for a while, I expect that you'll be able to find trainees to fill your vacancies. There is also a good chance that we'll get an infusion of people with at least basic mechanical and electrical skills – It will be fairly easy to train them for your needs. In the meantime we have an emergency. So how long until we have another satellite in orbit?"

"Like I said, we can finish the design in a week, build the thing in another week, and launch it several days later. By the way, I appreciate your discussing our Shavit launcher problem with the General Manager of the Israel Military Industries. That lit a fire under him and now the parts are being produced at a very nice rate."

"Maybe I will have to light a little fire under you too," Liebler said, "since you're asking for almost three weeks to launch that stupid satellite. I need it in less than two! Shall I ask the Armaments Authority to take over the project?"

"You have to give me priorities, Nitzan. We can't prepare all those passenger jets for mass transport, re-start the turbine blades plant in Bet-Shemesh, and set up titanium production all at the same time. We don't have enough people! You either have to postpone one of the other projects or wait three weeks."

"OK, don't get all excited," Liebler said. "You can ease up on the passenger planes for a couple of weeks and titanium production can wait a bit as well. Will that do it?"

"You have a deal," Itamar responded.

***

Avigdor Mizrahi walked over to 10 Downing Street - a short walk from his house. According to the butler, the lodgings had been assigned because it was so close to the P.M. A passageway through an internal courtyard connecting the two properties made the trip discreet as well.

Churchill was having tea when Mizrahi was shown into the sitting room. He accepted both a cup of tea and an armchair opposite the PM.

"It's a great honor to meet you, sir. You've been my hero since I was in grade school."

"You don't look that old," Churchill said.

"Since I haven't been born yet, it's a miracle I'm here at all."

"So it is true that your whole country was transported here from the future. It is the state of Israel - a Jewish state?" Churchill sucked on his cigar.

"Indeed it is. We succeeded in establishing it despite the fervent opposition of Britain."

"Not *my* opposition, Mr. Mizrahi. I've always supported the idea of a Jewish state in Palestine."

"Mr. Prime Minister, the 1939 White Paper prohibiting Jewish immigration to Palestine cost our people millions of lives without providing any benefits to Britain – the Arabs supported the Axis and kicked you out of the region anyway. This was one of those historical mistakes that are predictable but done anyway." Mizrahi sipped his tea. "As a show of good will, we ask that a full and complete annulment of the 1939 White Paper be issued immediately. If Britain demonstrates to the world her support for our cause, we can more easily support yours.

"We are going to transport millions of Jews into Israel very soon. Britain could be very helpful in this process" - Mizrahi leaned forward - "especially as many of the ships doing the transporting will be German. A safe passage from the Royal Navy would really simplify things for us. We will also need to use some of your troop transports to help us out in this matter. This shouldn't impose too much of a stress on the Empire, since they are idle anyway."

"The Germans have agreed to move the Jews under their control to Palestine using their own resources? How did you convince them?"

"Oh, we can be very persuasive. I assure you that we did not compromise with the Nazis on anything – That's not in our nature. We also do not believe in appeasement – If you have a mortal enemy the only way to deal with them is to annihilate them completely. That is the most humane way and the only way to a lasting peace."

Mizrahi smiled a predatory smile. "The Nazis had a demonstration of what will happen if they cross us, or try to cheat, and even they are not crazy enough to do that. But I am digressing. We can help you immensely in this war."

Churchill puffed on his cigar for a while without saying anything. What a strange twist of fate, putting this small group of oppressed people in a position of such great power. He suspected that Mizrahi, and the government that sent him, knew everything about Britain's problems both present and future. Better be very careful, he thought.

"So you'd like us to annul the 1939 White Paper, give German ships safe passage and contribute some of our own troop carriers. Is there anything else?"

"Mr. Prime Minister, we need to feed the close to seven million people that will be arriving in Israel soon. We also need energy. In exchange for our assistance in the war, we expect Britain to supply us, for a while, with food and oil. We want Britain to cede control of Kuwait to Israel. There are also a number of smaller issues, but these are the main ones."

Churchill smiled. "Mr. Mizrahi, you want a lot from us, especially considering the serious shortage of food in England and our difficulties exporting coal."

"Not really," responded Mizrahi. "The food shortage and problems exporting coal both have a common root: German submarines. Right now you are losing more shipping than you can build and it will become even worse. We can help you to help us and yourselves."

Churchill put down his cigar and leaned forward: "How do you propose to solve this bloody submarine problem?"

"Simple. We can pinpoint the position of every German vessel anywhere. If you attack only the wolf packs as they gather to sink your convoys, it shouldn't take long to sink most of the German U boat fleet or scare them into staying in port."

"That will help us in the short run, but I was hoping for more from your people, Mr. Mizrahi. The Grant and Sherman tanks the Americans give us would have been useless if it wasn't for the quantities. We are being beaten by German armor - How about giving us some of your wonder weapons which so impressed General Wilson?"

"Mr. Prime Minister," Mizrahi said slowly, "if we sign an agreement tonight, tank guns and ammunition shipments will start tomorrow, including drawings and instructions on how to install them. You could retrofit your existing tanks and kill any German tank, including models you have not yet heard about. It is more reasonable to improve the tanks you already have. New tank guns will give you a decisive advantage on the battlefield and be useful as soon as they are installed. And that's just one example of the kind of upgrades we can provide. As our relationship develops and mutual trust is built, we will be able to help you more."

"Mr. Mizrahi, I am glad we met tonight. I will present your proposal to the Cabinet tomorrow. If they decide to accept your ideas in principle, we will work out the details over the next several days. It would be helpful if you could put your proposal in writing, so the Cabinet can have all the details without relying on my somewhat defective memory.

"In the meantime, we need to determine what your formal status in Britain is going to be. Do you want to present your ambassadorial credentials, assuming you have them with you, to the King?"

"As a matter of fact," Mizrahi responded, "my country would prefer keeping a low profile for a while longer. Why not refer to us simply as Palestinians for the time being. My official status can be an emissary from Palestine or just a private business man engaged in business with His Majesty's Government. The Americans, I'm sure, will be interested in us, but there are advantages to keeping our relationship to ourselves. As opposed to the U.S. position we have no objections to Britain keeping its empire, as long as it is friendly to us. The U.S. may not be too happy with our assistance to you – it will diminish the importance of lend-lease and with it, their influence, on your policies. We don't want to attract attention – from the Americans or anybody else.

"We do insist on complete secrecy, at least until after our rescue operation in Europe is finished. The Empire is home to thousands of German, Japanese and Soviet spies. We will give you lists, but you will have to be decisive about acting against them – especially since some are in high places in your bureaucracy, including your intelligence services. Even with this information leaks may happen. I suggest that we work out the appropriate protocols as soon as possible. Israel will not tolerate any threat to the rescue in Europe. This will also preclude any written communications, at least until we work out an appropriate procedure with your security services."

Churchill looked both dismayed and surprised: "Sir, I understand your concerns. A list of spies will be helpful, but we will have to verify each one of them ourselves."

"Mr. Prime Minister, this is exactly what I was implying. By the time you weed those out it may be too late. So we need to keep this relationship secret until my government decides otherwise."

"Agreed. There will be only a very limited number of people that will know what is going on. Anything else we need to cover today?"

Mizrahi hesitated: "Our only immediate difficulty will be with current funds. We have significant amounts of currency, including American dollars and British pounds, but none of them are from this century. I suggest that your government establish a line of credit for us to draw on to be repaid in the near future. I assure you that you will get your money's worth very quickly." They shook hands and Churchill escorted his guest to the door.

After Mizrahi left, the British Prime Minister sat for a long while thinking about the current situation. He didn't like his country's position as a client of either the U.S or Israel – or both. To win the war Britain needed help. The Americans with their land-lease helped, and there was a promise of more substantial assistance in the future, but the price for this help worried Churchill. As things stood, the U.S. was building up a great military industrial capability and the P.M. could see how it would lead to American supremacy in the not too far future. He was also somewhat apprehensive of President Roosevelt's antipathy to the very idea of the Empire. Until now he had no choice but to accept American help and pay the price. The Israelis may have brought a solution. It would not be free but, at least for now, the price was fairly clear and not too high. The question in Churchill's mind was simple: could the Israelis' help free him from the need to accept American handouts and building up American strength at British expense? He didn't know the answer, it lay in the future, but he hoped that it would.

***

The Infrastructure Minister reviewed a plan submitted to him by the Electric Power Commission. It was a revamped version of a 1980s proposal to dig a canal from the Mediterranean to the Dead Sea using the elevation difference to generate electricity. The original plan called for a 500 megawatt power station. The new version proposed a 1500 megawatt power plant and three parallel water conduits. Two of these were envisioned as huge underground pipes and the third was to be a navigable canal passing by Beer Sheba.

In their former time-line, the much smaller plan had been opposed by several environmental groups, whose lobbying had scuttled U.S. loan guarantees for the project. The environmentalists' concerns were unwarranted: there was no danger of overfilling the Dead Sea. In fact, the Sea had almost disappeared by the time of The Event. Another claim was suspect from the very beginning: that the canal would change the climate so much that the Negev desert would disappear because evaporation from the canal would increase rain in the area. First, what was the problem with the desert turning green without all the artificial irrigation? And second, it was never shown that the miniscule amount of evaporation would measurably change the rainfall in the desert. There was a third claim, the one that finally scuttled the funding: that leakage of salty sea water from the canal would contaminate the aquifer and make the water under the Negev unusable. It did not matter that any leakage could be prevented by using appropriate building techniques or that the Negev aquifer was not used.

The Minister decided that he liked the new and larger power generation proposal. He still needed to present it to the full cabinet for approval and then find the money in the budget to build it. The hydroelectric project was a short term stopgap solution. He also decided to recommend starting development of the gas fields in the Mediterranean as soon as practicable – It shouldn't take very long to make the area safe. Israel was producing about ten thousand megawatts of electricity and would need at least double that amount within a couple of years. Natural gas would provide clean and abundant power.

***

Amos Nir brought the meeting to order. The cabinet had a number of issues on their agenda, and he began with the most important: "We've been negotiating with the Brits since last Wednesday. We've met with some resistance on a number of issues, but mostly we're making good progress. They've agreed to supply us with coal and oil through the port in Eilat and the Hadera pier. Food will go through the Suez Canal into Ashdod. To begin with, it will be mainly grain, rice, vegetables and fruit from the Far East, Australia and South Africa. We'll be getting Canadian cattle but will have to expand our slaughter houses to process it. Coal will come from South Africa and oil from Iraq and the Emirates. They are resisting ceding Kuwait to us and, to a lesser extent, transferring control of the Sinai Desert. In their view giving away any part of the Empire sets a precedent they don't want set. I expect that we will have to give them something more than upgrades to their existing weapons or threaten them directly, which, personally, I am in no hurry to do.

"On a different note, their Foreign Office is going to issue a new White Paper tomorrow, Tuesday, changing their Mideast policy. The new declaration will encourage Jewish immigration to Palestine. The Royal Navy is standing by to protect our ships. We convinced the Germans that any ships carrying refugees to Israel will fly the Caliph's flag in addition to the swastika and whatever else they chose to put on them. Nitzan?"

The defense minister took over: "We'll let the Brits know when one of our ships leaves port. We don't want the Nazis using our flag to transport supplies to Rommel in North Africa." The Defense Minister paused to look at his notes. "We'll have an additional satellite above the Atlantic in about a week and a half, this one with the ability to detect magnetic anomalies. Combined with our interception and decoding of German naval transmissions, the new satellite will let us pinpoint individual submarines. In the meantime, we are relying on optical imaging and radio intercepts, which works well enough, to locate U-boat wolf packs preparing to attack convoys.

"We also have Military Industries working at full capacity making 60mm hyper velocity cannon and ammunition to upgrade the British tanks. The first shipment went to Cairo just a couple of hours ago. I expect them to be installed in Crusader tanks and ready for action within a week. The quantities will likely not be enough to stop Rommel's advance but it will crimp his style a bit.

"Also, I think Amos and I found a solution to the British reluctance to give up Kuwait and the Sinai. It involves some waiting time but will ripen in a couple of weeks."

It was the Infrastructure Minister's turn. He presented the proposal for hydro-electrical power generation, which met with general approval. The Finance Minister interjected: "Don't worry about the cost of this or any other project. We are budgeting in shekels and can print as many as we need. I don't expect inflation will be a problem either – By the time the new currency hits the market, we'll have significant numbers of immigrants arriving, food and energy supplied by the Brits, and an economy growing fast enough to keep up with any inflationary pressures."

"Then we're in agreement to go ahead with hydro-electric power?" the Infrastructure Minister asked. Everyone nodded. "In the meantime we've made tangible progress in other areas. Two of our contractors are erecting temporary buildings to accommodate about five hundred thousand refugees. We'll be signing contracts in the coming week with four more construction companies. We expect to use the buildings for several years so we're building them to be as comfortable as possible, including indoor plumbing – much more comfortable than what the new immigrants got in the early days of the State. That's a strain on our construction industry, but with more labor coming in, we'll manage. Starting in about two weeks we'll be able to accommodate 40,000 new refugees a month - 200,000 once we're working at full capacity. We should be able to accept all of them within a year and a half. If necessary, we can triple this rate if some of the refugees live in tents. They won't have plumbing but people won't be staying there very long."

"By the time the first transports arrive we'll have a staff of clerks and instructors to help with absorption," the Absorption Minister added. "The Security Service informs me they'll be ready for screening as well."

The Labor Minister sighed. "Some of the unions resent the massive hiring since they haven't been consulted. A good example is the Military Industry Employees Union: they threaten to strike unless we guarantee that all the new hires get the same rights as those employed before the Event. As you know, current employees can't be fired. With the big population surge we're expecting, we can't guarantee everybody secure employment for life. The law allows us to employ temporary workers without contracts. The unions believe the current labor shortage will force us to accept their demands. I am about to issue an order suspending union rights and activities for the next six months using the emergency laws. We'll see how the situation develops after that."

"I was going to raise this question too," the Absorption Minister said. "Most of the new instructors we are training joined one of the two

Teachers' Unions, which are increasing their demands. An emergency labor order will help me too."

Amos summarized: "We seem to be in good shape generally, except for some labor trouble which we can neutralize for a while using the emergency laws. Hopefully everything will get sorted out shortly."

"I don't think we should use the emergency laws against the unions," the Finance Minister interrupted. "The last thing we need right now is a serious internal fight. Why not tell them that six million new immigrants are on the way? There's no reason to keep it a secret, which it won't be for long anyway. Once they realize the labor shortage will be gone in a couple of months, I'm sure their stance will change. If they're smart - and there are some smart union leaders out there - they'll stop fighting us and start thinking about organizing the newcomers. This will be the first time in our history that they'll have that opportunity and I think they'll be eager to do so." She leaned back in her chair and looked around the conference table challenging anybody to object.

"I am not sure you are right," the Labor Minister said mildly. "Our unions have been part of the establishment since the beginning of the state. We have companies that are owned by them. They know very well how to play politics and squeeze the government but have been steadily losing ground in the private sector. I think they'll try to use their power to paralyze the government, regardless of the labor market."

"Hannah's right," Amos said. "We may as well let the country know about the new immigrants. It will cause an upheaval, but we have to make the announcement sooner or later. May as well do it now. If after the announcement the unions relent, I'll be very happy. If not, we can still use the emergency laws.

"We're planning on taking all our people out of Europe within a year - and we should be counting on at least six million. When they start arriving by the hundred thousands, we'll have enough labor to accelerate the construction process and hopefully the unions will stop bothering us, at least for a while.

"We're going to be building like crazy, everything from housing to metallurgical plants to oil refineries. We've got to be self-sufficient as soon as possible – preferably within two years. We'll have to purchase some equipment, probably from the U.S."

***

"May I have your attention," the Reverend John Walker said loudly. He had gathered his group again to make several announcements. The crowd was noisy and cheerful. Most had just returned from a tour of several holy places in Jerusalem and were discussing their trip. "I want to tell you about the discussions I've been having with the authorities. Please feel free to interrupt at any point with questions." The room quieted down and everybody looked at him expectantly.

"The government recommends we postpone the tour of Bethlehem we've been planning as there may be trouble from Palestinian extremists. How many want to go anyway?" Most raised their hands. "Ok, we go tomorrow as planned. The bus will be in front of the hotel at 10 a.m.

"On a different note, I've been assured that anyone needing medical treatment will be treated free of charge at any hospital. I've also been instructed to tell you that anyone who wants to work will be issued an Israeli ID and work permit. There's a serious labor shortage and most of us will be able to find jobs. Any questions?"

"Do we have to work or is it a choice?" an elderly man asked.

"The way they explained it to me, all men over 67 and women over 65 will receive Israeli Social Security payments, which should be enough to live on. Anyone younger than that will have to work to get an income unless they are disabled."

"That's not fair!" one of the younger women exclaimed. "I have a perfectly nice job back home and don't want to work for these people."

"Dear Elizabeth," the Reverend said patiently, "you mean you used to have a job in the U.S. we came from. That world and all our sources of income there don't exist yet. We can't expect to live on charity here and be tourists forever. We need to contribute to the society we're part of. I recommend that everyone - including retirees - discuss the situation with the labor advisor that will meet with us the day after tomorrow. They promise to help everyone find appropriate jobs." The group looked somewhat surprised and dismayed but there weren't any more questions.

The weather was pleasant and the traffic sparse for their trip to Bethlehem the next day. There were two checkpoints between Jerusalem and their destination. At both of them Israeli soldiers boarded the bus and politely asked for identification. Bethlehem, the boys told the group, was dangerous, filled with terrorists prepared to attack civilians. At the second checkpoint an officer boarded the bus: "I highly recommend that you postpone your trip, sir. We have information attacks are being prepared in the territories under Palestinian control and you are taking a grave risk going there."

"Are you saying we are prohibited from going into Bethlehem?" Walker asked.

"No. This is a free country, and unless there is an emergency border closure, you are free to go. But, again, I highly recommend that, for your safety, you stay in secure areas." The officer shrugged: "I can't stop you, but you are taking an unreasonable risk."

"Thank you. I'll discuss it with my group," the Reverend responded as he climbed back on the bus.

"Sir," the bus driver addressed him after closing the door "I would like to say that the Israeli army always says these things to tourists. Our bus belongs to an Arab-owned company from Nazareth. My fellow Palestinians are not stupid; they don't attack tourists. They have nothing against you. It is the Israeli occupation that causes all these problems."

"Thank you, my friend," the Reverend smiled at the driver. "I suspected as much. Let's go."

The bus continued on its way and arrived in Bethlehem a little behind schedule. Reverend Walker guided his group around the streets of the ancient town and into the Church of the Nativity. "This is a sacred place," he told them.

The next thing he knew, there was an eerie quiet. He didn't know where he was. It took him a while to realize that a severed human leg, still dressed in pants was on the floor in front of him.

The quiet was the result of severe damage to his hearing – being less than ten feet from a suicide bomber can do that. His group was decimated. Most of them were seriously injured, ten were dead. The Reverend was one of the lucky ones. He was operated on three times in two days. They removed most of the nails and ball bearings that were imbedded in his legs and chest and reattached one finger that was hanging by a sliver of skin on his left hand. Nobody could cure his nightmares in which he relived the blast. He felt guilty for surviving and was afraid to fall asleep.

Chapter 9

On Thursday, June 26, 1941, six days since The Event Noam Shaviv was in his tent. His company was spread out over ten kilometers of the Egyptian border. Their chances of stopping anybody from crossing would be extremely unlikely if it wasn't for the electronic fence. This morning he had received a call from battalion intelligence: "We have reliable information that an attempt to cross into Egypt will be made today or tomorrow by a single infiltrator."

Noam transmitted the new information to his platoon commanders and an hour later drove along the line to check how the company was doing. As usual, he had remarks for his platoon commanders, but generally he was satisfied and let his men know it.

At two the next morning he got another call from battalion: "Your customer is on his way. Take care to get him alive. We need to see what he's carrying and we need to talk to him."

"Is he alone or is somebody leading him?" Noam asked.

"Funny you should ask, lieutenant," the intelligence officer chuckled. "He has an escort. We want the escort to go through unharmed and get back in. We need him to think that his mission was successful."

"You are telling me that now?" Noam was somewhat indignant.

"Well, I told you as soon as I heard about it. You know how the Security Services are – never share with anybody." The officer on the other end of the line sounded only slightly apologetic: "In any case, you have about two hours before they try to come through on the northern edge of your sector, so I'm told. Good Luck."

Noam's next move was to notify the platoon guarding the northern sector, where the Egyptian, Gaza and Israeli borders met. Next he notified the other platoons.

When the new platoon commander awoke Uri Dayan, the sergeant was slightly annoyed. He'd only had three hours of sleep after checking the guard positions for the umpteenth time, making sure that everybody was well hidden, quiet and awake – not an easy feat on night duty. The new commander wanted him to visit all the guard positions again, this time instructing them to keep their eyes open but not interfere with the expected infiltrators. The commander would organize a pursuit party to nab the courier.

An hour and a half later, close to sunrise, with gray light full of shadows, the two figures would have slipped through undetected if it wasn't for the combination of night-vision equipment, an electronic fence and the troops expecting something to happen. As planned, the two dark figures passed through the line oblivious to the alarms that went off in headquarters. The platoon commander, followed at a distance by Sergeant Dayan, trailed after them. The other five members of their squad took a parallel route, reducing their chance of being detected by the returning escort.

About a mile from the border the infiltrators shook hands and parted. Uri waited behind rocks as the escort passed by heading back into Israel. The sergeant fingered his radio: "He's on his way back - Be quiet and let him through."

Now they concentrated on the lone figure walking into Egypt. The commander ran through an adjacent wadi, emerging in front of the courier. The man was walking slowly, consulting his compass from time to time, relaxed now that he was in Egyptian territory. Uri got up and walked behind the dark figure. When he was less than twenty yards away, Uri shot him with a dart gun, one of about twenty issued to the platoon earlier in the day.

The courier collapsed noiselessly and was carried back to the platoon's base and into a waiting jeep.

***

Mohammad al Husseini was unhappy, not an unusual state of mind for him. Of the four people his group sent to contact German agents, two were apprehended at the Lebanese and Jordanian borders. That message had been brought by the Bedouin who was supposed to smuggle them across the border. Suspecting that this same Bedouin had sold out the couriers, Mohammad had ordered him killed as soon as the man left the house of his cell commander. The third courier may have been martyred or imprisoned by the Israelis - there was no way of knowing. Thanks to Allah the fourth courier passed safely into Egypt. The man who led him through the border, a long-trusted member of both Hamas and Islamic Jihad, was rewarded for bringing good news.

Suicide bombers were ready to strike. One had already been successful – that was another piece of good news. Mohammad did not know how many more were waiting or what their targets would be, but he was confident something would happen soon. He instructed his operatives to make sure that the strikes were effective: They must kill as many infidels as possible.

***

David Rothstein was surprised on Friday morning when his cousin called him at the hotel: "David, I have a proposition for you. Since our conversation last week I've been looking for something for you to do. I have good news: you have a selection of jobs. To be interviewed and to see what exactly is being offered, you need to go to the nearest branch of the Interior Ministry. That would be at the Azrieli mall. I will meet you there in about an hour, if this is convenient."

"You mean the Ministry has a job for me?" David was surprised.

"No, no. They will issue you an ID card and a work permit. I have to be there to vouch for you, so that the whole process will be completed on the spot. Otherwise it may take a week. After you have your papers, we will go meet with people at a number of companies that are interested in your skills. If you will want still more options, we will go to Haifa."

After a short pause David said: "I really appreciate this. Can't I see what is available first and decide about the ID later?"

"Most of the jobs are somewhat sensitive and they will not talk to you unless you are committed, at least to the extent of getting an ID. The process of issuing an ID includes a basic security check, without which nobody will talk to you, which is why I need to vouch for you."

"We could meet in about an hour and a half, but Shabbat starts around six, so I'm not sure how much we can accomplish today."

"Okay. See you at the Ministry at 9:30."

"Wait a minute," David hesitated. "Let me call you in thirty minutes. This is somewhat unexpected, and I want to talk it over with Rachel."

"OK." His cousin sounded cheerful. "I don't mind if we get your papers at the Ministry today and do all the interviews on Sunday. So take all the time you need."

"Thanks, Ze'ev."

Rachel was out for a short walk and some window shopping; she was tired of being cooped up in their suite. The boys were out on the beach. David decided to call his wife's cell phone. He hadn't tried using it in Israel before and hoped that it would work. When they bought it, it was advertised as a world phone. It did ring, and she picked up after a long delay: "Hello, who is this?"

"Rachel? This is David. Something came up and I need to speak with you. Are you far?"

"I am in front of the hotel looking at a nice store that sells Dead Sea cosmetics. I'll be upstairs in a moment."

"No, wait for me there. We can walk around the hotel and take a look at the boys while we talk."

When he saw his wife, David repeated to her his cousin's proposition.

"Well, I see no problem with that," she said "Why didn't you agree immediately?"

"Because I have a high security clearance in the U.S., which will be withdrawn if I get Israeli citizenship and getting an ID and a work permit are the first steps towards citizenship. Ze'ev also said that some of the jobs will be offered only if I am committed to staying here, and I am not sure I am."

"You are speaking as if we can return to the U.S. of our time. I don't think it's going to happen. Even if the Israelis knew how to go back, which according to what everybody says, they don't, they're not stupid enough to actually do it. I heard a discussion on TV: The longer we stay in this time, the more technology leaks, especially with the efforts to rescue the European Jews that were announced yesterday. If the country travels forward to our time, the rest of the world will have had all those years to develop this leaked technology, which means that Israel will probably have lost the edge over its enemies it enjoyed in our time-line. That would be a disaster. I think that we are here to stay and should act accordingly. Take the ID and work permit and look at what jobs are available." Rachel was slightly out of breath from the combination of a long speech and fast walk.

"You think that I should take one of the jobs they offer me?" David asked.

"No, I think you should listen to the offers and decide later. You were never happy working for someone else. The only thing that you were content with was being your own boss. Maybe you can set up your own business here."

"I can certainly try." David smiled.

***

The Chief of the General Security Service (the Shin Bet) and the head of the Institute for Intelligence, otherwise known as the Mossad (which means Institute in Hebrew), met for one of their regular meetings over a cup of coffee.

"We have the guy you told me about last week. I'm sorry the other one was killed while trying to cross the border into Jordan. Really stupid of him to cross through all the minefields. The first two that tried ahead of this bunch were arrested. We had no choice since the idiots tried to attack the border guard instead of just sneaking through. I don't think any more are coming." The Chief of the Shin Bet smiled. "Now it's your job to figure out what to do with the guy."

"I have a plan," responded the Mossad Chief, "but I will need your continued cooperation. The first thing we need to do is keep the courier unconscious until we are ready for him in a day or so."

"Agreed. We'll be ready as will our courier, Ibrahim."

***

When Ibrahim woke up he was slightly confused. He clearly remembered walking in the desert just south of the Israeli border into the Sinai, and then he woke up here, wherever here was. He was in a clean bed in an even cleaner room. There was a big flag with a swastika on the wall as well as a poster with verses from the Koran and a picture of the Grand Mufti of Jerusalem, Hajj Amin Al Hussein, in a sleek black uniform, next to a larger photograph of Hitler. Ibrahim had a splitting headache and a painfully sore spot on his calf, which was red and slightly swollen.

"What happened to me?" he asked as soon as a doctor entered the room – it had to be a doctor, with a white coat and a stethoscope.

"You were bitten by a snake in the desert three days ago," the doctor explained. You were found by Bedouin, who brought you to an Egyptian army post where they notified one of our agents. You were carrying some very interesting documents, which justified the expense and effort of bringing you to here. I hope that you will be able to explain all this to us."

Ibrahim noticed that the doctor was speaking Arabic with a German accent, which reassured him. "I want to see the Grand Mufti. Only to him can I disclose the message I am carrying."

"Don't worry, my friend," the doctor said. "You need to recover from the snake poison. You are among friends here. This is the base hospital of the Muslim SS Handschar division the Grand Mufti organized a while ago. He is now in Croatia and it will take him a while to arrive. You really need to rest." The doctor left and shortly thereafter Ibrahim fell asleep again.

***

The German ambassador, Von Weizsacker, was somewhat discomforted by the Duce's skepticism "But Il Duce," he said, "I am only repeating the main points of the Fuehrer's letter to you. The arrangements we want to make in Brindisi are in no way a concentration camp. We have an arrangement to transport all the Jews from Europe to Palestine, and Brindisi is the best port for it. I assure you this is a completely peaceful endeavor and will not involve Italy in any hostilities. We also do not require any active participation from you."

Mussolini was not entirely convinced: "You want to take over the port of Brindisi, including all the warehouses and the area around it. How can I allow Germany to establish a concentration camp on my territory? This is a breach of Italian sovereignty."

"But this is *not* going to be a concentration camp," Von Weizsacker argued patiently. "I propose that we prove it to you. Your co-operation will be a great expression of your good will for Herr Hitler and will insure growing friendship between our countries." The last phrase could be interpreted as a threat since the ambassador had instructions to settle this issue as quickly as he could. Ribbentrop's instructions were confirmed by Goering, so the ambassador did what he could.

"How do you propose to prove that it is not going to be a concentration camp?" Mussolini smiled his skeptical smile again.

"We will bring several thousand Jews into the compound, and they will be picked up by a British passenger ship within a day or two of arrival. Will this convince you?"

Mussolini was surprised and it showed on his face: "What do you mean by a 'British' ship? Is this some kind of code?"

"Sir," Von Weizsacker smiled, "this is another proof of our good intentions. The British are acting on the request of a neutral party to help evacuate these Jews. Apparently they too don't want them in Europe and have agreed to help us. It is up to Italy to enable this great project."

"I agree in principle," Mussolini paused, "but Italy will not spend one lira on this project. It will be your responsibility to house, feed and guard the Jews while they are on Italian territory. We will do nothing to help you, and I expect this not to disrupt our war effort at all. I am somewhat suspicious of the British ships. How can they cooperate with this while at the same time fighting us in Northern Africa?"

"The neutral party that's taking the Jews off our hands is in fact a powerful Muslim country." Von Weizsacker smiled triumphantly. "They will be the ones feeding the Jews, providing housing and guarding them. We're only building a perimeter fence. The Muslims will not venture beyond it. This arrangement will free our troops to help you out more decisively in North Africa."

"That's a powerful argument," Mussolini said firmly. "My preference would be to negotiate with these Muslims directly," Von Weizsacker started to raise his hand, "but I respect Herr Hitler's judgment and will not interfere in his plans."

Ambassador Von Weizsacker relaxed. He had done his part and the project could go ahead.

***

Jacob Hirshson did not say "I told you so" but he definitely thought it. His family and that of his friend Zalman Gurevich shared one room, also housing an old woman, her cat and a young couple with their baby. It was noisy and crowded with no privacy. It took two weeks after the Germans occupied Vilnius for the Lithuanian Jews to find out what their Polish brethren had already discovered: the Nazis really hated the Jews and did what they could to make life hell for them. The oppression started a couple of days after the occupation when they decreed that all Jews had to wear a white armband with a yellow star; several people who were caught without them got beaten up. Then came an edict making it mandatory for Jews to work in jobs assigned by the German occupation administration. Zalman lost his grocery store, which was now in the hands on one of his Lithuanian neighbors. The next order forced all the Jews of the Vilnius area into a ghetto that was much too small for the population. Actually it was two ghettos, one small, one large. Jacob was especially aggravated because neither of the ghettos included the Jewish neighborhood where he and his family had lived. They had to abandon their spacious apartment and move a couple of blocks into the larger of the two ghettos. Jacob and Zalman were lucky to have a room. People were living on landings and staircases. Food was also getting scarce. Jacob smuggled some in but only when older German soldiers were on guard. He was especially careful with the Lithuanian police and even more so with the Ukrainian guards.

"I heard a rumor today at work," Jacob confided in Zalman one evening. "One of the German Jews that came here through the Warsaw ghetto said that it is being evacuated. People are allowed to take one suitcase with them and are given some food for the trip. They are warned that the food has to last a week. He heard from a Polish railway worker that they are being transported to Italy."

"Wishful thinking," Zalman responded. "I don't believe these rumors. Germans giving food for a week! To Jews!"

Jacob did not respond. He also was not confident in the truth of this story – Why would the Germans move Jews to Italy? It made no sense.

***

Sergeant Bohdan Kovalenko stood at attention in front of his platoon commander and an SS officer. The SS man had arrived this morning to their quarters in Vilnius. Bohdan's unit was assigned guard duty at the Jewish ghetto. Bohdan liked it. It was easy work and he got to beat up Jews. It was true that in Podolsk, where he was born and grew up, he had worked for a Jewish food store manager. The Jew treated him well, and in the years of the great Ukrainian famine saved his life and the life of his mother by sharing the meager food he managed to find. Bohdan spent his childhood with the neighborhood kids, who were Jewish. He spoke their language and knew how they behaved. Still he hated them. The parish priest said that he needed to hate them and he didn't think about it much.

"Bohdan, we have a special assignment for you," the SS officer announced. "How is your Yiddish?"

The question scared Bohdan Kovalenko. Were they considering the possibility of him being Jewish? The fact that he was fluent in the language did not make him a Jew. The SS officer seemed to understand his concern: "Sergeant Kovalenko, we are looking for a good Ukrainian, faithful to our cause, who is fluent in Yiddish. According to your records, you are such a person. You'll be performing a very valuable service for the Reich."

Bohdan saluted and clicked his heels as enthusiastically as he knew how.

The SS man spoke with him for close to half an hour, most of the time in Yiddish. After he was certain that the Ukrainian sergeant was fluent in the language, the officer told him to get into the waiting staff car. Several weeks of grueling training followed, including radio communications and a variety of spy tricks. Bohdan was given false papers in the name of Boruch Katzenelson and memorized his new history as a native of Lutsk – one of the few survivors of the pogrom there almost a month ago. He was then brought into the Vilnius ghetto as a transferee from another ghetto in the Ukraine. His instructions were simple: spy on the Jews and report to his SS control. He was to go with the Jews when they were transported to Palestine and continue reporting as frequently as he could, using local contacts among the Arabs or, as a last resort, the radio transmitter hidden in his suitcase. Bohdan was promised an officer's rank and a rich reward when he returned from his assignment. He knew that if he failed, his family would pay the ultimate price.

Bohdan was not alone. The SS were taking precautions and planted a number of spies among the Jews. Some of the spies were Jewish. The number of Jews they were able to recruit was small. The Jews were not leaving families behind and the only leverage the Nazis could use was a promise of future payments. Several German Jews, who considered themselves Germans first, agreed to help out of a sense of patriotism.

The Nazis knew that the Caliph was powerful and they distrusted him and his motives. Himmler also wanted to find out as much as possible about the Caliph's weapons and technology, though he doubted that the spies embedded with the Jews would be useful for that purpose.

Chapter 10

The weather in Istanbul was pleasant: sunny and warm with a few clouds. Moshe Cohen got off a nondescript boat that blended in with the many fishing vessels coming and going in the port area. His documents showed him to be one Ibrahim al Taibeh from Palestine. He was in his late twenties, about 5'9", with brown eyes and dark, almost black hair. His suit concealed a heavily muscled physique. For the past five years he had worked for the Mossad. His native language was Hebrew, but he was fluent in Palestinian and Syrian Arabic dialects. He could speak German like a Berliner or with an Arabic accent. He could also communicate in Turkish, Greek and Serbian. He had been recruited to the Mossad from the Tel-Aviv Kameri Theater – his friend, and now controller, thought that he was far too good a performer to be wasted on a theatrical career. He had jumped at the opportunity to add some excitement to a life he considered dull and pedestrian and never regretted his decision.

Moshe wandered among the crowds of Istanbul, making haphazard turns and randomly changing direction. He knew the city well from previous assignments and it didn't change in a century. It did not take him very long to verify that he was not being followed. Then he proceeded to the German embassy.

It took him more than thirty minutes to get into the building. He was passed from the Turkish Army guards at the front gate to a couple of uniformed SS and from them to a German civilian. He was searched for weapons. The letters he was carrying were discovered and returned to him.

The civilian, a cultural attaché of the embassy, escorted Moshe into a small office with two chairs and a table – a fairly typical Gestapo interrogation room.

"Now, please explain to me who you are and what your mission is." Gustav Hildebrand sounded bored.

"As you were notified by your Foreign Ministry, I am Ismail Al Taibeh. I was sent from Palestine by the Grand Mufti's cousin with a message for the Grand Mufti, may Allah always smile on him. I must see the Grand Mufti as soon as possible. Your government guaranteed me safe passage and transportation and I expect to be on my way immediately."

Hildebrand was carefully examining Ismail's documents. "This is interesting," he said slowly. "Your documents seem new, not older than several weeks, and they were issued by the Caliph of Jerusalem. I thought the British held Jerusalem?"

"You are not up to date, my friend," Moshe smiled. "Our enemy has not been in charge for a while now. The Great Caliph rules Palestine and the adjacent territories."

The Gestapo man smiled a nasty smile. "I am not your friend, Ibrahim, assuming that is your real name. It says here that you are a major in the Caliph's guard. What are you doing here?"

"I told you once and I will repeat it, since you seem to be slightly hard of hearing: I was sent as an emissary to Hajj Amin al Husseini, the Grand Mufti of Jerusalem, with the full agreement and cooperation of your government."

"I heard you before. I think you are lying, and we have means to extract the truth from you. So tell me – what do the British want with the Mufti?" Hildebrand was not entirely sure that this was the right way to treat the visitor, but in his experience intimidation usually worked and was worth trying.

"Gustav Hildebrand, you have a choice, you can either keep playing your little Gestapo games or you can call the ambassador and let him decide. If you choose the Gestapo games, you will either die by the hand of the Caliph or be hanged with a piano wire around your neck by your own people. Neither execution will be pleasant, though likely the Gestapo way will be easier for you." Moshe Cohen leaned back in his chair and relaxed.

Hildebrand was conflicted. He was angry at the threat but also confused by the complete self-assurance, or rather arrogance, of the visitor. The major, as Hildebrand was already thinking of him, behaved as if he was in charge. Possibly he was bluffing, but his documents had an air of being genuine about them, including the fact that they were made of a smooth filmy material the Gestapo agent had never seen before, and Ribbentrop's personal invitation was received by the embassy only a day earlier. He decided to try a different tack:

"What is this book you brought with you?"

"This is the holy Koran," Moshe responded laconically.

"Is that so?" He leafed through the book, "And would you mind if I opened the envelope?"

"This is entirely up to you. I was ordered to deliver it sealed and untouched. Please read the warning on the outside before you open it."

Hildebrand examined the envelope again. There was an incomprehensible script he thought might be Arabic, followed by German. It said: "For the eyes of the Grand Mufti Hajj Amin al Husseini, may

Allah smile on him forever. Opening without authorization punishable by death." The seal consisted of the same script with crossed scimitars and a Hand holding a rifle.

"What would happen if I opened it now?" Hildebrand asked the major.

"You will die in the manner I described before." The major was as relaxed as ever.

Hildebrand toyed with the envelope for a couple of minutes pretending to study it. The envelope was made of the same strange material as the major's documents. Finally he made a decision: "Please wait here. If you need something, knock on the door. Would you like food or coffee?"

"Thank you. I am fine, but my patience is wearing thin. I suggest you go about your business as quickly as possible."

Hildebrand left, to pass this problem to his superiors.

***

Mizrahi had been negotiating with the British for almost two weeks. There was good progress on some issues and several disputes. Supplies of food and fuel had started flowing and, in return, cargo ships loaded with 60 millimeter hyper velocity guns, along with their armor-piercing ammunition, were leaving for the port of Alexandria. The British complained that they did not have enough time or facilities in Egypt to perform all the upgrades on their tanks. This had been partially resolved by shipping tanks from Egypt to Israel, retrofitting them with the new guns, and shipping them back.

The British government was still reluctant to cede Kuwaiti or the Sinai Peninsula. They did not refuse outright but kept postponing their decision to ask for meaningless clarifications while at the same time claiming that the territories were independent countries. In fact the British controlled the Egyptian government and it would take very little to make the Egyptian king sign a declaration selling the Sinai to Israel. The British had no idea why Israel wanted this piece of desert. The Egyptians were not interested in it either and would have sold it for a song if asked to.

Mizrahi knew the Foreign Office was doing its usual thing: playing for time and hoping for the best. Their situation in England had vastly improved since the negotiations began – food supplies, for instance, were almost at pre-war levels with shipments arriving from the colonies and Canada without interference from German U-boats. The pinpoint coordinates given to the Royal Navy by the Israelis made the submarines' life expectancy so short the Germans withdrew most of them.

The ambassador advised his government to claim "various production problems" and slow down the shipment of weapons. This was not too far from the truth: the plants were running at full capacity with maintenance suspended indefinitely. They could use some downtime.

His recommendations were considered by the Israeli Defense Cabinet.

"In the old days," the Foreign Minister offered, "I would have said that we have to stick to our agreement. If we slow down the supply of weapons, they'll be within their rights to slow down the supplies to us. In the current situation, I am not so sure.

"I believe that Mizrahi is right and the British do not intend to give us either Kuwait or the Sinai. They think that because we are Jewish we won't endanger their fight against the Nazis. I also have the feeling that they think of us as 'small Palestine' and of themselves as 'the great British Empire,' an attitude we supported by dealing with them fairly. We all know that's not the 'superpower' way!

"I recommend we slow the deliveries a little and make it clear we can increase them again – for a price. I estimate that it will take them less than a week to start yelling for help, not only because of slowdown of deliveries but because of a combination of less cannon supplied and their very high attrition rate."

"I agree," Nitzan Liebler interjected. "We now have two satellites in orbit over Northern Africa and are also flying regular drone reconnaissance flights. The British have only a vague idea how to use their armor. They have lots of first shot kills of German tanks with the new guns, but their tactics suck. Given the number of tanks, along with their reliability and range, our average battalion commander would have made mincemeat of Rommel's troops by now. The new guns damage the Germans, but not enough to stop them completely."

"Okay," Amos Nir summarized, "then our next step will be to slow the deliveries a bit and wait for them to yell. We'll offer them some tactical training to reduce their losses and request a fast, positive response on Kuwait and Sinai. To make their decision easier, we will offer to train their tank commanders in the Sinai. After we build bases there, a transfer of ownership will be only a formality. Of course, the Egyptian government will have to sign off on the agreement, but we'll leave that to the Brits."

The Foreign Minister brought up the next issue: "Avigdor Mizrahi asked for additional staff. He needs people he trusts to handle communications and paperwork. He bought a building in a nice neighborhood, so we have space, sort of. The building has been bombed and while it is being renovated we will be able to accommodate a small number of people there. I suggest we send six or seven people, including a communications expert, a trade expert and other staff I listed in the memo you all have in front of you."

"I agree," said Amos Nir. "We need more of a presence in London, and we also need to prepare for opening formal relations with the U.S. and the Soviets. That will require at least six additional staff people. I suggest we start with that and add more as necessary."

"How are we going to send them to London? I don't think we should ask the Brits for transport – especially as we need to transfer computers and satellite equipment," remarked the Defense Minister. "How about using one of the executive jets we have available?"

"Do they have the range for a return flight from London?" the Finance Minister asked.

"We have a choice," the Defense Minister said. "We can either use an Israel Aircraft Industries Galaxy 200 to fly directly over France – it has the range to go to London and back with some fuel reserve left, or we can fly over Spain. In that case, we have to refuel in London. My recommendation is to fly over France. At mach .75 and a ceiling of 45,000 feet it will be out of reach of the German fighters, assuming the Germans will even be aware of it."

"What if they have an emergency and have to land in France?" the Foreign Minister asked. "We don't want this plane or its passengers falling into the hands of the Germans. I would prefer the safer route over Spain."

The Defense Minister looked dubious. "Refueling in London is possible - we can use plain kerosene and put the additives directly into the tank. This will mean a much longer stay on the ground, giving the Brits a good look at the plane. I'm not sure we want to do that. The chance of an emergency on such a flight is about one in five thousand - they probably won't have to land in France. I suggest that we leave the decision to the experts at IAI."

Amos Nir closed the discussion: "I agree with Nitzan, the chances of an emergency landing are very small and exposure to the Brits is undesirable. If the engineers at IAI agree, I would vote for a direct flight."

"I have another issue," the Defense Minister said slightly apologetically. "It should be dealt with by the German negotiating committee, but there is no time. We had a communication from Eichmann. He is the main liaison with the Germans responsible for organizing the transports to Brindisi. In his radio message he complained that they are having problems rounding up Jews for transport to Italy. People seem not to trust the Nazis - no surprise there - and not many volunteer to go. We need to do something to help; otherwise this endeavor will take much too long."

The Absorption Minister was the first to respond: "There is one resource we haven't used yet: the Jewish Agency and other activists spread out all over Europe. It won't take very long to locate them. If we could persuade them, they could persuade their communities to cooperate. We will have, of course, to send people to the different political movements – the leftist, like the Hashomer Hatzair will not accept a Revisionist emissary."

"I think this is less of a problem than some of the Orthodox communities," the Minister for Religions responded. "I don't think that the anti-Zionist communities will yield to any persuasion by anybody. They think that if the Almighty wanted a state, he would perform a miracle and create one; It's not up to the Jews to create a state of their own. To make them move we have to send emissaries that speak their language telling them that the miracle happened and the state is here. This is not a problem we can ignore – They number close to two million."

"And how do we get to any of those communities?" Amos wanted to know.

"How about setting up a meeting with Eichmann at the Brindisi compound and telling him that we'll send our agents to deceive the Jews? These agents will be our liaison with the activists in Jewish communities," suggested the Defense Minister, "but I am reluctant to suggest we send the Ultra-Orthodox as agents – the sight of bearded Jews traveling all over Europe may be too much for the Nazis."

The Religions Minister nodded: "I agree, especially as few of the Ultra-Orthodox are trained for this kind of activity. On the other hand it would be enough, in my opinion, to send agents who are observant, know the history of the community they are visiting and can persuade the leaders that a miracle happened and the state of Israel is here, now. They saw it that way in 1948. These people are open to the idea of a miracle, which I think is really what it is anyway. Oh, and some of them had emissaries in Palestine. If we could locate their descendants, it might make the mission that much easier."

"I have a related question. Isn't the compound still being built? Do we really want to let this Nazi see what we're doing?"

"Hannah has a point," Amos Nir said, "But I think that psychologically it's a good idea to make him come to us and meet face to face. Maybe we can create an enclosure in the compound and meet him there, limiting what we show him?"

"That sounds much better," Hannah responded. "Who will talk to him?"

Nitzan Liebler thought for a moment: "I think that we have the right man there already. The commander of the facility is one Colonel Ephraim Hirshson. He speaks German, not like a native but well enough to be understood. His Arabic is good and he is a tough cookie and definitely the guy to deal with the likes of Eichmann. We'll need to tell him what we want from the Nazi and I believe he can get it."

***

The next time Ibrahim woke up, a couple of hours later, he felt much better. His headache was gone and his foot wasn't as red. He enjoyed the sensation of not being in pain. The door opened and a soldier in a black uniform came in. He put a bundle on the chair next to Ibrahim's bed.

"What is going on?" Ibrahim asked.

"Everything will be explained to you in good time," the soldier responded in Arabic. "Please dress and get ready to leave."

Ibrahim did as he was told. A bit later he was escorted to a small dining room decorated with swastikas and verses from the Koran. Within seconds a familiar looking man entered the room.

"Sit," the man pointed at one of the chairs at the dining table. "May Allah bless you forever. You deserve a good meal before going back to Palestine." The man took a seat opposite Ibrahim.

As soon as they were seated, servants, in the same black uniforms, started serving food.

"Do you recognize me?" the man asked.

"Your Excellency, I think that I am in the presence of the Grand Mufti of Jerusalem!" Ibrahim attempted to get up.

"Sit, sit," the Mufti said. "I am glad you recognized me. It is a good sign that I am known even in your own future time."

"Sir, you are not only known, but revered by us. You are our role model and we strive to fulfill your vision." Ibrahim' voice was slightly trembling with excitement.

"Now listen carefully," the Mufti said, extending a typed sheet of paper. "I have carefully read the books you brought. Here is a message for my grand nephew. You will have to memorize it. I'll also give you a handwritten note to show him. The note is written on and sealed in rice paper, so if you get caught on the way back just swallow it." He pulled out a fountain pen from his pocket, signed the flap of the envelope, finished the cup of coffee he was drinking and got up. Ibrahim jumped up from his seat.

"Sit. Finish your meal in peace. Later one of my aides will instruct you on how you will return to Palestine. May Allah be with you always."

"Yes, sir. May Allah the mighty and merciful smile on you forever." Ibrahim attempted a salute like he saw the soldiers give the Mufti.

The Mufti saluted back: "Allahu Akbar," he said as he left the room.

Later, after nightfall, Ibrahim was taken to an airplane parked on the runway of a small airstrip. It was dark except for the car's dimmed lights, but even in this light he could see the German Luftwaffe insignia on the plane. He had never before flown in such an old-fashioned airplane. It was uncomfortable, noisy and slow. The plane's windows were painted so no light could escape. Only the pilots could see outside. Ibrahim spent his time on the plane memorizing the message.

Finally they landed without cutting the engines: "This is as far as we go," the pilot said in German, with an adjutant of the Mufti translating. "Here is our position on the map. Walk southeast from here for about eight miles. It will be light soon - Be sure to hide during the day. As soon as it gets dark you can cross the border. You know how to get where you are going." The adjutant added "Allahu Akbar."

Chapter 11

Colonel Hirshson was busy. He hadn't been this busy since he was a bright-eyed and bushy-tailed second lieutenant preparing his platoon for an operation in Gaza.

Two weeks ago a small flotilla had entered the Italian port of Brindisi. The flotilla consisted of two large Israeli missile boats, two 3000 ton cargo ships, and two mostly submerged and invisible submarines. Under the watchful eye of the missile boats, submarines, drones and jets patrolling the skies above, the cargo ships were unloaded and returned to Haifa for a second run.

Hirshson was responsible for getting the construction done and setting up the facility. He had at his disposal a battalion of combat engineers with their heavy earthmoving equipment. Two infantry battalions were assigned to guard duty and navy and air force units kept a watch on the area.

The first engineering job was to create an earthen barrier about thirty feet high around the compound. It was built inside a perimeter fence erected by the Germans only a week earlier. The barrier would enclose an area two miles wide by three miles long, with the longer side being parallel to the sea and the port in the northwestern portion. The toughest job for Hirshson had been prepping space for a pre-fabricated concrete wall that was to separate the town of Brindisi from its port. He didn't like the idea of forcing blameless Italians from the surrounding area.

"Colonel," the mayor of Brindisi complained at a meeting called by Hirshson, in which a number of prominent citizens participated, "if you cut us off from the port we will lose our livelihood. This town needs fishermen going out to sea every morning."

"Yes," agreed the colonel, "and it needs its smugglers to return every morning too."

"You have to allow us access to the port. We will complain to the Duce," one of the town elders yelled.

"Please complain," Hirshson responded. "This arrangement has the Duce's full agreement. I am truly sorry he forgot about your needs, and I think you should complain to him."

"Dear colonel, we do not wish to be an obstacle to whatever plans you have for the port," the mayor added, trying a more friendly approach. "We only wish to help and hope you can at least allow us the use of some piers."

"How does this sound to you?" the colonel asked with a smile. "You can continue to use the northernmost pier and most of the warehouses as long as everyone in town reports to us information and rumors about military activity, and we will be free to take more land to expand the compound to the South?"

"We are in agreement," the mayor declared after a short consultation with the rest of the attendees.

****

Work went on uneventfully for a couple of days after the meeting. The concrete wall was almost finished and the earthen barrier extended half way around the compound. The barbed wire erected by the Germans was connected to a computerized alarm system to prevent infiltration. Another week would complete the enclosure. The refurbishing of structures was well on its way with some ready to house evacuees. Then Hirshson was ordered to set up a meeting with Colonel Adolph Eichmann.

The Israeli was too young to have witnessed Eichmann's 1962 trial, but being interested in history - particularly that of the Holocaust - he had studied the testimony of witnesses in the trial. He was proud and bitter - proud that the Mossad captured this son of a bitch and brought him to trial in Jerusalem, bitter that Eichmann had done his job as the main organizer of the 'Final Solution' so well. Most of Hirshson's family had been killed, thanks to Eichmann. Only his grandfather and a few cousins survived.

Hirshson had one of his soldiers, a German speaker, call Eichmann's office directly using a phone connected to the Italian system. It took a while to get through all the operators, but eventually a German voice announced: "Colonel Eichmann's office."

"This is the office of Colonel Abdul Rakhman of the Caliph's First Guard Division calling Herr Eichmann," the soldier said.

"Just a second," was the response.

Several minutes passed before a voice came on the line: "This is Eichmann. How can I help you?"

"You are to report to our main gate in Brindisi in three days to speak to the Colonel regarding your request for help with the deportation of Jews."

"I will see what I can do." Eichmann responded.

Looking at Hirshson, who nodded, the soldier said: "Herr Eichmann, you will either do exactly as you are ordered by the Caliph's guard or somebody else will answer your phone next time. We expect you here next Thursday at four in the afternoon." The soldier hung up.

"Very good," Hirshson was smiling. "You seem to have a natural talent for this."

"No, sir. I just hate them."

***

By the time of the meeting Hirshson had an office in one of the warehouse buildings of the port. Inside the entry door was a large waiting area equipped with food and thermoses with fruit juices, coffee and tea. The walls and floor were covered in expensive oriental rugs. The halogen lighting was adjustable.

A secretary's desk occupied a space in front of an ornate carved door leading to the Colonel's office. A lamp and a sophisticated telephone were the only items on its highly polished surface. There were two more doors in the side walls of the room.

Eichmann's car arrived at four in the afternoon sharp and stopped in front of the heavy solid truck gate in the concrete wall surrounding the port. A door in the gate opened and a soldier wearing a khaki uniform with a swords and rifle patch on his sleeve approached the vehicle, weapon ready.

"Colonel Eichmann is here to see Colonel Abdul Rakhman," the driver said.

"He may enter," the guard responded. "You and the car wait here."

Two men exited: Eichmann and his assistant.

"Only the colonel," the guard said.

"Surely my aide can accompany me?"

"You may bring in whomever you like," the guard replied with a cold smile, "but only you will come out alive. It's your choice."

Eichmann hesitated. He wasn't used to this kind of direct and brutal treatment except by superiors. But these people were barbarians and he had better be careful. They destroyed Wolfsburg so it stood to reason that killing Alois would be nothing to them. He went in alone.

Beyond the door was a large square enclosed by a concrete wall tall enough to conceal everything behind it. Only one building was partly inside the enclosure. There was a door in its stone wall with a big flag of the Caliph over it.

"Herr Eichmann, please hand over your side arm and the dagger," demanded the guard. "They will be returned to you when you are done here." Eichmann hesitated. They were on Italian territory after all.

"You have a choice," the guard said coolly. "You can proceed armed and be executed as an infidel bearing arms in the presence of an officer of the Caliph, you can leave now or you can follow our orders." He smiled and extended a hand.

Eichmann handed over his pistol, ceremonial SS dagger and, just to be safe, a pen knife he carried in his trouser pocket. It dawned on him that this was *not* Italian territory anymore.

The inner door opened and an armed guard in a bulky uniform beckoned, leading the Nazi officer through twisting corridors into the bowels of the building. He stopped in front of a heavy door, which opened silently.

"Herr Eichmann," the sergeant behind the desk said in good German, "welcome to our modest domain. The Colonel is busy and will call you in as soon as he is ready. Have a seat. If you need to refresh yourself, the facilities are there," he said pointing. "Please feel free to enjoy the food and drinks."

Eichmann sat in one of the comfortable chairs. He was annoyed – the secretary, who was only a sergeant, had not bothered to rise from his seat when he greeted a senior SS officer. The entrance door opened again and a man in an immaculate uniform entered. The sergeant jumped to attention: "Captain, Sir, the Colonel knows you are here." There were other people in the room, all ignoring him. Two were civilians. Another two were in uniform. Officers he thought, but could not be sure. Two were having a lively discussion in Arabic, about Italian women. His Arabic was not as good as his Hebrew and too limited to understand the details.

After waiting for more than thirty minutes Eichmann decided to use the bathroom. It was a complete surprise. There were polished marble mosaic floors, granite counter tops and gilded or maybe solid gold, fixtures - a room worthy of Goering set up for men of his own rank and below, and on a temporary base yet. Incredible. He used the toilet, which flushed by itself when he was done. The faucet, he discovered after some exploration, dispensed warm water when he held his hands under it. By the time he was invited into the inner office an hour later, the waiting room was empty and his mood was subdued. He had to report on his experience here in detail and he did his best to commit everything to memory, especially the self flushing toilet and smart faucet. He still hadn't decided how to interpret the opulent and luxurious amenities. He would have liked to tell himself that these were clear signs of decadence, like the Ottomans or the Colonial British. There was something that wouldn't let him accept this interpretation. He decided to reserve his opinion until after the meeting with Colonel Rakhman.

Finally the sergeant told him that the colonel was ready for him and led him into the inner sanctum. This room was big and matched the bathroom in its opulence. A stocky man in his late thirties sat behind an intricately carved desk.

"Heil Hitler." Eichmann clicked his heels in the Nazi salute.

"Herr Eichmann, I am very pleased to see you". Hirshson shook the Nazi's hand ignoring the salute. "Let's make ourselves comfortable," he said, gesturing at the leather sofa and armchairs arranged around a low table. Without apologizing for the wait, he politely inquired about Eichmann's trip to Brindisi. Eichmann was neither surprised nor annoyed. This was behavior he expected from superiors.

After a few minutes of polite chitchat, Hirshson got down to business. "Please describe to me the problems you claim you are having with our Jews."

"Well, Colonel, we are doing our best to round them up for transport to Brindisi. Since you limit the amount of force we can use, it is difficult to persuade them to come. You will either have to allow us to use somewhat more effective means of persuasion," - Eichmann smiled thinking of what he would do to the Jews if the colonel agreed - "or be prepared for a very slow trickle coming in for treatment. I also have to warn you that the Fuehrer's patience is running out. If the Jews are not gone soon, he may decide to restart our own treatment program."

"Dear Adolph - may I call you Adolph? There's really no need to get all worked up about the slow progress. As you can see, we are just getting ready to receive the Jews. If the Fuehrer decides to take care of them himself or use what you call 'more effective means of persuasion', I will destroy Munich. It'll be the Fuehrer's decision. Please remind him of our determination when you have an opportunity.

"On the other hand, I do understand your frustration. We are also impatient to finish this business. How about we send a large group of our agents, pretending to be Palestinian Jews, to persuade their leadership that this idea of moving to Palestine is the best thing that happened to them since Moses." Hirshson was waiting with a wolfish smile for the Nazi to swallow the bait – It would be great if he thought that the whole idea was his to begin with. It would be enough if Eichmann just thought that he improved it and made it workable – in either case, he would promote it enthusiastically with his superiors.

"Dear Colonel Rakhman, the basic idea is good, but its success will depend on your agents being fluent in the local Jewish languages, mostly Yiddish, fluent in Hebrew, and able to tell the Jews a believable story."

"Ah, I knew you were the man to ask!" The Colonel was beaming at Eichmann. "Your advice is invaluable! Assuming we can find people with the necessary skills, what kind of a story do you think would work?"

Eichmann was thinking as fast as he knew how: "As you know, every good lie has to have a basis in truth to be believable. Also, as our friend Goebbels says, the bigger the lie and the more often it's repeated the larger numbers of people believe it. I would tell the Jews the truth, but turn it on its head: tell them that the Caliphate is an invention of the Palestinians who, with the support of the Brits, fooled the Reich into giving up the Jews."

"I am somewhat dubious about that." The Colonel sipped some orange juice. "The Caliphate story is difficult to believe, unless, of course, you had personal experience like you did. It is even more difficult to believe that the Third Reich would be deceived by such a story."

Eichmann felt confident enough to now pour himself some juice as well. "You are probably right. We can dilute the story somewhat to make it more believable."

They discussed the details for a while, finally arriving at a mutually agreed cover story.

"We'll be sending our agents to as many Jewish communities as possible. They will leave as soon as I get word from you that they have safe passage. All of them will carry documents issued by the Jewish Yishuv in Palestine. To enable your people to identify them as agents and citizens of the Caliphate the documents will look like this one," the Colonel showed Eichmann a plastic card with his name and photograph. "The number on the Palestinian ID will be the same as the citizen's real ID number – just in case you need to cross check with us.

"These agents will have free travel rights between this port and every Jewish community."

Eichmann smiled: "You should also issue these ID cards, in German, to some of the real Jews, and send them back to their communities. They will be the most effective means of luring the rest of them."

"Herr Eichmann," Hirshson smiled an almost genuine smile, "you are a genius. We will definitely follow your advice."

Eichmann hesitated and decided this was a good time to obtain the information Himmler wanted. "Your facilities here are very comfortable and look quite permanent. I wish I could have an office like this."

Hirshson smiled: "Yes, I like comfort and see no reason to deny it to myself or my subordinates even in a temporary base like this one. We believe that a well-rested, well-fed and healthy soldier can be a formidable fighter. He has to be well-trained, dedicated and armed – and you can trust me that we take care of all these aspects of a good army."

"So you don't think that all this makes you soft?"

Hirshson smiled a wolfish smile: "I would advise you to ask our enemies about how soft we are. But they are all dead, so you will have to take my word for it."

Eichmann was at the point in this conversation where he could ask his question without it sounding strange. "You must have had some fierce battles. Only a short time ago Palestine was under British rule with a sizable garrison and hundreds of thousands of Jews to help them against you. I am curious how you could manage against such odds."

Hirshson did not answer immediately. He kept looking at Eichmann until the German lowered his eyes. Only then did Hirshson recite the answer he was instructed to give: "Dear Colonel, if the Great Mufti of Jerusalem thought that you need this information he would have already given it to you. It is not my place to override the Caliph's cousin's decisions."

Hirshson got up, signaling the end of the interview. As the Colonel was opening the door for his guest to leave the sergeant at the secretary's desk jumped up to salute: "Sir," he started in Arabic.

"Please speak German. It is polite to do so in the presence of our esteemed guest," the Colonel was smiling.

"Yes Sir. Captain Gamal reports that he just caught an Italian trying to infiltrate the compound to steal whatever he could. Shall we administer the regular punishment?"

"Did the Italian know what the punishment was going to be before he infiltrated?"

"Sir, there are clear signs in several languages outside the fence."

"Good. Please ask Gamal to make certain the man is not a spy. If he is just a thief, Gamal should round up his family and any friends he can find and administer the punishment in front of them. Then let everybody go. If he is a spy, tell Gamal to wait for me. We shall do the usual."

"What is the punishment?" inquired Eichmann.

"Oh, it's prescribed by Sharia: We cut of his left hand for a first offense. It is done in public with a sharp ax. His friends and family will be there to comfort him and treat him afterward. The Caliph's law is merciful. Of course, if he is a spy, we will interrogate him and then cut out his tongue and eyes as is prescribed by law. We are merciful and very infrequently kill our prisoners."

After returning to his car Eichmann gave orders to drive as fast as possible to Rome where a Lufthansa plane was waiting to take him to Berlin. He needed to report to Himmler on this first face to face encounter with the Caliph's military. He also had to warn his superiors that Munich would be in danger if the Caliph was displeased. It was depressing, on the other hand he will probably get to see Hitler again – to report about the Grand Mufti – and that might lead to a promotion. He had to think for a while. It was of paramount importance to present the information about the Mufti as being the result of his great interrogation and diplomatic skills.

***

The weather was nice and hot, not unusual for mid-July in Vilnius. Jacob and Zalman worked side by side at the cabinetmaking shop. Their supervisor, a middle aged German sergeant, was sitting outside smoking a cigarette and reading a newspaper. The sergeant demanded they do a good job of the repairs they were working on but otherwise treated them well. The workshop was busy restoring furniture brought by German officers from conquered Soviet territories. Most were high quality antiques from czarist times needing restoration after years of abuse as office furnishing. Both Jacob and, to a lesser extent, Zalman, were good with their hands. Both were trained cabinetmakers, though Zalman never used his training and Jacob used it only during the short time he ran his late father's business before it was taken over by the Germans. They found this job and were doing well enough to be made foremen – each with a small crew - by the sergeant.

"What do you make of the announcement this morning?" Zalman asked his friend. He was referring to the notices posted everywhere in the Ghetto, announcing the commencement of transports to Palestine.

"I almost believe them," Jacob responded, "though it's not clear to me how they can transport us to Palestine while they're fighting the British. The incentive they offer is irresistible. I don't like it. On the other hand, Günter told me that some of the smaller ghettos in Poland were emptied. According to his source, another Communist that works for the German railways, they were transported to southern Italy."

"You believe the stories our sergeant tells? He knows as little as we do and is even more afraid for his life – having been a member of the Communist party doesn't give him much standing here."

"On the other hand, he's never lied to us and his information about new repressions has always been accurate. If it wasn't for him, we wouldn't be able to smuggle food into the ghetto. He's warned us that the Gestapo was coming so we could hide. Also, he's not the only former Communist – There were more than 7 million of them in Germany before Hitler took over, so I believe his story," Jacob responded. "If they start reducing the number of rations for the ghetto by the number of people who are supposed to leave each day for Palestine, and if people don't actually leave, how long do you think it will take for all of us to starve? I believe they'll starve us as the notice said – I'm surprised they haven't done it already."

"Well, I was considering going to the forest," Zalman said quietly, "but with a wife and baby I can't go anywhere. My in-laws can't go to the forest either and my parents will resist going anywhere. Maybe if they hear that your family is going, they will decide to join."

"I don't think I'll go to the forest," Jacob said looking around. "Though both my mother and sister are in good health, the forest with all the bandits is not a place for an old woman and a teenage girl. I'm thinking of volunteering for the first train on Monday next week. We don't even have enough possessions to fill the suitcase per person that we're allowed, so moving will be easy. The only thing that worries me is that according to Günter's friend we will be transported in cattle cars. They'll supposedly supply water and give us food for the journey, but it's not going to be comfortable. I wish we had more information from a trustworthy source. I'm going to speak to my uncle today. I hope to persuade him and his family to join us. I'm hoping they'll treat the first transports well – if only to encourage people to volunteer."

Zalman was surprised: "You plan on going with the first train? That's less than two weeks away! I don't think I can make a decision fast enough to join you."

***

Commander Thompson was about to salute, but remembered in time that Churchill did not like formalities at his official country residence - the Chequers mansion.

"Sir, we have a request from the Palestinian representative to allow their airplane to land at Croydon. They want to transport several people to add to their mission here. They will be bringing equipment and requested full diplomatic immunity for both the personnel and equipment."

"Please inform the Air Marshal I want lots of photographs taken and to have our best aircraft designers on hand to take a look. They will need to refuel, and if we do the refueling slowly enough we can get a good look."

***

When the Israeli executive jet landed, a large party of British officials was waiting to meet it. But Avigdor Mizrahi was the first to approach.

"Had a good flight?" he asked the pilot that opened the door and lowered the exit ramp.

"Perfect. Good weather all the way and no other traffic in the air. Very easy."

"Good. I need everyone to help unload the equipment so you can take off as soon as possible."

They were done in eight minutes – there wasn't that much equipment and only one suitcase per person. While the Foreign Office bureaucrat was still shaking hands and welcoming the new arrivals the jet revved up its engines and started taxiing for takeoff.

"Leaving already?" a colonel from the British Air Ministry asked. "We are ready to refuel your plane."

"Thanks for the offer," Mizrahi responded, "but the plane doesn't need refueling. We appreciate the thought."

"Wouldn't it be safer to take off in daylight?"

"Not really. Thank you."

The aircraft was gone before the conversation was finished.

***

"So, what have we learned from their aircraft?" Churchill was smoking a cigar and drinking tea, relaxing on a terrace at Chequers.

"We know it can fly nonstop from Palestine to London - and back again without refueling - at an estimated air speed of 460 miles per hour, cruising at 45,000 feet, according to our radar. We definitely have nothing that can catch it. Of course these figures are only very rough estimates – our radar installation could see the plane when it was almost over the Channel. We don't have enough refinement in the system to see single planes at larger distances." The Air Marshal looked at the two men at his side. "These gentlemen tell me that the craft is powered by some kind of turbine, though we had no chance to examine it closely."

"What was your impression of the plane? Was it a military transport or a fighter?"

"The writing on the fuselage said 'IAI Galaxy 200'. I had a glimpse of the interior – very plush. We saw no armaments of any kind, though this is no guarantee that they didn't carry something we can't even identify as a weapon. In my opinion it is not a military plane at all, rather a passenger transport."

"I must add," the taller of the two experts said, "that these people could obviously accelerate our jet turbine engine project."

"I have no doubt that they could, if they were willing to share," Churchill said. "Do any of you know what their cargo was?"

The three men looked at each other again. The Air Marshall answered: "The cargo consisted of suitcases made of fabric plus several boxes about the same size that appeared to be made of aluminum."

He paused and then continued: "Sir, may I know who they are?"

"Well, this is somewhat complicated. The only thing that I can tell you is that they are a Palestinian outfit helping us in various matters. You are all sworn to secrecy and not a word of this may get out as per your briefing. Thank you, gentlemen. Your information was very interesting."

Chapter 12

David Rothstein returned from work to the apartment where his family was settling in. The consulting business he'd started was doing very well. He had decided not to accept any of the job offers presented to him. Instead, he was happily doing what he did best: helping companies design and build microchip manufacturing equipment. His expertise was highly valued before the Event and was even more valuable now that most of the other experts were in the future. David was surprised to discover that Israel had several microchip plants. They were small but sophisticated. All of them were expanding as fast as they could; competition was many years in the future and everyone anticipated Israel establishing commercial relations with the rest of the world – this would present infinite opportunities.

He was greeted by his wife. "You're just in time for dinner. Jake called ten minutes ago. He's going to pick up Josh. They should be here soon."

"How'd the house hunting go?" David inquired.

"Well, I saw a couple in Rishon L'Zion. There is one I liked and the price is right, but I need to research the neighborhood a bit more. I spoke to Ze'ev's wife - we will go together tomorrow. I'm really tired of this apartment and would like to move as soon as possible." Rachel was talking and setting up the dinner table at the same time.

"Well, maybe we should rethink our priorities. I have been car hunting today; spent a good five hours going from dealer to dealer in Tel-Aviv. Lucky they are fairly close together. But it's a lost cause; none of them have a car for sale. I thought I got lucky with the Ford guy – he told me on the phone that he had a couple of cars left, but by the time I got there he was sold out. We couldn't afford the price anyway." David sounded slightly depressed.

"How about a used car?" Rachel asked.

"Just look at the car section of the paper. It's empty. Apparently old cars sell before they get into the paper. I doubt that many people are selling – everybody knows that car imports will be dead for a while."

"While you were running around I was looking at houses and talking to people," Rachel said while still fussing with the food. "The real estate agent told me that some dealerships and large repair shops are buying junked cars and restoring them. We may be able to buy a Jeep, or an old

DeSoto or even a Mercedes. They are not cheap and I have no clue how safe they are."

"I don't have much choice," David responded. "I need a car to get to the different plants I am working with, though that may be temporary. I met a nice guy today - actually he took pity on me and gave me a lift. He's a civil engineer, works for a big firm. According to him the upcoming area is Beer Sheba and south. They have a huge contract to develop those areas and are extending the railway to the Sinai border. Maybe we should consider moving there; or at least somewhere closer to a main public transportation hub. It's too difficult to have to take at least three buses and a train to get anywhere."

By this time, the boys arrived and dinner began. For a while everyone was quiet, concentrating on their food, which was different than their meals in the U.S. had been. The supermarkets here were full of fresh produce, poultry and some fish. Bread and grains were plentiful too, but there was an almost total absence of beef. Israel was planning on importing beef from Argentina, like they did before the Event. In the meantime, only small numbers of cattle were coming in from Canada.

"Jake, how was your day?" David asked.

"Good, but its hard work. Try studying Hebrew at the same time as taking college courses *in* Hebrew. I'm just glad they offer some classes in English. By the way, I got a notice at college today to present myself at the IDF registration center next week. The guys say they'll probably let me continue with my studies for now and take me in the summer for training."

"I hope so," Rachel looked worried. "David, do you know anybody that could help?"

"Mother, this is not the U.S. We are in our own country now, and I *will* share the burden of defense with everybody else!"

"OK, OK, calm down," David smiled. "I won't interfere, even if I did know somebody.

"How about you, Josh? What were you up to?"

"I feel like an idiot. My Hebrew is lousy and I think that maybe I should quit high school and volunteer for the Army."

"Don't be stupid," Jake told his younger brother. "First of all, they won't take you – you're too young. Second, your Hebrew may be lousy, but it's much better than it was a month ago and will be even better next month. And if you don't graduate high school you can, maybe, sweep the streets – any decent job here requires at least a high school diploma. I don't think you'd like that better than having a hard time in school, so keep working on your Hebrew and you'll be fine."

"Yeah, maybe."

***

"Mr. Mizrahi, I appreciate you coming so soon." General Wilson rose from his chair to shake the ambassador's hand. "We have a problem that needs to be resolved."

The General was transferred to London only a couple of days earlier. He was promoted and given a post at the General Staff, but his main duty was to be a liaison between the Israeli ambassador and the Prime Minister. Mizrahi asked for him and Churchill agreed – he trusted Wilson and agreed that having been in contact with the Israelis and having visited Israel he was the most qualified person for the job. It was also agreed by both parties that for reasons of secrecy the P.M. could not be involved directly. Continuing meetings with a Palestinian business man would be noticed by foreign intelligence services. Neither Israel nor Churchill wanted the secret out. Not yet.

"Yes, we have a number of problems that need to be resolved." Mizrahi sat across the deck from the General.

"You'll be reducing the number of cannon and ammunition supplied to us. This is unacceptable. We have an agreement, which we respect. There haven't been any interruptions or delays in our supplies to you, have there?"

"No, General. Your side has been meticulous about keeping the agreement. We want to keep our part of the bargain but there's a problem. Actually there are several problems. Let me begin with what bothers us on the political front." Mizrahi paused for a moment. There was traffic noise coming from the outside - London was definitely reviving, making these negotiations more difficult. "Our talks regarding Kuwait and the Sinai are going nowhere. Your Foreign Office is dragging its feet, probably hoping that we will go away as suddenly as we appeared. Do you want us to go away?" He looked intently at Wilson awaiting a response.

"Mr. Mizrahi, I owe you an honest reply. My feelings are somewhat contradictory. Your help in Syria has been useful - though certainly not critical - and whatever trick you are using to spot the German submarines has considerably helped both the PM's popularity and our war effort. The Soviets are certainly benefiting by getting almost all the Lend Lease supplies without interruption and we're not losing transports on the way to Murmansk. I also admit that the equipment you are supplying has enabled us to slow Rommel's advance. On the other hand, we've paid you generously for this help. Shall I enumerate?" Wilson smiled.

"Please do."

Wilson looked surprised: "If you wish, though this is a very unusual way of negotiating. You are improving my position by letting me list all we do for you in return for your help."

"You may be surprised before we are done." Mizrahi smiled.

"Very well. We supply you with food and fuel – enough for a small country. We've also put fifteen large troop carriers at your disposal for a year. Shall I go into details of the food and fuel supplies, or is a general statement enough?" Wilson was smiling again. Clearly, the listing of the British supplies to Israel cheered him up.

"No need to go into details - I have them right here." Mizrahi pointed at his briefcase. "Your supplies to us amount to less than 20% of the surplus the Empire generates. And the troop carriers were sitting in port anyway since there are no invasions planned for the foreseeable future. So in fact, the British Empire is hardly bothered by supplying our demands.

"You also listed very eloquently the help you receive from us. If you wish, I can give you a rough outline of what happened in the reality we came from, when we were, obviously, not available to assist you."

General Wilson leaned forward in his chair: "Please do. I'm an eager student of history, especially military history, as you must know."

"If we had not arrived, Rommel would soon be very close to taking Cairo. You would eventually win the war but the price would be the loss of your Empire. Your holdings in the Far East, except India - which you lose after the war, fall to the Japanese. The Soviets advanced into the heart of Germany - and stayed there, controlling Eastern Europe for more than forty years.

"In my world the war ended in 1945 and the British Empire started falling apart immediately – mostly under American pressure, but also because 'Great' Britain, Mizrahi added, with sarcasm dripping over the 'great', was exhausted and impoverished by the war. America and the Soviet Union become superpowers dictating policy to the rest of the world, with the United Kingdom a junior adjunct of the Americans."

The two sat in silence for a while. "Thank you for the information," Wilson said finally. "I see that your presence will change things and will report to the Prime Minister accordingly. We must cooperate closely to advance both our causes. I am sure that Mr. Churchill will not allow the Empire to fall apart or let Stalin take over Europe." He paused collecting his thoughts: "For the sake of our long term relations I would like to clarify a number of points. If I understand you correctly, your government, or maybe it is only you, personally, did not like the world in which two superpowers ruled. Is that so?"

"You are absolutely correct, and yes, it is my government's position."

"Do I also correctly estimate that your government would like to change the course of history?"

"General Wilson, we want a better world for all. The world we came from was not pleasant: for more than forty years it was on the verge of a third world war and complete destruction. Each superpower supported its clients and fought wars using proxies, propping up bloody dictators and killing millions. Then the Soviets collapsed, and the vacuum was filled by Muslim religious fanatics, a resurgent Russia with imperial ambitions and Communist China with capitalistic tendencies and somewhat disruptive foreign policies. The world we came from has known no peace since the end of the current war. There was always fighting somewhere in the word, some wars were small and local and some were major. Not like the current one, but still serious with genocide on some scale happening all over the world.

"Our estimate is that a world without superpowers, with a number of strong countries, will be more peaceful than the one we left behind. People will still try to resolve their differences by force, but they will be less likely to do so if the blood they spill and the resources they squander are their own. We view the situation as the difference between two large feudal lords squabbling by inducing their vassals to attack each other. The lords have little to lose, and in the meantime people die. If there are no vassals, but instead, free democratic countries, wars between neighbors are less likely, since democracies tend not to be militarily aggressive. Do you think that Europe will go to war anytime soon after this war is done? Of course, there are no guarantees for the future, and human stupidity and hubris know no limits, but at least we want to try. We also know that only a minority of the countries existing now are democracies, but without superpowers and with better understanding of social dynamics we hope to help that number grow steadily."

"Mr. Mizrahi, I assume that you have practical steps in mind?"

"Indeed we do, General. We think that for the good of the future world the British Empire has to be preserved, at least for a while. It will have to be dissolved eventually, but the dissolution can be beneficial for everyone – including Britain. Colonies have to gain independence. It is our belief that if they are prepared for it and are granted it instead having to fight, both Britain and the colonies will gain and there will be a potential for a more peaceful world. We are not prophets and we may be wrong, but it makes no sense to repeat the mistakes that were made in our time. Please convey this message to Mr. Churchill. We are being open about our plans for the future and expect an open and truthful British policy in return."

"I would like to go back to the original reason for your visit," Wilson said. "How soon can the undersupply of cannon be remedied?"

"The rate of supply dropped by only 10%," Mizrahi said, "and if your troops had been using their tanks efficiently you wouldn't even notice the change. The problem is that your army has only a vague idea of how to use armor. As a result, Rommel - who is an expert in armor warfare - is beating you even though you have better weapons. The theories he is using were proposed by one of your own Liddell Hart, in the 1920s. His ideas were rejected by your establishment and the same establishment has only a foggy idea of how to implement them. The Germans adopted his ideas and developed them, which is what makes Rommel so dangerous, besides his personal talent, of course.

"If we increase the supply of cannon, you will keep losing tanks at an unacceptable rate and Rommel will come close to Cairo, or even take it, as this time-line is different from ours and there is no guarantee that history will repeat and hand you a victory."

"Actually I am one of the few military supporters of Liddell Hart. You are right though that the establishment rejected him. I assume that you have a proposal," Wilson said.

"Yes, we have a solution. We will establish, with your written agreement, a number of bases in the Sinai where we'll train your commanders in what we call combined arms operations. In the end, it will be much more effective than just increasing the supply of cannon." Mizrahi leaned back in his seat and relaxed. It was up to Churchill to make a decision, though the way the options were presented gave him little choice. Mizrahi assumed that if he persuaded General Wilson, Churchill would accept the General's recommendation.

"How long would it take you to set up a training program, assuming that we agreed?"

"We can start training the first batch of officers in slightly over two weeks. We suggest running several parallel courses for different command levels and for different specialists. It will take somewhat longer to set up the full curriculum." Mizrahi paused. "And it will take us a while to set up the shooting and maneuvering ranges. I think that we will have a full armor school running in about a month or so. That is, a month after the Foreign Office resolves to acquiesce to our modest requests."

"Why not start immediately? From what I saw of your troops and equipment, you must have an advanced armor school. Why not use it now?" Wilson asked.

"There are a number of reasons," Mizrahi paused for emphasis. "The main being that our trust in benign, or even rational, behavior on the part of the Foreign Office is extremely limited. The other is that our facilities are not designed to accommodate the number of trainees the British army will have to send us, and we would rather not have large, or even small, numbers of British military personnel in Israel. I am not sure we could guarantee their safety. Where we came from, Britain is not a very important power, a socialist country that is kowtowing to the Arabs and the left, making our relations, and our population's attitude, somewhat unfriendly. As far as we are concerned, you have to prove to us that you are better than the Nazis, since history tells us otherwise. There is also a security concern: we don't want large numbers of Britons realizing that we exist. Up to this moment you are the only Briton of this time that visited Israel. As long as the training is done in the Sinai by instructors that speak English, you will be able to sell your troops a reasonable story of who we are – that is if you think that any story is needed. Since most of our instructors speak English with a foreign accent you could pass them off as Americans or Russians or a mix of the two or somebody else all together."

Wilson seemed to accept the open, undiplomatic, show of anti-British sentiment. Sometimes it was an advantage to talk to a military man and not directly to the Prime Minister. He sipped his tea for a while saying nothing.

"If this is how you feel, why are you helping us at all?" he asked finally.

Mizrahi hesitated for a moment. "General Wilson, you are not Jewish and have no idea what it is to be Jewish in this world. Both your country and the U.S. know about the plight of Jews under the Nazi regime. What have you done to help them? Did you try to bomb the railroads leading to the concentration camps? No, you are too busy bombing German cities. You have the resources to bomb Berlin from time to time, but not Dachau. Neither you nor the Americans, or anybody else for that matter, have even told the Nazis that genocide of Jews, Gypsies or any other group, is unacceptable. The message to the Germans is clear: do what you want - we don't care. President Roosevelt sent a strong message when his administration refused to accept Jewish refugees. They sent them back to Germany. Britain had its opportunity in 1939. Opening Palestine to Jewish immigration would have saved Jewish lives and would have also told the Germans: 'We care.' Instead you published and enforced the White Paper, and Jews were forced to stay in occupied Europe. Is this not being an accessory to murder?

"The only reason we are helping you is that the Germans, or rather the Nazis, are much worse. You are only an accessory to their murderous policies, and you will, in the history that we came from, become an accessory to the Arab's attempt to murder the refugees that survive Hitler's holocaust. Our judgment is that the world cares not a bit what happens to its Jews or any other group that is too weak to protect itself. Just remember the slaughter of Armenians by the Ottomans in the First World War. For this reason we will help those that are least offensive, but only as long as they behave like civilized human beings."

The General looked somewhat shaken: "Mr. Mizrahi, I appreciate your candor. I have some things to say in Britain's defense, but maybe we should postpone this conversation. I will let you know the Prime Minister's decision as soon as possible. Some of the issues will have to be approved by parliament, which will take a while. I hope you can be patient."

"General Wilson, it has been a pleasure discussing these issues with you. We are in no hurry, please take your time. We are a democracy and we know how democracies work." Mizrahi shook the extended hand and left on his way to London.

***

The two young men that asked to be admitted to see Yitzhak Stern looked like typical Vilna residents, except for their bearing. There was a pride in their posture that their worn clothing and three day old beards could not suppress. Stern was careful of who was admitted to see him. It was a reasonable precaution. He was the leader of the left-wing Zionist youth movement Hashomer Hatzair in Vilnius and as such was the target of the Gestapo, who considered him a Communist. Though the Germans seemed to be leaving the Jews in peace, for now, you could never know what might happen next. For this reason Yitzhak urged his followers, of whom there were several thousand, to arm themselves and leave the ghetto for the forests to join the partisans there. Not many followed his advice. Obtaining firearms was next to impossible in a community that never favored armed resistance. Under the brief Soviet rule private ownership of firearms was outlawed, making guns scarce. The general hostility of the partisans didn't help either. In the summer of 1941 there were not many partisans in the forests surrounding Vilnius. Some of them were Polish and Lithuanian units that killed Jews on sight. There were several small units of Soviet army soldiers trapped behind German lines – they sometimes accepted Jews. You had to be very lucky to meet one of the small bands of Jews hiding in the huge forest. Even then it was not safe: the Germans, Poles and Lithuanians all hunted them down.

"Who are you and why do you want to see Yitzhak?" the young man standing nonchalantly in the entrance to the inner courtyard of the house where Stern had his headquarters that day asked.

"We were sent from Palestine, by the Jewish Agency, to contact leaders in a number of communities in Lithuania. Stern is the first we are visiting."

"Your names?"

"Yossel Lebovitz and Menachem Goldman."

"Wait here."

The young man was back in a couple of minutes: "Yitzhak will see you. I have to search you for weapons first."

After the search he led the two inside the courtyard, into a narrow door and up several flights of a dark staircase. They entered an apartment filled with people, like every other space in the ghetto. They passed through several rooms before stopping in front of a door. Their guide knocked.

"Come in." They entered the room. It was small, with a bed and a small table with four chairs. A young man with a head of wild hair sat at the table writing in a bound notebook. There was another burly young man sitting on one of the chairs.

"Please sit, I will be done in a moment." The man with the wild hair, who they recognized as Yitzhak Stern, pointed to the vacant chairs. They sat, with their guide next to them. Yitzhak kept writing for a moment, apparently finishing a thought, then put down the pen and closed the notebook.

"Gershon tells me that you come from Palestine. How did you get here and why have you come?"

"It is a long story. Maybe it would be best if we tell it in chronological order," Menachem, the older of the two guests smiled. "If you don't mind - it will make more sense that way."

"Go ahead."

"As you know, the Yishuv has been pressuring the British for some time to lift the restrictions of the White Paper. After the recent fighting in Syria, when the Palmach gave them critical help, they started negotiating with us in earnest. It took a while, but we arrived at an agreement. I don't know whether you can hear the BBC here, but a new White Paper was issued by the Foreign Office several weeks ago. Jews are now welcome to come to Palestine. The Germans agreed to move all the Jews under their control to Brindisi, Italy. From there British and German ships will transport them to Palestine. This is it in a nutshell." Menachem smiled again. "Now it is up to us to convince our people to go."

"Wait a minute. I have a number of questions. First: why would the Brits change their mind all of a sudden?"

"A number of reasons. They still have a problem with the Arabs, who despite the 1939 White Paper support Hitler and fight the Brits wherever they can. The other reason is that the Yishuv showed them that we are organized and can be of help. They realized that we can also cost them the Middle East if we rebel now. The British decided, wisely I think, that if the Yishuv is with them and is several million strong it will solve the Arab problem and be of help with the general war effort as well" Yossel, the other guest, responded.

"That sort of makes sense of sorts." Stern was still dubious. "What about the Germans?"

"Ah, this is a bit sensitive," Menachem said. "Do we have an absolute assurance of secrecy from all of you?"

"Yes," Yitzhak looked at his companions, who nodded.

"Just so we have no misunderstandings, what I am going to tell you cannot leave this room. If it does, it will cost many thousands of Jewish lives."

Everybody nodded.

"Our leadership sent an emissary to meet with a representative of Himmler. We offered him a deal: if they give us all of Europe's Jews, we will declare independence in Palestine. The Nazis had plans for Europe's Jews – you may have heard what was going on in Polish territories conquered by them in 1939 – and didn't agree easily to give their Jews a safe haven in Palestine. We finally persuaded them that it would be a great bonus for them if the Jews left without their intervention. The troops and resources they are wasting now on guarding you will be freed for the war effort. An agreement was reached and we are ready to move everybody to Brindisi in Italy and from there to Palestine."

"And when did that happen?" Yitzhak Stern was even more skeptical than before.

"We finalized our negotiations with the Germans at the end of June. Maybe you noticed their anti-Semitic propaganda stopped about then.

That was part of our agreement. Also there have been no pogroms since then, and food supplies have stayed at reasonable levels."

"How did you get here from Palestine?" the young man sitting next to Menachem wanted to know.

"We have an ID that was issued by the Palestinians that allows us to travel to any Jewish community in Europe."

"Please show me."

Menachem handed over his plastic ID card. It was closely examined by all three hosts and finally returned to him.

Yitzhak Stern was the first to speak. "If you don't mind we will talk later about who exactly sent you here. I want to make sure you are who you say you are. But this is for later. Do you expect me to tell everybody to get on the next train that the Germans claim goes to Italy? Based only on your unlikely story? You know I can't and won't do that."

"Wait a minute." Yossel rose slightly from his chair. "We ask no such thing. We expect you to send volunteers, people you trust, on that first train. They will be free to inspect the facility and ascertain that it is indeed run by our people and that we are transporting everyone to Palestine, as promised. They can even go to Palestine. We will assure their return here within a week or so to report. Then you make your decision. In the worst case, if your emissaries don't return, you will know not to trust the Germans' promises and resist them."

The interview went on for another hour or so. The visitors were interrogated on the situation in Palestine, who sent them, how did they get to Europe and other details. They apparently passed the test, since in the end Stern said: "I will give you the names of our delegation tomorrow. Come here at three in the afternoon."

"I hope this will not disappoint you," said Menachem, "but from here we are going to visit some of the other Zionist leaders, including the Revisionists. We want everyone to come home to Eretz Yisrael and will try to persuade even non-Zionists. Communists, Orthodox and all other Jews are welcome."

***

Jacob's mother was not at all happy about his connection with the Revisionists. In her opinion it wasn't much better than his involvement with the Communists in 1937. The Polish authorities arrested him for that and he spent a couple of days in jail. They released him after he promised to abandon his connections. Mostly it was because his parents pleaded for him. Being a teenager the Polish police couldn't do much anyway since his only crime was having been named by one of his friends. That experience didn't make Jacob abandon his interest in politics. He analyzed his previous support of the Communists and decided that he was wrong. The party did not support him in jail and after his release he heard from them only once. They threatened him to keep quiet about their activities, of which he knew nothing anyway. When the Soviet Union signed the Molotov-Ribbentrop pact he decided that these people were not much better than the Nazis. Jacob was also suspicious of the left-wing Jewish organizations, like the Hashomer Hatzair and the Bund. They all seemed to share a similar ideology, and by now Jacob was deeply suspicious of Socialism.

There was one Zionist organization that appealed to him: the Revisionists. It was a movement led by Ze'ev Jabotinsky and decidedly *not* Socialist. They also thought that Jews must be able to use force and trained their followers in the use of weapons and self defense. Led by Jabotinsky, they taught that the land of Israel will belong to Jews only after having been fertilized with Jewish blood; in other words, nobody will give them a country out of the goodness of their heart, they will have to fight for it. Jabotinsky also pushed for the immediate establishment of a Jewish state. It was not a popular view and the movement was small. Most Jews in Vilnius, like everywhere else in Eastern Europe, did their best to make a living and not to annoy the authorities and their neighbors. Jacob finally decided to join the Revisionists after he attended a public appearance where Jabotinsky said: "You can walk with us on the right or with the others on the left. The only ones in the middle of the road are horses."

Being somewhat stubborn and independent Jacob was not very popular with the Revisionist leadership in Vilna, but he was respected for his integrity, wisdom and ability to judge a situation beyond what it seemed to be. He was surprised at the weekly meeting of his cell when they were given the information brought by the Palestinians. He was asked, with another member, to volunteer for the first train to Italy. He was supposed to evaluate the truth in the Palestinian's story and report back to the leadership.

***

The mid-July day was hot; the cattle cars parked at the Vilnius railway station radiated heat. Sergeant Bohdan Kovalenko, now costumed as a Jew, was in the large crowd waiting on the platform. Like everyone else, he carried a package with his belongings and talked in Yiddish.

"I hope the train starts as soon as they load us," he said to the young man next to him. "If it doesn't move quickly, we'll be cooked alive in those cars."

"Maybe they won't close the doors," the young man responded. The pretty girl next to him was looking at Bohdan, who stood straighter under her inspection. He knew how to assume a perfectly straight-backed military stance, having been well-trained in his previous life in the Ukrainian guards.

"Is this your girlfriend?" Bohdan asked the young man.

"No, this is my sister Sheina, and this is my mother Sara," the young man responded. "I'm Jacob Hirshson."

"Boruch Katzenelson, from Lutsk."

"Were you there when the pogrom happened?" Sheina asked.

Bohdan was not surprised to hear that the pretty girl had a pleasant voice and spoke an educated Yiddish. "Yes, I survived by a miracle. Just ran out into the fields and hid there." He was practiced in his story and by now it came out naturally.

"Are you alone here?" Sheina inquired.

"Yes. My sisters and parents were all lost in the pogrom. I'd rather not discuss it."

"I am sorry!" Jacob exclaimed. "My little sister is sometimes too inquisitive."

Their conversation was interrupted by the station P.A. system: "Achtung! Achtung!" a German voice announced. "You will start boarding the train. Proceed to the cars immediately."

The train was loaded within an hour. About eighty people per cattle car - crowded but leaving enough space for most of them to sit.

Jacob looked around. In one corner of the car was an open-topped barrel of water. In another, plywood enclosed a hole in the floor. A notice printed in a variety of languages prohibited the use of the lavatory hole while the train was standing.

Jacob pointed out some writing on the wooden planks of the cattle car to Bohdan.

"Very interesting. It looks like we made the right decision to come on this train. According to this, the previous transport arrived someplace in Italy."

So that's what is says, Bohdan thought, hoping his inability to read Yiddish wouldn't be a problem.

"Are we supposed to relieve ourselves behind this piece of plywood with everybody just an inch away on the other side?" Sara complained.

"Yes, mother," Jacob responded. "It could be worse. The Germans don't usually care much about their own privacy, let alone ours. Don't worry, we will survive this."

Two SS officers stopped in front of the open doors of the cattle car consulting quietly. The only thing Jacob could hear was "heat" and "die". Finally the two left. A few minutes later The P.A. system announced "The car doors on the side facing away from the platform are wired shut. Do not attempt to open them. We will close the doors on the platform side with wire as well but will leave an opening for air. PAY ATTENTION: if anyone removes the wire, opens the doors, or tries to leave their car, everyone in that car will be executed.

"You were issued food packages. Make sure your food lasts you for at least seven days."

Chapter 13

Noam Shaviv enjoyed his work. He would have liked to have explored more design options for the building he was working on, but today was different. His yearly month-long reserve service ended only two weeks ago; it was more important for him to spend time with his wife and two boys. They were hoping the next one would be a girl. His wife wanted two boys and two girls - "balance the family". Noam wasn't entirely sure about having four kids, but he loved his wife and enjoyed the process.

"Hi, Shosh!" he yelled. "I'm home."

"So I hear," his wife, Shoshanna, answered. She was a nursing instructor at a nearby hospital and sometimes worked strange hours. She'd arranged to work only days since Noam came home so they could spend as much time as possible together. She was, as ever, full of energy and enthusiasm. "How did it go at work?" she asked.

"Good. I'm working on an interesting design. My team finished all the small stuff while I was away and now I'm annoying them a little by challenging some of the assumptions."

"They should be used to that by now."

"I heard some news at the office," said Noam. "We're negotiating a new government contract and, if we get it, my department will run it. The strange thing is that the government wants us to design an inexpensive building, preferably a duplex on a 600 square meter lot with fairly nice amenities. It makes no sense, since the land will cost more than the building itself, unless they build it in the desert."

"It sounds like they plan to build a new city, which makes sense. With all the people coming in we'll need to house them somewhere."

"I don't know," Noam hesitated. "Someone probably got a contract to design the city, but I have no idea who it may be. I'll have to inquire tomorrow. And I heard that the railways are looking into expanding their network by another five hundred kilometers south of Beer Sheba. But enough about my work. How was your day?"

"Normal," Shoshanna smiled. "Today we were preparing for a mass inoculation for polio. Teva, even with all their experience as the largest supplier of generic drugs in the 'old' world, still haven't produced the quantity of vaccine we estimate we'll need. I've been practicing my Yiddish - How does it sound? I discovered that I didn't forget everything my grandmother taught me."

Noam was amused. "Your Yiddish sounds funny to me. I only remember a couple of words, but maybe it will come back if I use it. I still remember Polish, I think. I got to use it a bit a couple of years ago - remember that project I did in Poland? It came back to me then like my dad told me it would. He says that no language you ever master is forgotten, only dormant until needed."

The next day at work Shoshanna was surprised.

"I have good news," her supervisor, the nursing school's administrator told her. "We've been instructed by the ministry to setup a new nursing school at another hospital. It'll need an administrator. If you want, the job is yours. I will hate losing you, but all the medical personnel that will be coming in from Europe will need re-training and you are one of the best in the business. Besides, I think that you deserve a promotion and there is nowhere to go here."

"I appreciate the offer, but I'll have to think about this and discuss it with Noam."

"Sure, sure. Think it over. I am certain that Noam will approve. In the meantime, whether you decide for or against, I need you to go there today to meet with the architects and the city engineer to discuss the needs of the new school. They want to put up temporary buildings, but you know the saying 'there is nothing as permanent as a temporary arrangement'. We don't want to be stuck with makeshift construction, especially as the ministry miraculously found the money necessary to build a nice school."

That evening the couple greeted each other with: "I have news."

"You go first."

"Sima offered me the post of administrator at a new nursing school they're going to build at our local hospital. They'll start construction in a couple of weeks. I need to give her my decision soon."

"That's great." Noam was smiling. "You finally get rewarded for all your hard work. It's also walking distance from here. I think that you should take the job."

"Not so fast." Shoshanna was serious. "It is not the same job I have now. The new job means longer hours and all kinds of aggravation, at least until the thing is built and running. What if we have more children? I still want my girls."

"Your word is my command, my lady. Shall we start working on that right now?"

"Can't you be serious for a moment?"

"Oh, I am serious. I don't see how a couple of hours more a week at work will prevent us from having more kids, especially if you're working closer to home." Noam was serious now too. "Anyway, the key to success in a job like that is not working harder but deputizing. Let your assistants do the work while you supervise. They will let you hire people right away?"

"I'll check on that. If they do, you think I should take the job?"

"Yes, I think you should. I'll do my best to help you, though with my news it will be difficult."

"News?"

"Well, I let you go first, now it's my turn. I was also offered a promotion today; or rather I was promoted without an option to refuse." Noam was smiling happily. "I was made a partner in the firm."

"Hey, this is great." Shoshanna was smiling now too. "Are we rich yet?"

"My salary will be half again as much, plus part of the firm's profits. There's a catch though; I'm now responsible for a huge project. You remember my speculation yesterday about who's going to design that new project and the railway extension? Well, the answer is: our firm. Jacobson, Amichai, Keshet and Shaviv. Sounds good, doesn't it?"

"Your name will be on the firm's building? Really?"

"Yes. They ordered new signs already. Now the catch is that it's going to be my responsibility to coordinate the different design teams. The other partners will help, but with Jacobson having celebrated his seventy-fifth and Amichai close to it, it will be up to the two younger partners to carry that out."

"But Noam," Shoshanna said, "your firm doesn't have enough architects and engineers for a project of this magnitude."

"You don't realize how right you are. The new city, or rather complex of cities, is supposed to be in the desert. We don't even have enough surveyors for the job. We're hiring right now, but the market is tight. Architecture and civil engineering were never that well-paid, so the pickings are slim. I applied today to the Ministry of Housing to issue temporary licenses to any qualifying architects and civil engineers among the newcomers. According to the immigration statistics I saw today, that should solve the problem. We'll have to revert to old pencil and paper techniques, but it will be doable."

"I wonder why the government chose to give such a big contract to a small firm like yours."

"Hey, we're not small. There are three active partners, with two very experienced architects advising us. The firm employs close to eighty people. Among architectural design firms we're considered big. Not the biggest, but big enough for the job. And we won the contract. After all, we're not going to build anything, just design and supervise. They're going to divide the construction between a number of builders. Maybe even get some foreign companies in on this. Besides, if we need to, we can partner with one of the other firms, or hire them as subcontractors. We'll see."

***

Ibrahim knocked on the door in Jenin. His friend and commander pulled him inside: "Allahu Akbar. I see you are back. How did your mission go?"

"I was taken by the guide to the Sinai and eventually arrived at a German base in Bosnia. I met with the Grand Mufti, may Allah smile on him forever. I completed my mission."

"Are you certain you were not followed here?"

"Yes. The Mufti's pilot took me into Jordan and landed in the desert not far from the Dead Sea. I walked across the border south of there and then hitchhiked to Jenin. At no time did I see anything suspicious."

"OK. I'll report to the commander. You can stay here for a while. I'll not be long."

***

Mohammad al Husseini listened quietly to the report. He was elated – Finally he succeeded in striking at the hated Jews and, hopefully, eliminating them altogether.

"You say that my great uncle met with Ibrahim. Did he give Ibrahim a message for me?"

"Ibrahim has a message, but he claims that it is for your ears only and will not tell me what it is."

"Stop wasting time then. Bring him here. But be careful - We don't want the Israelis getting wind of this."

Less than an hour later the courier knocked on his door

"Allahu Akbar." Mohammad greeted him. "I hear that you bring good news."

"Allahu Akbar, sir, and may Allah cherish you forever," Ibrahim responded. "I have good news indeed. But first I have to give you the message your great uncle, may he be in Allah's favor forever, gave me. Here is the sealed letter he personally handed me. He also made me memorize a message, in case I had to destroy the letter."

Mohammad carefully inspected the thin, postcard size, rice paper envelope. It was sealed with a gold leaf seal bearing the words 'Allah is Great' and the Mufti's personal crest with an image of the Temple Mount mosques. The top left corner said in German: 'The office of the Grand Mufti of Jerusalem, Chief Commander of the Muslim forces in Europe"; the right corner had the same text in Arabic. There was a signature across the seal on the flap of the envelope. He sliced the envelope open, without breaking the seal. Inside was a piece of rice paper bearing the imprinted seal of the Mufti as well as the address of his office in Sarajevo. The rest was hand-written and signed in dark green ink – the Mufti's favorite. He knew the signature from the many family papers he had seen. Being a careful conspirator, Mohammad pulled out a copy of his great uncle's letter and compared signatures. He had no doubt: both the handwriting and signature were authentic.

"Did you see what kind of pen my great uncle used to write this?" Mohammad asked.

"I saw him sign the back with a fountain pen with, I think, a gold nib. I don't know what make it was. I am sorry but I am not familiar with brands of fountain pens."

"That's fine, I wouldn't expect you to know that. You did a great job."

He read the letter. It was short and to the point, just like Mohammad expected a communication from the Grand Mufti to be:

My dear nephew, may Allah always smile upon you,

We were handed a unique opportunity to finish the Jews. My friend, Herr Hitler is doing a thorough job on them in Europe but it will be up to us to get the Dar al Islam rid of them. The lands of Islam will be liberated by the numerous Muslim SS divisions being recruited and trained in Bosnia. They will have advanced weapons the Third Reich is building with Allah's help and the knowledge you gave us.

We must train as many soldiers as possible to join the SS. For this purpose I instruct all the Arabs dwelling in the Jewish state prepare to leave for the Kingdom of Jordan. We are working on establishing our training camps there and want everyone to be ready to leave as soon as I give the word. In the meantime you should desist from any activity that may alert the Jews to our plans or cause them to attack us before we are ready.

By Allah's will your uncle,

The Grand Mufti of Jerusalem, Hajj Amin al Husseini

Sarajevo, July 7, 1941

Mohammad looked at Ibrahim: "What was the message you memorized?"

Ibrahim recited his message. It was the same as the letter.

"Did the Mufti say anything else?" Mohammad inquired.

"We had a conversation that lasted almost an hour. Mostly he wanted to know about the future and what kind of weapons the Israelis have. He seemed very sure about his plans. He told me that German scientist looked at the books I brought with me - by the way he thought that it was a great inspiration for you to send science books in German. The Germans are sure that they will be able to develop an atomic bomb very soon. That's one reason he wants everybody to get out of here – he plans on using it on the Jews and doesn't want any of our brethren to be harmed." Ibrahim paused, thinking. "That is all I remember, sir."

"Ah, that makes more sense. My great uncle is truly a great strategist. Now the order to leave for Jordan makes sense." Muhammad nodded to himself. "It will have to wait until the Israelis open the borders, but we should make all the preparations now. Tell the commander of your cell that we will have a strategy meeting tonight. He has to notify the others."

After Ibrahim left, Muhammad made a telephone call to Ramallah. "The package was successfully delivered; I need you to set up a meeting soon."

***

Moshe Cohen, aka Ibrahim al Taibeh, was tired of traveling. He had been transported in German military cars from Turkey to Greece and from there to Bosnia. Apparently the Nazis were trying to check up on him and were in no hurry to deliver him to the Mufti. Even after he told them to radio the Caliph to verify his identity they were still slow. Moshe suspected that they were bugging the site of the meeting. Now, after four days on the road, they were approaching Sarajevo where the Mufti was supposed to be.

"Major, we have a room in one of the local hotels ready for you. Not the best accommodations possible but not bad considering the barbaric conditions in this country." The German SS officer smiled as he opened the car door for Moshe.

The hotel looked like it was the fanciest place in town, although that wasn't saying much. The facade was pockmarked by bullets – a witness to a battle. At least all the windows were glazed, which couldn't be said of most of the other buildings in the area. Two huge Nazi flags hung from first floor windows and a couple of SS guards patrolled outside the front door.

"It looks like this hotel is well-guarded," Moshe said with fake innocence. "You have problems with criminals?" He knew that this was military headquarter for the Muslim SS.

"No, sir." The German made a dismissive gesture. "The Bosnians mostly welcome us, at least the Muslims do. Of course, there are always some malcontents, but this place is guarded because it's the temporary headquarters of the Muslim Hanjar 13th Waffen SS division."

"Oh, I will have the honor of staying in the same building as the Grand Mufti, may Allàh always smile on him."

The room was large and had been expensively decorated before World War I. Now it was a bit shabby but still livable. Moshe had no complaints.

"When will I see the Grand Mufti?"

"He will see you at supper, in about two hours. You may want to wash up, sir. There is a fresh change of clothes in the closet." The officer saluted and left the room.

Moshe decided to follow the German's advice. He showered and changed into a black suit that had been prepared for him. It fit well and he marveled, again, at the efficiency of the Germans.

At a quarter to seven there was a knock on his door. Another officer in a black SS uniform was outside. He saluted and said, in German heavily accented with Arabic: "Major, sir, the Grand Mufti will be in his private dining room soon. I have orders to escort you there."

They walked along a corridor and down a flight of stairs. To the right was the entrance to the hotel's main dining room, to the left a short hallway with a double door at its end. The SS officer opened that door for Moshe, announcing in Arabic "Major Ibrahim al Taibeh, your Excellency."

The Grand Mufti was seated at a table laid out for two. He rose from his seat and shook Moshe's hand. "Allahu Akbar. I heard many stories about you, Major. I hope they are true, otherwise I will be very sad to see you handed over to the Gestapo."

Moshe smiled. "May Allah always smile on you, Hajj Amin. I don't know what stories the infidels told you, but one thing is true: I come from your cousin, the Great Caliph of Jerusalem, with very good news."

The Mufti sat and gestured for Moshe to take the other seat: "You will have to explain yourself my friend. I was asked by the Germans about a Caliph in Jerusalem but the last time I was there the damned British were in control of Palestine. I need proof of your claim."

"The Caliph is actually your cousin, Jamal Husseini. Here is a letter from him. The rest of what I have to say is for your ears only." Moshe nodded at the SS officer standing at ease in the far corner of the room.

The Mufti tried to slice the envelope with a knife, but with no success. He inspected it carefully, finally saw the thin cord and pulled it, tearing the envelope open. "I've never seen such an envelope before," he said. "What kind of material is it that a knife can't cut?"

"Sir, I will explain everything when we are alone."

"I understand," the Mufti said. "I will read the letter first, and then I will decide."

> My dear cousin, may Allah the Merciful favor you forever
>
> I am writing this letter to you sitting in my temporary palace, where the British High Commissioner used to dwell. Due to a great miracle that Allah the Merciful bestowed upon us, I expelled the British and soon will be powerful enough to conquer the world. My emissary, Ibrahim al Taibeh, will tell you all the details of this miracle. I hope that you will come to Jerusalem soon as I wish to make you my first minister. Before I have the pleasure of seeing you here, I need you to perform a service for our cause. Ibrahim will explain all the details to you.
>
> Please keep the contents of this letter secret. After you finish reading give the letter and envelope back to Ibrahim, who will destroy it before your very eyes.
>
> The Great Caliph of Jerusalem
>
> Your cousin, Jamal AL-Husseini

The Mufti looked at Moshe then returned to the letter. After reading it several times he folded it, put it in the envelope, and handed it back to Moshe.

"Please do as the letter instructs," the Mufti said.

Moshe put the envelope on a plate and passed his hand over the envelope as he triggered an ultra violet light emitting diode in the heavy ring on his left hand. The reaction was almost instantaneous: the chemically treated Mylar de-polymerized, turning into a grayish dust. The performance would have been impressive to most people even in the twenty first century. The Mufti was stunned.

"I want to know everything you can tell me about the new Caliphate. What am I supposed to do before I travel to Jerusalem? How did the Caliphate came into existence?"

"Your Excellency, I have a surprising story to tell you, but I have strict orders to do it only in complete privacy." Moshe again nodded at the SS officer standing guard in the corner.

"Hasan, please leave us alone," the Mufti ordered.

The officer hesitated for a moment, then saluted and left.

Moshe turned on the bug detector in his ring. It blinked red. He moved around the room, and finally stopped at the table: "Excellency, would you please move aside?"

The Mufti moved his chair away from the table. Moshe looked under the table and pulled out a box the size of a cigarette pack. He opened it and pulled out the battery. The LED in his ring turned green.

"We can now continue our conversation without anyone listening in."

Moshe poured water into his glass from a carafe on the table: "About six months ago your cousin, Jamal, found a time portal in a cave in the hills near Nablus. It opens into the same place, but eighty years from now. The time portal can be traversed in both directions and is large enough to transport a passenger car."

"Did he find a Caliphate in this future time?" the Mufti asked impatiently.

"No. What he found discouraged him so much that he almost killed himself, but Allah the merciful inspired him and Jamal found a way to correct the situation."

"So, what was the terrible thing he found?"

"He found seven million Jews controlling a state from the Mediterranean Sea to the Jordan River. The Arabs have an autonomous little territory around Jenin, Nablus and Jericho. The Jewish state is very advanced and very strong. In fact, it is so strong that the surrounding Arab countries fear to attack them."

"What happened to our plans? Why did the Germans allow this to happen? How could the British allow a Jewish state?" The Mufti was indignant.

"I am coming to this, your Excellency. If history takes its course the Germans will lose the war without exterminating all the Jews, many of whom come to Palestine, doubling their numbers there. The Allies, after winning the war, feel guilty for allowing Hitler to kill so many Jews. They also are unwilling to accept the Jewish refugees into their lands. So the successor of the League of Nations grants the Jews' request for an independent state. The British had to withdraw but tried to help our cause as much as they could. The new Jewish state withstood our attacks and grew stronger and larger from year to year, while we grew weaker." Moshe paused for a sip of water.

"So what was Jamal's great inspiration?" the Mufti asked impatiently.

"Your cousin realized that the time portal presented an opportunity to change history. He could let Germany win the war and strengthen the Arabs in Palestine. He had the means to do that – All he needed to do was bring back through the portal advanced weapons and soldiers from the future to form the core of an invincible Arab army. I am one of those from the future that followed Jamal Al-Husseini. There are thousands like me - engineers, scientists and trained soldiers."

"Ah, I see. So the Caliphate is real. What is the next step then?"

"I need to tell you more before we get to the next step." Moshe reached into his suit pocket and pulled out the Koran he brought with him: "This is no simple Koran. If you open it to page 100 you will find that there is another book hidden inside. That book is a concise history of World War II. It was printed in 1999 and contains an interesting analysis of how the Germans lost the war. I suggest that your Excellency read it before we continue this conversation."

The Mufti looked through the book, stopping, as instructed, at page 100: "I suggest we have dinner now," he said, "and renew this conversation tomorrow morning."

***

The next morning Moshe was escorted by the same SS officer to the Mufti's suite.

"Sit my friend," the Mufti gestured at one of the armchairs next to a coffee table. "Shall we continue?"

"Just a moment." Moshe turned on his ring and scanned the room. It was clear.

"Yes, we can continue now," Moshe said. "Do you have any questions?"

"Still the same question: what is the next step?"

"First, I need to update you on what has been done already: we destroyed the Jews in Palestine – our extermination system is much more efficient than Herr Hitler's. We also told the British to get out and leave us alone – which they did after a demonstration of our abilities. The next step was to stop the German effort to get rid of the Jews in Europe. Our methods are more efficient but more important, it will free enough of their resources to win this war."

"Was the 'accident' in Wolfsburg somehow connected to this?" the Mufti inquired.

"Yes. It was our way of forcing the Germans to obey our request to ship all the Jews in their jurisdiction to Palestine, where we will take care of them. You see, it will take them less than a year to do that, with minimal diversion of resources. In 1942, when they'll face a critical phase in this war, they will have enough forces to make the Soviet Union collapse. If not, you know what will happen. It happened once already."

"Interesting," the Mufti mused. "A couple of days after the 'accident' Himmler asked me if I knew anything about a Caliph. I told him that I had not been in touch with Palestine for a while. It seems to me," he continued dreamily, "that after the Germans win the war we could take over their domain and rule the world."

"The Caliph's exact sentiments," Moshe agreed, "and that is why all this has to be kept secret. We are not strong enough yet to take on the world. You will likely be invited to see the Fuehrer and he will ask you about the Caliphate. We left them with the impression that we are incredibly powerful, which is true in a sense, but they can't be allowed to know the truth until we are strong enough. After that it will not matter what they know. You are to tell the Fuehrer that the Caliphate came to power as a result of Allah's miracle, but you will learn the details only after you visit Palestine. Promise to enlighten him after your return here.

"The Caliph also needs you to tour Europe, including the countries allied with the Germans, and see to the safe passage of the Jews to Palestine. Just be careful not to mention Wolfsburg to anyone – it is to remain a secret until the Caliph decides otherwise. We want the Jews to think that their dream of a home in Palestine is being fulfilled, so that they will come willingly. This way, as small as our numbers are, we can deal with them effectively. After you finish your tour, please come to Brindisi in Italy. We have set up a transit camp for Jews there, on their way to their final destination. You will be welcomed there by our troops and put on a transport to Palestine."

"I will do as the Caliph wishes," the Mufti said. "I have much admiration for my cousin and his inspiration, may Allah guard him. Are you going to accompany me on this tour?"

"I am sorry," Moshe responded, "but my orders are to proceed to Brindisi and from there to Palestine. Experienced undercover operatives are needed to deal with our enemies, and I will be very busy for a while. I'll appreciate your assistance with transportation. It is likely that a fishing boat can pick me up in Dubrovnik and get to Brindisi in less than a day."

"It will be my pleasure to arrange it." The Mufti rose from his armchair and shook Moshe's hand, smiling and blessing him repeatedly.

Chapter 14

The two ministers, Defense and Absorption, finished their tour of the Brindisi facility. They arrived in the early morning on a small military transport and now were treated to a meal in Colonel Hirshson's office. It was a working lunch.

"You are quite well organized here," the Absorption Minister said, "but I have seen large numbers of refugees that seem to have been here for a while. Is there a transportation problem?"

Hirshson sipped his coffee: "Not really. When we started at the end of June we were getting about ten thousand people a day. It was mostly due to the limitations of the rail system. As you have seen we can now accept four trains at a time, which makes our theoretical capacity close to fifty thousand in a twenty-four hour period. We can transport about twenty nine thousand per day, on average, by ship to Israel. This includes British shipping, German ships, one Italian ship we persuaded them to give us, three of our own converted cargo ships and the cruise ship that was stuck in Haifa during the Event. The problem is that this is on average. In practice the round trip to Israel takes these ships between seven and ten days, depending on the weather and how long it takes to load and unload them. Which leaves us with substantial numbers of refugees waiting here for transport – the facility is almost empty at times and sometimes contains close to a hundred thousand.

"You've also noticed that we are processing them here for security instead of Haifa, as was originally planned. The immigrants are waiting for shipping here anyway, so we use some of the time to filter out possible spies and such. After they get into Israel the environment is less controlled, they have some of the families waiting and there is a higher likelihood of someone slipping through."

"You're receiving more than ten thousand a day now, are you?"

"Like I said, when we started in June it was ten thousand. Now we are in the end of July and the number is more or less steady at twenty-five thousand. Our first priority was to remove as many Jews as possible from the Polish ghettos, especially the big ones in Warsaw, Krakow, Lodz and Bialystok. We also got a fair number of people from concentration camps. They have been under German occupation since 1939 and it wasn't a picnic. We had large numbers of starving and sick that needed urgent medical attention – hence the large rehabilitation facilities. It got so bad that we had to ask any doctors and nurses that were among the refugees to assist us.

"By now, I think we've gotten most of the sick out. The Germans aren't starving them anymore, so the general condition of the people that arrive now is much better."

"I was interested in how you developed the reception procedure," the Defense Minister asked.

"Well, we have to be careful not to show either the German or Ukrainian guards or the train crews what is going on. So the first step when a train arrives is to get these escorts into a sealed holding room guarded by our forces just outside the facility. We also keep them happy with food and a little Schnapps – not too much, as we don't want them to become drunk and unruly, just enough to make them slightly fuzzy.

"With them out of the way we tried, at first, the German technique of opening all the cars at once and guiding the crowd inside. This may work if you use dogs and beat people, but it didn't work for us. There are always old or sick or disabled immigrants who need help. People are milling around the platform and it takes an unreasonable amount of time. An average train holds about 2500 immigrants; it took us close to an hour to clear them off the platform. We needed to get the procedure down to twenty minutes max.

"The system we use now - and are still refining - is opening the cars in pairs, starting at opposite ends of the train. The occupants of each car, usually about eighty, are led by two soldiers into the facility. You may have noticed that we have an intermediary yard behind the first wall, with a second wall and an offset gate, just to make sure that outside observers can't see into the facility. We also don't allow any air traffic within several miles of the facility."

The Defense Minister looked thoughtful: "Do you have difficulties with people refusing to go to Palestine. After all, they come from a time where Palestine had a bad name: sands, camels and Arabs – not a very civilized country."

Hirshson thought for a moment. "As long as we were getting desperate, starving people, the mere fact that we fed them and treated them well was enough. They didn't really care where they were going as long as it was not into the clutches of the Nazis. Most of them were passive.

"The situation is different now. The new arrivals are not starving and some are having second thoughts about going to Palestine. We had a large group from Lithuania that wanted to go to South Africa where they have family. This group refused to get on their ship and was threatening a hunger strike."

"How did you deal with that?" the Absorption Minister asked.

"We told them that they can either go back to where they came from on the next train or go to Palestine and arrange travel to wherever they want from there. They didn't want to return to Lithuania and decided that since Palestine is part of the British Empire, getting from there to South Africa wouldn't be too difficult.

"We've had no other problems so far. It's a sad fact that these people know that they are not wanted anywhere in the world. There were a number of families who wanted passage to the U.S. and thought they would be allowed in since they have family there. We told them the truth: that they would be turned back into the clutches of the Nazis. They believe us. It happened before and many people know the sad story of the SS St. Louis."

The Absorption Minister looked dubious: "What do you do if some of the scouts the communities are sending are skeptics or not Zionists? I would imagine that the Communists, Bundists and some of the ultra-Orthodox have no desire to go to Palestine."

"We encountered this already. More than once. We use different techniques with different groups. The ultra-Orthodox are actually the easiest to deal with. We have representatives of the major Hassidic sects here as well as some of the Lithuanian rabbis. They have a lengthy theological discussion with the emissaries and do their best to persuade them that this whole arrangement is a miracle: we have the Nazis and the British – neither one a friend of the Jews – collaborating in the middle of a bitter war to bring Jews to Eretz Yisrael. This argument never failed yet.

"The leftists are sometimes more difficult. They would like to go to the Soviet Union or sometimes prefer staying where they are to going to Palestine. We deal with them by posing a number of questions: Do they know what happened to the German Communist and Social Democrat parties under Hitler and do they expect to be treated differently by the Nazis? Can they go to the Soviet Union or anywhere else for that matter, from the places they live in now? Why not go to Palestine and then go to the Soviets? After all the British and the Soviets are allies in this war.

"After they think about the answers for a moment their choice is to recommend that their organizations move to Palestine."

***

Jacob and Bohdan stood side by side looking out the door of the cattle car. There wasn't much to see. In front of them was a concrete wall that Jacob estimated to be at least ten meters high. People on the other side of the car reported seeing a similar wall. The train had been stopped for about five minutes and there was a commotion outside. The German and

Ukrainian guards that had accompanied them from the Vilnius ghetto were marching off and the engine crew was leaving as well. The train was being surrounded by armed soldiers in drab green uniforms. There were no insignia on the uniforms.

The station's PA system came to life, announcing in German, "Please be patient. It will take us a while to open the cars. If there are people that need urgent medical care, please wave a handkerchief from the car's door. You will be fed soon."

"High time for that," Bohdan commented. "They promised seven days travel and it is eight by now. I'm starving."

"We all are," several voices responded.

The cars were opened in pairs. It took fifteen minutes before the car containing Jacob and his family was opened, spilling everyone out onto the concrete platform. Soldiers were busy opening the next car.

"Follow me!" a soldier yelled to Jacob and the group from his car. "We need to clear the platform so that the others can be released from their cars." The group followed him through a gate in the high wall and saw... another wall. They were now in a square surrounded by tall concrete walls and two gates, another opposite the one they entered and about fifteen yards to the right. Quietly, the group followed the soldier through the second gate.

"This is amazing," Jacob exclaimed when they left the concrete square. "This is unbelievable!" He was not the only one surprised. They were standing on the edge of a large plaza surrounded by tall warehouses. In the distance low structures were visible. A large flag with the Star of David and two blue stripes was fluttering in the sea breeze coming from a stretch of blue water visible in between the buildings.

"A prayer shawl!" somebody in the crowd exclaimed pointing at the flag.

"No," a soldier corrected them in Yiddish. "It's the flag of the Jewish state. Welcome home."

The crowd was confused. Some were crying, others staring in disbelief. They were startled when the soldier yelled at the top of his voice, "Please follow me. You will want to wash up and have supper. During the meal we will explain to you what will happen next."

They followed him into one of the buildings surrounding the plaza. Inside they found sinks and toilets, beyond that were several large halls with tables and benches and a cafeteria counter. The delightful smell of food greeted them. The soldiers accompanying each group directed them to one of the halls.

The entire crowd from the train had been divided into groups of roughly 500 per dining room. After they had been served and were eating, a sergeant climbed on a podium by the food counter and introduced himself in classical Lithuanian Yiddish. "I am with the quartermaster company of the Palestinian Defense Forces responsible for Sector 3 of this repatriation facility. The guys next to me are my assistants who will do their best to answer any questions you may have and to help you. After the meal, please move up the staircase to the right - Anyone needing assistance, please assemble by the double metal doors. You'll find showers and disinfectant on the second floor. We do not want lice and such in this facility. After cleaning up, you will be escorted to a dormitory. We will wake you up tomorrow morning at 7 am. Please assemble here for breakfast and further instructions. I hope that your stay here will be pleasant and not too long. As soon as possible you will board ships and be on your way to Eretz Yisrael. Any questions?"

A pandemonium erupted with everybody yelling at once. The sergeant raised his hand and turned up the volume on the P.A. system: "Please quiet down. Raise your hand if you want to ask something."

"How about seeing a doctor?" "My wife is pregnant!" "I have a stomach ulcer!"

"Every new immigrant needing medical assistance can see a doctor. On your way to the dormitories please knock on the door with the red Star of David. Inside you will find people to assist you. I will see you all tomorrow. If you have more questions or need help, please ask one of the soldiers." The sergeant waved to them and got off the podium.

"I don't believe it," Bohdan said to Jacob. "Jews took over Palestine? When did that happen? Why would the Germans deliver us to these Jews?"

"Let's go upstairs and pick up a brochure," Jacob said to his family. "Maybe it will have some answers."

***

"153 please." The uniformed guard in front of the glass door called the number of the ticket Jacob was holding. It had been given to him this morning when, after breakfast, his group entered the big waiting hall as instructed. To obtain the number he had to give his full name, the full address where he used to live as well as the names of the family members that came with him. Now he approached the guard, who checked the number on his ticket. "Are you alone or is your family here?" he asked.

"My mother and sister are with me."

"Bring them with you, please, to room number 5."

"Thank you." It had taken almost an hour of waiting for this short exchange, not that Jacob noticed the passage of time. The room was cool and well ventilated, though without windows. There were brochures explaining possible education options in Palestine as well as employment that might be available to them.

The family went through a glass door into a long corridor with numbered doors on both sides, entering the room with a five on the door. It was a small office, with a desk and four chairs. The young man behind the desk rose to greet them, offering his hand: "Please sit. Would you like to drink something? Water, tea, coffee?"

The Hirshsons took the seats offered but refused the drinks. Jacob was curious about the somewhat unusual desk – it had a glass surface with a darker rectangular area in front of the official.

"Your names, please," the civilian official asked politely.

"Sara Hirshson," Jacob's mother responded, taking charge. "My son Jacob and daughter Sheina."

"And where are you coming from?"

"Vilnius, Lithuania."

"What was your address there?"

"In the ghetto we lived on Strashuna Street 19, apartment 9. Do you really need to ask all these questions? We answered them just an hour ago."

The young man smiled. "Sorry for the inconvenience. I'm just making sure that the guard sent me the correct people.

"Did you leave any family behind in Vilnius?" the young man asked, looking at the glass surface of his desk.

"My brother-in-law Chaim and his family are in the ghetto. I sincerely hope that they will follow us soon. He's stubborn. I wish I could send him a message from here."

"Jacob Hirshson," the young man asked, "are you a scout for the Revisionist movement in Vilnius?"

Jacob was startled and defensive. "Yes, is something wrong with that?"

"No, nothing wrong, but you understand that we have to make sure that you are who you say you are."

The young man was again looking at the desk surface in front of him. "Did any of your friends come on the same train?"

Jacob hesitated. "Arye was supposed to come with me but was taken ill at the last moment."

After a somewhat longer pause the Palestinian said. "Is this Arye Levitan you are talking about?"

"Yes."

"What are your dates of birth, starting with you Mrs. Hirshson?"

Sara recited her birthday as well as those of her children.

The man finished tapping on the keyboard, then picked up the phone on his desk and dialed a number. He spoke in fast Hebrew and the family caught only a couple of words.

"Please follow me," he said to the Hirshsons. "The commander of this facility wants to meet you."

"Is there a problem?" Jacob asked.

"No, no. No problem whatsoever. Please come."

They followed the young man into a new, one story building that was obviously a military facility. Soldiers hurrying in all directions; a big, glowing map of Europe filled one wall, with strange symbols scattered all over it.

The family stopped in front of a desk. "Sergeant, these people are here to see the chief."

"Yes, I'll take care of them." The woman got up from her desk, smiling at the family: "Please follow me. The boss is busy with some unexpected stuff. There will be a short delay. In the meantime, please make yourself comfortable." She opened a door and led them into a comfortable sitting room complete with a sofa, several armchairs, and a coffee table.

"Please feel free to take anything you want," the woman told them, pointing to a large credenza with food laid out. "A bathroom is through this door." She showed them around and then left.

Jacob looked at the room. It didn't have windows but was lit by several skylights. Five minutes later a door they hadn't notice before opened. A man in his early thirties came in. He was wearing a uniform similar to the others but had small, silver wings on his chest and three brass oak leaves on a red background on his shoulders. His face was smoothly shaven and he had a receding hairline.

"My God! Ephraim!" Sara gasped.

"Yes, I know," the officer said with a big smile "The resemblance is there. I am Ephraim Hirshson, but not your husband. We are related, though I am somewhat at a loss to pinpoint how."

The room was silent for a while. Ephraim was examining his family and they were too stunned to say anything as they stared at him.

Jacob was the first to recover. "We are related? I don't recall anybody from our family going to Palestine."

Colonel Hirshson sighed. "I'm not an expert in genetics, but it seems certain that I share some genes with you – otherwise why the resemblance?"

Sara smiled. "I think I know where the resemblance to my Ephraim, may he rest in peace, came from. He told me that when the Great War started his first cousin decided to go to Palestine rather than enlist in the Russian army. He went the long way, through Turkey, and Ephraim never heard from him again. You must be his descendant."

They were interrupted. "Sir, we have an intrusion alert."

"Again? Who and where?"

"Messerschmitt fighters, five of them approaching low over the water. About 250 kilometers and closing."

"Excuse me. This is the second time this week. The Germans are very persistent and don't learn." He left the room after giving a stunned Jacob a quick hug.

"You have a funny look on your face." Sheina was smiling at her brother. Being seventeen and adventurous had its advantages, among them a willingness to accept strange stories at face value. She recovered her composure before her elders did.

"Yes. Very funny," her brother responded. "He looks like family and I was a bit surprised."

"He looks exactly like your father," Sara exclaimed.

"Well, mama, not exactly. But the resemblance is there." Jacob hesitated. "At least we will have family when we get to Palestine."

By the time colonel Hirshson returned, the family was mostly recovered and immediately started questioning him about Palestine and about his family there. They had a lot of questions, which the colonel tried to answer without lying or disclosing the truth – speaking to his young grandfather was confusing enough. After a while Hirshson asked to speak to Jacob privately in his office. "Zionist business, you know."

"OK, Jacob I know that you are a scout for the Revisionist group in Vilnius. They gave us a list of people to expect. There was supposed to be another one on yesterday's train, but he didn't come – ill, I understand?"

"That was Arye. He came down with a bad case of food poisoning. Not surprising given the stuff the Nazis are feeding us. I decided to go by myself."

"I'm glad you did. We'll let you and the other scouts from Vilnius examine this facility. Everything will be open to your group, except some of the military installations. Your group will be allowed, if you wish, to board and examine the ship that is waiting in port to pick up the next contingent going to Israel, er, Palestine.

"I hope that you'll be done with your inspections quickly. It'll take us some time to show you some documents of the Nazis' plans for the Jews of Europe; these are most convincing. Families of the other scouts are on their way here, and we'll meet with them later in the day. We would like you and the other scouts to return to Vilnius as soon as possible, but I have to be absolutely certain that you are convinced that the best thing for Jews now is to come to Palestine. It'll be up to you to make our people come here. We have limited time before the Germans lose patience and revert to their original extermination plans. After that happens all hell will break loose."

Jacob was thoughtful. "I have to return, but my mother and sister do not. Will they go on to Palestine by themselves?"

The colonel smiled. "That would be entirely up to you and them. If they want to wait for you here, we'll provide them with a private apartment. Or they can leave on a ship sailing today and reunite with you in Palestine at my father's house. The families of all scouts will have to decide where to wait."

***

"So, your name is Boruch Katzenelson, from Lutsk?" the clerk asked. She was probably in her thirties, but he couldn't tell for sure. He was too nervous.

"Yes, this is my name."

"And you survived the Lutsk massacre?" she asked.

"Yes. I ran into the fields and hid in the grain."

She was making notes as he was speaking. He couldn't see what she was seeing in the desk's glossy surface and it worried him a little.

The woman smiled at him. "Don't be so nervous, you are among friends now. Can you tell me how you got to the Vilnius ghetto?"

"Yes. I was picked up by a Ukrainian guard patrol when I tried to look for my family. They transferred me to the Germans and the Germans put a bunch of us on a truck to Vilnius."

"Did you befriend anybody at the ghetto?"

"Actually a good friend of mine, Jacob Hirshson was in the same car with me when we arrived here." He hesitated. "His sister is really nice and I think likes me. I like her too."

"Very good, Boruch. Please take a seat in the next room. It won't take long."

Bohdan sat on a padded chair in a small room with no windows, brightly lit by invisible lights. There were a number of newspapers on the table in the corner, but they were all in either Hebrew or Yiddish – not knowing how to read either he couldn't tell the difference. He was worried. The Germans told him that he would encounter a bunch of Palestinian Jews or, maybe, a bunch of German allies. One of his assignments was to determine who was running this operation and report to his masters. Something was wrong. He couldn't put his finger on what it was. Maybe the Palestinian soldiers didn't behave the way he expected Jews to behave or maybe it was the fact that their rifles seemed to him more advanced than the weapons the Germans were carrying. He was ready to accept that these Palestinians were really something else. Maybe the allies the Germans mentioned. That seemed wrong too; they spoke Hebrew and Yiddish and treated the refugees like family.

After the door to the waiting room was securely shut, the clerk, otherwise known in the Israeli Internal Security Service as a Talker, picked up the phone. "I think I have a live one here."

"I'll be there in a moment."

A few minutes later a short, skinny man came into her office. He was in his forties and had many years of experience interrogating people disinclined to give out information. When they did talk, they mostly tried to deceive. He didn't rely on his experience and instinct alone. An array of electronic stress measuring equipment was at his disposal.

"Dahlia, I would like to see the recordings from your interview with this Boruch character."

He looked at her computer monitor. "The guy is stressed and lying. He has no clue what the Hebrew and Yiddish signs say, completely uninterested in the newspapers. I don't think he knows how to read. What about his story?"

Dahlia pointed to the display: "The holocaust database has a Boruch Katzenelson, who died in the massacre in Lutsk. The dates match our guy's story as does his description of his family. The problem is that he was among the 300 that were murdered there several months ago. I think that he's not who he says he is. Shall I check with Jacob Hirshson? Maybe they are good friends and something is wrong with our records?"

"Don't bother. I can see he's lying. The Boruch Katzenelson of Lutsk went to a heder for several years and was on a Soviet list of religious Jews. What are the chances he didn't know how to read Hebrew?"

The short man knocked on the door of the adjacent room and entered without waiting for a response. "Come with me," he ordered Boruch, who jumped up from his seat.

They exited the room through a different door, one that opened only after the short man pressed his thumb to a plate by the lock. After walking through several corridors, Bohdan found himself in front of a heavy steel door that opened when they approached. Inside, several guards, seemingly unarmed, looked him over after nodding to his companion. Then the two of them entered a room with only a table and two chairs. It had a mirror on one wall and was lit by a luminescent ceiling.

"Please sit. If you tell me the truth, you will be fine. If not..."

"I didn't do anything wrong. Why am I here?"

"I haven't accused you of anything." The man switched from Yiddish to German. "But I need to have truthful answers to the questions the nice lady asked you. You see, I am not nice and I don't like people wasting my time. So, what is your real name?"

"I told her already, I am Boruch Katzenelson."

"Right. And you are from Lutsk."

"Yes."

"You must have known everybody there?"

"Well, not everybody, but yes, I knew lots of people." Bohdan was recovering a bit. These people seemed to be what they said they were: Jews. How dangerous could Jews be?

"Do you remember the names of those who were with you in the heder?"

"Some. It was many years ago, before the Soviets took over, in 1922, I think"

"And how long did you study at the heder?"

"Only three years. It was prohibited after 1924."

"Good. Very good. Now, please spell this word out for me." The interrogator put a magazine on the table and pointed to its name.

Bohdan was sweating. "I, I don't know how to read Hebrew."

The interrogator pulled a pen knife from his pocket and started cleaning his fingernails: "Do you know how many ways there are to pull out someone's fingernails?" he inquired.

"No - I, I don't know." Bohdan stammered. "I am from Lutsk. I really am."

"I believe that you may actually be from Lutsk, but your name is not Boruch, So what is it?"

"I am Boruch."

"If you insist, I can teach you, you know, about the fingernail business, and before you lie to me again and make the lesson inevitable: Boruch Katzenelson died in the Lutsk massacre in June. So again: what is your real name?"

Bohdan was thinking furiously. Apparently these Jews knew more than his German masters expected. It was also clear to him that this short, wiry man, who moved like a cat, had the power and the will to do to him anything he wanted. Bohdan's only thought now was whether he should tell him the truth or continue pretending to being Jewish.

His thoughts were interrupted by the interrogator. "I know you are not Jewish and I know much more than that. So will it be the truth or a nice lesson?" The man was smiling, a very unpleasant smile that sent shivers along Bohdan's spine. Still he hesitated. "Go ahead, I'm listening."

Bohdan told about his childhood in the Jewish neighborhood, the many Jewish friends he spoke Yiddish with, how the Germans discovered his language skills and sent him on this mission, threatening his family if he failed.

After Bohdan was done with his story the interrogator slapped him on the back: "You see it wasn't so bad after all. Don't you feel better now that you don't have anything to hide?"

Bohdan was surprised that he was actually relived. He expected to be sent to a jail cell now that the interrogation was over. Instead, music started playing and the interrogator took a small box out of his pocket and placed it next to his ear, stopping the tune. "Yes," the man said, "go ahead."

"We found your guy in the SS database. He was a sergeant with a Ukrainian guard unit. Fairly smart and not trigger happy it seems, at least there is no verified record of him killing anybody. I need more time to research him."

"Thank you" the interrogator said.

He was still smiling when he looked at Bohdan again: "I promised you a lesson if you lied to me. Well, I don't know if not telling the whole truth can be considered lying. I think that it is the same. What do you think, Sergeant Bohdan Kovalenko?"

"Sir, please, I was afraid to tell you I was in the Ukrainian SS. I was afraid you would kill me if you knew. I will tell you everything and do anything you want."

"I am sure you will."

The door to the room opened and a tall, heavily muscled man came in: "I see that you are done," he addressed the interrogator. "I guess it's my turn."

Bohdan expected the man to beat him up – that was what he would have done – but he was only asked more questions. The sergeant did not dare lie again. He wasn't sure what these people knew or which questions were traps. He was sure that another lie would bring terrible suffering. He wasn't that fond of his German masters anyway. But he was worried about the fate of his family.

The interrogator assured him that they would find a way to keep his family safe. Bohdan wanted to believe them.

At the end of the day, Bohdan was escorted to a concrete building separated from the rest of the sprawling complex. Inside this jail he had a reasonably sized cell, with a desk on which to write detailed reports to his German masters, reports dictated by the military intelligence officer that had taken over from his interrogator. It was Bohdan's responsibility to rewrite the reports so that the Germans would not suspect that they were fabricated and transmit the encoded reports on his radio set once a week in

Morse code from a special room. He was very diligent in his work. He sincerely hoped that the skinny, short man forgot all about him. He also hoped that his German masters believed his reports and left his family alone.

There were several radio sets similar to his in the radio room he used. Apparently he had not been the only spy caught in the Jew's security net. Many spies were not caught. Those who were Jewish and used their proper identities were extremely difficult to detect. One item that would have been a clear giveaway was a radio transmitter but the Germans issued them only to very few of their spies. The rest were supposed to use local Arab contacts to communicate with their German masters. As far as the Security Service knew none of the Jews tried.

Several Germans using their own names and pretending to be Jewish did get through. The high degree of assimilation of the German Jewish community made post Holocaust records somewhat fuzzy and unreliable. These were trained spies and could have used local connections if they would have traveled to Mandatory Palestine. As it happened they found themselves temporarily helpless in 21st century Israel.

***

"Sir," Hirshson's second in command said dubiously, "I think that we may have a security breach. Our people overheard the crew of the German freighter Tannenfels talking about their last visit to Haifa. They were discussing the size of the city and the fact that it was brightly lit at night. Most worrisome was the fact that they saw a couple of Israeli flags on some of the buildings and on one of our naval ships. It seems that they put their binoculars to good use. Is there anything I should do about this?"

"Let's see. There's no way for them to send a radio message – the jammers we installed on all the foreign ships will take care of that and our people on board will see that it is not disabled. The crews know that they will die if they don't follow the exact course we prescribed. So, in my opinion, the danger of information leaking is quite small."

"Sir, the Germans are not stupid and will, eventually, realize that something is not kosher," the officer insisted.

Hirshson was losing his patience. "They certainly will, and they'll be right, it is more like halal," referring to the Islamic definition of foods allowed for consumption by Muslims. "Whether it will happen because somebody on one of the ships finds a way to communicate, or, more likely, through their spies in Britain, or even some that will slip through our security, is immaterial. Our time will run out. We need to make sure that when it does, there are few Jews left vulnerable. I'm sure that some people will decide to stay where they are and will pay the price. There's nothing we can do about that. The scouts have increased the numbers willing to escape by so much that we will soon have problems shipping everybody.

"In the meantime, we need a reevaluation of our transportation and housing capabilities. I believe we'll reach about fifty thousand a day soon. This means that our refugee population here will grow by ten thousand a day. We need to accommodate them. As I ordered you yesterday, I need plans for expanding the base. In a couple of months we may have to keep close to a million people here. I hope it won't come to that, but we have to be ready in case it does. I'd rather have them waiting here than in territory controlled by the Nazis."

Chapter 15

A group of fifteen scouts sent by the Vilnius Jewish groups went to the railway station in Brindisi, from there to Rome, and from Rome, on a commercial flight, to Berlin continuing on a military transport to Warsaw. They were harassed by the Germans only once – When they got off the plane in Warsaw a Gestapo agent checking their documents took them to a small office and questioned each of them at length. The Israeli who accompanied them threatened the Nazi, but to no avail. The man seemed to be ignorant of what their ID cards meant. The whole debacle ended when the door opened with a crash and a SS major stormed into the room. "Are you crazy?" he yelled at the confused Gestapo man. "These are representatives of a friendly foreign power. I am taking them with me. You will report to your superior and ask to be punished for this. I will make sure that you go to the Eastern Front for this stupidity." The Gestapo agent opened his mouth but closed it when two more SS came into the small room.

In Vilnius the scouts were escorted into the larger ghetto and left there. Jacob immediately went to the headquarters of the Revisionist movement on Strashuna 25, not far from where he had lived in the ghetto. He was greeted with surprise. "That was a fast trip," the young guard in the inner courtyard said. The three leaders of the movement, its chairman, secretary and defense coordinator, were also surprised. Jacob told his story. He did mention that the commander of the Brindisi facility was his relative and explained that he was the son of a cousin who had left for Palestine at the beginning of the Great War.

The discussion of what to do and how to do it took up the rest of the day. By the time they were done, it was too late to go anywhere. The ghetto was under curfew and breaking it meant, if one was caught, spending a week or so in jail on half rations.

The next day Jacob went to visit his uncle Chaim's family. The visit was difficult. None of the family members were Zionists and they saw no good reason to move to the backwards land of Palestine. At yesterday's meeting everyone had been dubious about his story. They had difficulty believing in a large compound in Brindisi free of Germans or Italians let alone a British troop carrier waiting in port to transport Jews to the Promised Land. They were finally convinced by Jacob's eagerness to return to Italy and his story about his relative. An equally convincing argument, at least for his uncle, was that if he didn't like Palestine he would be able to go somewhere safer and more developed. Chaim conceded that there was no future for them in Vilnius.

"I can't tell you all I saw. You will understand when you get there. But please, go as soon as you can. There is a train later today, do your best to be on it."

"Will you come with us?" Chaim asked.

"I wish I could, but I want to convince as many of my friends as I can to go. There are also Grandma's cousins. Everyone should leave as soon as they can. When I've met with everyone here, I'll go to the ghetto in Kaunas with some others that came back from Italy with me. There are people there that know us and will believe what we say. We are trying to save as many as we can."

"You're not staying here then?" Jacob's cousin Tzipora asked.

"Oh no! I don't want to die! I'll do my best to get on a train after we are done in Kaunas. Probably in two weeks. When you get to the compound in Italy, tell my mother and sister that I will be there as soon as I can. They'll get reports about me every couple of days but will want to hear from you."

Chaim hesitated for a day, but in the end decided he trusted his nephew and got on a train with his family. So many people had been contacted and convinced by the Jewish agents, that the Germans started loading a hundred people per car, which made the passage very hard.

Jacob's friend Zalman was convinced more easily. After their conversation he got on a train as soon as he gathered his extended family.

Not everyone in Vilnius and Kaunas believed the story. There were people who knew Jacob and other members of the scout group, mainly through their Zionist organizations. They listened and got out as fast as they could. Other groups, including the Kaunas Yeshiva and, paradoxically, the local Bund leadership, concluded the whole thing was just propaganda and refused to go. The head of the Yeshiva changed his mind after meeting with two agents who were making the rounds of religious institutions.

A large portion of the Bund members ignored their leadership and went anyway as word spread about the scouts and as their friends left. Those unaffiliated with any political or religious group – a large majority in both cities – were mostly leaving as well. The Germans were of some help, in their usual brutal way. They cut the rations while at the same time allowing the Ukrainians and Lithuanians to beat up Jews. They tried to be careful not to kill anyone, but they really didn't care.

Jacob's family decided to wait in Brindisi. They studied Hebrew. Both Sheina and Chaim's daughter Tzipora were making great progress. Their parents were acclimatizing at a slower pace. Their main concern was with finding good jobs when they finally got to Israel. They did not want to be a burden on anybody and state handouts were an alien idea to them.

***

Jacob's group, like others that operated throughout Europe, carried with them a short wave radio transmitter. Theirs was state of the art for 1941, made by Blaupunkt and supplied to the Caliph by the Germans. Other groups carried German, British or American made radios. The group's leader, an Israeli, used it to send messages to the Brindisi base. The messages followed a predefined pattern and reassured the people in Brindisi that the team was OK. Since the pattern of the messages was agreed upon before the groups left and was calculated to last for a month, there was no code to break and the Germans could not send a fake message without being caught.

The group Jacob traveled with consisted of four people: Mordechai, a native of Palestine, was the leader and carried the radio, Jacob from the Revisionists, Hirsh Goldstein from the Zionist Halutz movement, and Rabbi Zerah Litvin from the Yeshiva of the Forty in Vilna.

They finished their assignment in Vilna a week after arriving there. They spoke to all the leaders and did their best to convince them to go. It was time to cover more territory. The plan was to travel from Vilna to Mariampole, from there to Kaunas and then return to Vilna. Some towns had no Jews – they had already been deported by the Germans to one of the larger ghettos. This made the job a bit more manageable.

The three Vilna natives carried letters from their respective organizations attesting to their membership and explaining that these organizations asked their members to move to Palestine. They also had personal connections they used. Mordechai was there to witness to the safety of Palestine and to persuade those who wanted to go to America or other places that they would be able to do so from Palestine. It also helped that people who arrived at the Brindisi base were encouraged to send letters to their friends and family. Many did.

Their mission went well. Traveling in a horse drawn cart was not the fastest way, but it aroused minimal suspicion. They went unmolested from ghetto to ghetto delivering their message. The Germans and their helpers, the Ukrainian and Lithuanian police, recognized their special ID cards and mostly cooperated, though from time to time the group was subjected to verbal harassment.

They arrived in Kaunas almost two weeks after leaving Brindisi. It was close to the end of August. The sky was leaden and a fine rain was falling.

Something was different here. Instead of inspecting their IDs as usual and letting them into the ghetto, the Germans politely but firmly escorted the group to a truck and took them to the Ninth Fort.

The Fort had been built by the Russians as a military fortification before the First World War; it was never used for its intended purpose. After the Russian Empire disintegrated, beginning in 1924, the Fort was used as a prison by the independent Lithuanian state. The Germans used it as a torture and extermination camp. Jews, Soviet prisoners of war, Gypsies and other undesirables from the surrounding area were brought to the Ninth Fort, "interrogated" and executed.

Mordechai, the "Palestinian", was the only one in the group familiar with the Fort's infamous history. He was shocked to discover that the facility seemed to be busy. All the guard towers were manned – some by Ukrainians and some by Germans – and prisoners were going about their business in the inner courtyard where the truck stopped and the group got off. They were searched and all their meager possessions were confiscated – including the special ID cards and the radio. When Mordechai protested, a guard hit him in the stomach with his rifle butt and proceeded to break his nose and split his right ear. At this point the prisoners were separated and locked in solitary cells. Mordechai, as the leader, was locked up in a cell under the main staircase. Three times a day, when the prisoners ran down the stairs to be counted, the noise in the cell was deafening. The rest of the time Mordechai couldn't fall asleep because of the reverberating noise of footsteps. This went on day and night.

Jacob spent two days in his cell. It had a small window with a reasonable view of the fields and he could hear noises from the outside. On the second day he heard shots. They came from the right, but no matter how hard he tried he couldn't see what was happening. It sounded like a machine gun, then single shots. After about an hour the machine gun again, then single shots again. The sequence repeated the whole day. In the evening his cell door opened and he was taken to a small room with no windows. A table and chair were in the middle of the room. He was told to wait standing in the corner. Several hours later a dapper looking civilian accompanied by a uniformed guard came in. The civilian sat in front of the table, took out a notebook and a pen from the elegant leather briefcase he was carrying, and started the interrogation.

"What is your name?"

"Jacob Hirshson."

"Is the information on your ID card correct?" he showed the card to Jacob.

"Yes."

"Who gave you this card?"

"A clerk at the Palestinian transit camp in Brindisi."

The questions went on for several hours. The interrogator was polite but relentless. He kept repeating the same questions in different forms trying to catch Jacob in an inconsistency. Finally Jacob decided that he couldn't stand on his feet anymore and instead of answering the next question asked the interrogator for permission to sit on the floor.

The response came from the guard. The rifle butt hit Jacob in the stomach and he found himself on the floor gasping for breath.

"Since you asked for it, you may stay there for a couple of minutes." The interrogator went on with his questions.

Sometime later in the night the first interrogator was replaced by a new one and the questioning continued.

Jacob wasn't sure what they wanted. He did exactly as he was instructed before they left Brindisi: answer all the questions truthfully, conceal nothing and don't worry about giving the Germans new information. Everything he knew was known to them already.

When he was returned to his cell it was daylight and he had no idea how long he had spent in the interrogation room. He legs barely moved and he was so tired that he ignored the bowl of watery soup that was waiting for him on the floor, collapsed onto the thin mattress and was asleep within minutes.

Jacob woke up when the door to his cell opened with a clang.

"Get up you lazy Jew," the guard yelled.

He led Jacob down the stairs and into the internal courtyard where a truck was waiting. His two colleagues from Vilna were already in the truck, which started as soon as Jacob climbed in. Twenty minutes later they arrived at the Kaunas railway station. The officer who rode next to the driver returned their possessions and IDs and told them to board the train waiting in the station.

"Don't get off the train until you get to Vilna. If you do, we will bring you back here. The second time we won't let you go so easy."

Jacob screwed up his courage and asked: "Where is our friend Mordechai?"

The German smiled. "We released him yesterday and suggested that he wait for you, but he chose to take the cart and start on his way to Vilna. He will probably get there at about the same time as you."

The train started not more than ten minutes after they boarded and slowly proceeded on the track to Vilna. The three relaxed in their seats. The other passengers looked at them with a mixture of respect and suspicion: wasn't everyday that you saw civilians being put on a train by an SS officer, never mind that one of them had a beard and was wearing a black fedora – obviously a Jew. The group was worried about Mordechai. It didn't seem like him to leave them at the Fort. There was nothing they could do about him at the moment and discussing this in the presence of others was out of the question. Since they were left alone, the three went to sleep fairly soon and woke up only when the train stopped.

"Where are we?" inquired Rabbi Litvin. "This doesn't look like a station".

They were in a fairly large clearing in the woods. Angry voices sounded from the front of the train, followed by a shot. Ten minutes later four men entered the car. They were dressed in remnants of uniforms and armed with rifles and a submachine gun.

"Papers," demanded their leader in Lithuanian.

They perfunctorily looked at everybody's papers and quickly zeroed in on the three Vilna Jews.

"What have we here," the leader smiled after carefully examining their ID cards. "Jews from Palestine. Very interesting. Maybe you can be of some use to us. You are coming to our camp. Get up and go with Marek." He pointed to a big smelly guy with a rifle. He was smiling wolfishly daring them to refuse. They obeyed and the partisan directed them, in Polish, out of the car and to a group of his comrades waiting under the trees at the fringe of the clearing. Another shot rang out from the car next to the one they just left.

"This is what happens if somebody refuses our request," Marek said. "Oleg is a nice guy but has no patience."

***

The messages from Jacob's group in Lithuania came in the first three weeks then stopped for a day. The day after that a message came in, but the code was wrong. The security people at the base decided to wait one more day - mistakes happen and the code sent was similar to the one used a week before. The next day they had a message, again with a wrong code. Colonel Hirshson called Eichmann to find out what happened.

Eichmann denied knowledge of anything unusual having happened but promised to investigate and call back as soon as he had something.

"Colonel Eichmann, you will call with an update twice a day starting at six in the afternoon today. I hope, for your sake, that you find out where our agents are. And don't try concealing the truth from us. We have ways of finding out what is going on. If you lie to me it will end badly for you and many others."

Eichmann called before six. He sounded somewhat agitated. "Colonel Rakhman, I just found out that something happened in Kaunas. Since I can't get to the bottom of it from here, I am flying there in an hour. I will let you know tomorrow morning at the latest what I found."

He called early the next morning. According to Eichmann the agents were on a train to Vilna that was stopped by Lithuanian partisans, who abducted the group.

Hirshson was not sure whether or not Eichmann was lying. The voice analyzer indicated high stress, but that could be the result of fear of the Caliph's reprisal for the loss of any agents. After reporting to Gad Yaari, Hirshson went back to Jacob's family. "We never leave a soldier behind enemy lines. I'm sure that Jacob and the others will be extricated." He did not add "Whether they are alive or not."

***

The next morning colonel Hirshson was again on the phone with Eichmann.

"Colonel Rakhman, I have somewhat strange news. This is what I found out about your agents: Apparently the Lithuanian authorities in Kaunas got information that fake ID cards similar to the ones issued by you were used in the area. When a group of four people arrived at the ghetto and displayed their ID cards they were detained and transferred to one of our units for interrogation to make sure the cards were authentic. It took two days to verify their authenticity. Then your people were released and put on a train to Vilnius. It seems that the train was stopped by partisans and your people were taken off the train and abducted. We are still looking for them."

Hirshson was quiet for a moment considering the information. "Herr Eichmann, you may not know it, but the Caliph never abandons his citizens. I see two possibilities in this situation. The first is that your story is true. The second is that some overzealous official decided to make our agent and the Jews disappear and hopes to gain information from them. We are sending a team to Lithuania. You will arrange for their air transportation. If your story is true, we will know it as soon as our team arrives on the spot. Trust me on this: we have the means to know when people are lying to us. If a German is responsible, you still have time to return the missing people to us, unharmed, with only those directly responsible paying the price. This offer will expire by the end of the day today.

"If this is indeed the doing of Lithuanians, I expect you to do all in your power to get our people back unharmed. We will not retaliate against you if our people are returned unharmed within two days. If they're not, we will exterminate the guilty along with their families and neighbors. The Germans involved will be treated like the traitors they are. And you know what we do to traitors. If one of our people is harmed you will be held responsible. Just to remind you: the ratio is one hundred to one."

Chapter 16

"Let me first update you on the general situation." Amos Nir said. The cabinet meetings were somewhat more relaxed these days. The Prime Minister didn't let anybody relax too much – the situation was fluid and there was much to do.

"It is about two months since the Event, and I think we are doing well, all things considered. First the immigration situation: the Mufti and our agents in the ghettos did a great job for us. The Germans and their allies are shipping people at a rate we didn't expect. The Mossad has to be congratulated on a well executed operation. As a result though, the repatriation facility in Brindisi is at capacity. We don't have enough shipping to move people at the rate they are arriving, so we need to expand the facility. The difficulty is that the complex already resembles a sprawling city, and if we enlarge it even more, we will have perimeter control problems. As it is the Italians are unhappy and we have a full infantry battalion, four anti-aircraft batteries and an Air Force Kfir wing tied up there. Any ideas?"

"We have a landing strip in the center of the Brindisi camp," said the Transportation Minister. "Why not use some of our passenger jets to pick up immigrants? They are ready to go and if we use enough of them it will relieve the pressure. It is also a good idea to exercise some of the planes and pilots."

"Isn't it dangerous?" the Infrastructure Minister asked. "We will be flying in airspace controlled by the Germans. Even if they don't harm the planes they may see them, which isn't a good idea."

"Actually it is not a bad idea," the Defense Minister said. "We ignored the airlift option, but that may have been a mistake. If the passenger planes are accompanied by fighter jets and if we use our radar carefully we can avoid detection or worse. The advantage is clear: we will finish moving our people home in less than eight months. I think it is worth the risk."

"I agree," Amos said, closing the discussion of the subject.

"The next point: the Afrika Corps is doing much better fighting the British than in our timeline. They got an infusion of two Waffen SS divisions, both of them Muslim, from Bosnia. Not the best fighters but much better than what they had in our history and more ferocious than the Italians. They also have more supplies. The presence of our passenger transports causes some confusion. The Brits are hesitant to shoot at German shipping whether or not they're displaying our flag. As a result, more are getting through and Rommel is not suffering from the same shortages as in our history. There is a real danger that he will be in a position to attack Cairo much earlier than we expected. If the German attack happens before March of next year, Cairo is likely to fall. The Brits are not ready and don't have enough forces to stop him."

"I suggest that we wait and see," Nitzan Liebler responded. "The first two batches of British trainees left our new armor school in the Sinai a week ago and are already having an effect on their troops' performance. The graduates are also training others in a facility they set up east of Alexandria. In addition, if we're done with the Brindisi facility by February 1942 as we expect, the confusion over shipping will end and the Brits can start sinking more German and Italian transports."

"That sounds reasonable. We'll table that for the moment and go on to the next item. The Russian front worries me a bit. Our satellite images show two SS divisions and several regular infantry battalions moving east from Poland. All these troops had been busy exterminating our families in the original history but are now free to attack the Soviets. There is another complication: the German railway system is not clogged with transports of Jews to camps in Eastern Europe. This has greatly improved the supply situation of their army in the east. In our history Moscow and Leningrad barely survived. What if one of them falls now?"

"Maybe we have no choice but to intervene directly," the Finance Minister said.

"That's not so simple," responded the Defense Minister. "The fighting is far away and we don't have airfields in the area. This makes effective air support impossible. I don't think we should endanger our troops."

"I had something different in mind," the Finance Minister smiled. "Wars aren't won at the front. The actual fighting is only a manifestation of industrial and economic power. What if we disrupt the Germans' source of oil? The refineries they're using in Ploesti, Romania, are easily within our range. We don't have to destroy them – that may cripple the Germans too much - just damage them enough to slow them down. If that isn't enough, we could also damage their synthetic oil production facilities in the Ruhr. As an alternative we could attack the synthetic fuel plant in Leuna, Saxony-Anhalt."

"That is an idea," the Prime Minister paused, "but I see a problem. If we do the damage too late, it will not help the Russians; if we do it too early, the Germans may figure out who did it and kill some of our people still in Europe."

"I have an idea," the Transport Minister looked very proud of his insight. "What if we use propeller-driven bombers dropping regular iron bombs, with a laser guided one mixed in here and there. That way they are not likely to suspect us. We can convert a couple of our old Stratocruisers for the job. After all, they were originally developed as the B-50 bomber by the U.S. in 1947. If we can disguise them as British, the only danger will be losing them to anti-aircraft fire or malfunctions."

"I'll have a talk with Itamar Herz," said the Defense Minister. "Maybe we can solve this problem. Probably using several old DC3 transports would be better. They are older designs than the B50 and much smaller. Properly painted they may fool the Germans."

"It is decided then: we damage the Romanian refineries and, possibly, the synthetic oil production. Let the military and historians figure out when and how much."

Amos closed the meeting.

***

The Chairman of the Palestinian Authority called the meeting to order. The group was seated around a big conference table in his Ramallah office. All the factions were represented, including those supposedly opposed to the Authority, like Hamas and Islamic Jihad.

"Brothers," announced the Chairman, "I have grave news. My office received a letter from the Israeli government. Let me read it to you. We can discuss the implications later:

Jerusalem, August 19, 1941

Dear Dr. Mazen;

I am hereby notifying you of a number of judicial and administrative decisions that may be of interest to you.

As of July 10, 1941, the military courts have been reviewing the cases of convicted terrorists currently serving life sentences, whose acts resulted in death or injury. The prosecution invoked paragraph 3.4.1.7 of the emergency regulations, allowing it to ask for the replacement of a life sentence with the death penalty.

As a result, 357 prisoners (see enclosed list for names) have been sentenced to death so far. I will send you updated lists as soon as they become available.

Let me assure you that the death penalty will only be enforced if our citizens are harmed. If such a tragedy should happen, we will execute convicts belonging to the organization or organizations that participate in such an attack. The names on the lists I enclosed are in the order in which the death penalty will be enforced in case of an attack. We will execute twice the number of convicts as the number of civilians killed or injured in any attack.

You may rest assured that our intentions are peaceful. It is with deep sorrow that I have to notify you of the execution of 16 members of Hamas, as a result of the attack at the Church of the Nativity in Bethlehem. The full list is enclosed. You will note that Ahmad Darwish, who ordered the operation, was among those executed.

I hope that you will be able to rein in the extremist in your ranks to prevent any additional deaths.

Yours Sincerely,

Minister for Internal Security"

The Chairman paused and looked at each of the men at the conference table: "As you understand, this changes the equation. If we continue our resistance by the same means we have used for so many years, we will cause untold devastation to our own friends and families. I urge each one of you to study the lists carefully. You will find that many of your relatives are at the top of the respective lists."

Muhammad al Husseini was the first to respond: "I reject this threat. The Jews are too weak to enforce it. We can go to their Supreme Court and appeal all these unjust convictions. We can also appeal to the international community and apply pressure through Israel's allies - that's always worked in the past. My group will continue our operations – we have to revenge the death of Ahmad Darwish. Besides, every one of us that dies in this holy Jihad becomes a martyr with seventy-two virgins awaiting him in heaven."

The room was silent for a moment. Nobody wanted to contradict this patriotic speech.

"As I said, it will be up to you and your organizations to decide how to react," the Chairman said finally. "I will order the forces loyal to the Authority to stop all operations immediately.

"By the way, Muhammad, your uncle warned us not to make trouble now and to wait for his return. Are you going to disobey his order? What if the Israelis arrest you? It's happened before and may happen again. You will probably be sentenced to death this time around – they know a lot about you. Should your second in command go on and attack some unworthy infidel? And by the way, an appeal to their Supreme Court would be useless as it has no jurisdiction over military courts that operate outside Israeli territory. The West Bank has not been annexed by Israel, so there is no appeal."

"I would like to point out to all of you that even if Israel were not blocking all outside communications we would get no help from outside," said the Palestinian Foreign Minister. "Some of us have been open about destroying the Jews, while others pretended to negotiate with the Jewish state, but our final goal was always the same: to get rid of them for good.

"You may consider it a miracle that the world never took us to task for this desire, but it is really very simple: nobody thought that the Jews deserved a state of their own or that they even deserved to live. There were some exceptions, but they were in a small minority. The Allies agreed to the Jewish state out of guilt for the Holocaust and because the Jews would have probably established one anyway, but the Jewish state has always been a pariah. That's why the leftist organizations support us no matter what we do and this is why we could continue to terrorize Israel without rebuke. It is funny, really, how anti-Semitism was condemned but the destruction of the State of Israel was a legitimate goal. Remember, it was anti-Semitism that served us so well.

"I am sad to inform you that the situation has changed. In the world we're in now, we are at the Israeli's mercy. They're a superpower with advanced weapons and technology, not to mention nuclear capability. Do not forget that the Jewish population of Israel will almost double shortly, increasing their strength. If they decided to kill us all, they could get away with it. Nobody cares about hundreds of thousands of Arabs any more than they care about millions of Jews. The world now thinks Palestinians are the Jews living here. Our friend and ally – anti-Semitism - is still there, but against a Jewish superpower we are nothing. I'm still not quite sure why the Germans are letting all these Jews go. Muhammad's explanation based on the Mufti's conversation with our emissary is that they want to concentrate all the Jews in one place and then drop a couple of atom bombs on them. I pray that this is so."

A stunned silence lasted for several minutes. It wasn't every day that this group heard a realistic evaluation of their situation. It was very pessimistic and sounded true.

"How do you mean 'several hundred thousand Arabs'?" asked the leader of the Islamic Jihad finally. "Our own population surveys show that there are more than a million Palestinians in the Gaza strip and at least as many in the West Bank!"

This time it was the Chairman's turn to respond: "My friend, you believe our propaganda? The West Bank holds at least thirty percent less Palestinians than we claim. The actual birth rates were much lower and emigration much higher than reported. Gaza is not relevant since it did not get transported with us to this time. An Israel with twelve million Jews has no demographic problem with us. Actually they never did but we convinced some of them otherwise – enough for our purposes.

"But back to our main issue. I recommend that you tell everyone in your organizations that from now on any blood they spill will come back to haunt them, immediately and directly. The blood of their brothers will be on their hands."

"What if the Jews decide to exterminate us?" asked an older man, the leader of a small Marxist faction.

"There is nothing we would be able to do except die with dignity." The Chairman surveyed the crowd. "That is why the Grand Mufti's advice is so wise – keep quiet and don't get into fights you can't win. I agree with his estimate that the only way to defeat Israel is with nuclear weapons. To use them with minimal harm to our people we will have to get out of this area as soon as the border is opened. I only hope that we can convince our brothers living in Israel to follow our example."

The meeting dispersed after that statement. It seemed that the sacrifice of a small Palestinian state for the dream of a large one without Jews was for naught. The years of struggle and bloodshed were wasted, as were so many Arab lives. It was depressing. Some of the attendees were considering the option to end it all in one glorious act of violence worthy of a real Jihad. Never before had these leaders considered martyring themselves for the cause. It was safe to assume they would find a way to stay alive, as they always did. The Mufti was their only hope. Pray to Allah that his plans will succeed.

***

Dr. Ahmad Mazen didn't like the current situation one bit but thought that maybe he could change it. It was all a question of politics. The Grand Mufti may have been correct about the Germans and their atom bomb, but in the meantime something had to be done about this terrible change in Israeli policy. They should not be allowed to hold his brothers hostage to future terror acts. The Palestinians should not be held back in their efforts to liberate their land and push the Jews into the sea. He had an idea. It was simple and only required a couple of telephone calls. His first was to his long-term collaborator and agent in the Peace Now movement.

"Hello Shlomo. This is your old friend. How are you?"

"Oh, it's you. Haven't heard from you in a long time. I'm fine. How are you and how can I help you?"

"Shlomo, in a moment I will fax you a letter I received from the Minister of Internal Security. Please read it carefully. You will find that it breaks a number of your laws and constitutes inhumane behavior towards our people. I know that your organization has good lawyers and recommend that you start a two-pronged offensive. A request to the Supreme Court for an injunction to suspend the letter, or whatever other legal action they can come up with, and, in parallel, demonstrations and grassroots resistance to this policy. We will also have the Arab members of the Knesset as well as the left wing peace parties raise hell in the legislature. It's immoral and illegal to hold prisoners' lives hostage."

"Consider it done."

Mazen thought some more. He was a historian with a specialty in the Holocaust. Several of his papers explaining how it never happened had been very well accepted in the Arab world. He knew this period well and estimated that none of the great powers, including the U.S. and Russia, would be supportive of the Jews, and certainly would not support the draconian measures against his brothers. The problem was, he didn't have access to the great powers. He did have access to their ambassadors though. Mazen thought that if the American and Russian ambassadors publicly oppose the new "Hostage Law" it would help his friends in Peace Now. It might also help them gain some votes in the Knesset. In any case, no harm would be done. He called the American embassy, and after that he called the Russians.

***

The four citizens of the Caliph disappeared in the vicinity of Kaunas, so testified the chief of the local Gestapo. He was extremely nervous and looked afraid. Inspector Saul Unger looked at his voice stress indicator and made a decision. "Everybody out. You," he pointed at the Gestapo man, "stay here."

The Germans tried to protest, but Eichmann ordered them to obey. Those who were still not convinced of the Caliph's power, the Major that governed Kaunas being one of those, were swayed by two explosions. The first, the smaller of the two, destroyed an SS barracks two streets away from the building they were in. The second destroyed an empty bunker at the Ninth Fort. The force of this explosion shook the town. The timing was perfect, as the plane that released the two laser-guided bombs received its cue from one of the Special Forces.

"You better listen carefully to what I have to say," Saul declared. "This is the last warning you will get from the Caliph. One more case of hesitation in obeying my orders and we will execute everybody here."

There were several German officials in the room, including Eichmann. Three members of the Israeli Special Forces, dressed as Caliphate soldiers, were also present. All the Germans got up and left. Outside another trio of Israelis stood guard. One of them escorted the Germans outside the building. The Israeli group took over, unceremoniously expelling the Gestapo, local Lithuanian police and the German Governor's staff. The building that used to be the German regional headquarters, the headquarters of the local Gestapo and of the Lithuanian police was now controlled by Israelis.

"Relax," Saul told the Nazi in good but heavily accented German. "I know it's not easy to be calm in the presence of the Great Caliph's inquisitors, but you will be okay if you speak the truth. Let's begin." He put a standard polygraph harness on the German. A thin cable connected it to a small hand held computer. The whole thing was plugged into a power outlet.

"Now, what is your name?"

"Hans Klemper."

"When were you born?"

"February 2, 1904."

"What color is your hair?"

"Brown."

"Did you have anything to do with the disappearance of our citizens? Yes or no only, please."

"No."

"Do you know anyone who may have been connected to their disappearance?"

The German hesitated: "No."

"Another lie and you will lose your tongue." Saul smiled a cold smile. "Let's try again. Do you know anyone who may have been connected to the disappearance?"

This time the German did not hesitate: "Yes."

"Who is this person?" Saul asked.

"Walter Huber."

Saul looked at the display. He had all the names of German and Lithuanian officials in the area. The man named was an SS major.

"Why do you suspect the major?"

"He is responsible for intelligence in the area and has all kinds of connections. He may have decided to gather some information on his own. I'm guessing, but this is the best I can do."

"Who else do you suspect?"

"Captain Andreas Niemetzkas of the Lithuanian police."

"Why him?"

"He has connections with the Lithuanian partisans. I was watching him for a while but did not arrest him in the hope of gathering more information about the bandits."

The next to be interrogated was SS Major Walter Huber. After the normal introductory baseline questions Saul wanted to know whether he was involved with the disappearance. The Major, a tough customer, tried to evade a direct answer: "I told a number of people that it would be a good idea to get some intelligence from these Jews."

"Give me a list of names, please."

"Well, let's see. I spoke to Hans, Andreas, Gerhard and maybe some I don't remember."

"Who is Gerhardt?" Saul asked.

"Lieutenant Gerhardt Hartle is my adjutant. He disappeared yesterday. Our troops are looking for him – I suspect that this is the work of bandits. Gerhardt is inexperienced and, I am afraid, given to long walks. He may have been taken while walking in the forest – I think I remember him saying something about mushrooms."

"Walter, my friend," Saul smiled his unfriendly smile, "do you know what the penalty is for lying to me?"

"No."

"I will forgive you one attempt. The second time you lose your tongue. My associate," Saul pointed at one of the three soldiers standing guard, "has the appropriate tools and will relieve you of the instrument of your lies right here."

The soldier smiled as if pleased to have an opportunity to use the wicked looking combination pliers/cutter he produced from one of his pockets.

The major bridled: "You can do no such thing to an SS officer. You will die if you try."

Saul looked surprised: "Are you threatening me?"

"Take it as you will, but I am not answering any more questions." The Nazi seemed unconcerned.

Saul nodded to his soldier, who moved quickly. Before the SS man realized what happened his right hand was held firmly. When the German tried to free himself he was rewarded with a pair of swift punches. Now he was bent over from a punch to his solar plexus and bleeding from a broken nose.

"If you resist, Ahmed here will have lots of fun with you. You will be much better off just letting him do what he needs to do," Saul said calmly.

Before the German could respond Saul nodded and the soldier cut off the index finger on his right hand.

It took a while before Major Huber stopped shrieking and recovered enough to continue answering questions. Saul decided to wait until his subject regained his breath, stopped retching and was able to hold the gauze pad the soldier gave him to stem the bleeding.

"Where is your adjutant Gerhardt?"

"He was on the same train as the people who disappeared. Nobody has heard from him since then."

The Lithuanian Police chief was next. Having heard the German's distress through the open window and having seen his sorry state, Andreas did not try to conceal anything but knew very little.

***

While Saul was interrogating the obvious suspects and later talking to inhabitants of the ghetto, a second group, consisting of a forensic expert and five Special Forces soldiers went to the site where, according to a Lithuanian who had been on the train, the transport had been stopped and the abduction had taken place.

A week had passed so they didn't expect to find much, if any, physical evidence. The forensics expert looked carefully on both sides of the track. There were clumps of broken branches where the tracks entered a small clearing in the dense forest.

"Are the Lithuanian partisans active in this area?" the Special Forces lieutenant asked.

"No, not really. As far as I know this was the first time they stopped a train. They didn't attack it or derail it either. Just placed a couple of big trees across the tracks. The passengers cleared it in five minutes after they were gone."

"How many people did they take?"

"Well," the Lithuanian looked at his fingers and murmured to himself, "the three Jews with special permits, an SS officer, two Lithuanian civilians and two young women. That's all, I think."

"How do you know the Jews had special permits?"

"The bandits were looking for them. They asked everybody for their papers, and nabbed the three as soon as they showed those fancy cards."

"You said three Jews? Are you sure there weren't four?"

"Oh, I'm sure. I sat two rows behind them in the car. Actually, since they were put on the train by a German officer nobody wanted to take the fourth seat next to them. It was empty."

"Did the German officer put up a fight?"

"No! Are you crazy? It was a big band of bandits. Maybe a hundred. The German had no chance. But, since you mention him, I do remember a funny thing: the bandits did not take the SS man's pistol. I thought it was strange - why let him keep his gun?"

By this time the forensic guy was done so the lieutenant thanked the Lithuanian for his help and offered to escort him to his village.

"Thank you very much, but there's really no need. The forest is safe. I doubt that there is a human being within fifteen miles outside of my village."

***

The teams met in the evening at the Gestapo building.

Their commander, a Special Forces captain, informed the group that while they were doing their jobs his team had checked the building for bugs, prepared it for defense and also set up a command center.

"Now let's hear from Saul," the captain said.

"I have some conflicting information and some clues." Saul paused to look at his notes. "From the testimony of the Germans I can only draw some preliminary conclusions. It seems that a SS lieutenant Gerhardt Hartle is missing from the same train as our guys. He is probably involved in this but I still have to determine how. His boss, SS Major Walter Hubel, is smart and tough. He managed to partly fool the lie detector. If a person convinces themselves that a fantasy is true, the machine will say it is true. It is also possible that he was smart enough to formulate his orders to this Gerhardt as general wishes and is now able to tell us, sort of truthfully, that he never ordered the abduction. He almost outsmarted himself by refusing to answer questions.

"By the way, Sergeant Zohar," Saul was very serious now, "I want to file a formal protest with your commander. There was no need to be so brutal with Hubel. I asked you to break his index finger. You should not have beaten him the way you did and certainly shouldn't have cut off the finger. It is one thing to use violence when necessary, quite another to take pleasure in torturing your subject. Your behavior was not fit for a member of the Israeli Defense Forces."

"Sir," the sergeant was surprised. "You know who this Nazi is. I read only a couple of pages from his file. He was trained in Dachau and a couple of other camps in interrogation techniques. His file says he was commended on his achievements. Who knows how many innocent people he's tortured to death already? And here in Kaunas, if it wasn't for our time accident, he would have become notorious for torturing prisoners at the Ninth Fort. They killed tens of thousands there, and he was personally responsible for a significant number of those deaths. I think that I was very mild, all things considered."

Saul was about to respond, but the captain was faster. "Sergeant, I will let this go. This time. You've had your warning and any repetition of this kind of behavior will have consequences." The captain looked at each member of his team. "We don't want to become like these beasts. All of you have to understand that we are in a precarious situation and orders will be obeyed exactly as given. If you have doubts, ask for confirmation. The only time you are allowed to improvise is if you are cut off and all by yourself, which I sincerely hope will not happen.

"OK. Lieutenant, what do you have to report?"

The lieutenant told them the Lithuanian witness's story: "The thing that worries me is that he is sure there were only three of our people on the train. Somebody is missing and we don't know who or how."

"It was difficult to find anything after a week," the forensic investigator said. Forests have the ability to repair themselves fairly quickly. But I found a couple of clues." He explained his findings for a couple of minutes. "Judging by the broken branches, I can say with reasonable certainty that the partisans waited for the train at the edge of the clearing. The group couldn't have been larger than 10, maybe 20 people. Our guys were definitely taken off the train at that spot – I found a bunch of polyester and rayon fibers. I don't know why one of them was allowed to leave wearing synthetics, but in this case it was useful.

"There is a faint trail of broken twigs and a couple of cigarette butts that leads to the northwest from the abduction spot," he pointed the direction out on a map, "but I have no idea how far they went or if they kept the same heading. It's not likely they did. This forest is too dense for a straight line path and they wouldn't be that stupid anyway."

Saul was thinking aloud: "If your Lithuanian is not lying, there is only that one small village and the town of Kasiadorys. I assume that he exaggerated the distance to the next town, just as he saw maybe a hundred attackers where there were at most twenty. It makes no difference as far as locating our people. Assuming they are hidden in the forest, there is only one way we can locate them."

***

Just after ten the next morning, Saul and the forensic expert were huddled in front of a monitor. They had requested that one of the surveillance satellites be diverted to scan the forest, giving them images in both infrared and visible light. Now they were trying to determine if something unusual was evident. It took another two hours before they found something.

"There are two suspicious spots," Saul reported to the captain. "One is north by northwest of the point where the abduction took place, the other directly north. Both areas had discoloration and signs of smoke on the daylight images and showed up as bright spots in night time infrared." He paused, as if hesitating, then continued: "Yesterday I spoke to a number of people in the ghetto. It seems that a number of Jews left the ghetto at the beginning of July. They are rumored to be in the forest, but nobody knows where. We may have just found them. But we don't know which encampment is friendly. I am afraid that we will have to investigate both.

"There is also some negative information in the sense that none of the ghetto residents saw the group or heard of them. I believe that they never entered the ghetto and were taken to a different location. We will have to investigate this as soon as we can."

***

While the investigating team was doing its work in Lithuania, Hirshson called Eichmann. "Herr Eichmann, you were less than truthful with me. I want to know what happened to our agent. We have evidence of only three being on the train. Where is the fourth?"

"Colonel, I truly don't know. I wasn't aware that they were separated. Please let me make some inquiries and I will call you back as soon as I can."

"Herr Eichmann, I reported these events up my chain of command and I have orders to act. You and your superiors will not find my actions pleasant. I may be able to give you some time, but not much."

Eichmann sounded cool. "What actions are we talking about?"

"I think that you know. Munich is on my short list and there are some lesser alternatives. But don't let me delay you."

"Colonel Rakhman, please excuse my question, but how important can these Jews be to you? After all, they are only Jews and destined to disappear soon anyway. Why the fuss?"

Hirshson was furious and let it show in his voice: "Eichmann, what we do with the Jews is our business. The important matter is that your country showed a blatant disregard of our agreement and of the sanctity of both a Caliphate citizen and people under its protection. One of the four is a citizen, the others, whatever their fate may be in the near future, are now under our protection. Your country, or some of its officials, committed a mortal crime against us. The sooner this is resolved the better for you. And I mean you personally." He hung up without waiting for a response.

***

The small force moved out at dusk. Their commander decided to split his men three ways: five, with him in command, to go to the northernmost encampment; five, commanded by the lieutenant, to the spot near Kasiadorys. Saul, the forensic expert, and three soldiers stayed in the Gestapo building for communications and control. They were also responsible for guarding the building.

The two strike forces piled into commandeered German cars and started towards their respective destinations. They could ride only part of the way, traversing the last ten miles or so on foot. Each soldier carried night vision goggles and donned them as soon as it became dark.

In his group, the lieutenant led the short line of shadows. They walked carefully, making as little noise as possible. It was difficult, considering the density of the undergrowth. Without the night vision equipment, they would have made enough noise to alert animals miles away let alone human sentries they assumed were much closer. As it was, the slight crackling of broken twigs and tree limbs being carefully moved aside blended in with the forest's night noises.

Progress was slow, complicated by the marshy terrain they encountered from time to time. They could not walk through that too fast – their boots made loud squishing noises, getting louder the faster they moved. The group took almost six hours to cross the distance from their car to the vicinity of the encampment. By the time they got there, dawn was still a couple of hours away; it was still pitch dark.

The group spread out and carefully approached the encampment from three directions. The lieutenant noticed a man standing next to a tree and circled, approaching the figure from behind and rendering him unconscious with a sharp strike to the side of the neck. A blow like that had to be measured carefully – too strong could kill a man or make him a quadriplegic for life. He caught the collapsing sentry, only to discover it was a woman. He signaled to the rest of the force to continue with their search. They found another sentry at the other end of the little camp and disabled him as well, without alerting anyone. A short survey showed entrances to three dugouts. The lieutenant posted sentries at two of them and proceeded to enter the third with another soldier. They found six people sleeping on wooden platforms. He fingered his throat mike and ordered the soldiers that remained outside to enter the other dugouts. They reported ten more people – a mix of men and women. He took off his night vision goggles and turned on a powerful flashlight, waking the people in his dugout. They were startled and frightened, crying out in Yiddish. He calmed them down as best he could and instructed the soldiers to take care of the group. They looked dirty, undernourished and suffered from an array of small but debilitating injuries: small infected cuts, a broken finger, a shallow stab wound. While his soldiers were busy gathering and treating the refugees, the lieutenant radioed the captain to report his findings. He had found another group of Jews; the captain was facing the Lithuanians.

***

The captain's earpiece came alive about a hundred yards from the target. Now he knew that the encampment in front of them was the real target and informed his troops. He decided to deploy his small force in two groups. He and Sergeant Zohar circled around the camp. The other three waited on the southern edge. When he was in position, the captain signaled the others. It took them about five minutes to disable the four guards. It was easy work made even easier by the fact that two of them were asleep.

There were five dugouts positioned around a rough stone circle that contained the cooking fire. Coals were still smoldering, giving off a rich woody smell but also overwhelming the infrared equipment. They switched to light amplification vision. There was a guard sitting next to the entrance to one of the dugouts, his rifle on the ground, smoking a foul-smelling cigarette. Zohar circled through the outskirts of the camp and carefully crawled towards the guard.

When the captain saw the guard slump with the cigarette still smoldering in his slack hand, he signaled his soldiers to take up positions on top of the four unguarded dugouts. They had stun grenades ready – Saul had requested that the Lithuanians be brought back alive if possible. He needed to interrogate them.

The officer entered the little dugout by himself. The dim light was enough to see by, after it was amplified by the night vision goggles. There were six men in the underground space. The ceiling, which was made of heavy logs and sealed with moss, was about six feet above the floor. On the outside, the structure was covered with dirt. The space was small, about ten feet by ten feet, with wooden bunk beds on one side and several crude cabinets on the other. Two men were sleeping on a bunk. Three others were on the earthen floor. He took off the night goggles and turned on his flashlight. Two of the men were apparently not asleep at all. They were pretending, laying in wait for someone to either enter the dugout or try to escape. Both jumped the Special Forces officer at the same time. He saw a reflection of light and moved aside just as a blade cut through the air next to him. The other attacker also had a knife, and in the small space, with people lying on the ground, the Israeli could not move freely to fight both of them. The second knife imbedded itself in his chest.

The other three men were also awake and tried to get up to help but could not. They were tightly bound. In the meantime the first attacker was pulling a pistol from a holster on his hip.

The shot was thunderous in the pre-dawn quiet of the forest. It was accompanied immediately by four loud explosions and bright flashes of light as the stun grenades went off. Each of the soldiers rushed into his assigned dugout ready to kill anybody opposing him. There was not much opposition. The inhabitants were only half awake and temporarily deaf and blind. It took less than two minutes to pacify them.

Sergeant Zohar rushed into the dugout his captain had entered. He found the commander sitting on a pallet and calmly cutting the ties that held the prisoners.

"Sir, what happened?"

"A stupid mistake," admitted the captain. "I should have used the stun grenade instead of letting my ego rule. I assumed the guards were asleep since they were breathing regularly and not moving. They were not, and now I will need a new breastplate for my body armor. This piece of dog's excrement," he pointed at the SS officer unconscious on the floor, "managed to shoot me while his friend here stabbed me. No matter, it's a lesson we will discuss at debriefing back home."

Three abductees were accounted for. They were not in good shape though. The SS lieutenant had interrogated them and was not gentle. They had not eaten much in a week and were tied up most of the time. Rabbi Zerah Litvin was missing the pinky on his left hand. The wound was infected and the rabbi was feverish and delirious. Hirsh Goldstein was missing two of his front teeth and Jacob had a dislocated shoulder and what seemed like hundreds of small cuts all over his body. He was feverish as well, though not delirious.

After all the Lithuanians and the German were bound with their hands tied behind their backs with plastic straps, the Israelis marched them towards the nearest road. Rabbi Litvin had to be tied to a stretcher. Jacob could barely walk: even with his shoulder back in place, he had several badly infected cuts on his feet and walking was painful. All of the liberated men were given emergency tetanus shots and a hefty dose of antibiotics.

Two trucks were waiting for the group. Saul sent them driven by two of his soldiers, who were replaced a couple of minutes later by the lieutenant and his force who returned from their mission. The hapless group of ghetto refugees was left to walk for a while. The Germans did not have another truck on hand to bring them back and the command car used by the lieutenant could only hold five passengers. It was still going back and forth delivering the dirty and tired Jews when the trucks carrying the captain and his group arrived at the Gestapo headquarters.

***

In the early afternoon the Israelis were trying to decide what to do next. Two of the rescued men were coherent and told the story of their trip to the Ninth Fort, interrogation and release. They also told their rescuers that Menachem supposedly left by himself the day before they were released. Neither they nor the Israelis believed that.

The Lithuanians and Gerhardt, the SS lieutenant, were locked up in the basement cells of the Gestapo building.

Saul started the debate. "I want to interrogate Gerhardt and see if he acted alone, or if, as I believe, he was instructed by Major Hubel."

"And what if Hubel is involved?" the captain wanted to know.

"Kill him," contributed his second in command.

"Not so fast," responded Saul. "We will report to Hirshson and do what we are ordered. My guess is that it will not be simple. The guilty parties, of which there are many, will have to be made an example of, so others will not dare follow in their steps."

"Okay. Go ahead and see what Gerhardt tells you. In the meantime, I'll call the colonel and report. We'll have to go to the Ninth Fort and see what we find there. I have a bad feeling about this business."

***

"Lieutenant, please calm down. I am not going to do anything bad to you, yet. I want just to ask you a couple of questions." Saul poured tea for himself. "Would you like some?"

The young Nazi nodded. Saul poured tea in a glass, added two spoonfuls of sugar and put the glass on the table in front of his subject. He then proceeded to release the Nazi's left hand from the plastic strap that held it tightly to the arm of the chair he was sitting in: "Please don't imagine that you can free yourself. Sergeant Ahmad would really like you to try." Saul smiled and Gerhardt shivered.

It took only three questions to clarify the situation: Gerhardt decided he was going to be a hero and answer no questions. He wasn't familiar with a polygraph. It required the interrogator to ask questions that were unambiguous and required only a "Yes" or "No" response.

"My dear Lieutenant," Saul said softly, after his first question about age had been met with silence, "if you don't answer the next question, the sergeant will cut out your tongue with the nice tool he has. Show him please, Ahmed."

Zohar pulled out his modified pliers with the two blades welded on the front edge.

"He will pull it out and then clamp down the blades. No big deal really, but you will not be able to speak after this procedure. Ever. And I have no leeway in this. The law is clear, and we have to obey it."

"What law? You are barbarians! How dare you threaten me with torture? The master race will not tolerate the likes of you!"

Saul was very calm now, with his voice even quieter than before. "It is the law of the Caliph, and master race or not you are now being interrogated by one of His inquisitors." He paused to sip his tea. "Your superior, Major Hubel, thought nothing about talking to us and giving you away."

"You are lying to me. The Major would never talk to dogs like you."

"Would you like to hear his testimony?" Saul asked. He was sickened by the thought that Zohar might have to carry out the threat. If the German did not start speaking they would have no choice – a threat had to be carried out or their reputation and power over the Nazis would be ruined.

"Yes."

Saul put a small tape recorder on the table and pressed the Play button. Anticipating this problem he had prepared and edited a copy of Hubel's testimony.

The SS lieutenant listened carefully. The tape started somewhere in the middle of Hubel's questioning and went through the part where Zohar beat him up, ending after he gave Saul Gerhard's name. At that point Saul stopped the tape.

"This is a fabrication," yelled the Nazi and threw his empty tea glass at Saul, who easily evaded it. The SS man tried to get up from his seat and would have overturned the table but Sergeant Zohar was faster. A single blow to the shoulder and another to the nose and the German was gasping for breath. Zohar took out his tongue tool and forced the Nazi's mouth open. The Nazi, who had no problem torturing Jews, was now shrieking in a surprisingly loud, high-pitched voice. As Zohar pushed his pliers into the Nazi's mouth a foul smell spread in the room. The sergeant stopped and stepped away from the Nazi. He started laughing. "Our hero has shit and pissed himself."

After this experience Gerhardt did not object to answering questions and he didn't lie.

***

A couple of hours later the captain reported to his team the orders they had received from the Brindisi base: "We are to go to the Ninth Fort and get to the bottom of this affair. By now it is certain that this was not a local decision. Whatever Gerhardt or anybody else says, they were acting on orders from above."

"Colonel Eichmann, my orders come directly from the Caliph's headquarters, so please listen carefully.

"We will leave for the Ninth Fort now and you will accompany us. We know that the orders to interrogate and abduct our people came from higher up, not from anybody in Kaunas. This is a serious breach of your agreement with the Caliphate and requires a thorough investigation. After we are done I will report to my superiors and they will decide what to do."

Eichmann sounded surprised. "I don't have the authority to let you into the Ninth Fort or anywhere else besides the Kaunas ghetto. You will have to wait. I must contact my superiors and get their permission, which I'm not sure will be forthcoming."

"Colonel, one of my orders is to kill you on the spot if you don't cooperate. We will do that as soon as my interrogator is done with you. Shall we start now or do we go to the Ninth Fort?"

"But this is unreasonable. I have my orders and I have to follow them. You don't have the right or authority to do anything to me." Eichmann was pacing back and forth. He sweated heavily and looked pale.

"You seriously want to test that statement?" The captain smiled cheerfully. "Who do you think will rescue you if we start the interrogation now?

"As to having no authority: this is your second lie to a Caliphate officer. You lied once already to Colonel Rakhman. This may have sealed your fate anyway, but I will give you a chance to redeem yourself. So, shall we go or shall I call the interrogator?"

Eichmann sat down. Now his face was calm. "If you torture and kill me, the consequences will be catastrophic. You won't be able to go anywhere from here – all cooperation and transportation is on my authority only. And my superiors will likely rescind our agreement regarding the Jews."

The captain smiled: "Well, the consequences will certainly be catastrophic for you. You will be dead after having been tortured by the best in the business. I would like to remind you that it was the Fuehrer who ordered you to cooperate with us and everything you do is on his orders. I very much doubt that he will suddenly decide to sacrifice a city to the incompetence of his subordinates."

Eichmann got up from his seat. "Captain, you passed my test of loyalty. I apologize for the aggravation, but I had strict orders to make sure that you are faithfully executing your agreement with the Fuehrer. We can now go to the Ninth Fort."

The Israeli could only admire the brazen lie. For the time being he decided to let it go. The inspection of the prison camp was a much more urgent affair than getting even with Eichmann.

***

The captain, Saul, the police investigator, Sergeant Zohar and a soldier drove to the Ninth Fort in Eichmann's car, with Eichmann squeezed between Zohar and Saul. Their visit was shorter than anticipated. When approaching the fort they heard machine gun fire and then several pistol shots.

When they arrived at the fort ten minutes later they found themselves in hell: a group of SS soldiers was standing on the edge of a large pit dug out next to one of the tall walls surrounding the fort. In the pit a group of prisoners were shoveling lime on top of more than a hundred dead bodies. This was the explanation of the gunfire they heard on approach. This was also what Jacob heard when he was there earlier. A quick calculation suggested that in the last week the Germans had murdered more than four thousand people. They were digging yet another pit next to the one that was half-full.

Eichmann was proud: "As you can see we are quite efficient in dealing with enemies of the Reich."

"Who were these people?" the captain asked after a little while, when he could trust his voice not to tremble.

"Oh, I don't know exactly. We can ask the commander when we speak to him. Here he is." A medium height, non-descript man in a well pressed SS uniform was walking towards them. "This is SS Captain Gratt, the commandant of this facility."

"Captain Osama Ramadan, Company A, the First Battalion, Tenth Division of the Caliph's army," the Israeli saluted. "Pleased to meet you."

"Captain Ramadan is here to investigate the disappearance of their operatives. I expect you to fully cooperate with his team." Eichmann sounded sincere, but Saul noticed that his eyes flicked to the side. Something wasn't kosher.

The Israeli requested, and was granted, a full tour of the fort. It was filled to its considerable capacity. Thousands of people were incarcerated in the underground casements and the drier cells above ground. The team could not easily determine who these prisoners were. One thing was certain: their life expectancy was not great.

They started their questioning with the commander. Eichmann was not allowed in the room and was told to wait in the car. This somewhat rude treatment of a superior officer seemed to surprise the SS captain, but he said nothing. When questioned, he freely admitted that the four men had been brought to the fort by an SS detachment.

"We interrogated them as gently as possible to make sure that they are who they said they are. As soon as we ascertained their identities we let them go."

"All together?" asked Saul.

"No. The man name Mordechai was released on his second day here. The rest were released the next day. He departed on his cart as soon as we let him go."

Saul looked at Captain Ori Ben-Zvi, otherwise known as Osama Ramadan. Ori nodded and Saul pulled out the polygraph harness from his bag. Captain Gratt objected to wearing the harness and was promptly whacked in the face by Zohar. He was so surprised that he forgot to protest.

"Captain, we are here to get to the truth. As you can see, we have the means of getting to the truth and we will discover it no matter what the cost to you. I would prefer to do it quickly and painlessly, but if you prefer it the other way, we can do that too."

The fort commander regained some of his composure: "You will be shot for what you did, Colonel Eichmann's authority notwithstanding. You can't expect to beat the commander of this facility and get out of here alive."

Ori nodded to Zohar, who smiled and broke the Nazis nose.

"Gratt you are learning what Herr Eichmann and others learned before you: never talk back to a Caliphate officer. Never. We've wasted enough time. Answer my interrogator's question. Truthfully, please. The punishment for lying is the loss of your tongue so be careful what you say."

The SS man didn't resist but stuck to his version of the story. After ten minutes Saul was certain that he was lying, that Mordechai had never left the fort. He and Captain Ben-Zvi quietly conferred in the corner of the office. Then Ori said "Sergeant Ahmed please remove this man's tongue. We are getting a bunch of lies from him."

Gratt jumped at Zohar and it took all of the sergeant's skill to pacify him. They made enough noise for the soldier standing guard outside to poke his head into the room to see if they were okay.

When Gratt came to he was tied to his chair and couldn't move. Zohar approached with his tongue cutting tool and made the Nazi open his tightly clenched teeth by the simple expedient of pinching his nose. A screwdriver prevented the murderer from closing his mouth. When Gratt's tongue was pulled out and he realized that it is about to be cut off he started making frantic noises.

"Would you like to amend any of your answers?" asked Saul.

Gratt nodded, though his head couldn't move much.

"Sergeant please let him speak."

Zohar let go of the German's tongue and smiled at him: "I will be quicker next time. Don't you worry."

"Captain Gratt if you have something to say now is the time."

Gratt's voice was trembling. "It is really not my fault. A stupid guard beat your man to death. I had nothing to do with it."

Saul thought for a moment: "Good. Let's start from the beginning."

It didn't take long to discover the truth: Mordechai was beaten by a guard on arrival to the Ninth Fort. His three companions told the Israelis about that. His injuries were not serious and definitely not life threatening. The interrogators at the fort knew that Mordechai was not like the other three men and tried to pump him for information about the Caliph. He died suddenly during the interrogation. Saul and Ori were sure that Mordechai was about to crack and spill his secrets. He must have decided to commit suicide with the implanted poison tooth rather than tell his torturers the whole truth, which would have cost millions of lives.

There was another thing the team decided to investigate: who were the prisoners at the fort. It didn't take long to find that out. The SS kept meticulous records and captain Gratt was very cooperative, especially after Eichmann made no comment about his broken and still bleeding nose.

A great majority of the fort's inmates were ethnic minorities, mostly Gypsies, a couple of hundred Communists, or, rather, alleged Communists – several Lithuanians but mostly Poles and several Jews. A contingent of Soviet prisoners of war was also there awaiting their turn at the pits.

There were two issues left: What was Eichmann's role and what to do for punishment.

***

The investigating team and Eichmann got back to the Kaunas ghetto by the end of the day. The captain made his report to Hirshson and waited for orders.

Eichmann was summoned to the Gestapo headquarters at 7 in the morning.

"Colonel, we received orders. You are to take the whole Gestapo and SS contingent from the ghetto to the Ninth Fort. Assemble all the personnel from the fort near the pits. You will read this to them."

The captain handed a printed page to Eichmann.

"After that you can return to your duties."

"Pay attention: the assembly has to be at ten in the morning tomorrow. Please be punctual and don't leave anybody behind either in the ghetto or at the fort."

Eichmann quickly read the text of the speech he was supposed to give: "I am glad you realize that none of what happened was intentional. We regret the death of your man, but it was just an accident. I am sure the Fuehrer will appreciate your restrain in this matter. I have a small objection, though. We can leave the ghetto to its own devices for a short time. The Lithuanian and Ukrainian guards will see to the population's safety and we have only a small contingent here anyway. The fort is another issue. We must leave some guards in place otherwise there will be chaos."

"Don't worry," the captain reassured him. "The cells are locked and we will make sure that everything is peaceful. It should take you no more that fifteen minutes to read the speech. After that everything goes back to normal – I am sure that the prisoners won't even know that the guards were away. What would you expect from sub humans?

"One more thing I need to mention. The Jews at the fort have to be released at once into the ghetto. Also notify Herr Himmler that when the Caliph ordered all the Jews transferred to him he meant all of them. No exceptions."

***

The next day close to five hundred people were gathered at the Ninth Fort pits. They stood at attention in neat rows prepared to listen to Adolph Eichmann. Eichmann was there. He looked at his watch. It was precisely 10 in the morning. Captain Ramadan waved to him from about a hundred yards away. The captain stood close to a corner of the perimeter wall and moved around the corner when Eichmann started his speech, leaving a laser designator attached to a pole discreetly stuck in the dirt at the corner. Ori was fifty yards along the wall when the explosions came. They didn't sound too bad – the tall, massive wall gave him ample protection. By the time he returned to his position at the corner of the wall it was all over. The combined napalm/explosive bombs left not one of the murderers alive. In fact there wasn't much left of them at all.

The captain ordered his soldiers to get the keys from the prison office and release the prisoners. He wasn't sure how long the inmates could survive in this environment, but this was the best he could do for them.

On the plane back the lieutenant wanted to know why they had to deceive the Germans: "Sir, why not execute them properly? Why lie to them?"

"Well, my friend, would you go quietly to your execution if you were armed and had a numerical advantage over your would be executioners? Besides, these Germans are mass murderers and deserve to be treated as such. They may wear uniforms but they're no soldiers."

"I am not sure all of them deserved to die," said the lieutenant. "I am sure that there were innocent clerks among this bunch."

"What do you mean 'innocent'? They may not have shot anybody, but they facilitated the murder. In any case, this is the chance you take by associating with murderers. Our justice, in this case at least, had to be somewhat crude. Hirshson told me that it had some effect. He got a call from Himmler of all people. The guy was very angry, but calmed down quickly when Hirshson told him that if he makes a fuss we will investigate some more and maybe find that he was behind this operation. In which case we will ask the Fuhrer to behead him."

Chapter 17

Jacob was recuperating from his injuries. The infected cuts were healing, aided by the antibiotics he received for ten days. He was weak and still unsteady on his feet but did his best to walk around the small infirmary. He visited the gym next door as often as he could. The other members of his team were in the infirmary as well.

Two weeks after his return from the mission to Lithuania, Jacob was ready to travel to Israel. While he had been away and recuperating, his sister had studied Hebrew and was now fairly fluent. His mother was less proficient but had made friends with some of the other women in the facility and was in the process of organizing a training program for them. She thought that studying Hebrew was essential to their future and wanted the other women to study as she did. The women's group also included his uncle Chaim's daughter and Chaim's wife. Since their Yiddish contained a fair amount of Hebrew it made learning the new language easier but also imbued it with a definite accent.

Chaim was reading up on Palestine and trying to figure out what kind of business he could setup when he arrived there. The brochures they got were a new publication. They presented the most pertinent information without mentioning the state of Israel or time travel.

When the day for their departure finally came, on September 10th, 1941, the family was surprised. They had expected a three or four day journey on a German or British ship. But the bus carrying Hirshson's extended family and several others stopped at a small terminal building nowhere near the sea. The real surprise came when, after having their ID's checked one last time, they came out on the other side. An enormous airplane was waiting for them. It carried the name "El AL" in both Hebrew and Latin letters.

Some of the new immigrants hesitated and some flat out refused to embark – they wanted the ship they expected. The prospect of flying terrified them. These were taken back and put on a ship. Most of the immigrants got on the plane without further comment, though Jacob wanted to know how come such a huge airplane existed without being famous all over the world. He wasn't the only one who was surprised and curious. They were promised an explanation after boarding the plane.

The Airbus A380 jet had been configured to carry more than 900 passengers. The seats were small and cramped together, but to these people it seemed the height of luxury. They didn't complain that no meal was served and were grateful for the water and juice the flight attendants gave them.

A short film informed them about the time displacement event and the strange fact of going to an independent Jewish state. Some of the passengers were skeptical and some wanted proof that wasn't forthcoming except in the form of the huge aircraft itself. After drinks were served, another film introduced the immigrants to some aspects of life in Israel.

The flight to Israel lasted only three hours – the Israeli jet did not have to follow set routes and made the best time possible. They were warned by the captain that they would see other aircraft marked with a Star of David and should not be alarmed – these were their armed escorts. The escort pilots waved to them – with the passengers waving enthusiastically back.

When they approached the Israeli coast the captain pointed out major features - the Tel-Aviv marina with its boats, the skyscrapers and other notable sights. The new immigrants paid little attention – they were overwhelmed by the size of the metropolis – it was many times larger than Vilnius as seen from mount Gedeminas, or any other town in the Baltic countries. Most were stunned by the experience.

After the plane had taxied and connected to the unloading sleeves of the terminal building everybody tried to get out at once. The captain had to ask several times to take it easy before the crowd calmed down. The passengers wanted out; they were eager to see the Promised Land. What they saw was the inside of a modern terminal building, unlike anything they had ever seen.

It was a fairly long walk to the passport control area. The crowd was separated into lines in front of the windows – everybody's ID was checked and compared to a computerized list.

"Your family is waiting at the exit from this hall. Go to marker number 10 - you will see it when you get through the sliding door," the young woman in uniform told Jacob. Most new arrivals were also told to meet family. There was a significant number whose relatives could not come or who had no surviving family members in Israel. They were directed to buses that took them directly to immigrant villages.

When the Hirshsons entered the main hall of the terminal they saw a tall, yellow pole topped with the number 10 written in large letters on a placard. There were a number of people waiting there, looking eagerly at the crowd of newcomers. A stocky man in his mid sixties, about 5'7" with a receding hairline and a shortly trimmed gray beard walked quickly towards them: "Welcome to Israel! I am Ze'ev." He shook hands with Jacob. The rest of the family was introduced as they walked to a nearby parking lot. The whole clan piled into a minibus and was driven to Ze'ev's home in Hertzlia Pituach, an affluent suburb about ten miles north of Tel-Aviv on the Mediterranean shore.

On the way, Ze'ev tried to clarify the family relationships. He explained to Jacob and the others that in his time-line Jacob was his father. They had already met Ze'ev's son: Colonel Ephraim Hirshson, commander of the Brindisi base. Ephraim was Jacob's grandson, named after Jacob's father.

"All this is giving me a headache," declared Sara, "but at least it explains why your Ephraim looks so much like my husband, may he rest in peace."

***

Ze'ev Hirshson was somewhat of an oddball. He had not followed the path most common for young men in Israel in the late 1960s. Instead of enlisting in the Army at the age of 18, as required by law, he chose to try to get into college before his compulsory service. It was partly due to a character defect: he never obeyed orders and was not happy with a situation where everyone could order him around – which is how he viewed the Army. There was a solution: It would not be easy to accomplish, but if he succeeded he would enter the Army as an officer. Anyone who passed a difficult week of psychological and leadership tests could qualify for officer training. This enabled them to apply to study particular specialties at an approved college, becoming a member of what was called the "Academic Reserve". The real problem was getting accepted: each year more than 2000 candidates competed for 400 slots in the program. He could of course enlist like everybody else and apply for officer training later but that would mean serving as an enlisted man for a long while. Completely unacceptable to Ze'ev.

His parents encouraged him to try, partly because they hoped that his studies would put him in a relatively safe position in the army and partly because of the prestige of graduating from the elite Academic Reserve program. They were pleased when he passed all the military tests and was accepted to study mechanical engineering at the Technion, Israel's most prestigious engineering and science university.

Things turned out a bit different than anticipated. Ze'ev was wounded early in his military career, before graduating from college. A shootout with terrorists had left him with an injured foot that should have led to his discharge. He resisted, unwilling to give up his coveted spot in the program. In the end he succeeded in staying in the service, thereby also preserving his place in college. Since he was unwilling to sign up for five years of professional army service in his chosen profession – again, the desire not to be told what to do – he ended up in a combat infantry unit, serving only the minimum time.

After the army, he was considered a hotshot at his first job - graduating from the Academic Reserve didn't harm his career prospects. Four years later he was running the company's Research and Development unit.

For the same reason he wanted to be an officer in the army, Ze'ev kept climbing the corporate ladder: the higher up you go the fewer people telling you what to do. By the time he was thirty he'd become a vice president for R&D of Consolidated Manufacturing, where he started his career.

He would have loved to be his own man, but Israeli industry of the 1970s and 1980s was dominated by relatively large corporations – such as Consolidated, with sales in excess of $80 million. Consulting engineers were rare, and usually were retirees from large companies. Not wanting to work outside his profession Ze'ev didn't have a choice and stayed with the company.

At one of the numerous seminars he attended in his career he was offered an opportunity to go to MIT for a couple of years to work on a PhD and, like the MIT professor that invited him said, "have some fun". Ze'ev decided to take a chance and go to America.

Six months after moving to Boston he met Linda. They were married before the end of the year. By the time Ze'ev finished his PhD, the couple were the happy parents of a boy, with another one on the way. Ze'ev set up a consulting company, which did very well. Five years later, the company he had worked for in Israel was in trouble and he and several friends managed a leveraged buyout. Ze'ev led the company, buying his friends out within ten years. Just before the Event he was expanding his company from its traditional business of steel and iron into advanced ceramics. He thought that the electronics and defense markets for these materials were going to expand and the company had a chance of becoming a leader – if it invested in research and was not afraid to tackle new technologies.

The Event changed little in his business perception, except making the metallurgical business more attractive – it wasn't a commodity anymore. The company's abilities were unmatched and being the only steel maker in Israel was a huge asset.

***

When they arrived at the house Ze'ev introduced everybody to his wife, Linda. It took a while to sort out how to address each other. Jacob looked like Ze'ev's father when Ze'ev was a little boy, but Ze'ev also remembered him when he was eighty. Calling this young man "Father" was strange, and he was not really Ze'ev's father, not in this reality. It was even stranger for Jacob. His mother saw the resemblance and, most of all, some of the mannerisms of her son in Ze'ev, and was not shy about pointing it out to everybody. But Jacob's instinct was *not* to call this older man "son". They finally settled on calling each other by their first names.

It took a long lunch with several glasses of wine in the spacious dining room for everybody to relax. There was a multitude of questions, asked mostly by the women who naturally took over the conversation.

Sara wanted to know everything about her grandson's family. Linda obliged: "We have five children. You met our eldest – Ephraim. He graduated from the Technion and Ze'ev had great hopes for him in the business, but he decided to stay in the Army. I don't really like the idea of my son being a soldier, but it's his life. He is also married and has a daughter. They have a house not far from Jerusalem. I visit his wife frequently while he is away – she is expecting their second child and I worry about her. Our second child is a daughter. She is a nurse, married, with two young boys. They live in Holon, not too far from here. The next one is also a daughter. She lives in Jerusalem and is a reporter for a newspaper there. The second youngest is a son. He lives in Beersheba and runs a plant that belongs to my husband's company. You will meet the youngest son soon, I hope."

Both Sara and Chaim's wife said in unison: "Jerusalem!?"

"Yes, we will go to see Jerusalem soon" Linda responded. "Probably we should go out and do some shopping first. You'll need light dresses for this climate. How about a shopping trip tomorrow?"

"Great!" Sheina was eager, as was her cousin Tzipora.

"Wait, wait." Sara was uncomfortable. "We have no money. How can we buy clothes?"

"You're family - Don't worry about it. I'll pay for now and you can teach me to cook. I've heard stories about your kishka and gefilte fish. So don't worry. We will go shopping and have lots of fun."

"So that's settled," Ze'ev said. "I have to be at the Ministry of Industry tomorrow. May I suggest that while the women go shopping with Linda, Benjamin, our youngest, can take you two men to get some new clothes. He's a fairly successful menswear designer. He'll take good care of you. Then we can all meet at the Sheraton for an early dinner at, say six?"

Linda said to Jacob and Chaim: "Benjamin knows clothing but don't pay any attention to his politics. He is a socialist, a lost soul."

On that note Ben joined the party. He looked nothing like his parents. He was tall and thin, with a big mop of dark hair, dressed in slacks and a silk shirt with a colorful kerchief around his neck.

After the introductions, he sat next to Sheina. "I wish my mother had volunteered me to take you out on the town tomorrow. A beautiful girl like you - and your cousin of course - would be much more fun than the two guys."

Linda heard that. "Benjamin, dear, stop flirting with your aunt. Our new family will all be out of bounds for you." Benjamin looked slightly offended, but didn't dare to contradict his mother – not many people did.

The family moved from the dining room to a veranda in back of the house giving a view of the beach. A path led to white sand only a hundred feet away.

Jacob wanted to know what happened in the reality from which his new family came. Ze'ev was the one to answer this question. He chose his words carefully but everyone was depressed anyway. It's not easy to hear that if not for a time accident you were destined to suffer and eventually be murdered.

Linda quickly switched the conversation to more pleasant subjects: life in Israel, life in Lithuania and families. They stayed until late discussing the future, which cheered everybody up.

By the time everyone was ready for bed it had been dark for a while and was fairly late. The house was big. It had been built by a foreign ambassador who needed to accommodate his large staff. There were three stories topped with a canopied observation deck - very pleasant in the humid summer. Below it, on the third floor, were several small bedrooms, a couple of bathrooms, and a large sitting room. The second floor held four more bedrooms, two connecting bathrooms, and a game room for the kids. The master suite, Ze'ev's office, the dining room, a library, family room, and kitchen were all on the ground floor. Two double garages plus utility and storage areas that doubled as a bomb shelter took up the basement.

The newly arrived relatives were taken to the third floor, which Linda had cleaned and furnished with fresh linen, toiletries, and flowers. "Feel at home," Linda told them. "You can stay here as long as you wish."

Despite being tired it took the newcomers a long time to fall asleep. They were shaken and surprised by the new reality, barely believing what had happened to them.

Chapter 18

Mizrahi sat in a comfortable armchair in the drawing room at Henry Wilson's house, having been requested to meet with the general. He was sipping the gin and tonic Wilson had offered after Mizrahi informed him that the Israeli government expected its representatives to avoid grape products, such as wine or brandy, unless they were certified Kosher. He was also smoking his pipe. Mizrahi gave up smoking several years ago – it was becoming impossible to smoke in public places and Ruhama was not happy with his pipe anyway. In 1941 England a pipe was acceptable and there was some reasonable tobacco to be had. He would probably have to stop when his wife came over, but in the meantime he happily slipped back into his habit. It also had the advantage of gaining time in a conversation. Just fiddle with the pipe while you think.

"Mr. Mizrahi, the Cabinet decided earlier today to cede sovereignty over the Sinai Peninsula to your government. An agreement with the Egyptians to make it all legal is being finalized as we speak. They will cede it to us and we to you. So the secret of your existence will not be compromised." Wilson sipped his tea with a grimace.

"This is good news, General. I will inform my government as soon as possible."

Wilson leaned forward. "Mr. Mizrahi, we have known each other for a while now. You state your position clearly and do not play devious games. I would like to ask you a question and, please, do not take offense. Why is your government insisting on sovereignty over Kuwait? It's causing Mr. Churchill no end of problems. If we understood your goal, maybe we could find a compromise."

"Believe me, General, everyone will benefit from this arrangement."

"What if the Prime Minister can't pull it off? You've heard Holbrook's speeches. If he succeeds in taking control..." General Wilson trailed off. "What would happen if we refuse?"

Mizrahi put down his drink, emptied the ashes from his pipe and started reloading it, playing for time. He was slightly surprised, but only slightly. Churchill's claims of danger to his rule, especially from Lord Holbrook, were grossly exaggerated, though he did have his difficulties and possibly was really worried. But the real problem, in the ambassador's judgment, was the Prime Minister's reluctance to give up even a tiny piece of the Empire. He worried, correctly as it turned out, that the British people would forget his great leadership and only remember that he surrendered the Empire. Churchill was also likely annoyed by a request he didn't understand.

"Well," Mizrahi said finally, "we are a patient people. Nothing bad will happen immediately. My government's current perception of the British Empire as a basically benign and friendly power is built on your current cooperation. If we can't come to an agreement, we will assume that your government is hostile to us, or rather that Britain learned nothing from past mistakes and will keep doing the same things it did in our timeline. How this will influence future relations is an open question."

"You see, the Prime Minister has some difficulty justifying such a high price for your assistance." General Wilson was about to add something, but stopped.

"If you want to negotiate," Mizrahi smiled a somewhat predatory smile, "don't forget that I am from the Middle East and haggling is in my blood."

"I will take that into account," Wilson smiled too. "Maybe I should bring some help to these meetings – it seems that I will need it."

Once back in his office, Mizrahi picked up the satellite phone and called the Foreign Minister.

"Avigdor, do you know what time it is here?"

"Yes I do, but this is important. We will have the formal agreement on Sinai in a couple of days. Kuwait is another matter. Churchill explores the possibility of giving us a flat denial. I threatened him with a hostile stance. As of now, we will continue to negotiate. You need to consider what to do next. I suggest waiting several months, maybe until January of 1942. When the Germans advance close enough to Cairo, Churchill is likely to re-evaluate our relationship. I also suggest that we tell Churchill why we want Kuwait. I think that a big part of the problem is his resentment of a demand without an explanation."

"I will present this to Amos tomorrow morning. Send me a written report and a recording of your conversation with Wilson."

Chapter 19

The meeting was tumultuous and disorganized. Heisenberg had called them together after inspecting the Wolfsburg site and becoming convinced that some kind on nuclear technology was involved in the city's destruction. He wanted to convene this assembly of physicists now, at the end of July, 1941, so as not to lose initiative. He knew that if he waited longer, his rivals in the Army would likely seize control of the available funds.

The auditorium at the Kaiser Wilhelm Institute in Berlin held close to sixty of Germany's leading physicist all trying to speak at the same time. Finally Heisenberg yelled: "Quiet please. Let Dr. von Weizsacker finish."

Carl Friedrich von Weizsacker repeated the statement that had caused the uproar in the first place: "According to our measurements at the Wolfsburg site, it is still radioactive. I think that it is possible that the bomb that exploded there was enhanced, containing uranium or another radioactive substance."

"Dr. Weizsacker is forgetting his own patent application from the beginning of the year. It seems to me that this was, undoubtedly, an atomic explosion." Dr. Kurt Diebner sat down after delivering his remark.

"We have proof enough to state that a bomb based on nuclear fission is possible. I suggest that with this knowledge we should start working on our own bomb immediately," interjected Dr. Walther Gerlach, a member of Diebner's team.

The assembled scientists seemed to be in agreement.

"The Kaiser Wilhelm Institute will approach the authorities to obtain funding and we will proceed as quickly as possible. I believe, like all of you, that uranium was involved in the explosion, but we need more research to verify whether it was the primary explosive or just an incidental ingredient." Heisenberg signaled the end of discussions and of the meeting.

Diebner and his team were not happy. They were afraid of losing their independence. As it was, Heisenberg had his own team at the Institute in Berlin, funded through the Post Office of all things, while Diebner was working independently under the Army in the town of Gottow. He decided to act quickly, meeting with Dr. Paul Harteck, the Army's chief physicist, to discuss the matter.

"I don't trust Heisenberg," Diebner said. "The man was never devoted to the cause of the Fatherland. Now he is saying that more research is necessary into the possibility of an atomic bomb. To me it is cut and dry. We should be working on duplicating this bomb, not investigating if the Wolfsburg explosion was indeed atomic."

"I am not as sure as you are," Harteck responded. "In my opinion we should let Heisenberg do what he wants. He is a very gifted physicist and has an excellent team. There is a great advantage to keeping our present structure. Two teams are better than one, and I am sure that given the necessary resources you can develop the bomb as easily as Heisenberg can, assuming, of course, that such a bomb is possible."

***

Gad Yaari was busy, but not as busy as he had been during the last several months. Israel was at peace, sort of, and in no immediate danger of being attacked by its neighbors. A great war raging in Europe was about to spread to the rest of the world, but Yaari felt somehow isolated from it.

The illusion was shattered on a Sunday morning. It was August 3, 1941 - the Fast of Tisha B'Av –the fast in memory of the destruction of the temples and various disasters that had befallen the Jews. It had been deferred this year. The ninth of the Hebrew month of Av fell on a Saturday and according to Jewish law its observance was deferred until the next day.

Yaari's secretary ushered in General Zvi Kaplan, the head of Military Intelligence, who greeted his friend and superior with a casual "How are things going?"

"Ah, this is exactly what I was going to ask you. What was so urgent that you needed to see me on an hour's notice?"

"I think that something is happening in Germany that may put us, and the world, in serious danger." Kaplan paused to remove a sheaf of papers from his briefcase. "Look at these satellite images taken yesterday." He pointed at two photographs, "This is a research facility in Gottow, south of Berlin and southeast of Potsdam. In the last couple of days the traffic there has increased significantly and it looks like the facility is being expanded."

"And the significance of this?" Yaari inquired.

"This is where one of the German nuclear weapon teams is based. According to our communications intercepts the German Army is putting in a large base next door to house guards for this facility. They had almost none only a week ago. According to the bugs we placed on their telephone system, the Kaiser Wilhelm Institute is suddenly getting lots of resources for the Heisenberg team."

"Ah," Yaari smiled ruefully. "The bulb went on in my head, finally. This is a serious problem. We have to alert the government." He picked up his phone. "Liat, I need to speak to the head of the Mossad. After you get him make an urgent appointment with the Prime Minister."

***

"What's up, General?" asked the head of the Mossad.

"Let me ask you a question: Did you hear anything about unusual German nuclear activity lately?"

There was a brief silence on the other side of the line: "Funny you should ask. I was about to call Zvi Kaplan when your call came in. To answer your question in one word, yes. I think that we need to brief the Prime Minister."

Yaari looked at his watch. "If he is not busy, I'll try to make the appointment for fourteen hundred hours. That okay for you?"

***

"All of you had a short briefing about why we are here. I don't want to waste time, so we will start with the historians. The question is: what do we know about the German nuclear effort during WWII?" Amos Nir sat back and waited for one of the three historians to say something.

The three researchers invited to the meeting looked at each other. The oldest decided to take the plunge first: "The historical record is contradictory. We have some evidence that the Nazis were far from developing a bomb. It relies mainly on secret recordings of conversations between German scientists held after the war at Farm Hall, England. From these recordings it is clear that they were very surprised by the Hiroshima bomb. Also, that Heisenberg wrongly calculated the amount of radioactive material necessary for a bomb. He corrected himself and arrived at the correct number only several days later. I find this contradictory."

"In my opinion they were much closer to a bomb than previously thought," one of the other historians cut in. "We have documents that were released recently by the Russians that clearly show the Germans had a good understanding of the physics involved. Heisenberg's collaborator, von Weizsacker, even tried to patent a bomb design in the beginning of 1941."

"Yes, then there is the Thüringia experiment," the third historian added.

"What was that?" Amos inquired.

"In March of 1945 German scientists tested a nuclear device in Thüringia, in eastern Germany. Several hundred concentration camp inmates and prisoners of war were killed. Most historians and physicists don't think it was a full-fledged nuclear explosion. More likely it was a bomb that fizzled, but it still was a bomb."

"I assume that the names of the scientists involved in the project are known to us?" asked Yaari.

"They had a number of projects. This probably slowed them down. They also lacked resources. But the answer to your question is yes. We have the names."

"The bomb project seems to be getting all the resources it needs now," remarked Zvi Kaplan. "Is it possible that our bombs on Wolfsschanze and Wolfsburg did it?"

"In our history the German Army was interested only in projects that would produce weapons in the immediate future, so they did not devote much of their scarce industrial resources to nuclear projects. This was exacerbated by Heisenberg's opinion that it would take many years to produce a bomb. These two factors combined to starve the projects.

"We changed their assumptions. They have apparently concluded that the two weapons used by the Caliph were nuclear in nature. This gives them an incentive to put resources into the project. On the other hand, our help to the British anti-submarine warfare paradoxically freed lots of industrial abilities. In our history Germany spent significant resources to build submarines, at least until 1943.They've given up on this almost completely. That leaves them with reserve capacity to use to develop an atomic bomb." The historian seemed to be done.

"Any questions?" asked Amos.

"I don't know if historians are qualified, but I'll ask a question anyway," said the head of the Mossad. "How can we stop the Nazi nuclear effort, without tipping them off to what is going on?"

The oldest historian responded. "The only thing I can advise you to do is to make the German leadership stop the project of its own volition. Shouldn't be too difficult with their command structure – It's hierarchical but has several competing authorities. That creates all sorts of opportunities. That's about all I can tell you off the top of my head. We'll do more research and I'm sure can find an opening."

***

Moshe Cohen arrived in the Brindisi compound expecting to go home. He was only slightly disappointed that he could not. It was not the first time in his career that orders changed overnight and he knew it would not be the last.

Colonel Hirshson invited Moshe to his office. After they were both equipped with the mandatory cup of coffee, he extended a sealed envelope. "This arrived for you yesterday. I also got one, with a short notice that your team will be here in a day or two and to give you all the assistance you require, including transportation to Venice. I have no idea what this is all about and prefer not to know. Good luck with whatever it is you are going to do."

In his little apartment in one of the new buildings Moshe finally opened the envelope. It contained new orders and pages upon pages of information he had to memorize. According to the orders he was to take a small group of Mossad operatives and enter Germany within the week to stop their nuclear projects. The papers had information on the key personnel involved in these projects, along with fairly detailed instructions. They laid out the plan he was to follow but left room for initiative. He had the freedom to improvise.

While waiting for his team to arrive, Moshe collected further information and made plans. He contacted the Mossad's main office a number of times asking for documents and more information. He felt lucky that the communication satellite was operational. It gave him both a secure phone line to the Mossad and access to their databases. He also could do some research on the internet – at least the part of it that traveled back in time with Israel. Since a large part of the web had been cached on Israeli servers it was now available to Moshe. When the members of his group arrived with equipment and documents, Moshe was ready.

***

Breaking into the main building of the Gottow Physics Facility was easy, especially for an experienced burglar. The alarm system was antiquated by 21st century standards and was bypassed in a couple of minutes. The three men, dressed in Wehrmacht uniforms, spent less than twenty seconds in front of the locked door – that was how long it took to bump the lock. No one noticed anything unusual – not really surprising considering the dark night and blackout. The guards outside the perimeter probably saw them enter the complex, but they were just three soldiers and attracted no special attention.

Once they were inside, one of the privates put a long lab coat over his uniform and proceeded up a staircase. The burglar followed closely, with the officer following the other two at a distance. They walked quickly and confidently to an office on the second floor. This wing held only offices and a few night lights. The other wing containing several labs was fully lit and busy.

In the office, the burglar found a wall safe hidden behind a picture and went to work on it. The captain and the private in the lab coat stood in the corridor, seemingly deep in conversation, but in fact looking for intruders.

The safe was easy pickings, only slightly more difficult than the office door lock. The burglar inserted a sheaf of typed and handwritten pages into a pile of documents in the safe and relocked it.

They were back on the street in less than twenty minutes with the alarm system reset and no one the wiser.

Their next objective was a residential apartment building in Gottow. This is where several of the physicists working at the facility lived. Some, like Kurt Diebner, the director of the facility, and his close assistant, Walter Gerlach, kept their homes in Berlin, using their apartments in Gottow only intermittently.

The team entered the apartment building easily, careful not to attract attention on the deserted street – someone casually looking out a window could ruin the whole operation by noticing something out of place. The almost total darkness of the blacked out town helped, as did the addition to their uniforms of military police breast plates – they could pass for a legitimate patrol. After entering the building they walked up to the fourth floor; using the elevator would have saved time, but the noise could attract unwelcome attention or be later recalled as unusual by one of the tenants. After examining the lock of apartment 4D the burglar took out a cut-down key and quickly bumped the lock. The noise made by his rubber mallet on the key was barely audible and opened the door in an instant, leaving no telltale scratch marks that normal tools could leave, especially if used in a hurry in almost full darkness.

The burglar entered the apartment, the officer and the private stayed in the small foyer just beyond the entry doors. The burglar carefully examined the space for good concealment places – not too obvious, but not impossible to find either. Finally he settled on the desk in what was obviously a study. He took out the top right side drawer and using small office pins attached a piece of paper to the underside of the desk. He replaced the drawer and the team was gone.

***

The head of the Potsdamer Gestapo was annoyed by this haughty intruder in his office but there wasn't much he could do about it. You dismissed a full SS colonel at your own peril. Karl Maria von Tretow was not just an SS officer but also an arrogant Junker.

"Heinrich," the colonel addressed the Gestapo man, "you have not been doing your work very well. I always thought the Gestapo was filled with lazy bureaucrats and it seems that you may be a good example of one."

"Karl," the Gestapo man tried to counter the colonel's insulting familiarity, "I think that this is a very bad joke. Why are you here?"

The colonel sat down, without invitation, on one of the chairs in front of Heinrich's desk: "You will call me Colonel von Tretow, or just Colonel, Heinrich."

The head of the Gestapo office in Potsdam was not a very senior member of the organization and visibly wilted at this haughty reprimand. He realized, somewhat belatedly, that if von Tretow decided to shoot him on the spot he would likely get away with it.

"Excuse me, Colonel, I meant no disrespect. I still want to know why you are here and why you accuse me of not doing my job."

"Ah, my friend, I did not accuse you of not doing your job. Just of being somewhat slack about it. A case in point: are you familiar with currency transfer regulations?"

"Yes, of course."

"But not everyone with responsibility is enforcing them as diligently as they should. And you, my friend, are one of those."

"Why are you accusing me? I am a patriot and do my job very well." The Gestapo man knew what good work he was doing. And he really didn't know much about von Tretow. In fact he knew nothing about him, except that he was here, wore a uniform and was extremely arrogant. "But before we go on, I would like to see proof that you are who you say you are"

"Finally you are starting to think," the colonel chided the Gestapo man. "This is a question you should have asked fifteen minutes ago. Here are my papers. Please check them out carefully. You don't want to repeat your mistake; you may not have another chance. Remember to always check everybody's papers – don't assume anything."

The Gestapo man looked carefully through the documents. They identified SS Colonel Karl Maria von Tretow as deputy head of the Office of Racial Purity - an extremely powerful outfit, given great latitude. Not even high-ranking party members were safe from them.

"I'll have to telephone your office in Berlin, just to make sure."

"Good, good. You are beginning to redeem yourself in my eyes," responded the colonel.

The Berlin office confirmed that Colonel von Tretow was indeed one of their own but refused to disclose his whereabouts. The Gestapo chief decided that it was likely they didn't know where he was – these people were secretive even among themselves. And von Tretow was senior enough, and apparently well connected enough, to do his own thing.

"So, Colonel, how may I help you?"

"Heinrich, it is I who want to help you. We are conducting an investigation in Potsdam and surrounding towns, like Gottow. I need you to notify me immediately if anything unusual comes to your attention. I am relying on your professional acuity, so don't disappoint me. This is a matter of paramount importance to the Fatherland. Please pay special attention to large financial transactions and let me know if anything interesting happens." On that note, he marched out of the office.

The Gestapo chief sat motionless, thinking for a couple of minutes. After deciding what to do he alerted his network of informers and settled for a long wait.

***

Moshe Cohen chose the identity of Karl Maria von Tretow very carefully. The colonel was a real person, who indeed worked for the Office of Racial Purity. Moshe could pass for the colonel, if properly made up and if the examination wasn't too close. The ID he displayed in Potsdam was a duplicate of Tretow's actual document, preserved in the Israeli archives. They even used Tretow's photograph. Tretow was an ideal choice: According to reliable historical records, on August 25, 1941 - the day Moshe met with the Gestapo Chief of Potsdam, Tretow was on his way to Dresden, where he had family.

The colonel had stopped at a small inn in Luckau for refreshments. He always stopped there – the place served excellent weizen beer that Tretow liked and their food was very good. He had left his car with the inn's filling station attendant to fill it up before continuing on towards Dresden.

Tretow liked to drive fast, and his Mercedes coupe Kompressor delivered a lot of speed. In the middle of a sharp turn he heard a loud pop and felt the car swerve into the turn, threatening to flip. He tried to regain control but the steering did not respond – there was an oil slick on the road. He stepped on the brakes and the pedal went down to the floor with no effect. The Mercedes slammed into a tree. The resulting fire eradicated all evidence of the small radio-controlled charges attached to the front left wheel of the Mercedes and to the hydraulic line leading to the same wheel.

A third charge under the fuel tank ensured a fire. The stop at the inn proved fatal for the colonel. No one could prove that he hadn't stopped in Potsdam on his way.

After Moshe and his two pretend body guards were done fixing Tretow's car and causing his accident they went to Berlin. From his previous visits, many years in the future, Moshe knew Berlin quite well and the city looked familiar even in this time period. Armed with historical information and maps, the three Mossad agents drove into the Alexanderplatz district. Despite the Nazis' efforts to clean up this notorious red light part of Berlin, it was as rundown and seedy as ever. They found the hotel they were looking for on Keibelstrasse and rented a room. These places were decrepit, but, if properly handled and slipped a couple marks, the clerk wouldn't immediately report the new guests to the police, as required by law. Moshe knew that the team would be able to stay for only a day or two, but that should be enough for their purposes.

His only concern was their car: a member of the team bought it from a dealer in Dresden. The dealership was chosen for its size, which made it likely that the buyer would not be clearly remembered. The late model Mercedes was registered to Johan Bock – the name on the Mossad agent's papers, and also the name of a Dresden resident. According to German records, the real Bock, a party member since 1931, was supposed to be killed in the battle of Smolensk several weeks later. The mission's planners knew that it was more than likely that the purchase and registration of the car and its disappearance at a later stage wouldn't attract attention. What concerned Moshe was the car's appearance: while it was suitable for Colonel von Tretow it stood out in the Alexanderplatz neighborhood. They did their best to muddy it and give it the appearance of neglect. The license plates they had used in Potsdam, and that carried a group of numbers and letters assigned to the SS in Berlin, were replaced with one identifying it as an unmarked vehicle of the Berlin KRIPO – Kriminalpolizei, the Police criminal investigation unit. Criminals in the know, who were the ones likely to be interested in stealing it, would not be stupid enough to touch an undercover police vehicle.

The next day after dark the three drove to the Karl Wilhelm Institute on Boltzmannstrasse in Berlin. It was on the other side of the city from their lodgings, but Moshe figured that if they use the car with falsified KRIPO plates, they should be able to move around Berlin safely – just blend into the not too thick night traffic. It took them about fifteen minutes to break into the building through a back door, go to the second floor, and deposit thin packs of typed and handwritten pages in two safes.

The next day, the team left Berlin by train. They dumped the car into a lake next to the Wannsee district of Berlin, with no license plates attached.

Car theft was not unknown and would raise no particular suspicions. They used a pair of pocket sheet metal shears to cut the false plates into small strips and distributed them among Berlin's numerous canals. The team had a set of documents identifying them as Wehrmacht soldiers returning to their units in Slovenia. They changed into civilian clothing at Lubliana and, with a set of Italian documents, traveled to Trieste where they boarded a fishing boat waiting to take them back to the Brindisi base.

***

Several days after the Mossad team left Germany a sum of a 150,000 Reich marks was transferred from a Swiss bank to the account of Dr. Walter Gerlach at the Gottow branch of the Dresdner Bank. If it wasn't for the Gestapo being on the lookout for something unusual, the transfer might not have been noticed. From time to time Dr. Gerlach received large amounts of money as consulting fees. Though 150,000 was twice as much as he had ever received, it wouldn't have attracted attention. As it happened, the bank routinely reported the foreign currency transaction to the Gestapo and the report ended up on the Potsdam chief's desk the next day.

The chief of the Gestapo in Potsdam followed von Tretow's instructions: he called the office in Berlin and asked to speak to the colonel. After proper identification he was transferred to an assistant. This was the first time the Gestapo man heard that von Tretow had died in a car accident just hours after their encounter. He told the assistant that he called for personal reasons and hung up.

The chief of the Gestapo in Potsdam was ambitious and decided that the colonel's demise might have created a great opportunity.

His next move was to ask the International section of the Gestapo to investigate the bank in Switzerland and find out who owned the account from which the money originated. In the meantime there was no time to lose: if Gerlach became aware of the investigation he might flee or destroy evidence. He decided to act carefully, hopefully without endangering his career. Not being a fool, the chief of the Potsdam office realized that arresting Gerlach for receiving money from Switzerland might be risky – if he was deemed important enough and if there was a legitimate reason for the money transfer. This would mean no promotion or maybe even a demotion for the chief.

When the Potsdam Gestapo team arrived at the facility in Gottow they were, at first, refused entry. The Wehrmacht was guarding the complex and allowed only people with special passes inside. It took several calls to Berlin and the angry intervention of Mueller, the head of the Gestapo, to get them inside. Mueller intervened just on the principle that the Wehrmacht should not tell the Gestapo what to do and where not to go.

Heinrich decided to start by searching Gerlach's office. He might find something useful and if he didn't, no harm would be done to his career.

At first Walter Gerlach refused to open his safe: "The contents are secret and highly sensitive Army research. I can open it only on the orders of the director of the Institute, Dr. Kurt Diebner."

Diebner agreed to the search – he, at least, was a loyal Nazi. He did order that nothing from the safe leave the building. They had to read the documents in Gerlach's office.

After almost three hours the Gestapo technical expert examining the documents called his chief: "Sir, I have found a couple of very strange documents. I need you to come here and read them." He refused to say anything else, which the Gestapo chief knew was a sign of the information being explosive. He was not disappointed. Apparently Dr. Gerlach was in contact with a foreign intelligence service, probably British, and was acting on their behalf. The documents indicated that the whole pretense of making uranium weapons was a British idea to force the Reich to waste precious resources. Gerlach wrote, in his own hand, that the uranium weapon idea was far-fetched and, if at all possible, would result in a weapon after many years and many millions of marks in research. Other documents showed that Diebner, though a supporter of the Party, had agreed to go along with this fraud in exchange for a significant amount of money deposited in a Swiss bank account.

The information was so important that Heinrich, the Potsdam Gestapo chief, called Berlin to make an urgent appointment with the boss himself. While he was on his way to meet the head of the Gestapo, his team searched Diebner's safe and the Gottow apartments of both scientists. Diebner's apartment yielded a piece of paper that was almost overlooked in a superficial search – it was pinned above the top drawer under his desk. The only thing on it was a number and several capital letters.

This information was relayed to the chief via telephone while he was waiting in Gestapo Chief Mueller's office. It did not take the Gestapo foreign department very long to identify a small bank in Geneva – the initials of its name were on the paper found in Diebner's desk. The bank admitted to having a numbered account, but would not give out any details without the appropriate code.

It took another two days for Mueller to get permission to arrest the two physicists and to perform a full scale search of the Gottow facility. The Army objected, but presented with incriminating documents, the Army chief physicist had to agree that closure of the facility and a full search and investigation were a reasonable precaution.

Documents found in Gerlach's safe indicated that the analysis of the Wolfsburg incident was falsified by Dr. Weizsacker of the Kaiser Wilhelm Institute who had made the presentation that claimed Wolfsburg was destroyed by an atomic device.

Further searches at the Institute uncovered an interesting piece of evidence: a report written by Weizsacker stating that the huge explosion over Wolfsburg had been caused by conventional chemical explosives. He speculated that the explosives, all five or six thousand tons of them, were teleported to a spot about a thousand feet above the Volkswagen plant and then activated. In support of the theory the report cited clear evidence of nitrate residue all over the area. It also pointed out that tiny remnants of steel brackets, covered with a residue of heavy elements, strongly suggesting the use of a quantum teleportation device.

The evidence mentioned in the report was indeed to be found at both the Wolfsburg and Wolfsschanze sites, having been recently spread at night by a low-flying silent and undetected stealth jet.

The experts within the Gestapo speculated that Weizsacker had not published his original conclusions but decided instead to claim that the explosion was atomic because he held a patent for an atomic bomb. Even though the patent was shared with the Institute, if the Reich did manage to make the device a reality, the scientist would make a huge profit.

By the end of September, 1941, the Uranium project was over. Hitler told his underlings that his instinct concerning this "Jewish" science was correct. There was nothing to it - the Reich should waste no more resources pursuing it. Teleportation, on the other hand, was a different issue. Heisenberg, an innocent victim of the plot and an expert in quantum physics, was appointed to head the project and instructed "to stop all work on atomic weapons and dedicate all available resources to the development of teleportation." There were not that many resources to dedicate, as the Fuehrer did not trust theoretical scientists and saw no reason to spend significant resources on developments that would not be useful in the ongoing war. Neither Heisenberg nor any of the staff, who knew better, dared to point out that this order was based on pure fantasy. The other physicists did not try to correct the terrible mistake either. No one wanted to put their neck on the block and be associated with proven spies and enemies of the Reich.

***

On September 29, 1941 Amos Nir attended a combined Military Intelligence and Mossad briefing.

"I think that we are in good shape," Zvi Kaplan, the Chief of Military Intelligence, said. "It seems from our intercepts that the Nazis dismantled their nuclear effort and have no plans to proceed."

"We have done a very thorough job," added the head of the Mossad. "A number of their leading scientists disappeared in the Gestapo labyrinth and others, like the chief Army scientist who had been a staunch proponent of nuclear development, are silent on this issue. I think we have nothing to worry about. Except if they develop teleportation. That would be interesting.

"This operation was fairly easy. We have a serious technological advantage, which helps, but the main advantage we have is knowing who is who and what is about to happen. That advantage will be gone soon, since we are changing history quite vigorously. Next time we will have to do much more planning and it will be a lot more dangerous."

Chapter 20

Colonel Hirshson presided over a weekly meeting to assess the progress of Operation Moses. He started the meeting formally: "Today is Thursday, September 30, 1941. I hope that this meeting will not be very long – tomorrow is Yom Kippur. It starts tonight at 5:54 pm. I would like to finish this meeting by 3 p.m. to give everyone time to prepare. We will start, as usual, with area reports. Ukraine first."

The young woman responsible for organizing the Ukrainian exodus shuffled a pile of papers: "The evacuation is slow. The devastation from the recent fighting is slowing us down. Trains are running in the western Ukraine, but in the eastern part, including Kiev, the Germans are still working on restoring the tracks. We estimate that about a third of the Ukrainian Jews have already arrived and the rest are eager to come. Obviously living under Soviet rule for several decades has made these people eager to get out. The famine of 1932-1933 left them scared and the Communist party purges of 1937 undermined their trust in the party, any trust they may have had left, that is. Our only difficulty right now is moving people to the railways. The urban Jewish population is mostly gone. We have to use local resources – horse drawn carts mostly. The Germans assigned a number of trucks to this project, which helps. I think that we will be done by January, or sooner if the trains start moving again."

"The Baltic countries, Belarus and Western Russia next."

"We are done with about two thirds of Lithuania and Belarus. Our main limitation is the same as in the Ukraine, the availability of transportation. We're still finding isolated pockets of anti-Zionists, mostly hardcore Communists, that are not willing to leave. My estimate is that once everyone else is gone, those people will reconsider. In any case, this is a very small portion of the population.

"Latvia and Estonia present a different problem. A large part of the Jewish community there is assimilated and, especially in Latvia, very proud of their German heritage. So far we've only been successful convincing the religiously observant and the active Zionists to evacuate. The rest are waiting. I think they'll leave before too long. The locals are extremely unfriendly and the Germans can't restrain themselves very well in this environment. We've rescued a third as of last Friday. It's slowed down to a trickle now, but there were not that many Jews there to begin with. At the current rate they will all be moved by December, I think.

"Thank you. Romania and Hungary, please."

A middle-aged, tired-looking, bookish man nodded. "It is slow-going, especially in Hungary. Like Latvia, a large percentage of Jews there are completely assimilated. Since the Horty regime stopped oppressing them as requested by the Germans, we are having trouble persuading the two thirds of the population who aren't religious or Zionist to move. We were lucky to find a descendant of a famous rabbi from the area – he was of real help. The rest are refusing to leave their comfortable homes. I don't see how we can force them.

"We tried persuasion; we even showed them a documentary of what happened in German-occupied Poland before our intervention. They were impressed but still decided against trying to persuade their community to leave. The Polish experience doesn't apply to civilized Hungary was their point of view. Documentaries of transports from Hungary to Auschwitz didn't have much impact either since the Germans are not demanding Jewish blood."

No one had any idea how to get the Hungarian Jews to move short of asking the fascist Horty regime to forcibly deport them, so the discussion moved on. Hirshson made a note to discuss this issue with Yaari and possibly ask Horty to deport the Hungarian Jews.

"It is different in Romania. There are several famous rabbinical schools there with well-respected leaders. As you remember, you gave us approval to transport ultra-Orthodox rabbis from Israel directly to Romania. That did it. The heads of the yeshivas were convinced and persuaded the observant community to follow. The rest are still hesitating, but I think that they will leave soon: they're already feeling isolated and scared by the Antonescu regime. We have three German passenger ships taking people directly to Israel. The emigration should be completed by mid-November."

"The Balkans, please."

"Bosnia and Croatia are done. I guess that the combination of local pro-Nazi regimes, Muslim SS, and Croat murderers were enough to get our people moving. These were small communities anyway. Serbian Jews are also coming due to the partisan war there and the German repressions. Bulgarian Jews are not moving at all. The Bulgarian government shielded them from Nazi persecution even before we intervened and is definitely friendly now. The population feels safe and isn't interested in Israel.

"We had better luck with the Greek community; mostly because of German repressions there. Most of them have already left. Same goes for Montenegro and Albania."

"Poland?"

A tall bald man smiled sadly: "We have no problem persuading the Polish Jews to leave: in western Poland they've been living under German occupation since 1939. They are so eager to leave that we had to establish priorities with the community councils. The Germans simply don't have enough trains going to Italy to accommodate everyone who wants to leave. We started with Krakow – it is, as you know, the seat of the German Governor General for Poland who was irritated by all the Jews, so we took them out of there as soon as we could. I can report that as of last Friday both Krakow and the Warsaw ghetto have been completely evacuated. Lodz is three quarters done. We'll start moving people from small towns as soon as we're done with the larger ghettos. My estimate is that about three quarters of the Polish Jews have been evacuated."

"Good. The low countries and Denmark are next."

"We have a somewhat difficult situation," the woman responsible for the region said. "In our history, the Germans did not act against the Danish Jews - there's no imminent danger we can point to, so all 7000 of them are reluctant to move. On the other hand, the Dutch and Belgian communities were not given a choice – the local police rounded them up and deported them, to what amounts to concentration camps.

"As of today we have trains full of immigrants running from Holland and Belgium. Nothing from Denmark. At the current rate the Dutch and Belgian Jews will be out of danger in a week."

"I think that the Danish Jews are safe where they are, at least for the time being," Hirshson said. "France and Italy are next."

"We probably would have had a serious problem in France, with so much of the community assimilated, but the Germans and the Vichy government did the job for us. A large part of France has been occupied by the Nazis for over a year. They've been deporting Jews to Poland. The remaining community needs little persuasion to come to us. The Vichy part of France is not much different. The French police have been enthusiastically finding and deporting Jews. When we arrived, the community, or what remained of it, was mostly eager to go. I think that about 80% of the Jews that were still remaining in France are safe now.

"Italy is a different story. Our presence here has an advantage; we can, and did, send a large number of emissaries to every community. Including some places in southern Italy that have only a few Jewish families. On the other hand, the fascists, despite a lot of anti-Semitic talk, haven't actually done much against the Jews. The population is generally friendly and they don't feel that they are in danger. Personally I think they are right, unless the Germans occupy Italy. We tried to be discreet in our dealings with this community – let them know that they can escape to safety but not make a big deal of it. We don't want the Catholic Church to discover what we're really doing and try to stop us. The Vatican was upset when the Croatian Jews left the death camps and actively tried to stop them from getting onto our boats in Dubrovnik. Who knows how the Church will react once they figure out who we really are."

Colonel Hirshson nodded in agreement: "I think you are right. I also think that I skipped Czechoslovakia."

"Yes, I was eagerly waiting to report and thought you didn't think it important enough," smiled the girl that was responsible for the area. "We have two distinctive areas. In the Czech part, we have a steady stream of immigrants. The Germans have been in the country for three years and started oppressing the Jews as soon as they got there. By the time we appeared, a large portion of the community had already been deported to either Theresienstadt or Poland. The rest relaxed when we came on the scene and the oppression eased. But we will have everybody out before January 1942.

"The picture is different in Slovakia. Their ruler, the Catholic priest Father Tiso, paid the Nazis to collect and deport the Slovakian Jews. By the time we arrived, some had been deported to Polish concentration camps but most of the community - about 50,000 - still remained. They needed no urging to go. As soon as we persuaded the leadership that we are for real, everybody left. We are done with Slovakia."

"Good. Finally, Germany and Austria."

"There is not much left for us to do in either country. There are still some Jews there but most left as soon as we offered them the opportunity. The remainder are either in hiding and very difficult to find, or are so sure that they are 'Germans of the Mosaic persuasion' and so patriotic that there is no way to make them leave. Our operation in both countries is winding down."

Colonel Hirshson looked at his watch. It was time to get ready for the Day of Atonement. "The chance of the Nazis discovering our bluff increases daily. Thanks to all of you we are doing fairly well. I wish you all an easy fast and to be inscribed for a good year in the book of life." Ephraim Hirshson wasn't observant, but Jewish culture was deeply ingrained and the traditional blessing came naturally.

***

Three days later colonel Hirshson's telephone blinked its red light: "Hirshson here."

"Hi Ephraim. This is Gad."

"Oh, hi chief. My red General Staff phone was blinking, but I didn't expect you on the line. How are you?"

"Fine, thank you. I hear that you are doing well too."

"Yes. We are a bit crowded here, but this is much better than the alternative."

"Ephraim, you think that your deputy can run the base for a week or so?"

"I am sure that the Major can run it until it's closed. He is a good officer and manager."

"Good, good. I think that you deserve a short vacation. Your wife is complaining she hasn't seen you for five months. Hop on the next plane and come home. The orders are being delivered to the base teletype as we speak. Don't forget to visit the General Staff the day after tomorrow. Call my secretary for details."

Hirshson knew his superiors well enough to realize it wasn't his wife's loneliness they were concerned about. But at least he'd get to see the family before finding out why he was wanted.

Chapter 21

The Minister for Industry and Infrastructure looked at his watch. It was time to start the meeting.

"I welcome all of you. Please be seated. You were invited to this meeting for an update on the current situation and to improve our communications. First an update." The Minister gestured to a young man waiting in the wings, "My assistant will do the honors."

"The situation for today, September 29, 1941, is as follows: Our total industrial output is up by about 40%. Both exports and imports of industrial products are zero. Inflation is currently at less than one fifth of one percent…" The assistant went on for a while with statistical information.

Ze'ev Hirshson interrupted. "We all know the statistics. Maybe not to the second decimal point, but we know them. Can we go on to the next item on the agenda?" A murmur of agreement went through the crowd of thirty industry leaders.

"Fine" the Minister said. "I only wanted you to hear the statistics one more time because they point to a problem: we need a drastic change in our industrial makeup or we face a crisis. Before the Event we imported most of our industrial needs. This included everything from heavy earth-moving machinery to silverware. We paid for it mostly with earnings from the export of high tech and pharmaceuticals, plus a considerable income from tourism. All that is impossible now and will stay so until we establish diplomatic and trade relations with other countries."

"It's the government's decision that made trade impossible," a tall heavyset man said. "If you open the borders we can do business again as usual."

"No, we can't," the Minister responded. "The world is at war and many years behind us in technology and science. We could not buy a D12 Caterpillar bulldozer no matter how much we paid – They'll start making them in the U.S. in about seventy years, assuming we haven't messed everything up. We also can't buy a Toyota or a digital clock. If we open our borders now we will be, with a little advertising, able to export anything we want, but we would not be able to buy one modern item. Some of the machinery available now may be useful and we will be able to buy raw materials.

"This is the reason you are here. We need to achieve industrial independence as soon as possible. The government wants to support you in this effort, if you are ready to cooperate."

"What kind of support?"

"We'll place orders with the companies that agree to participate in the program. The orders will be for items you're capable of making in small quantities or close to being able to make. If necessary, we'll advance you the capital you need to fill the orders. That will be the first phase. In the second phase, or maybe concurrently – depending on your response – we'll fund, again, through loans, development of manufacturing capabilities. For example: we can produce fair numbers of computers but have only a tiny capacity to make specialty hard drives. We would like to be able to make computers for export when the time comes as well as in numbers sufficient for internal consumption. We also need to make mass storage - hard drives or something else. There's no industrial base for that at all."

"Sounds good to me," the president of a large consumer electronics and appliance manufacturer announced. "How do we go about it?"

"I suggest that you split into small groups and discuss the matters pertaining to your industries in greater detail." The Minister paused for a moment and then went on. "You may have noticed that most of the people present here today represent large and medium sized firms. I would like to clarify that you are not the only ones that will be eligible for government loans. We are holding meetings with as many businesses as we can manage, mostly locally, and are doing our best to induce them to participate. The government will publish a simple set of criteria that will allow businesses to apply for loans, technical assistance or other help. We want to eliminate what is called 'crony capitalism' and will do our best to prevent public funds going to businesses that have little chance of repaying them."

****

Ze'ev Hirshson found Consolidated Manufacturing on the list and went to the assigned office. He was surprised to find himself alone with a Ministry employee. Apparently no other plant had similar interests.

"Dr. Hirshson, a pleasure to see you." The man seemed awfully young to Ze'ev. Everyone under fifty looked too youthful.

"I hope it will be my pleasure to meet with you," Ze'ev responded somewhat grumpily. He didn't trust the government to do anything good – in his opinion they only collected taxes and then wasted them on strange projects and bureaucrats. "Let's finish this quickly. I have a dinner reservation at six in Tel-Aviv with my new family. Can't be late for that."

"I won't impose on your time too much. Here's a list of things we would like to order from Consolidated. It's divided into three categories. The first is comprised of steel castings slightly beyond the upper weight limit of what you can make now – these are mainly turbine housings for the new hydroelectric plant and some other parts related to it. The second is a large quantity of medium-sized parts, mostly engine blocks and other automotive parts, and the third is machining of these castings.

"I would appreciate if you have your staff go over the list and tell us what you need to be able to make them in the quantities we want to order. If you are not interested, we will have to find somebody else, though I admit that this will be a serious hassle for us with your company the only steel foundry in Israel."

Ze'ev looked quickly through the list: "I think we can handle this. On the other hand, it seems strange to me that the Ministry chose to ignore our capability in industrial ceramics. We have been supplying the army with ceramic armor for a number of years now and most of the integrated circuit manufacturers are using our materials as a base for their chips."

"Dr. Hirshson, we didn't ignore anything. You will undoubtedly be approached by electronics firms with requests for large quantities of those materials. The Ministry of Defense has its own program. We're trying to interfere as little as possible with either the free market or other government entities. The chip manufacturers will be able to arrange financing to support your expansion, if necessary."

"You are somewhat inconsistent. Why buy engine blocks directly from us but not ceramics? You could let whoever is assembling automobiles buy the engines."

"We are hopeful that very soon there will be at least one car factory here, and we are preparing the infrastructure to enable their operation. This is not necessary with ceramics consumers as the infrastructure exists already."

Ze'ev thought for a moment: "I have no idea who you have in mind to make cars in Israel, but my company would certainly like to be on the short list. Let me know about that as soon as possible. Our response to the rest of the list may well depend on it. Also, I'm not sure I want the government to loan me any money. With a firm order I can probably arrange private financing at interest rates more favorable than yours. We'll look into this as well."

He got out of the office and went to look for his car. He panicked for a moment when he didn't see it in the spot he remembered. "I'm getting senile" was the thought that passed through his head. Then he remembered, after a couple of seconds, that his wife took his SUV to go shopping with the family and that he had driven her Jaguar to the Ministry in Jerusalem. It was parked right where he remembered leaving it.

***

"Hi, David, this is Ze'ev."

"Oh, hi, Ze'ev. How are things going?"

"Good, though somewhat confusing. I'd like you and the family to come to our house for Shabbat dinner. It'll be a big crowd. My relatives from Vilnius are here. Benjamin will be here, as well as Shoshanna and husband."

David hesitated. "We have a transportation problem."

"No, no. Don't worry about that. Shoshanna will pick you up – They live practically around the corner from you. They'll also take you back, unless you want to stay the night."

"In that case it'll be our pleasure. Thanks for the invitation."

"Good. They'll pick you up at about 4 pm on Friday."

After he hung up, Ze'ev thought for a minute and made another call, to his son Chaim in Beersheba. Chaim was busy but promised to come for the next Shabbat dinner – when more of the family would have arrived.

"Listen, son, you won't be able to postpone meeting your relatives until next Friday," Ze'ev joked. "I need you at the main office on Sunday. I called a general management meeting to discuss the Ministry's plan. I would appreciate your input."

Chaim knew his father well – this was not an invitation. His father's polite request was often an order and not complying would have consequences. In Ze'ev's experience as a company commander in the Army and a veteran manager, people were more willing to accept orders if they were worded politely.

"I'll be there."

"After we're done, we'll go home to meet the new family. See you Friday."

***

On Friday night with the table set and everyone assembled, the women lit Shabbat candles. Not all of them participated in the traditional ceremony. Shoshanna and young Aunt Sheina excused themselves. The rest lit two candles apiece. It was the first time in Ze'ev's memory that such a light shone from the table – a sure sign of the size of his new family.

He still had difficulty absorbing the situation, but it did not seem as absurd as it had only a couple of days ago. He even managed the introductions with reasonable decorum, he thought.

Ze'ev said in Yiddish. "I would like you to meet my daughter Shoshanna, who teaches nursing, and her husband Noam, an architect, also, my cousin David from America, his wife Rachel, and their two boys." He then repeated the same in Hebrew, just to make sure everybody understood.

The conversation went on in several languages at once. Apparently David Rothstein's Hebrew was the worst and he did his best to speak Yiddish. To his own surprise he was fairly fluent in it.

Sara shook hands with everyone enthusiastically, and then asked David: "Are you from our side of the family?"

David was confused so Rachel answered for him: "You remember your cousin Bertha? The one that married the crazy Zionist Eliezer Rothstein in 1937 and emigrated with him to Palestine immediately after the wedding?"

"Yes. But we heard nothing from them since."

"That's because after the Arab attacks in 1939 they moved to America, to Boston – Eliezer's cousin lived there at the time and sponsored them. David is their youngest. They tried writing to you a number of times, but Lithuania was by then under Soviet control and they never received a response."

Jacob was seated next to Noam and after a while inquired about Noam's job. "I'm a partner in a large architectural firm. We're working on the plans for several new cities."

"Must be a really big firm."

"We have over a hundred employees and are hiring as fast as we can find qualified people."

"A hundred people to design several cities and, you said earlier, railroads and such? That doesn't sound like very many."

"Most of the design these days is done on computers - You have seen a couple at the house here, right? We also subcontract some of the detail work to experts – the rail projects, for example, we gave to a small firm that specializes in such stuff."

"We saw computers here, but I don't know how they work or what they can do."

"Would you like to come to our Tel-Aviv office on Sunday? I can show you how we use them."

"I'd love to," Jacob responded enthusiastically. "I studied civil engineering in Vilnius. I'd love to see how things are done here."

"Do you know anything about surveying?"

"That was one of the subjects we studied. I can't claim any great expertise or experience but I am familiar with the techniques used before the war."

"I might have a job for you. I'll pick you up on Sunday at, say, nine in the morning and we'll see what we can do."

Ze'ev, who had been listening quietly to the exchange, decided to intervene: "Jacob, don't be in a hurry to accept the first job offered. I know my son-in-law. He's a good officer and treats everyone as if they were his soldiers."

"And who does that remind me of, Captain Ze'ev Hirshson, Sir!?" Linda said from the other side of the table, smiling at her husband.

"Right, right, just joking," Ze'ev smiled back at his wife. "What I was saying, Jacob, is that you'll have many opportunities. The country is experiencing the greatest labor shortage in memory, especially of engineers. You might even want to consider starting your own business."

"I would like to eventually, but I've a lot to learn first. It may be a good idea to work for somebody else for a while."

"Hear, hear," Noam agreed. "If you plan to work in the construction business, for instance, you have to be licensed and know the laws. We can take care of that. There's nothing to prevent you from going out on your own later."

"Besides going into business I have this idea of enlisting in the Army. I was hoping that somebody could explain to me the options." Jacob was a bit unsure. "The experience we went through at the Ninth Fort was very educational. I have the feeling that nothing is as important as participating in the defense of our people."

"Wait, wait," both Noam and Ze'ev said together.

Ze'ev continued, "Don't take what I am going to say the wrong way, but by participating in our economy you will be making the state stronger. If this is the angle you are looking for, consider where you can do the most good.

"You are almost 21, which is a bit old for a new recruit. They'll probably take you but I doubt that you will have a chance to do much of anything. If you go into the construction business, where you have some training already, your contribution will be much more significant."

Jacob just shrugged, unconvinced.

"Jacob, stop talking crazy," Sara interjected. "Your father went to fight in the Great War and look what he got for his trouble: gas poisoning and early death. I don't want to lose you."

"Mama, papa didn't go voluntarily. The czar's army took him and they treated their soldiers badly. If I enlist it will be in our own army to defend our own people. Don't worry, I'll be careful. Ze'ev, is there a chance for me to discuss this with Ephraim?"

"Probably. I'll have to find out how to contact him. We exchange email but I don't know how to call him – he never gave me a phone number for the base and his cell phone doesn't work in Brindisi."

"Wait a minute," Jacob interrupted. "What is email and what is a cell phone?"

"It will take you a couple of weeks to become familiar with all this. The short answer is that email is a message you send from your computer. Cell phones, or more correctly cellular phones, are phones that connect wirelessly."

"There's so much to learn." Jacob sighed.

***

Ze'ev spent Sunday in his office, pulling up data on the company's reserves and trying to work out a reasonable plan for expansion. It felt good to be at the center of activity; the offices were busy with people coming and going. Sunday was usually the busiest day of the week, with weekly coordination meetings for the different plants.

This Sunday meeting surprised him. Ze'ev always remembered his bad experience with a company president that feared the young and energetic. This memory made him do his best to support them. He was sure that they viewed him as "the Old Man" but he didn't feel old. His creative juices were flowing and he was ready for action.

The surprise came from his V.P. for Research and Development. "I don't completely agree with Ze'ev's idea of starting to manufacture fiberglass cars as soon as possible. It's true that we have some corporate experience with making plastic body cars, but that was many years ago and a failure. Without government subsidies we wouldn't be able to sell even one of those monstrosities. If we jump into this immediately, our product will be as bad - or worse - than the originals."

"And I suppose that you have an alternative?" Ze'ev was not exactly pleased with this unexpected objection but not very annoyed either. The young man was showing independence and, since he was smart, might have a solution to the problem, which had bothered Ze'ev as well.

"Well, I have an approach. How much of a solution it is depends on the definition of the problem. If we define the problem as 'We want to be a major player in the automotive market,' then I have an idea."

"Good. Let's hear it."

"Several background remarks first. It's good for us to make auto engines. We have most of the machinery and know-how to make small quantities right now. The only thing we're missing is aluminum casting capability, which, as you know, is necessary to make modern engines and transmissions.

"There are several small plants that have the ability we need but not the size, and we don't want to rely on outside suppliers anyway. This leads to another issue: Israel has enough steel scrap to last us a decade, but very little aluminum scrap. We need to develop smelting ability and develop external sources for bauxite ore. This will enable us to make aluminum from scratch and not rely on scrap.

"I'm not against marketing automobiles immediately as long as we make them different. How about electric cars? Our ceramics and composites division has been supplying computer battery makers with the necessary parts for years. It wouldn't take much for us to go into the business ourselves. I'm sure that an electric car with a range of several hundred miles and reasonable speed would sell well. It'll give us a foothold in the market and allow future development of more sophisticated models."

"An interesting idea," Chaim Hirshson nodded, "but I'm a bit worried about the magnitude of all this development. We have limited human resources, which we have to divide between all these projects; assuming of course that capital isn't going to be a problem. I can't see us developing both an electric car and a conventional one. We'll have to decide very soon which approach is best for us as a corporation."

"I agree with Chaim in principle," Ze'ev smiled at the R&D manager, "but he's not taking into account the new immigrants. There are very gifted engineers and scientist in that crowd. True, they are not up to date on the latest technology, but in some cases it doesn't matter. For example, we need to double our steelmaking capacity within the next few months. We can't buy another arc furnace from Europe but we can duplicate the ones we already have. A couple of mechanical engineers working with mechanics and welders can do it fairly quickly and efficiently with 1941 technology. Same goes for the electrical parts the arc furnace needs. It's also important to budget for and prepare to educate the newcomers. They'll make an important contribution to our company if we treat them right. Which reminds me: we have a number of very good automotive engineers coming and I'd like to hire all of them." Ze'ev looked at the Human Resources manager: "Most of these people used to work for Citroen and speak mostly French. I'll appreciate you being ready for them. They'll need to learn Hebrew and English as fast as possible."

The meeting went on for a couple of hours with spirited and open discussion unrestricted by rank or position. In the end, the R&D manager was charged with developing a detailed plan of action. The Human Resources manager was told to develop a list of personnel needed and start hiring by the end of the week. A new office of Education Coordinator was created with an eye to bringing new immigrant engineers and scientists up to speed on technology the company would need quickly.

Ze'ev used some of his connections at the Technion to arrange special courses for immigrants hired by Consolidated. The company would pay for them and the Technion was more than happy to provide some of its graduate students with additional income.

Chapter 22

Ephraim Hirshson's plane landed at Ben-Gurion airport in the early afternoon. He had spent most of the flight sleeping in an aisle seat of the first row and was first off the plane. Rank had its privileges.

After going through the passport, or, rather ID control, he ran to the exit door. The hall for arriving passengers was crowded with new immigrants and families. It took him a minute to see his wife, who was frantically waving to him. After hugging and kissing he finally had a good look at her: "I see that the baby is growing, and you look lovely as always."

"You flatterer! I love you too."

It was a relatively short and uneventful drive to their home in Mevaseret Zion just west of Jerusalem. For the first time in months Hirshson could relax, but something was bothering him. He didn't know why he had been called home so suddenly. He questioned his wife about her health, but she was fine and told him that the rest of the family was in good shape as well. "You have very nice ancestors, you know. We spent a day sightseeing in Jerusalem, including a couple of places tourists rarely see. We stopped at that nice restaurant off Jaffa Street you like so much. Your great-grandmother and Aunt Sheina confuse me a bit. They don't seem to be overly observant; they don't dress very modestly and sometimes eat dairy right after meat, but both prayed for almost an hour at the Western Wall."

"My great-grandfather and grandfather were militant atheists. My father, you may have noticed, is also an atheist, though not of the militant variety. I think that the poor women were oppressed at home and not allowed to practice, which resulted in this somewhat mixed up behavior."

"Wishful thinking my dear husband. Neither Sara nor Sheina are the oppressed types. It's more likely that Sara ruled the household and her husband did what she wanted him to do. You think you're much different from your great-grandfather?"

"Yes, yes. I know that women rule. No more arguments about this. Did you meet my grandfather and great-great-uncle too?"

"Yes, we had a big family dinner at your parent's house only a couple of days ago. Chaim is a nice man but seems to be troubled – I think that he is worried about making a living and is too proud to accept help from relatives he doesn't really know. Your grandfather confuses me no end. I knew him when he was in his eighties and now he is back with us, only he is twenty-one. I try to think of him not as your grandfather but just as a close relative - That works most of the time."

"Yes, that confused me too, probably even more than you. After all I knew him for most of my life and the young man resembles the grandfather I knew not only physically but in his mannerisms as well."

"Oh, by the way, Jacob mentioned that he would like to get your advice about enlisting. He is hesitating but wants to participate in the common defense, as he put it."

After he was sure that it was not a family emergency that brought him home, Ephraim decided to be patient and enjoy himself. He was scheduled to meet with his bosses in two days. They'd tell him what was going on.

****

"Please wait here," Major Liat Cohen instructed Ephraim Hirshson. "Gad will be with you in a few minutes."

Five minutes later Liat emerged from her office. She was smiling as she led him through her office and to a door on the right. Ephraim knew the other door led to Gad Yaari's office but he had never been through it. They entered a large conference room. Four generals were at the table: Gad Yaari plus the commanders of the northern, central, and southern commands. Everybody rose as Yaari announced: "Colonel Ephraim Hirshson, you have been promoted to the rank of Brigadier General. Congratulations."

His old rank insignia were replaced with new. After much backslapping and a toast with wine, the ceremony was over.

"Now," Yaari smiled at the new general, "there are a couple of things we need to discuss."

The chief of general staff relaxed behind his desk: "Please call in the others," he instructed his secretary. General Zvi Kaplan, chief of military intelligence, and the head of the Mossad came in. A couple of seconds later the general commanding the Air force and the Navy commander joined them.

Yaari opened the discussion. "Gentlemen, so far we've had an advantage. This has changed now. The history of this time-line deviated from the one we know, mostly because of our actions to prevent the Holocaust.

"The government concluded there was a serious danger of Moscow and/or Leningrad falling to the Nazis, which could lead to the collapse of the Soviet Union. A decision was made to intervene. We painted a couple of our old Stratocruisers, the ones we bought from Boeing in the fifties, in British colors and made them sort of look like Lancaster bombers – at least from a great distance. They bombed refineries and fuel depots in Ploesti, Romania. There was a danger of Germany recognizing that these were not what they seemed, but fortunately no one got close enough to do that – the escort jets shot down a couple of Messerschmitts that tried. There may be repercussion though, as the planes flew above the flack, which Lancasters can't do. We'll deal with that later if need be.

"The operation was a success in that Germany lost its major source of fuel for at least three weeks. We figured that would slow them down enough to give the Russians a chance. To make sure they did slow down, we also bombed a synthetic fuel plant in the Ruhr. The damage to the plant was repaired in a couple of days, but we destroyed a month's worth of production reserves as well."

Zvi Kaplan hung a large map of the Ukraine and eastern USSR on the wall. "In the history we knew, the Germans surrounded five Soviet armies near Kiev. This happened on September 16, 1941, when Guderian's Panzer Group 2 and von Kleist's Panzer Group 1 met east of Kiev, completing the circle.

"This time, both Guderian and Kleist are moving much slower. On September 16 they were still more than fifty kilometers apart. Soviet troops, retreating from Kiev, attacked Kleist's panzers and slowed them even more. Our satellite images show that neither Guderian nor Kleist maneuver as much as they did in our history and consequently are suffering more losses. Because of lack of fuel they are spending much longer just sitting there waiting for supplies. They eventually completed the encirclement of Kiev, but only on October 2.

"The net result of this small difference is that instead of taking about 650,000 prisoners, along with two thousand tanks and almost a thousand pieces of artillery, the Germans only captured about 200,000 prisoners and maybe five hundred tanks and about the same number of artillery pieces.

"This being October 4, we still don't know what the Soviets will do with their 'extra' troops and materiel. One thing is certain: history has changed in a major way."

The head of the Mossad picked up the reporting. "We are getting information from Germany, some of which is coming through Zvi's intercepts, that indicate Hitler still thinks that Kiev was a major victory - which objectively it was, just not as big as it could have been. He congratulated all involved, and, most significantly, promised his armor commanders to increase fuel supplies for operation Typhoon, that is, the attack on Moscow. Our conclusion is that the Soviet's good luck was the result of a simple fuel shortage. Another important piece of information is that Typhoon has been scheduled for October 7 – in our history it began on September 30.

"The winter war will go badly for the Germans, much worse than in our time, unless Stalin does something exceedingly stupid. Our analysts estimate that if it goes badly enough, the Germans will ask the Caliph to help them. It's also likely that we'll see less German assistance with trucks or shipping – they'll try to squeeze the last drop of fuel for their army."

"It's my assumption that our government will refuse help to the Germans," Yaari said. "This brings me to the main subject of this meeting – the Brindisi base. Sometime in February or early March of next year we'll probably discover that the Nazis are not friendly to the Caliph anymore. We expect that this will happen either because the Caliph will refuse their request for assistance, or, more likely, because they'll realize who we really are – the government is considering establishing formal relations with several countries fairly soon. The Germans will stop cooperating with our rescue efforts. We have to get everybody out of Europe by the end of the year."

"I don't think we can do that," Hirshson interjected. "There are communities that won't move."

"Are they in real danger, or, rather, will they be in real danger when the Germans become hostile?" Yaari asked.

"Difficult to predict," the Mossad man responded, "but we probably can intimidate the Axis regimes directly, without nuking the Germans again. It's either taking this chance or using force - German force - to evacuate them."

"Fine. I will report to the government and let them decide.

"Now the next issue." Yaari hung a map of southern Europe on the wall: "What do we do if, after realizing that we are not friendly, the Nazis decide to attack our base?"

"Why would they? It makes no sense," the Air Force commander asked.

"As one who has had direct contact with them, I can tell you that they are definitely not rational," Hirshson pointed out.

"I agree," Yaari said. "We need to prepare a defense. And don't tell me that the Air Force can do it all by itself. Don't underestimate the Germans. Ephraim, get your staff to prepare a plan. Everybody here will assist. Think of this base as a beachhead for the future invasion of Europe by the Allies – whoever they may be at the time."

***

Amos Nir was in conference with the head of the Mossad when the Foreign Minister arrived: "Come in," he greeted the Minister. "Our meeting got more complicated than I expected and your input will be helpful.

"We were discussing how to prevent Hitler from declaring war on the U.S. in December. We came up with several ideas, but none of them is guaranteed."

"We have a number of options," the head of the Mossad said. "The Mufti is still running around Europe making sure that every single Jew is moved to Brindisi – We could have him try to convince Hitler that it would be folly to declare war on the U.S. Or we had the idea of giving Hitler's astrologist a sudden revelation of what is going to happen a couple of days before the Japanese attack Pearl Harbor. After his prediction comes true, he should have no trouble persuading Hitler that a declaration of war would result in a catastrophic loss for Germany. The last suggestion we discussed was sending an American businessman with good ties to the Nazis and known as their supporter - someone like Henry Ford or IBM's Thomas Watson - to convince them that the U.S. wouldn't attack Germany if Germany doesn't declare war. I'm not saying that all these ideas are doable, but we need to decide which approach is most effective."

"I don't think any of those ideas would work," the Foreign Minister declared. "It's futile to try convincing Hitler, and I've said so in the Cabinet meeting. Hitler's decision to declare war on the U.S is inexplicable. Germany gained nothing from it and lost a lot, allowing Roosevelt to get actively involved in the war in Europe. The Japanese have certainly not asked for German involvement or help. Historians and psychologist have speculated for years why he did this crazy thing. My approach is simple: the man is crazy, therefore unpredictable and uncontrollable. Nothing we can do will persuade him. I think that the full Cabinet has to discuss this again, with input from our resident psychiatrist and the Mossad." He looked at the Prime Minister: "In the meantime I have news we have to discuss."

Amos addressed his advisors: "Okay, thank you for your input. I guess we'll see you at the next Cabinet meeting."

When they were alone the Foreign Minister again expressed his opposition to interference with American involvement in Europe. He presented the common wisdom position: if the U.S. doesn't get involved, there will be a real danger of the Soviets crushing Germany and dominating all of Europe, not just its eastern half. They had a similar conversation in the Cabinet meeting, with the Foreign Minister remaining in the minority. Most of the cabinet members accepted the Prime Minister's opinion that it would be a good thing to prevent U.S. involvement in Europe. After all, it was Roosevelt that agreed to give Stalin, whom he trusted for inexplicable reasons, all of Eastern Europe.

Amos tried to persuade him that Soviet dominance would be unlikely. In the end he presented his plan, which he hadn't yet disclosed to anyone. After a heated discussion the Foreign Minister agreed that, with some modifications, it was a good plan.

Next they discussed the Kuwait situation. Amos wanted to pressure the British government immediately while the Foreign Minister accepted Mizrahi's position that they should wait. They briefly discussed the issue and Amos agreed that it was probably a good idea to wait a bit.

The next issue on the agenda was somewhat of a surprise for the Foreign Minister. The Minister for Internal Security joined them, as well as the head of the General Security Service.

"Nathan," the Prime Minister asked, "what is your opinion of the Peace Now demonstrations?"

"I think they are stupid, but I always thought they were. They think that if we cancel the decision to execute murderers when a new terror act is perpetrated the murderers will just go home? For some reason these idiots always blame us for everything. It is always the 'poor, oppressed' Palestinians."

"I am glad that you agree with me on this, but we have a larger problem here. The last demonstration at Rabin square in Tel-Aviv had more than thirty thousand participants, and the number of their supporters is growing. Now the Arab parties and the leftist peaceniks in the Knesset are organizing for even larger demonstrations.

The Foreign Minister nodded: "I've even gotten a couple of telephone calls from the Russian and American ambassadors. Since they are, by our own definition, private persons, they may decide to support this movement. I don't like it at all."

Amos Nir looked at his colleagues. "We may have a surprise for these guys." He nodded to the Security Services man.

"As you know, we have good sources in the Palestinian organizations," the head of the GSS stated. "One of these alerted us to unusual activity by the Palestinian Authority a while ago. We pinned a micro transmitter on Muhammad al Husseini, the Hamas guy from Jenin, when he was on his way to meet with the chairman of the Palestinian authority. This is what we recorded…" He started a small tape recorder and played back the conversation between Muhammad and Dr. Mazen coordinating the operation to contact the Mufti. Everybody in the room, except for the Foreign Minister, had enough Arabic to understand the gist of the conversation. The Foreign Minister waited for a translation.

"About a month later, there was a meeting of all the Palestinian leaders in Mazen's office. They swept the office for bugs but didn't think of long distance laser eavesdropping."

"What is that?" the Foreign Minister asked.

"Oh, it's a simple device – You point a laser beam at a surface that vibrates when a sound is made, like a window pane, and, with proper calibration, can hear everything said in the room.

"But this wasn't the only means we used. One of the participants carried a bug in his clothing." He played back a recording of the meeting.

"After everybody left," The GSS man continued, "Mazen made several telephone calls."

Amos Nir took over at this point: "I think that if we disclose the whole thing to the public, we can stop the protests for good."

"I wish it was so simple," the head of the GSS smiled a sad smile. "The liberals, or rather the Marxists, are a religious lot. They never change their minds no matter what, and they never let facts confuse them. They also don't care if the Palestinians are the ones that initiate terror attacks."

"We might not be able to sway the true believers, but the great majority of those who come to these demonstrations are just people who want peace and think that if they wish strongly enough it will actually happen. If they abandon the movement there will not be enough support for the rest do anything."

***

The large conference room was noisy, filled to capacity with business leaders and some of their staff.

"Ladies and Gentlemen, please take your places. We have a lot to discuss and little time." The Foreign Minister waited for the conversations to stop. "You were invited here because your companies were all exporters before the Event and some have experience in areas we are interested in. The Cabinet made a decision that will impact on your business activities.

"The government has decided that certain products may be exported and sold outside of Israel. The conditions will be the same as they used to be for defense items before the Event. For those who don't know: the export of every item will have to be approved by the Ministry of Defense and the Ministry of Trade and Industry. In departure from pre-Event practice, all foreign deals and contacts will be managed by government-owned corporations set up abroad. For example: if a company wants to export shoes to Timbuktu, the Ministry of Trade sets up a trading company in Timbuktu and all exports go through that company. Each exporter will have a separate government-owned company in the destination country. Smaller exporters will share a trading company. The ownership of these corporations will be transferred to you after the state of emergency is over. We are setting this up to insure that future information doesn't leak out, at least until after we are done with the Germans, and possibly, the Soviets.

"We also want to set up several industries locally. These industries will need equipment we don't have and can't make fast enough. The government will purchase the necessary equipment abroad and sell it to you. Any questions?"

Ze'ev Hirshson was the first. "I'm the president of Consolidated Manufacturing. We need raw materials that we used to buy from Europe before the Event. I assume that you will help us to set up a procurement operation in Britain and Africa for these materials. Is that correct?"

"Not entirely," the Minister responded. "You give us a list of what you need and, if you have it, information on where to find it, and we buy it for you. You will be able to attach a representative to our missions. At this time only the government will have access to the outside world. One piece of advice: before you try to buy something abroad, check if it's already available locally and if it isn't, can it be made here. We have to become self-sufficient in a hurry."

"Does that mean that the government will set the prices for all imports?"

"Not really," the Minister responded. "We will start by charging you the lowest price in shekels you used to pay before the Event. As exchange rates get clarified, we'll modify the prices, after a consultation with your companies. We hope to be out of this business fairly quickly – as soon as diplomatic relations are established with the rest of the world."

"You mentioned the auto industry," Ze'ev asked. "Is there a change in the government's policies as described three weeks ago?"

"No change. We expect some entrepreneurship from the captains of our industry, and this time around there will be no subsidies to make lousy cars here. Just think of the possibilities: our population has almost doubled and there are no cars being imported. If you manage to make reasonably modern cars at a reasonable price..." The Minister smiled. "And after the war is over you will own the world market, at least until the Chinese catch up."

"So we still get loans on the terms that were offered in the original plan?"

"The short answer is 'Yes'. The slightly longer answer is that the government will not loan money to companies that obviously have no clue what they are doing or that won't have the means to repay the loans in the future."

After the meeting was over the Minister asked the CEO of Teva to join him in his office.

"Abraham, we need you to be the first," the Minister told the executive. "You have several drugs that will sell like crazy and are also impossible to reverse engineer with 1941 technology."

"Good," Abraham Hasson responded. "I have production capacity about eight times larger than local consumption. We must export to survive. Where and when do we start?"

***

Avigdor Mizrahi had been busy. He had moved his staff from the house near Downing Street to a leased mansion on Hanover Square. There was an option to buy, which might become important if Israel decided to use this house for its permanent embassy. Mizrahi found a real estate agent at the synagogue he attended from time to time in Golders Green. Beth Hamedrash was a small and relatively new congregation, established in 1934. Most of its members were refugees from Germany; Mizrahi was just one more foreigner among them. Being a Palestinian was a bit unusual, but the community was diversified enough and new enough not to look too closely into his business – especially since he discouraged inquiries.

He explained to the agent, a London native, that he needed a large house with a private garden, separated from its neighbors and in the center of London to be used as a combined office and residence. The agent asked what he was going to do there – just friendly interest from a fellow Jew. Mizrahi presented his cover story: He was a businessman from Palestine, importing and exporting goods; his business was doing well and he needed both an office and a place to live.

When he saw the house for the first time in early August he rejected it. It looked awful – Most of the windows were broken and part of the roof was missing. No doubt there was extensive damage to the interior as well. In his judgment repairs would take too long and the house was probably too big. It took more than a week of looking at alternatives for Mizrahi to take a second look at the house on Hanover Square.

Closer inspection revealed two wings. The northern wing, facing Hanover Square and Princess Street, had taken a direct hit from a German bomb and was wrecked. The blast had also done significant damage to the southern wing facing Hanover Square and Hanover Street, but the basic structure was still sound. Mizrahi decided there were advantages to taking over a damaged, empty house. The price was low which fit his image as a businessman, even if cost was not really a major concern since the British Government provided a line of credit. The whole structure, when restored, would be big enough to house the embassy of a major power with an enclosed courtyard that could provide parking for a future fleet of official vehicles. Under the guise of repairs, modern communications and security equipment could easily be installed.

The remodeling would have taken forever without support from Churchill's office. With it, the basic structure was repaired by the end of September, with work left for Mizrahi's Israeli crew. His staff was now up to eleven, including a security expert as well as communications and computer engineers. They installed networking equipment, satellite antennas, surveillance cameras and intrusion alarms, none of which were visible from the public areas of the building.

On Thursday, October 9, 1941, the Israelis moved into the building.

On Monday Mizrahi received a telephone call from the Foreign Office inviting him to meet with the Foreign Secretary, Anthony Eden. Instead of accepting the invitation, Mizrahi asked to speak to Eden.

"Sir, I can't connect you," the woman stammered. "The Secretary of State is not available. I suggest that you come tomorrow at 11:00 am and discuss the matter with him then."

"Please tell the Secretary that he is invited to my new office. We just inaugurated it and I would be honored to see him here tomorrow at 11:00. I take it he does not have any other engagements at that time."

"Sir, I will give him your message." She sounded indignant.

An hour later Mizrahi's phone rang again. "Mr. Mizrahi," Eden sounded like he was about to lecture him on something, "what is it with inaugurations and you inviting me?"

"Mr. Secretary, we just moved into our new offices and I would be honored if you came here. It is only fitting that our first guest be the British Secretary of State for Foreign Affairs. It is also much better for security. At this point in time it may look somewhat unusual for a humble Palestinian to be visiting you."

Eden thought for a moment and accepted the invitation.

The next day, at 11:00 a.m. sharp, a black Bentley stopped in front of the embassy. Security cameras identified Anthony Eden in the back seat and the gate swung open.

Their conversation took place in a small reception room. It was brightly lit by full spectrum lights - cheerful, despite the overcast October sky. Eden accepted a glass of Champagne and was introduced to the unofficial embassy's First Secretary as well as the Military Attaché.

After brief pleasantries Eden went straight to the point. "Gentlemen, the British government has decided, as a gesture of generosity and friendship, to settle the issue of the Crown Protectorate of Kuwait. I suggest that we leave the details to our subordinates."

"Mr. Eden, I tend to take care of most of the details myself. I suggest that we settle them now and leave the drafting of legal documents to our subordinates."

Eden considered whether or not to be offended and decided not to be. "As you wish, Mr. Mizrahi. Kuwait is our protectorate. Has been since the last war. So we need the agreement of the ruling sheikh before we can transfer the protectorate to you. This will take some diplomacy and, like everything in the Middle East, time."

"But Britain has explicit transferable treaties with the ruling family of Kuwait. Your country can unilaterally transfer those treaties to us. We then become the protecting power. It can be accomplished in a day. We have all the papers drawn up. The only thing missing is the British Crown's seal and appropriate signatures."

Eden wasn't ready for this approach and thought furiously of how to respond. The Foreign Office counted on at least a year for negotiations with Sheikh Abdullah Al-Salem Al-Sabah. By then, they hoped the issue would be moot.

There was no real reason for their reticence. The oil discovered in Kuwait in 1938 hadn't proven to be commercially viable. The war stopped any further exploration and development. Politically Kuwait was insignificant, only a small speck on the map surrounded by many larger British protectorates, including Iraq. But it was against the Foreign Office's policy to give away anything, especially to these insolent Jews. If only they were still dealing with the small Palestinian Jewish community: They could be easily ignored.

It took longer than one day but by the last week of October, 1941, the agreement was signed. The British would notify the Kuwaitis of the changes in the protectorate when - and only when - Israel told them to do so.

***

Avigdor Mizrahi was surprised by the sudden British initiative with Kuwait. His guess was that Rommel would have to come close to Cairo before the Empire would be willing to trade Kuwait for Israeli help. He was curious why Churchill had suddenly decided to move on this issue. His guess was that the news coming out of Russia had scared the British government – If the Soviets collapsed, which didn't seem impossible, Britain would be left alone and Israeli assistance would become vital. So they decided to placate a powerful ally. Of course Eden tried his best to drag out the negotiations, but the quick conclusion of the agreement indicated that Churchill did not support this policy.

The British government did not know, of course, that due to the Israeli attack on Ploesti and resulting German fuel shortages the Soviet front was holding better than it had in the original history. On October 10, 1941, the Germans made an effort to wipe out a pocket of Soviet forces trapped in Bryansk, some 250 kilometer southwest of Moscow. In the original history they had succeeded, taking about 50,000 Soviet prisoners of war. This time around, the Red Army used some of their forces from the Kiev pocket to counterattack the German pincers. The Bryansk pocket was evacuated through the resulting breach in the German ring. The net result was a loss of several thousand troops for the Germans and a rescue for most of the Soviet force. There was also a more important change: the Red Army learned that standing in defense to the last man was not a feasible policy. Even Stalin seemed to concede this point after hundreds of thousands of his soldiers got out of encirclement and lived to fight another day. The German Army Group Center was still advancing, but not as fast as in the original time-line. Fuel shortages were severe, impacting on everything. Logistics were relying mostly on horse-drawn transports – no news there. Now though, panzers were often idle, waiting to be refueled, and the Luftwaffe had to ration its ground support for fear of running out of high octane aviation gasoline. They cleared the Vyazma pocket on October 19 but instead of taking 650,000 prisoners, 1000 tanks and 4000 artillery guns, the Nazis captured only less than a 100,000 men and almost no equipment.

The war in the East was not going well for the Germans but they didn't know it yet. Hitler announced on October 20, ten days later than in the original history, that the war in the East was won.

***

Amos Nir opened the Cabinet meeting. "Hanna, gentlemen, there are a number of issues we have to decide today. First, an update: the Germans have been much more efficient than we expected. As of last week, ending October 24, 1941, we have taken in about four million refugees. The railroads in the Ukraine are functioning, though not at full capacity. The Brindisi base is receiving about 40,000 people a day. This is about the limit of our capacity to transport them to Israel, so as things stand now we are balanced. At the current rate, we'll be done with Operation Moses by December of this year. There is a caveat though. As you all know, the Nazis are less successful than in our original history. This, paradoxically, may interfere with our rescue efforts since it will take them longer to conquer the areas where they previously exterminated Jews. It is possible that they won't conquer some areas at all. We will have to wait and see how things go. The net result may be that more of our people will be trapped in the Soviet Union, ending Operation Moses earlier than expected.

"We are running behind in building our refugee cities. We need to prioritize - It seems that we can either build housing or industry. We don't have enough capacity to do both."

The Industry and Infrastructure Minister cut in. "I disagree. We don't have enough capacity if we stick to modern construction techniques. Up to now, I've met resistance from several people here to employing the newcomers in construction. These are smart people that will learn fast. I see no reason not to have them build their own houses."

"I think that's a great idea," the Finance Minister said. "Make it a community project – We can have expert construction workers instructing and the community builds their own houses."

"But that means using cinder blocks and all kinds of outdated technology, since we don't have enough capacity to make prefabricated elements," the Absorption Minister objected.

"Sure, but it's better than having these people live in tents while waiting for housing, and then wait some more because we don't have enough skilled construction crews to build their workplaces," responded the Industry Minister. "If we let them work on their own housing, we can use the skilled crews to build the factories we need. Granted, it is not very efficient, but it will be done faster than otherwise, and, as a bonus, I believe it will boost morale among the immigrants."

Amos Nir stopped the discussion: "I think that this is a good idea and we should try it. Since the rails to Central Sinai are laid already, we may as well start the first experiment near the Refidim Industrial center. It's time to replace the tent city with a real town. I would also encourage entrepreneurs among the new immigrants to start their own businesses – construction and others as well. They will need supervision and licensing, but there are lots of skilled people out there that are eager to do something. The Infrastructure Ministry will take care of it. Please report your progress to the cabinet next week.

"The next item on our agenda is Japan, or rather their attack on the U.S.," continued Amos. "There are several decisions we need to make. Should we intervene to keep the U.S. from entering the war? The head of the Mossad, our psychologist and the chief of the history team are here with a detailed analysis of our options. Let's invite them in and see what they have to say before we go on."

The head of the Mossad took a seat at the conference table. "We performed a detailed analysis of what would happen in four different scenarios. The first is: we do nothing. In this case, most likely Japan will bomb Pearl Harbor on schedule, the U.S. will declare war on Japan and probably Hitler will declare war on the U.S. We are not one hundred percent sure about Hitler's declaration since we changed history quite a bit and his declaration made limited sense to begin with.

"The second scenario is: we prevent the Japanese attack on Pearl Harbor. Absent the attack, the U.S. stays out of the war.

"The third scenario is: we allow the Japanese attack and America's reaction to proceed as before but intervene to somehow prevent Hitler's declaration of war. This will in all likelihood prevent the U.S. from declaring war on Germany.

"The fourth and last scenario is the most complicated: we allow the Japanese attack on Pearl Harbor to proceed, but interfere with the Japanese actions after the attack and prevent Hitler from declaring war on the U.S."

"I have a question," the Industry and Transportation Minister said. "Why intervene at all? Just let history go the way it is supposed to go – like in your first scenario."

"This is the question," responded the head of the Mossad. "In our time-line the U.S became a superpower because of its involvement in the war. Spurred by their war effort, America developed new technologies, culminating with the atomic bomb. Its industrial base grew and since its armed forces were a major component of the Western allies' occupying armies the U.S. became a major influence in post war Europe. Paradoxically, the U.S. technological and scientific effort also helped the Soviets to become a superpower since the Soviets had such a good spy network. Out of the war, it's unlikely that the U.S. will invest the necessary resources in the Manhattan project, delaying their atomic bomb indefinitely. On the other hand we are sure that by now the Americans know that the Germans are working on teleportation and not an atomic bomb. This should reduce the incentive to build the bomb.

"U.S. participation also helped the Soviets in that Roosevelt gave Stalin all of Eastern Europe. Churchill objected, but being a junior partner in the alliance he acceded to Roosevelt's policies. If the U.S. is not a party to the European war, it will be up to Churchill, and probably us, to reign in Stalin.

"With no American participation, the outcome in Europe will be different as well. Left to its own devices, Britain will not be ready to invade Europe in 1944. This will lead to a longer war and probably more of Europe occupied by Stalin. Unless we do something about it."

"Like what?" The Finance Minister asked.

"We have a number of options in this regard. I suggest that this issue be left for a future decision."

"Are you suggesting that a world with Stalin's forces occupying all of Europe is better than the world we came from?" the Finance Minister asked sarcastically.

"No, what I am saying is that we can insure with a very high probability that the Soviets go no further than the old German border."

Amos intervened. "Please continue with your analysis."

"If we prevent the attack on Pearl Harbor there will be even greater repercussions in the Far East," the head of the Mossad continued. "Japan will continue building its empire and will also continue its genocide of the Chinese and other people it conquers. Depending on the means we choose to prevent Pearl Harbor, they may be able to continue for many years, slowly exhausting themselves until they collapse. It will be a mess that we have very little means to prevent.

"There is also a real possibility that Japan will attack the Dutch and British colonies even if the attack on Pearl Harbor doesn't happen. After all, the main reason for this attack was their need for oil. This hasn't changed.

"The third scenario, with Hitler not declaring war on the U.S., looks a bit better. The U.S. will concentrate on defeating Japan and will likely be done with them in a couple of years. This scenario has the advantage of decreasing the likelihood of the U.S. becoming a superpower, also limiting America's ability to pressure the British into giving up their empire. In our time-line Britain gave up mainly because of economical reasons: it could not both support the empire and pay its war debts. The Brits' position is somewhat better now that their shipping is not being sunk by the Germans. We project that without Roosevelt's pressure, Churchill will hang on to the empire, at least for a short time. We also think that our intervention in the war makes him more likely to stay on as Prime Minister until well beyond the end of the war. In our time-line he was defeated mainly because the British public was exhausted by the wartime deprivations and bloodletting as well as the disappointment of the Empire falling apart."

"What is your recommendation?" Amos asked.

"It seems to me that the best outcome for both us and the rest of the world will be to have Hitler not declare war on the U.S. We will get a world that will have three almost equal powers: the Soviet Union, the U.S. and the British Empire. Israel is going to be the fourth – how equal or not to the others only the future will tell. A slow dissolution of the Empire, less violent and abrupt than in our time-line, will be beneficial for everybody. This will also be a world where we will be the only nuclear power, for at least 10 years, and between three great powers there will be space for a fourth one.

"We can also slow down, or possibly stop, the Manhattan project. If we accelerate the U.S. victory over the Japanese so that the conflict is over by 1943, or is limited to a Japan surrounded and cut off from the mainland, the need for an atomic bomb will be gone and the huge expenditures of the Manhattan District Engineering project will become unnecessary, especially if there is no perceived threat from a German nuclear program. Hopefully the project will be canceled. We will have to give the Brits and Americans lists of Soviet spies in their nuclear projects. This will slow the projects to a crawl even if they decide to go on with it. Some of the spies, like the German mathematician Fuchs, were crucial and their absence will have significant consequences. I put a 10 year limit on us being the only nuclear power due to the simple fact that as soon as we open our borders, information will leak and everybody will try to build a bomb. It will take the great powers a while, but they will get it in the end. Of course, with no war going on and no immediate urgency the budgets will be limited and this will extend the time frame of these projects."

"How do you propose improving the American's position in this war without our direct involvement?"

"We will have to be involved, but not in the sense of using our forces to fight. There are points in history where a small push can send everything on a different path. We have identified several balance points in the Japanese attack on the U.S. This is what I propose ..." The group listened attentively.

"Thank you. I am sure we all appreciate your analysis.

"Ms. Katz," the Prime Minister addressed the psychologist, "I take it that you disagree with something the head of the Mossad said?"

"I do," Mina Katz smiled at the Mossad chief. "We discussed this issue before and we still disagree. I think that the Mossad's estimate of a 10 year lead-time on the nuclear issue is optimistic. I have no doubt that their scientific analysis is correct, but I think that as soon as information starts leaking out, the great powers will be in a race to develop nuclear technology. It is unreasonable to think that they will forgo, or postpone, the acquisition of the ultimate weapon because of budgetary restraints."

"How long do you think it will take somebody to develop a bomb?"

"I'm not an engineer, but judging by our history, probably the same time, or slightly less, than it took the U.S. in our time-line. Let's say four to five years from the time they decide to go. The information they'll get from our libraries will reduce their expenses, but the time frame will probably stay the same. Unless, of course, we decide to make all our libraries classified. Even then spies will get the information."

"I tend to agree with Mina," said the historian, "and would like to add that the same is true for every other technological advantage we have."

The head of the Mossad rose slightly in his chair. "I still don't agree. Some of our advantages are so big that it would take the world 20 years to catch up – satellites, microchips and computers are good examples. As to nuclear technology, we differ in our estimates of what the world will think is important. Will the U.S. invest in the Manhattan project, or computers or pharmaceuticals? The government doesn't have the resources to do everything. Especially in peacetime and with the FDR-induced recession still dogging them. The Soviets and the Brits have even less resources.

"I'll give you an example of false technological 'catching up': We know that the Brits, the Americans, and the Germans are all working on jet technology. We also know that left to their own devices the British would have a flying jet in about three years. The fact that they saw something of our jets will help them. The time estimate will be down to a year or two if we open our borders and allow information to get out. But we need to remember that the distance between our jets and theirs will still be about fifty years of technological development. I am being cautious estimating it at fifty years - It may be as much as seventy. What is more important is the fact that technology and science you learn from a book is different from that you develop yourself. The most important elements of any scientific and technological development are not available from textbooks. You may be able to find the basics of a nuclear bomb in a library book, but how to build the extremely accurate switches necessary for a plutonium device is classified and not easy to come by. Another problem is uranium enrichment – this also takes time and special equipment that they will have to develop or buy from us."

"I think that we all understand the different positions on the issue of the technology gap," Amos interrupted. "Anyone have anything to add regarding the options we were discussing earlier?"

"Yes," the historian jumped in. "I have a remark about the Mossad presentation. It was somewhat black and white. The U.S. has already developed a serious industry as part of their lend-lease program, which the Soviets at least will need for a while. So whether the U.S. gets into the European war or not, it will have a sizable industrial base by 1943. I agree with the head of the Mossad to the extent that this industry will not be as big or dependent on the government as it became in our time-line. This will tend to reduce the U.S. government's control over the industry and the industry's ability to spend money. With less jobs dependent on military production Congress may be more reluctant to raise taxes to pay for it. Also, if the U.S. is not in Europe - and we meddle some, the cold war may not develop – which will slow everything considerably.

"Another issue we need to deal with is Hitler's declaration of war on the U.S. We don't have a complete understanding of why he did it and so have no sure way of stopping him, short of killing the maniac. Killing him will cause a huge perturbation of the time-line with unpredictable results.

"We have a theory that goes as follows: Hitler was frustrated for a while with the U.S. It wasn't formally at war with Germany but in practice assisted Germany's enemies as if it was. This assistance included land-lease and escorting British and Soviet ships. As far as Hitler was concerned the U.S. couldn't do much more against Germany. It had no armies to send overseas, and what small forces it had ready are going to fight Japan. Hitler probably estimated that as soon as the U.S. had the means it would declare war on Germany no matter what he did.

"From this perspective it actually makes sense for him to declare war. Such a declaration would allow German submarines to attack shipping as far as U.S. coastal waters. There is no downside as the U.S. is not ready for action.

"If this theory is correct, Hitler may not declare war in this time-line. The Brits using our satellite information have sunk so many German submarines as to make the whole enterprise not worthwhile. We have seen a sharp drop in submarine attacks since we came on the scene. With no clear advantage, as short term as it may be, Hitler may decide against a declaration of war or not consider it at all."

"I have another remark," Mina Katz said, "in regard to U.S. participation in the European war. We didn't have a third war initiated by Germany in our time-line. An important reason for this was, in my opinion, the way Germany was defeated in WWII. It was a defeat in the first total war in human history. Almost each and every German experienced the air raids, bombs and occupation. Unlike after WWI they saw their enemies marching through their streets. To repeat this performance we may need the Americans. If they are out of the European theater, we, the Brits, Soviets and possibly the French may not be able to inflict enough pain to prevent a third round."

The discussion went on for hours. It was dark by the time the Cabinet finally voted. It was not unanimous, but a decision was reached.

Chapter 23

The speaker looked at the crowd in front of him. Rabin Square was full, with close to a hundred thousand people. It didn't really matter how many came. The peace movement was gaining momentum. Ambassadors from the United States and Russia were on the platform, along with the heads of two Arab parties and a couple of left wing peace advocates.

"We may yet win," thought the speaker, "and make this oppressive government give back all the lands it took from the Palestinians. We will finally have peace." The "peace" mantra was an old one and he almost believed it.

He started his speech: "Dear friends, this is the third time in as many months we have come together for peace. More and more people are supporting our cause for freedom and democracy. I call on the government to free all the unjustly detained. Cancel the 'Hostage Law' now! No Hostage Law!"

The crowd cheered. The speaker raised both arms into the air. The crowd chanted rhythmically: "No law! No law! No law"

The speaker lowered his arms and made soothing motions with his hands. "Let's hear from the Russian Ambassador. He is here as a private citizen and has graciously agreed to express his opinion on this issue."

The Ambassador rose from his seat and approached the microphone, the crowd cheering.

"My friends," he began, "I am honored to speak at this event. As you know, my country and I personally have always supported your desire for peace. I would like to remind you that at this very moment the Soviet Union is fighting for its life against the barbarian Nazis. It is our duty to help anyone fighting these animals and to oppose everyone who supports them. As we speak, thousands of people are dying in this war.

"I have grave news for you. It has come to my attention that the Palestinian Authority and its affiliates actively support the Nazis."

The crowd, quiet up to this moment, started booing. The ambassador waited patiently for the booing to stop and, when a semblance of peace returned, continued. "The so called 'peace loving' Arabs you are trying to liberate have sent emissaries to Nazi Germany with information on how to make an atom bomb to help them win this war. Their only objective is the destruction of this state and all of us with it."

His last words could not be heard. The crowd was screaming accusations of lies, provocation and propaganda heard through the general hubbub. That was the end of the rally but not of the scandal.

The next day the local media carried detailed reports of the ambassador's speech. He was accused of lying to prop up the government. He protested and gave the press audio tapes as well as transcripts and translations. There was no doubt that the tapes were authentic – Dr. Mazen's voice was clear and well-known.

The peace movement tried to defend itself, claiming that their intentions were good and peace negotiations with the Palestinians were desirable. The leftist parties tried to claim that the whole thing had been staged by the government. The Arab parties did their usual thing and accused the Jews of attacking the Palestinians.

The public seemed not to buy any of the claims. The next rally in Rabin Square managed to attract only its organizers. Peace Now was deeply shaken. They suddenly realized that Israel had an irreconcilable enemy in the Nazis, and the Palestinians were cheering this enemy on and doing their best to annihilate the Jewish people. The Arabs learned nothing from history and would, given an opportunity, repeat it. Only this time they hoped that all the Jews would die.

Amos Nir was satisfied. He knew that all the bleeding hearts would sooner or later find some other cause to make a fuss about, but at least for now they were licking their wounds. He was also hopeful that Peace Now would find fewer supporters among the new immigrants than they would have without the truth coming out. The newcomers were not very interested or moved by the rights of people bent on destroying their newly found state. Some of them though would keep their left-wing politics and follow the locals in their stupidity, but at least this little incident might reduce their numbers.

The Foreign Minister called the Russian Ambassador. "Vladimir, I appreciate your candor at that rally. You did us and your country a great service."

"Nathan, I did it for my country. Every word I said at that rally was true. I appreciate you trusting me with the tapes. I hope that you didn't forget our agreement?"

"We will do as you asked us. No member of the Russian embassy or any other Russian citizen will be forced to go to the Soviet Union when we establish relations with them. I completely understand your reluctance to face Stalin's NKVD and agree they would not be gentle with you."

***

The Cabinet was about to disperse with only one item left on the agenda: the American Issue.

Amos opened the debate: "Since we decided in the last meeting to establish formal relations with the Americans our researchers and planners came up with a possible approach." He nodded to the Foreign Minister: "Please tell us what they propose."

"I would like to give those of you that are not very familiar with this period of U.S. history a short summary of the country's, and particularly President Roosevelt's, attitude towards Jews.

"Starting with the late 1930s the U.S. refused to accept any Jewish refugees from Europe beyond the established quotas – which were very low. The only exception was made for world-renowned scientists like Albert Einstein and even his entry was difficult. In fact even the meager quotas were not being filled because of requirements that Jews couldn't comply with. One example is the requirement of getting a declaration from the police that they don't have a criminal record. Would you expect the Gestapo to issue such documents?

The SS St. Louis was probably a better example of how the U.S. treated Jews: None of its passengers - all refugees from the Nazis, were allowed to enter the U.S. and were eventually returned to the Nazis. The St. Louis was a test – Hitler wanted to check if anybody cared. He had a perfect demonstration of American Anti-Semitism and indifference and decided that the U.S. would do nothing to prevent the extermination of the Jews. He was right. In this regard the U.S. and President Roosevelt should be held partially responsible for the Holocaust.

"This sad history not withstanding this is what the experts found out and propose to do…"

***

Jonathan Brown had been born in Detroit, Michigan, in 1950. He graduated Medical School at the University of Michigan in 1976 and did his internship in internal medicine at the Albert Einstein Medical Center in New York, where he also met his future wife, Ruth who was doing an internship in pediatrics. It was love at first sight.

Jonathan was always a Zionist and considered himself an Israeli. He was somewhat disappointed the first time they visited Israel – the Israelis thought he was an American and not really a part of the "family".

Ruth was slightly less enthusiastic than Jonathan. On the other hand she was moderately observant and described Israel as "the only place in the world where I can behave like a normal American – go shopping at a mall and have a snack at a kosher MacDonald's."

It was their dream for a while to make aliyah. The only delay was finding jobs in Israel. In 1985 they both got offers to join the staff of the Soroka Medical Center in Beersheba. It took them all of five minutes to decide to go.

By the time of the Event they were both well established, middle-aged doctors, respected at their hospital and by the medical community.

The telephone was ringing. Jonathan looked at the clock - it was seven in the morning. His work day started at 10. This call was too early. He picked up the phone.

"Dr. Brown?"

"Yes."

"My name is Dan Levine. I work for the government and would like to meet with you. I apologize for the early morning call, but I really need to speak to you and didn't want to miss you."

"What do you want to discuss?"

"I can't tell you over the phone. We need to meet."

Jonathan was dubious. He was not sure this caller was legit and was reluctant to risk meeting him. On the other hand, if a meeting in a safe place could be arranged, why not. "Where would you like to meet?"

The stranger was ready. "How about the hospital cafeteria at 2 pm. It shouldn't be too busy."

"I'll need to check my schedule. If you give me your phone number I'll call you back directly."

The man gave Jonathan a number in Tel-Aviv, apologized again for the early call and hung up.

At this moment Ruth came out of the bathroom. She was done with her morning shower and was dressing for her day at a children's clinic – she started at 8.

"Jon, who was it? Don't scowl - it couldn't have been that bad."

Jonathan smiled. "Just a crazy person who wants to meet with me but won't say why. Calling at seven in the morning. Imagine that."

"Did he give you any information?"

"Yeah. His name is Dan Levine and he works for the government. He wants to meet me at two in the cafeteria. I promised to call him back. What do you think?"

"Very secretive, was he?" Ruth thought for a moment. "If he really works for the government he will keep bugging you until you agree, so you may as well do it graciously. Just make sure that he is whatever he says he is."

"He sounded very polite but persistent. I guess I'll call him and agree to the meeting. What can happen in the cafeteria? It's fairly busy and there is a security guard."

***

Dan Levin extended his hand. He was about six feet tall, the same as Jonathan, but unlike Jonathan's spare frame Dan had the physique of a wrestler. Jonathan judged him to be in his mid forties, with a face easily forgotten: nondescript brownish hair, brown eyes and a straight nose. If he met Dan in a crowd he wouldn't give him a second glance – an average man.

"Jonathan Brown, but you know that already. How can I help you?"

"Let's grab a coffee and maybe something to eat and discuss my business at leisure."

They picked up trays and five minutes later sat at a corner table. The cafeteria was half empty, with enough people to put Jonathan at ease but not enough to intrude on their privacy.

"What part of the government do you work for?" Jonathan inquired.

Dan pulled out his wallet and put an ID card on the table. Jonathan read it carefully. The picture was of Dan, though dressed in a suit and wearing a tie, not the windbreaker he was wearing now. It said that Dan Levine was an employee of the Ministry of Foreign Affairs.

"What would your ministry want with a humble physician?"

Dan smiled. "Before I describe my business in detail I need a favor from you." He pulled out a sheet of paper from the inner pocket of his windbreaker. "Take a look at this and tell me what you think the patient is suffering from?"

The paper was printed on both sides. It had descriptions of symptoms, results of an autopsy and the patient's response to treatment. Jonathan read it twice before responding. "Well, first, this seems to be a medical history that is quite a number of years old. We stopped using Digitalis, or rather Digoxin, many years ago. Some places still use it for heart failure, but the advanced countries have better medication. It's way too dangerous since a small mistake in dosage can cause serious side effects. There are test that were either not performed or are missing. Some are standard blood analyses and especially immune system tests – these were not available before the sixties. So it kind of dates this record. The other comment I have is that the patient wasn't managed very well.

"As to the diagnosis: the patient obviously suffered from a number of ailments. The history you gave me covers only about 4-5 years. He has heart failure, hypertension and possibly metastatic melanoma – which probably killed him. But the main thing that jumps out at me is that he was severely misdiagnosed as having polio. I think that it's more likely that it was Guillain-Barré syndrome. The rest of his condition, except for the melanoma, may be the result of incorrect treatment, or rather neglect of that one problem."

"Are you sure about the polio?"

"Well, the chances, in my opinion, are about 70/30 that it was Guillain-Barré. That's the best I can do with this piece of paper."

"Okay, let's assume you are right. How should the patient be treated?"

"That would depend on how long the patient suffered from the syndrome."

"Let's say for about 20 years before the beginning of this report."

Jonathan fidgeted in his chair. "This is a long time. I'd have to examine the patient if he were still alive – which he's not, judging from the autopsy report. There are therapies but their success depends on too many factors to give you a reasonable estimate."

Dan finished his coffee in a gulp. "Thank you very much Dr. Brown. I'll probably contact you again and explain what this is about. I have to admit that your diagnosis was surprising and I have to seek instructions on how to proceed."

"And don't forget a second opinion," Jonathan smiled, "though it is not likely to help your dead patient."

***

Dan Levine called his superior as soon as he got to the privacy of his car.

"How sure was the doctor about this not being polio?" his boss asked.

"He was pretty sure, 70/30 according to him. He would need to examine the patient to be entirely sure and, most importantly, he would need to run a blood test that doesn't exist there.

"By the way, we selected this doctor because besides being an American he is a very good internist. He recommended a second opinion. I agree."

"Okay" said the voice on the other side of the line. "Find a specialist and get a second opinion. We'll decide what to do after we have that."

***

The next day Dan met with an immune system specialist at the Hadassah Ein Kerem hospital in Jerusalem.

After carefully examining the page the specialist gave Dan the same diagnosis as Jonathan Brown: the patient likely suffered from Guillain-Barré syndrome. To be entirely certain and to determine to what extent the condition was treatable the patient would have to be examined and several tests run.

Dan left the Hadassah hospital for his office in Tel-Aviv. At the end of his hour-long drive he had a plan, but one element was still missing. He reported to his boss and suggested that they prepare some things immediately so that when the missing element became available they wouldn't lose time.

"Go ahead," the boss said. "If Jonathan Brown agrees, we'll find a suitable candidate. As a matter of fact, I will start some inquiries now. If he doesn't agree… well, I know you well enough. He will be with us."

***

After a long meeting with the General Staff, Ephraim Hirshson called his deputy at the Brindisi base: "I need you to prepare plans to defend the base. Make use of the General Staff's planning division and intelligence. We may be attacked by the Germans in the next couple of weeks or, at best, several months. Take into account an increase of the garrison – probably double what we have now, but the final decision is up to us. Update me daily on your progress."

"Sir, I expected you here in a day or two. Is there going to be a delay?"

Hirshson worded his response carefully. "I am not sure about a delay, but there are a couple of things I need to take care of, including arrangements for additional forces. You'll probably have a week more of freedom from me."

From the General Staff he drove to his father's house. He was scheduled to visit with his wife for a Friday night dinner but had made a special appointment to talk to Jacob. Ephraim didn't support Jacob's desire to enlist but decided to answer questions without trying to influence him.

Jacob was waiting for him in the living room. "Thank you for coming. I appreciate you taking the time from your busy schedule."

"You are welcome, but no need to thank me. You would have done at least as much – We are family. I'll do my best to help you."

Jacob was quiet for a moment, collecting his thoughts. "You know, the experience I went through at the Ninth Fort and the interrogation in the forest changed something in me. After we arrived here, this change was pushed a bit further by the week of education we got to catch up to 'modern times'. I was never a hateful man, but something changed. It seems to me that eliminating the Nazis is the most important thing I can do now. I mean direct elimination, like killing them, not just hurting them by improving the economy of Israel."

"Is that why you want to enlist?"

"Yes and another reason: I don't ever want to feel helpless again in the face of our oppressors. I believe that being a soldier in a Jewish army is a good way to achieve this."

Ephraim said nothing for a long while. Jacob waited patiently.

"I understand how you feel. After all, I enlisted in the professional forces for similar reasons – call it patriotism. And don't think that my parents were not against my choice of a career. I'm not sorry that I chose to be a soldier and I would do it again, but sometimes it's hard. You lose your freedom of choice. You have to obey orders. They'll take you away from home and family for a long time. The army takes care of you but also leaves you very little choice of what you can or can't do. Even now as a newly baked Brigadier General I have limited choice and have to obey orders."

Jacob was embarrassed. "I'm sorry. I noticed that you had slightly different epaulets but I have no idea what the rank signs are. Congratulations on your promotion."

"Thank you. You are the first member of the family to know. I only got promoted today."

Ephraim glanced at his watch. "I will have to leave in about twenty minutes. My wife expects me for dinner and will kill me if I'm late, so let's try and make the best of the time we have. We can continue this conversation on Friday – we will be here for Sabbath dinner".

"I really have a couple of simple questions. But first, don't think that I am completely ignorant of what an army is. I may be young but I have some experience and I heard a lot from my late father. I would like to know what to expect if I chose to enlist."

Ephraim smiled. "It's been a while since I was in the predicament of being a young recruit. In any case, things changed since then. I did spend some time with the Instruction and Training command. That was about seven years ago, so take my information only as a general picture not an accurate prediction. At the time you enlist they will give you a medical. If you are found healthy and your medical profile is determined to be 97% you will be sent to basic training."

"Wait," Jacob interrupted, "why 97%? As far as I know I am 100% healthy."

Ephraim scratched his head with an amused look on his face. "Being a Jewish male you are missing a tiny piece of your original body. This makes your medical profile 97%. If you ever meet a male IDF soldier with a profile of 100%, he will turn out to be an uncircumcised Christian. There are some in the IDF."

Jacob smiled. "That sort of makes sense. So what is included in basic training?"

"You are close to 21, which means that you won't get the same training as the 18 year olds. It will still be infantry training, but not as long and not as hard as for the youngsters. There are several basic training courses for older recruits, people with lower medical profiles and those that have professions the army is interested in who are not going to be infantrymen. It is quite certain that with the abbreviated training you won't be accepted into a combat unit. Which will leave you with a number of choices, including attending army courses and becoming a technical specialist, like an auto mechanic."

Jacob looked disappointed. "I wanted to volunteer for one of the elite units, like Golani or the commandos."

"Ah, I see that you researched the subject." Ephraim shook his head. "I don't think they will take you because of your age and limited Hebrew. But this is my opinion. You can try and see what happens."

Jacob nodded: "Well, thanks for the information. I'll think about this. Maybe I should go to the induction base in Tel Hashomer and talk to them."

"That's a great idea. Call them first and ask to make an appointment with captain Ezra Vilnai. If they make difficulties tell them that you're my relative. He will know the answers to all your questions."

Jacob smiled. "Isn't this nepotism?"

Ephraim smiled back. "Sure. A little, but it doesn't count. If I asked them to actually do something it would have been unethical. This is just treating a relative well."

**

Jacob got his answer from the army recruiting office in a couple of days. It was disappointing. After a long conversation with one of the personnel assignment officers he was offered a number of options, which boiled down to a simple answer to his question: he didn't have a choice – all new immigrants under the age of 25 were inducted into the army for service periods that varied with age. In Jacob's case he would have to serve at least six months.

After he reported to the base he would go through several weeks of basic infantry training and be assigned to a support unit. To serve with a combat unit he needed six month of basic training and then advanced training – longer than his whole service. There were provisions for volunteers but an application would be considered only after he successfully finished basic training.

After mulling the problem over Jacob decided to wait until he was done with his basic training. It seemed to him that if he demonstrated good abilities and persisted in his efforts he had a chance to be accepted into a fighting unit.

It didn't take Ze'ev and Noam very long to persuade him that while he was waiting for his induction into the IDF he could prepare for the possibility of continuing as a civilian after his short military service.

**

Two months later Jacob Hirshson had his surveyor's license. The whole family had celebrated the opening of his new office in the central Sinai city of Refidim. His army service was still several months away. In the meantime he was being drawn into the new business. It seemed to him now that this may be as patriotic as serving in the armed forces. He also recognized that this perception might change after he was part of the IDF.

Uncle Chaim was working for Jacob as an operations manager. The new surveying business was in great demand as construction was booming. Jacob had the business savvy to hire every qualified new immigrant he could find, even before he had his business license or an office. He paid them a salary while they got their licenses; now he had nine surveyors working for him. The funds had come from Ze'ev in the form of a loan and line of credit. He had no doubt that his money would be repaid soon. Chaim was still somewhat unhappy with the idea that his nephew employed him. Jacob's father never worked together with Chaim and Jacob didn't either. That was partly due to Chaim being observant and Jacob's father an atheist, but also because of different interests. Chaim was settling in though, and his mood kept improving as he realized that Jacob really needed him.

Jacob's mother Sara seemed happy keeping house, which was all she'd ever done. The family lived in one of the new houses in Refidim. The city was a sprawling affair. Buses were ubiquitous and polluted the desert air with their fumes and noise. Everybody was looking forward to the numerous tram lines promised.

Sheina, together with her cousin Tzipora, was studying computer science at Beersheba University. It was hard. They were busy all day long, five days a week and kept studying in their dorm on weekends. There was a lot of catching up to do both in Hebrew and in science studies. But they were happy and had even found time to go out and make friends.

***

Days after his paternal relatives had moved to Refidim, Ze'ev went to meet his mother's family. They arrived at Haifa's newly expanded port passenger terminal, which was barely coping with the tens of thousands of new immigrants arriving daily. Ze'ev walked for a long time, comparing the faces he saw to old pictures. He walked by them several times without recognizing them before deciding to ask one of the numerous volunteers for help. The three people approaching the counter in response to the public announcement didn't look familiar. Ze'ev introduced himself.

"Yes, yes," the man responded. "I was told by the people in Brindisi that you would meet us here." Nachman Frumin accepted that they were related but didn't accept the relationship with his heart. His wife Tzila was just happy to have someone in this incomprehensible new land whether they were family or not. Their son Wolf, eighteen years old and proudly independent, didn't worry about new relatives. He was interested in learning more about the amazing gadgets they'd seen. All three were relieved to hear that the seventeen year old girl connecting them to these new relations was safe.

Esther, the missing link, had been on a field trip with friends when the Germans attacked their small town near Vilnius. Their guide, a Communist friend of Wolf's, took the girls in his charge east, out of danger. In the history Ze'ev knew, Esther spent the war in Uzbekistan, returning to Vilna to meet and marry Jacob in 1947.

Still unsure of the relationship, the family settled in for the drive to Ze'ev's house in Hertzlia. Nachman, a grain merchant and generous supporter of the Labor Zionist movement back in Belarus, was amazed that the state had actually come to be. Wolf had lots of questions about local politics. Tzila just seemed to enjoy the drive.

They communicated mostly in Yiddish, with a smattering of Russian. A road sign for Jerusalem excited them, it was in Hebrew and English, but apparently they could read both languages – knowing Polish meant that the Latin alphabet was familiar to them. Even Wolf, the self-proclaimed communist and atheist, wanted to see Jerusalem immediately. Ze'ev had to disappoint them but promised a trip to the holy city later in the week.

The dinner at Ze'ev's house was a crowded affair. Both Sheina and her mother attended. Jacob couldn't come and promised to join the next clan gathering.

After dinner at his house Ze'ev got to the business of explaining their family tree to his new relatives. It helped that one of Tzila's cousins used to own a photography shop and a number of pictures survived the war. It took several hours to convince the newcomers that Ze'ev was indeed their grandson. Wolf was slightly taken aback that Ze'ev was named after him – East European Jewish tradition prohibits naming a child after a living relative. He may have proclaimed himself a Communist, but this didn't make him any less Jewish. Having someone named after him meant that he was dead. It bothered Wolf.

Ze'ev tried to explain to the Frumins their daughter's fate. All they knew was that she had left on a trip to a town east of Druya in Belarus, where they lived, on Friday. The war started on Sunday morning. They hadn't seen her since. Several other girls from her class that had gone on the trip were also missing.

Ze'ev explained that Wolf's friend, the teacher on the trip, was an agent of the NKVD – the Soviet secret police. He knew more about the Germans than he let on while teaching history at their school in Druya. When they heard the first announcement of the German attack, he told the girls that by the time they get back home, the town will likely be occupied by the Nazis. He also explained that judging by how they behaved in Poland the Jew's chances of survival were bleak. He offered them a choice: those who still wanted to go back could take the horse and cart and go. He promised to take the rest into deep Russia, far away from the fighting and the Germans. The girls, who were all Jewish, debated their options for almost an hour – that was how long it took their teacher to make the necessary arrangements. When he came back most decided to go.

The teacher kept his word. In the general disorder of the Soviet withdrawal under German pressure he used his NKVD credentials to get the girls on one of the last trains evacuating the families of Soviet military personnel to the east. He went on the train with them as far as Moscow. There he had the local office of the Ministry of the Interior provide the girls with valid Soviet documents and recommended that they keep going. They joined masses of refugees trekking east. The only advantage they had were the documents. Issued in Moscow they gave the girls a better chance of obtaining food on the way.

Esther Frumin, with a friend, kept going until they got to Samarkand, the capital of Uzbekistan. She went to a nursing school there. The school offered some food to students, which was a major factor in her decision.

In the history Ze'ev knew, his mother only returned to her home town in 1944. There she found her aunt and cousin, who had been in Russia when the war began. Everybody else was dead. She met Jacob in Vilnius in 1947, marrying him several weeks later. They left the Soviet Union in 1956 and went to Israel. Ze'ev was their only child.

***

The Frumins stayed with Ze'ev and Linda for two weeks. They spent most of their time at the local immigrant absorption center studying Hebrew and getting acquainted with modern Israel. Benjamin took the men shopping, while Linda had a grand time with Tzila.

Two weeks after their arrival and before the Frumins moved to their new house in an immigrant town in the Galilee Linda invited both sides of the family for a Sabbath dinner. She made sure that everybody would be there and arranged transportation from Refidim and Beer Sheba. Ze'ev had his doubts. His mother's family came from a small town in Belarus and would, probably, feel uncomfortable with the more sophisticated residents of the big city of Vilna. But his fears were completely baseless. To his surprise Wolf and Jacob had a lot in common and Wolf also quickly zeroed in on his beautiful relative Sheina. Jacob seemed to approve and even switched seats with his sister so she could seat next to Wolf. The dinner was a success.

Wolf asked Sheina what she was doing.

"I'm a student at the University of Beer Sheba. I and my cousin Tzipora want to study computers. In the meantime we are studying Hebrew, math and other subjects. Hopefully we'll enroll in the Computer Science course next semester."

Wolf was impressed. "I would have nothing against a college education. It makes life so much easier."

"So enroll in college. It's also fun. Lots of new people to meet, though we study hard." Sheina smiled. "You could even apply to my university."

Wolf frowned. "I wish I could but in three weeks I have to report to start my Army service. Maybe after I'm done with that…"

How old are you?"

"Eighteen last month. I want to serve in the Jewish Army. We all felt helpless and defenseless when the Germans came. Even the stupid Belorussian police could do what they wanted with us. I never want to feel like that again."

Sheina smiled again. "You're brave. You know in what branch of the military you want to serve?"

"I really don't know much about the Israeli armed forces but according to your brother there are a number of elite commando units. I'll do my best to get into one of those."

Sheina nodded. "Yes, Jacob wanted that too but he's too old or something. Maybe he'll succeed in getting in anyway. I still have a year before they call me up."

"You're seventeen?" Wolf's eyes sparkled. "I see that the dinner is finished, would you like going for a walk?"

Sheina smiled. "I thought you'd never ask."

They came back to the house well after midnight. Jacob was waiting up and met his sister at the door. "You shouldn't stay out so late. I know that this area is relatively safe but you never know."

"I would have protected her." Wolf responded.

"And who will protect her from you?" But Jacob could barely hide his smile.

After two weeks, the Frumins moved to a new immigrant town in the Galilee. After having discussed his situation with Jacob, who could be his son but was also mature and had some experience, Nachman accepted Ze'ev's offer of a loan and several weeks later was well on the way to setting up a wholesale business. His two brothers arrived a couple of weeks later and joined him in his new endeavor.

Ze'ev was slightly worried about his eighteen year old uncle Wolf. The boy was a hothead and an idealist, not well-suited or prepared for army service, or so Ze'ev thought. In the old history, Wolf had been one of the first in their town to be shot when he came to the defense of a rabbi who was being beaten by a Nazi soldier. His parents were worried sick by his plans to join a commando unit. They still hadn't heard from their daughter. She might be alive, but there was no way of knowing. Now their only surviving child was in danger. They were informed that their son, as an only child, would not be permitted to serve in a combat unit without their written authorization. Nachman, who had served in the Tsar's army during the First World War, was suspicious of the promise.

***

Despite all the family events, Ze'ev wasn't neglecting his business. This was an opportunity to make Consolidated into a world-class corporation, much larger than it had been. Things were going quite well on most of the expansion projects. The new metallurgical complex being built in Refidim was progressing well. They were building their own equipment – arc and heat treatment furnaces and even sand molding machines were within Consolidated's capabilities. Electrical transformers and regulating equipment would be supplied by other companies.

Ze'ev was concerned with the company's ability to manufacture machining equipment. He would have preferred to buy it but the only suppliers were in the far future. A solution was suggested by one of his engineers: install computer controls on old machines to modernize them. The problem was that the available old equipment was really old and worn out. A source of new old-fashioned machines was available in Britain and the U.S. but it was inaccessible until the government implemented its import plan. Consolidated was not idle while they waited. The company had obtained catalogs of machining equipment available in 1941 and was planning a modernization program based on machines they would be able to purchase in the near future, assuming the current isolation would be lifted soon.

In the meantime, the company was making money supplying parts for the new electric trolleys being built at a former bus assembly plant in Ashdod. These were copies of German-made cars purchased for the Ayalon light rail project in Tel-Aviv. Luckily for everyone the cars were supplied with enough drawings and technical information to make reverse engineering easy.

Ze'ev was worried about his decision to invest a major effort in the development of an electric car. They had been working on it for several months now without coming up with any brilliant ideas. They were stuck with old lead-acid batteries. The company had no expertise or materials to develop a high-efficiency, inexpensive means to store energy. Several possible ways presented themselves to solve the problem: find a partner with expertise in batteries, find a completely new source of energy or try to develop a hybrid. All three options were looking worse than when they started the project and Ze'ev was leaning towards starting work on developing a regular car.

Consolidated had a partner of sorts in Tadiran, a local conglomerate that produced batteries and electronics, both consumer and military. Ze'ev wasn't happy with the cooperation: Tadiran knew how to make lithium batteries, but these were expensive and there was no sign that the price would come down any time soon. Plus the management of the battery plant expected Consolidated to fund expansion but was reluctant to sign an exclusive agreement that might lower costs to make the use of these batteries feasible.

At a recent meeting at the Technion Ze'ev had heard a rumor of a new source of energy being developed by the physics department. There was one person he hoped would enlighten him in this matter. He also wanted to ask a couple of questions that had been bothering him for a while. So he drove up to the campus in Haifa.

***

"Hi, Yitzhak. How have you been?"

"Hi, Ze'ev. I'm fine, despite some people here trying to drive me nuts. And how are you?"

"Good, good. I am sorry I haven't been in touch, but things are a bit hectic these days."

"Tell me about it." Yitzhak smiled. "So, what brings you here today?"

"Two things actually." Ze'ev was still not entirely sure he wanted to discuss this with anybody, not even a good friend from college. But here he was, so best to get on with it. "The easy part first. I've heard from a number of people that you are working on an interesting source of energy. They were mad at you, but that's a different issue. Is it true?"

Yitzhak fidgeted in his armchair and made a move like he was lighting a cigarette, though he had abandoned the habit many years ago. "There is something to it. A doctoral student of mine came up with this crazy idea of Zero Point Energy, this is..."

"Like in a couple of science fiction books?" Ze'ev interrupted.

"Well, sort of. It is a theoretical possibility, though not easy to implement. All those virtual particles that pop out of nothing exert measurable force on the real world. You know about the Casimir effect where two metal plates placed very close together in a vacuum will either attract or repulse each other? The question is how to harness their energy.

Say, would your company be willing to give us some money to research this a bit more?"

"That would depend on how much and how soon we can expect a result."

Yitzhak Wisotzky picked up his phone: "Arye, there's someone here I would like you to meet. Could you come to my office?"

When Arye Kidron came into the Professor's office, he was introduced as the guy who "sent us all into the past." Kidron wasn't happy with the introduction but had to agree that the description was accurate.

"If that's the case, then before we go into energy sources, I would like to ask the second question I had when I came here." Ze'ev looked at the two physicists. "Are you guys sure it actually was time travel?"

"What do you mean?" Professor Wisotzky asked. Arye Kidron was conspicuously silent.

"One reason I always thought time travel was impossible is causality. You can't reverse cause and effect. The classical example is, you go back in time and kill your grandfather before he has children. Then you were never born so never killed your grandfather and so it goes.

"Yet, here we are apparently back in time and meeting our ancestors. I'm sure that my father will marry long before my mother gets out of Russia - Why shouldn't he? The situation that brought them together in the first place doesn't exist anymore. So I shouldn't exist, but here I am." Ze'ev was done and looked expectantly from the older physicist to the younger one.

"You think you have existential problems," Yitzhak Wisotzky smiled, "wait 'til you hear my story. I discovered that my great aunt Sophie whom I remember distinctly never existed. That was a shock.

"But it is not completely inexplicable. We are talking about the quantum universe here. Just observing something changes it, and our time travel episode was a huge interference. So anything is possible in the sense that we may have changed the past just by going there. Not that I can explain exactly how this happened."

Now Ze'ev was seriously intrigued: "So maybe it wasn't time travel after all. What do you think, young man?"

Arye Kidron was inspecting his fingernails and took a while to respond. "Time travel is the simplest answer, but I am still working on alternatives. I really don't know enough to discuss this right now."

Seeing that Arye was reluctant to discuss his work, Ze'ev changed the subject back to energy. "How close are you to finding that 'Zero Point' source of energy? I'd happily finance the research if it is likely to lead to something practical in the foreseeable future."

Kidron considered how to word his reply. "We are fairly advanced on this. The Industry Ministry bankrolled the initial research so you'll have to iron it out with them and our lawyers before you could profit from it."

"Leave the legal and business stuff to me," Ze'ev said impatiently. "But I'll need a short written summary of the current state of affairs - what needs to be done and what results can be expected. In short, send me a research proposal."

Arye smiled. "Will do. I haven't done much about this since the Event – no money for experiments and such, just thinking."

Chapter 24

The Chief of General Staff supported Ephraim Hirshson's request to see the German fighting machine first hand despite strong opposition from the Defense and Foreign Ministers. They thought that satellite data and spy plane overflies produced enough information and there was no need to risk the life of a good officer, one that would be hard to replace.

"If you are killed or injured we will have great difficulty replacing you – at least in the short run. If you are captured by the Germans it may become catastrophic for us and the hundreds of thousands of Jews still trapped in Europe," said Nitzan Liebler.

"Injury or death is a soldier's normal combat risk – that's something that shouldn't influence the decision," responded Hirshson. "If an armed force is unwilling to risk its soldiers' lives, especially for a good cause, it becomes impotent. As to being captured: we can arrange for me to wear a British uniform of the Jewish Brigade or better – a neutral uniform. Maybe American. If I carry a micro transponder you'll be able to rescue me before anything bad happens."

"I'm not sure it's for a good cause," responded the Defense Minister. "What's wrong with the information we are getting now?"

Ephraim hesitated, not wanting to offend anyone. "Look at our own history: if we were to judge just by numbers and armament we would have lost the war of independence and a couple of wars after that. We would have won the second Lebanon war easily. We didn't, because dry statistics tell you nothing about the spirit and leadership that are the real forces behind every army. This is what I want to try to learn. Knowing about how the Germans fought from books is not enough. If I'm supposed to defend the Brindisi base and maybe do something bigger, I need to understand them."

The Defense Minister thought for a while and, somewhat to Hirshson's surprise, agreed.

Ephraim Hirshson spent almost a week with his family. The next week he was an observer with the British forces in the Libyan Desert.

***

"What's new, Erez?" General Hirshson asked his second in command even before his feet were off the plane's ladder.

Major Erez Zuckerman shook the hand his commanding officer offered. "Not much since my last report. I do need to update you on two recent developments though."

When they were in Hirshson's office Erez showed him an order that had come through the command line that morning. It authorized Hirshson to call Eichmann's replacement – Colonel Alois Brunner – and give him permission to forcibly deport all Jews remaining in Europe to Brindisi. This was a response to Brunner's telephone call demanding permission to do so. Since Hirshson was absent at the time and Erez knew no German and wasn't authorized to talk to the Germans he told the "secretary" to take a message and promise a response soon.

The other matter was somewhat more complicated: "We received a telephone request from a Mr. Howard Snyder, an American correspondent working for the New York Herald-Tribune. He wants to come here and do a story about our operation."

"Ah, we should have expected something like that to happen sooner or later," Hirshson responded. "Did you speak to him?"

"Yes. I told him that we would get back to him shortly."

"Good. I'll call him tomorrow. What do we know about him?"

Major Zuckerman looked at his notes. "He's apparently Jewish. His father emigrated from Russia and changed the family name from Schneider to Snyder. He is involved with the American Jewish Committee and a couple of other Jewish organizations. His wife, Golda, is a member of Hadassah. The guy is 43 years old. They have two kids. That's it."

"This gives me an idea." Hirshson made a note on his calendar. "I'll have to call somebody in Israel before calling Snyder. In the meantime I want to go through the base's defense plans."

For a while both officers looked through the computer printouts and maps of the proposed new fortifications. Hirshson appeared more and more concerned: "Major Zuckerman, I appreciate your hard work and imaginative planning, but we will have to modify this plan drastically. I must tell you that I was impressed and am somewhat worried by the Germans' fighting spirit. They seem to be unable to give up even in the face of certain defeat and often succeed winning a battle by pure bravery and persistence. I also gained respect for their command. We always knew that Rommel was a gifted tactician, but he also has some very good officers under him and the soldiers admire and trust him."

Hirshson pointed at the map of the base on the table in front of him. "If they decide to attack us it will likely come in two waves: the Italians will probably attack first. We should have no big problems pushing them back. The next major attack will be German and by then they will have information from the first attack. In theory we can deal with them indefinitely – our advanced weapons and all that crap. In practice though, we will suffer casualties and it will soon become a war of attrition. I don't think we need that. Any static defense can eventually be breached, and our technological advantage may not be big enough to make us invincible to a prolonged pounding by a determined enemy.

"What is the best defense, Major?"

"Offence, of course, sir." The Major was smiling. "If only I was allowed to plan an offensive and not just defend this facility."

"I'm glad we agree." Hirshson nodded at the plans in front of him. "Let's plan for an offense to take as much territory as possible as fast as possible. I also want you to consider what might trigger a fight. We can wait for them to attack, or we can choose another trigger. Present me with options. Another thing, plan on having two infantry divisions, a couple of armor battalions and a wing or two of air force support at your disposal. Before you do anything else, make sure that the joint command center for infantry, armor and air force is functioning properly. This should make planning that much easier."

***

The next day General Hirshson called Liat Cohen at the General Staff. "Liat, after reporting to Gad on my North African experience I sat in on part of a conversation with his next visitor. Please tell Gad that I may have a candidate for him."

"Ephraim, if you wait on the line I will let Gad know and see if he wants anything specific."

"Hi Ephraim, how are you getting used to the peace and quiet of Brindisi?" Gad Yaari sounded like he was smiling.

"It's shocking," Hirshson also smiled. "I found a good candidate for our friend."

Hirshson told his boss about Howard Snyder. "You should have a full report now on your computer. If our friend is interested I will call Snyder and setup an interview in Brindisi."

"Please do that. Our mutual friend doesn't want to lose any time. We were lucky to find anybody that is even remotely suitable."

Next Hirshson tried to call Snyder in Rome. It took almost an hour to get through. After the fourth ring, a woman's voice answered in heavily accented English: "Press office. How may I help you?"

"Mr. Howard Snyder, please," Hirshson said in his Israeli accented English.

"Just a moment, I will see if he is here."

Less than a minute later a man came on the line: "This is Snyder."

"My name is Hirshson. I am calling you back, as promised, from the Palestinian Refugee Organization. How can I be of help?"

"Thanks for returning my call. You people took your time but no matter. I guess no harm was done. I'd like to come to your refugee base or camp or whatever it is you call it and take a look at your operation."

"You are welcome. Please don't forget to get a pass from the Italian police. Without it, the Italian guards outside the facility will not let you in." Hirshson checked the note in front of him. "You need to see an Inspector Giovanni Poncetti at the central police building in Rome. It will take you at least three days to get the pass. I suggest that we meet this Thursday."

***

Jonathan Brown and Dan Levine stepped out of the Boeing 727 onto the Brindisi landing strip. The weather was pleasant, though the wind was picking up and promising a storm. Light clouds raced across the sky. Jonathan, on his first visit to the 1941 world, looked around curiously. He saw non-descript concrete buildings, fairly new judging by the old warehouses next to them, and a long landing strip – also concrete. There were people everywhere. Most were in army uniforms, taking care of heavy construction equipment parked under curiously constructed sheds. There were also guards.

Dan led them through a door in a tall fence made of pre-cast concrete pieces. They were challenged by guards on both sides of the fence. Dan's ID was apparently good enough to let them pass.

On the other side of the fence were more buildings – a mix of new and old Italian construction. The large plaza was teeming with civilians in what looked to Jonathan as somewhat shabby and old-fashioned clothing. It took him several minutes to realize that most of these people were lined up to board a ship moored at a pier of the Brindisi harbor. The ship carried a Nazi flag as well as a Palestinian one – a gold Star of David on a divided white and blue field. The combination looked incongruous to Jonathan.

Finally they arrived at their destination: a concrete building at the edge of the plaza, next to a tall concrete wall.

Inside they passed through a long corridor and arrived at a suite of offices. Hirshson greeted them in his office and offered refreshments. "Gentlemen, I have arranged your meeting for tomorrow. I'll greet Snyder and immediately transfer him to your tender care. I have no need or desire to know what's going on. Lieutenant Aviva Bashan will show you around the parts of this base that may be shown to our guest. Please learn them well – you'll be on your own tomorrow and are supposed to make Snyder believe that you are 'natives' here.

"Just to make sure: I am Ephraim Hirshson and I work for the Palestinian Refugee Organization – no mention of military titles or Israel. All personnel have been instructed not to speak to this guy, to pretend not to know English. The refugees will be free to say whatever they want – don't interfere with them. Last thing: on no condition will you take him to the other side of the wall – where you landed."

***

Howard Snyder arrived at the external gate at noon. The Italian guards admitted him and he went on to the inner gate – guarded by the Caliph's troops. For this occasion they were armed with old British Lee-Enfield rifles and dressed in British uniforms. The uniforms came from old IDF stores – they had been used by the Israeli forces as late as 1967. They looked well worn and mended, as befitted a poor Palestinian community.

One of the guards took Snyder to Hirshson's office. On the way Snyder got a glimpse of a refugee train pulling into the special station, but the guard kept moving and he had no choice but to follow him.

"Mr. Snyder, welcome to our modest installation. I am Ephraim Hirshson of the Palestinian Refugee Organization." Hirshson extended his hand.

Snyder's handshake was firm: "Thank you for inviting me. I'm sorry I was a bit short on the phone the other day. Had nothing to do with you, just a problem with the Italians that got me annoyed.

"I have a ton of questions for you and I would like to see and interview some of the refugees."

Hirshson smiled apologetically: "I am a bit busy just now. We are short on people and have lots of refugees to deal with. In any case, I probably wouldn't be able to answer most of your questions. I am only a local manager. There are two people here that know the operation better than I do and they also speak English much better that I do."

A knock on the door interrupted Snyder's reply. Jonathan and Dan came in. Hirshson introduced them as Dr. Jonathan Brown, a medical doctor with the Organization, and Dan Law, a senior manager based in Palestine. The two led Snyder out and into an office down the corridor.

"Mr. Snyder, would you like something to drink? A sandwich maybe?" asked Dan.

Snyder smiled. "I feel at home already. We didn't say two words and here you are trying to feed me. My grandmother did that all the time. My mother too. Thanks. I'll take a cheese and turkey sandwich, if you have it, and a cup of coffee."

"Sorry," Dan shrugged. "We are kosher here, so it's either cheese or turkey but not both and if you get turkey you don't get cream with your coffee."

"Oops, it is just like home. Okay, turkey sandwich then and black coffee."

"Are you Jewish?" Jonathan inquired. Not being a trained operative he was not given access to Snyder's file for fear that he might let on some information they were not supposed to know and alert Snyder.

"Oh yes. My father came to the States from Russia and quickly changed his name from Schneider to Snyder. He was hopeful that an 'American' name would let him more easily get into the printing business, which is what he was doing in Russia."

A young woman wearing a baggy British style uniform came in carrying a tray loaded with meat sandwiches, mayo, mustard and a pot of coffee. She put the tray on the table in the middle of the room, smiled at the three men and left.

"That was quick service." Snyder remarked.

"Just the time it took to carry the stuff from the kitchen. We feed thousands of people every day, so three more are not a problem."

After lunch they toured the facility, at least the part that Snyder was allowed to see. He interviewed several of the refugees. These were mostly from Holland and were happy to have left the Dutch concentration camps.

By four in the afternoon they were done with the interviews and Snyder was preparing to leave for the train station.

"Mr. Snyder, may I ask your impressions of this installation?" asked Jonathan.

"Dr. Brown, I am very impressed. I'm especially impressed that both the Germans and the British are cooperating. Maybe you could even negotiate a peace between them."

"You think that would be wise?" Dan asked.

"Well, I don't really know. I'm just a lowly reporter for the New York Herald. It seems to me that preventing bloodshed is always a good idea, though in the case of the Nazis I do have doubts.

"At any rate, I will write a report of my visit here. It will be as glowing as I can make it and will either not be published or will appear at the bottom of page 17 on Sunday. But that's life. Jews are not very high on America's list of priorities."

"Mr. Snyder," Dan began.

Snyder interrupted him: "Please call me Howard."

"Okay, Howard, Dr. Brown and I are going to the U.S. and could use the help of someone like you."

Snyder thought for a moment. "There are lots of people I could introduce you to but you probably know most of them. There are Jews in America that support the Palestinian cause. As a matter of fact I myself am a Labor Zionist."

"That's not the kind of help we need. Jonathan needs to discuss an important matter with a U.S. physician that is also a Vice Admiral in the Navy. We are looking for an introduction."

Snyder was quiet for a long while. Finally he said: "What is it that a Palestinian doctor would want with a Navy Vice Admiral?"

Dan responded carefully: "I'll tell you but you have to promise that the information will stay with you until I give you permission to expose it, and that may be years from now or never. Exposure of our mission will not only harm Jews but will also harm the U.S. and you personally. Are you sure you want to know?"

Snyder didn't hesitate. "Yes, I want to know, but I'll keep your secret only if it doesn't involve treason against my country. This is also a condition for me to help you."

Dan looked at Jonathan who said "It's really simple: we discovered, purely by chance mind you, that we may have a cure for some of the ills that plague President Roosevelt. The Admiral in question is his personal physician and an introduction to him may ease our mission of helping the President. No treason there."

Snyder got up from his chair and was now pacing back and forth. After a while he said: "I am somewhat skeptical that a medic from the land of camels and sand dunes would be able to cure what the best minds in America can't."

"Why not?" Jonathan sounded offended. "I graduated from the one of the best medical schools, did my internship and residency at the Montefiori Medical Center in New York – I'm a good doctor. Don't forget that the Hadassah Hospital in Jerusalem attracted the best Jewish doctors from Europe. In Palestine we have a unique combination of American and European knowledge."

Snyder stopped pacing: "Okay, let's assume you persuaded me. I'm easy. And let's assume that I may be able to give you a couple of names in D.C. I don't know your Admiral but I think I know people who know him. What will you do next?"

Dan answered "We would get to Washington as soon as possible to meet with him. I'm positive that after he hears what we have to offer he will be glad to accept our assistance."

"And what's in it for you?" Snyder inquired in a somewhat calmer voice.

"Very soon we will have close to six million new Jewish immigrants in Palestine. We need resources to support them for a while. It won't be long before our economy will flourish, but in the interim we will need assistance. The U.S. can help us. Roosevelt has showed us no great friendship up to now. We think that if his health improves and it is attributed to our help, he could be much friendlier and give us some of what we need."

Snyder thought for a short while. Finally he pulled out a pocket appointment book: "Can you make it to New York by November 13th? That will be Thursday."

***

Amos Nir got up from his desk when Ahmad Mazen entered. The Prime Minister shook hands with the Palestinian Chairman and gestured for him to sit in one of the easy chairs around a coffee table. He asked for tea, Mazen wanted coffee. They were silent until the refreshments were served and the door was closed.

"I am gratified that you want to resume our peace negotiations," Dr. Mazen said. "It is the right thing to do for both our peoples. I take it that your government changed its position on releasing our prisoners and removing settlements."

"That's not exactly why I invited you," responded Amos. "I think that we should abandon the charade of peace negotiations. After all, you were more than happy to let the Nazis drop an atom bomb on us."

Mazen moved uncomfortably in his seat. "That was just talk. We need to calm the extremists. There is really nothing to it."

"Ah, but that statement isn't accurate." Amos smiled. "Tell me, Ahmad, do you consider yourself a Palestinian refugee?"

"It's not a question of what I consider myself. I am a Palestinian and my family was expelled from Lod. So, by definition, I am a Palestinian refugee."

"But you personally were not expelled from anywhere. You were born in a refugee camp near Ramallah, under Jordanian rule. You were not even a glimmer in your father's eye when our war of independence happened."

"You just said it yourself, Prime Minister: I was born in a refugee camp among other refugees and so I am a refugee."

Amos Nir sipped his tea for a moment looking at the Palestinian Chairman. He seemed to be satisfied with his righteous response. "Dr. Mazen, you are a historian with a Ph.D. in the history of the world war we are in the midst of. Can you give me an example of another group in history that had third and fourth generation refugees? The twentieth century will be more than satisfactory."

Amos Nir kept sipping his tea, giving Mazen ample time to respond.

"I don't understand your question, Prime Minister. Every group of refugees that has children…" Mazen trailed off.

He started again: "If refugees are not exterminated, they multiply, have children, the children have children and so on. I still don't understand what you are saying."

"Okay, I'll explain." Amos picked up a cookie. "You know that in our timeline after the end of this war about 13 million ethnic Germans were expelled from Eastern Europe. They became refugees. Can you point out to me where their refugee camps were located in, say, 1980."

Mazen was shaking his head: "Amos, you know that there were no refugee camps for them. They were allowed to resettle and live normal lives."

"True, but they were not allowed to resettle in the countries that expelled them. They were absorbed by either Germany or Austria. Some went to other places, but it is telling that there are no accurate records of who went where.

"Let me ask you another question: In 1948, after Israel declared independence, the Arab countries started expelling Jews. The final number of Jewish refugees was close to eight hundred thousand. In which camps were they housed in 1980?

"In 1947 Pakistan separated from India. Millions of Hindus and Moslems became refugees. In which camps were they housed in 1980?

"These are just some examples out of many. If you give me the name of just one such place, we can arrive at a peace agreement in an instant."

"You know that none of these people were in refugee camps in 1980." Mazen was angry now. "What is the connection between all these people and the Palestinians?"

"None really." Amos was smiling now. "Except that the general rule emphasizes the exception. The Palestinians are unique in their status. They remained refugees, living in camps on UN handouts, for generations. The same UN also did nothing to help them move to other countries and, in fact, discouraged them from moving. A clear violation of their human rights.

"I have to remind you of another piece of history: Israel was ready to accept the UN partition plan; The Arabs, including a great majority of those living in Palestine at that time, refused and attacked. The Arab side lost the war. I don't want to get into the question of whether your people were expelled as you claim or left at the urging of their leadership as our historians claim. It is immaterial why they left. What is important is what happened next.

"There was no difference either ethnically, linguistically or culturally between the Arabs of Palestine, Jordan, Lebanon, Syria or any other neighboring Arab country. From this it would follow that your people could be absorbed by those countries and you would have been born a citizen of Jordan. No second, third and umpteenth generation of refugees, no misery and living a hard life being fed by the UN.

"The problem was that your Arab brethren hated Israel so much that they made your people into a tool of war. There was also some tribal hatred and fear of competition, but that was a side issue. Preserving them as refugees was vital to keeping up pressure on Israel. The UN cooperated. They set up a unique institution just to take care of you. I am saying 'you' because the term 'Palestinian' didn't apply to Arabs until the late 1960s – as you know the Palestinian national identity was invented by Arafat, an Egyptian himself. Very few of your people were granted citizenship in the

Arab world and you were always treated as pariahs there. Your people were cruelly abused by the other Arabs and left to their own devices. Those Arabs would do it again. That calamity started only seven years from now and was perpetuated by the forces in power now in the Arab world."

Mazen jumped out of his armchair. "What you are saying are partial truths mixed with lies. I don't have to listen to this."

"Mr. Chairman, please calm down. I'll be done in a minute and then we have to discuss a number of important issues, but the historical background is necessary."

Amos waited for the Chairman to sit back in his seat. "There is just one point left that I can't resist making: in the timeline we came from you claimed you wanted to set up a state that was supposed to live in peace with us. You know that that was impossible for a simple reason: the four or six hundred thousand original refugees multiplied into many millions. Only a fraction of these lived in the territories under your control and there was no way to absorb the others without massive help from the other Arabs. That help was not forthcoming – They gave you money to fight but never really wanted you to build a healthy economy. But I am done with this, and unless you want to add something, I suggest we move on to the real reason for this meeting."

"Mr. Prime Minister, I don't agree with most of what you said, but it would be a waste of time to argue. I don't see why these issues have to be discussed now."

"Mr. Chairman, I wanted to present to you the background before attempting to arrive at some kind of agreement. In your discussions with the other fractions - you know what discussion I'm referring to - you considered leaving for Jordan. Is this still on the table?"

Mazen looked surprised. "I will have to think about this and confer with my colleagues. Would you consider such an option?"

"We probably would," said Amos. "The territory you vacate would come in handy, and we would have no more security headaches. That would be worth a lot to us. Your people would become citizens of Jordan and stop being despised refugees."

Ahmad Mazen had a crafty look on his face. "What about the total embargo on export of knowledge?"

"We can work around it. If you leave with just basic possessions and the knowledge in your heads, you're free to go right now."

Mazen was surprised. "You're not afraid of our scholars taking all they know and building a great Palestinian state that may defeat you in the not so far future?"

Amos smiled: "Be realistic, my friend. First, you will be a bunch of Arab refugees from Palestine crossing over into Jordan or Lebanon or Syria. Maybe even Egypt. How do you think your brethren will receive you? You will number over seven hundred thousand and I expect that you will be treated exactly like your ancestors in 1948. Even if your census numbers were correct and there were two million Palestinians, you really think that the Arab rulers of here and now will share power with you? Or even feed you? Even if they wanted to, how would they do that?

"As to creating a great state: the first order of business, after you are herded into refugee camps, will be fighting for supremacy between your different factions. The remnants of this fight will be sent to attack us. How soon do you think you will have your state and how much will your superior knowledge, without the requisite industrial infrastructure, help you? And by the way, forget about the Nazis helping you. They don't care what happens to any of the Arabs and are busy fighting for their own survival – a fight I assure you they will lose."

Mazen hesitated for a moment. "Why are you telling me all this? You said just a moment ago that you would be happy for us to leave."

"And so I would, but it would be cruel to create a new multi-generational refugee problem. It would be worse in this timeline since the international community is not aware of you and doesn't care; you would get very little assistance. I can't take upon my people the responsibility and guilt of genocide. You've cost us many lives and keep educating your children to hate us and sacrifice themselves, but my conscience would not allow me to let you all die in the Jordanian desert."

"Then we stay," Mazen pronounced, "and try to negotiate a peaceful arrangement."

"You think it's possible? You think Hamas and even your own Fatah will let you rule or even live if you really strive for peace with us?"

Mazen didn't answer. After a while he asked quietly: "Why did you invite me here?"

"I think I have a solution to our mutual problem, a solution that will allow your people to leave with all their possessions, including their homes. You will even be able to take with you your universities with all their equipment and books."

Understanding came suddenly into Ahmad Mazen's eyes. He got up and started pacing. It took him a couple of minutes to calm down.

"Time travel," he said after sitting down. "To where and when do you propose to send us?"

"I'll be frank with you. I had much more time to think about this than you have. I'll explain my position and let you go back to your office and think about it.

"We can't send you back into the near history. There are several reasons for that. I will mention only two: if we send you, say into the middle of the First World War you will find yourself trying to do several things at the same time. You will have to defend against the Ottoman Turks who will not take your intrusion lightly. You will have, at the same time, to provide for your population and establish an organized state. You may not survive or, at the least, pay a very high price for this attempt.

"Our other concern is that you would screw up the timeline so much and so close to us that the result would be unpredictable."

"Okay, what about going back 2000 years?" Mazen asked.

"Basically the same thing, you end up in the middle of the Roman era having to fight and we risk disruption to our timeline.

"As you know we are in an area that has been populated for thousands of years. No matter how far back we go, someone will be here to resist you, except if we go back to the end of the last ice age – about 11 thousand years back. The advantage is that very few humans are around, so no resistance, but there is a disadvantage: the climate is going to be colder than we are used to. If you prefer a warm climate and no human competition at all, we can transfer you about 120 thousand years back. Or as far back as necessary to insure both your survival and ours. Of course, we will provide you with enough supplies, animals and seeds to enable you to build a prosperous society.

"Please consult with your people, ask your scientists to verify what I said. When you make up your mind we will invite your scientists to participate in the decision. We will send back instruments to make sure things are as we think they should be. Your people will be a party to all the decisions."

"What if we decide to stay?"

"That will be disappointing. I promise you that we will not tolerate terrorism. Those of you who will not accept this will either die or be deported to the neighboring countries. We will also make you stop the hateful education in your schools and adjust your radio and TV broadcast

282 - The Shield

– no more hate propaganda. Our Jewish population is growing and by the end of the year we will be about 14 million strong. You will most likely be assimilated, especially as the Arab world will be different. We will not allow incessant wars against Israel. If need be, we will destroy any hostile regimes. I don't mean that you'll convert to Judaism, but that you will learn how to live as a peaceful minority in a democratic Jewish state.

"I expect a response by the end of November. It will take us a couple of months to make the preparations, if you decide to go, that is."

***

Hirshson was done reviewing the base defense plans when his telephone rang.

"Ephraim please hold for Gad," Liat Cohen's voice said.

The Chief of General Staff came on line a couple of seconds later: "Hi Ephraim. How are things there?"

"Relatively quiet. We have about 25,000 people coming through every day.

"By the way, I spoke to Alois Brunner, Eichmann's replacement, and gave him the okay he requested to deport the rest of the European Jews to us. I also told him, and I hope you don't mind, that the previous formula is still in place. If they kill a Jew a hundred Germans will die and he will be among the first."

"Ah, that was a good idea," Yaari chuckled. "And how did our Nazi respond?"

"He didn't. I hung up on him. Since he didn't call back I'm assuming that he took the threat seriously, as he should."

"Good." Yaari paused. "Anything cooking with the Italians?"

"Not that we can see. All seems to be quiet."

"How is your plan going?"

"Funny you should ask. I just finished reviewing it. Looks good. It should be on your computer in a moment."

"Ephraim, we need you to come here. You can get on the refugee transport tomorrow afternoon. I'll expect you at the General Staff at 8 in the morning on Tuesday."

After they hung up Hirshson marked the appointment in his calendar for Tuesday, October 28, 1941.

***

Hirshson's defense plan was reviewed, amended and approved – all at the same meeting. He was a bit surprised that the Chief had him come all the way from Italy just to approve the plan. But the meeting was not over yet.

"Gentlemen," the Chief of General Staff said in a loud voice to cut through the conversations going on as everybody relaxed, "we are not done here yet. Please pay attention."

The eight generals and various assorted aides attending the meeting stopped their chatter.

"I will let Zvi explain what our next assignment is." Yaari nodded at the Chief of Military intelligence.

"We were ordered by the government to start strategic planning for a European campaign." Zvi Kaplan paused to let his audience absorb the surprising news. "I will try to present to you the basics of our thinking. Please feel free to interrupt – we are in the early stages and any input is welcome."

"What do you mean by 'European campaign'?" asked the commander of the Navy.

"At this point it would be any fighting in Europe involving our forces," replied Zvi Kaplan. "The other difference from Hirshson's plan is that it would be offensive and not defensive.

"The plan we just approved assumes that at some time in the not too far future the Germans will discover that the Caliph story is bogus. They may try to verify what our intentions are, but it is likely that as soon as they ascertain that they've been deceived by Jews they will attack the Brindisi base. It's arguable whether the Italians will participate, but it's not important either – to attack us the Germans will have to invade Italy. Hirshson's plan does exactly what it was supposed to do: make the Nazis pay a very high price on the way to Brindisi and finally stop them far enough from the base to prevent a direct assault on it.

"As you all remember, our initial plan was to turn over Brindisi to the British sometime in early 1942. By then they should've defeated Rommel, though not yet control all of North Africa. If we stall the Germans somewhere south of Rome, the Brits would be able to finish off in North Africa and start their advance up the Italian boot in the second half of 1942.

"Things have changed since that plan was formulated. Operation Moses is winding down and will be done by the end of December, 1941.

The Cabinet decided to establish open diplomatic relations with Britain, the U.S., and the Soviets by mid-January, 1942. Others will follow but that's not our concern here. The German response is. We assume that as soon as they verify their spies' reports about us, they will attack. If we follow the old scenario the German army will be well fortified in Italy by the time the Brits are ready to attack. You all know how difficult it was even for the combined British-American forces to dislodge them in our time-line. It will be much more difficult for the Brits alone, made even worse by the fact that the Germans are not as exhausted as they were in our time-line – this is before Stalingrad and the other big defeats."

"Why the rush to disclose our presence to the world? If we wait another six or seven months the original plan will work just fine."

"If you'll excuse me, Zvi, I will take this one. It is an important question," Gad Yaari interjected. "There are two reasons. The first is that the Government decided to do so and it's not debatable. And secondly, no matter when the German attack happens, if we stick with a defensive plan they will occupy most of Italy."

Zvi Kaplan looked at his notes. "I see that you guys are impatient so I'll make this as short as possible. Of course you will pay for this with some homework." He smiled. "Okay, here goes the bombshell: the Cabinet instructed us to prepare plans for the event of a government change in Italy. Don't ask me how. Just assume that the Italian king orders Mussolini to resign and appoints Pietro Badoglio or somebody else prime minister. Also assume that Mussolini is going to be out of the picture and that the new Italian government refutes its treaty with Germany. Any questions up to this point?"

After a moment of silence Ephraim Hirshson said "It would need a miracle for Victor Emanuel to appoint Marshal Badoglio two years ahead of schedule and without Italy being invaded by the Allies. But assuming it happens, the Germans may attack. So what have we gained?"

Zvi Kaplan chuckled. "The key word is 'may'. Our estimate, which agrees with the Mossad's, is that if this miracle happens before our identity becomes known to the Nazis, they may be angry but not actually attack. There's really nothing for them to gain from such an attack, as long as Italy doesn't become too cozy with Britain. The probability of a German attack will grow from about 40% to a certainty when they discover that the Caliph is Jewish.

"Our assignment is very simple: devise a military plan, to be implemented after the Italians break with the Germans and before Germany attacks that will prevent German occupation of Italy. Since the attack may happen as early as the end of January, 1942, we will be on our own – the Brits will have nothing to spare to help us. In fact, their perceived military situation may become worse due to the Japanese."

Chapter 25

Captain John Morgan of the Second Armored Company, Third Regiment of the Second Battalion of the British Seventh Armored Division, Eighth Army was standing in his Crusader tank's hatch observing the battle developing about a quarter mile in front of him. In the last week his company, with the support of several infantry and artillery units, steadily pushed Rommel's forces west, towards the town of Matruh. They were now about 40 miles west of the village of Fuka, still about 300 miles east of the Libyan border. Morgan hoped to be in Matruh by nightfall and, if the German resistance continued to be sporadic and ineffective, to reach the border in two or three days.

Something was going on in front of him. It looked like the lead tank of his scout platoon had been hit by something. Morgan scanned the horizon and identified a Panzer IV, or at least the top of its turret, sticking out above a rocky outcrop on the south side of the road. The targeted tank spun around. Apparently it was only a damaged track – easily repaired if not under fire. The tank's commander was well trained: as soon as he realized what was going on he stopped the tank and found his opponent before the panzer had time to fire a second shot. The Crusader's 60mm gun fired and Morgan enjoyed the fireworks' display as the German tank exploded. By now he was used to this: the new guns seemed to penetrate the German armor regardless of the point or angle of impact and most of the time ignited the ammunition inside.

The commander's hatch of the damaged Crusader opened and a man climbed out. He jumped to the ground and went to the left side of the tank. "Good", thought Morgan, "examine the damage and do something about it."

In the meantime two other tanks of the scout platoon started moving forward to shield the crew while repairs were done. They didn't make it on time. Two machine guns opened up from both sides of the road about 200 yards in front of the stuck British tank. The commander was hit and the rest of the crew would have no chance if they tried to leave the tank now.

As the two other machines were trying to target the machine gun nests, all hell erupted around the rest of the column. It looked to Morgan like the earth opened and hundreds, or maybe even a thousand, German soldiers in black SS uniforms jumped out of concealed trenches. Molotov cocktails (which Morgan recognized only as bottles filled with gasoline with a lit rag attached) flew at his tanks. Machine guns opened up on all sides moving down his supporting infantry.

"Mayday, mayday!" Morgan yelled into his radio. "We were ambushed by a superior force."

The brigade operator responded: "Please give us more details."

Morgan had to switch between his company and headquarter frequencies and report on what happened while organizing a defense. At moments like this he wished that tanks had space to carry a radio operator.

Twenty minutes later the remnants of his force – three Crusaders, two trucks with infantry, one six pound cannon and a truck with ammunition – were in full retreat. They needed to go back only about a mile before encountering the main body of their battalion. The Germans were hot on their heels and attacked the battalion which, despite the warning Morgan gave them, was not ready. It was a rout.

The tent housing battalion HQ was hit by a German artillery shell at the same time Captain Morgan's force was attacked. German infantry was pouring from the desert and tanks were appearing from hidden dugouts to support the assault.

John Morgan tried to contact the division HQ, but it was either too far away for his tank's transmitter to reach or wasn't listening on his frequency.

***

Gad Yaari picked up his phone: "Yes, Yaari here."

"Sir, this is Colonel Simha Shalom, Military Intelligence. We have disturbing information from the Egyptian front. Our drones picked up a battle close to the Libyan border – the British have been seriously beaten. That was about two hours ago. As far as we can see - and judging from radio intercepts - the British command either doesn't know what's going on or doesn't care. There are no signs of preparations to stop the advancing Germans."

"Good surveillance job. Colonel, please transfer a full report, including aerial imaging, relevant maps and estimates to my computer."

Next Yaari called Liat Cohen and gave orders for a general alert and a limited emergency staff meeting. The Chief of Military Intelligence and the General commanding the new North Africa command were in his office an hour later. The Navy and Air Force commanders arrived soon after them.

Yaari let Colonel Shalom do the information presentation. After he was done and had left, the Chief of General Staff asked, "Well, Gentlemen, any ideas or observations?"

The Commander of Military Intelligence spoke first. "The Brits' situation looks lousy. As you ordered, our liaison in Cairo notified their command of the threat. His official rank is only Colonel and he's nominally responsible for training, so the good General Auchinleck either didn't get the message or didn't think it important enough to act upon. Since the Colonel is also nominally a member of the Jewish Brigade and Auchinleck has no knowledge of our presence, I can see how the warning was ignored. We asked the Foreign Ministry to instruct our ambassador in London to warn Churchill as soon as possible.

"To tell you the truth, I don't think all these warnings will do any good. Look at the map: If the Germans keep moving at their current pace, they'll be in El-Alamein by tomorrow evening. The only thing that can stop them is fuel shortage, but I have a nasty suspicion that Rommel hoarded fuel while slowly retreating and will have enough to keep going. The Brits can disrupt his advance to some extent using their air force, but they really don't have enough aircraft to do serious damage."

"Okay," Yaari was looking at the map. "Let's assume Rommel reaches El-Alamein by tomorrow night.

"In his place I would go directly for Cairo and send a minor force to Alexandria."

"What do the Brits have to oppose him?" asked the Commander of the Navy.

Zvi Kaplan pulled out a sheet of paper from his briefcase: "In theory they have most of the Eighth Army in the area. The problem is that it's disorganized. Their command suffers from overconfidence and stupidity.

"Instead of being patient and amassing a significant armored force armed with the new guns, they threw them into battle piecemeal – as they became available. Rommel was surprised by the kill rate the British achieved, but he learned and adapted. The almost twenty thousand Muslim SS troops he got allowed him to develop a tactic similar to what the Russians used on the Eastern front: deep, layered defense with massed infantry attacks using anti-tank weapons - Molotov cocktails in Rommel's case. Apparently the Muslim soldiers don't mind dying – maybe the Mufti promised them seventy virgins in heaven.

"In any case, in our timeline Montgomery won at El-Alamein because the Germans were exhausted, low on fuel, and couldn't conquer his defenses. The situation is different now. The Germans aren't nearly as exhausted and they have two fresh SS divisions to help them. The British don't have a well-manned or organized defense line.

"Right now, after the British lead forces were ambushed and annihilated, there's nothing between the Germans and Cairo, Alexandria or the Suez canal."

Yaari sighed. "I see. Let's take a look at the aerial images."

After a short silence the Air Force commander said, "If we come down on the Germans before they reach El-Alamein, we can destroy most of their force. Look how they are strung out along the main road. There's not much choice there: sea on their left and desert on the right. The desert will probably slow down tanks, or damage their tracks very quickly, so I can see why they keep to the roads. Same goes for artillery that may sink in the sand. Why is the infantry confining itself to the single road?"

"Probably because they haven't been attacked from the air," Zvi Kaplan responded, "and the road will get them to where they are going much faster. It is true that light trucks and cars can negotiate most of the rocky terrain next to the roads, but there's no incentive for them to take that route, except for patrols and reconnaissance."

Gad Yaari made his decision. "I'll call the prime Minister. We need the Cabinet's permission to get involved. I need a detailed plan for aerial and naval operations by 7p.m. That gives you four hours.

"We need to stop this column before they leave El-Alamein otherwise they'll disperse and will be much more difficult to destroy. One more thing: we will attack at night. No need to expose our identity in a day attack. It will also be safer that way."

The Navy Commander asked, "What do you expect me to do? I have nothing that can destroy this column better than the Air Force."

"Destroying the column is not enough. While the Air Force is busy with the ground forces we need to cut off the German's lifeline to Italy. That will be your job. Ask for air support if you need it. Also plan on at least one ship capable of carrying a helicopter for rescue missions. I know, I know," Yaari waved at the commander of the Air Force, "You always take care of your own, but in this case it may be as far away as the Tunisian border..."

"Is that as far west as we can go?" The Air Force General wanted to know.

"Yes, you need to destroy everything in sight. It stands to reason that if we get involved it should be the end of the Axis in North Africa."

"I think that it's safe to assume that after the first night's work the assault on Cairo will be cancelled. We'll assess the results and decide what to do in the morning. If Rommel loses about half of his force he's done. I would let the Brits take over from there. If we do all the fighting they will never learn and will be seriously beaten in Europe in a year or less. Of course this is a political decision and the Government will have to decide."

***

"Gentlemen, how are things going at home?" Mizrahi asked his guests. The group arrived that morning on a specially scheduled flight from Israel and was now sitting in his living room at the embassy.

"Nothing much is new," Jonathan Brown responded, "except that we have millions and millions of new immigrants."

Dan Levine smiled: "Right, everything is about the same as usual. People still complaining about hard life and inept politicians. And car prices are going up."

Mizrahi switched to business: "The two of you are booked on a Pan Am flight from London to New York. It leaves tomorrow evening and, if everything goes well, will land in New York on November 13th. You should be well rested – the flying boat has beds in First Class."

Jonathan made a quick calculation: "Are you sure of the dates? We are going to be flying for two days?"

"No," clarified Mizrahi, "the flight is not non-stop. It stops in Iceland and in Nova Scotia to refuel and rest.

"I will likely be very busy tomorrow, so let me give you the tickets and your passports. These are genuine British diplomatic passports for Jonathan Brown and Dan Law. You are both attached to the British embassy in Washington but need not go there or contact them, except in case of trouble. The ambassador has been informed that you are VIPs and if you request his assistance he should extend all help possible. Your mission must be important – I had to call in a couple of favors with Churchill – but don't tell me what it is.

"So, good luck. My driver will take you to the airport tomorrow. Oh, by the way, your suitcases were marked as diplomatic pouches, so no customs checks anywhere."

They said their goodbyes and Mizrahi left. He had an afternoon appointment with Winston Churchill. The news he was bringing was not good.

***

"Mr. Mizrahi, you requested an urgent meeting. What brings you here?" Churchill was sipping a brandy and looked relaxed. London looked lively these days. Even the traffic had picked up. Not much merchant shipping got into England through the Mediterranean but petroleum products were arriving in adequate quantities around Africa.

"Sir, I have grave news from North Africa."

"Last I heard our forces were slowly advancing and pushing this confounded Rommel west."

"Yes, that was yesterday. The situation changed abruptly early this afternoon." Mizrahi went on to tell the British Prime Minister about the collapse of his forces and the danger to Cairo and Alexandria.

"Our General Staff estimates that the Germans and Italians will be in Cairo and Alexandria in a day or two and will control the Suez canal, at least the Egyptian bank of it, in three or four days."

Churchill lit a cigar and calmly looked at Mizrahi: "Mr. Mizrahi, we British don't give up easily. I'm sure that General Auchinleck is organizing a defense as we speak, but just to make sure I'll send him a message as soon as we're done here."

"Good," Mizrahi got up. "I've been instructed by my government to give you this information in the hope that it will assist Britain in mounting a defense. I have also brought with me aerial photographs of the area from El-Alamein to the Tunisian border. These should be of help in your actions." He laid a large manila envelope with the photographs on the coffee table.

The next day at ten in the morning the embassy phone rang. The Prime Minister wanted Mizrahi to come to his residence for an urgent meeting as soon as possible.

This time Churchill was pacing around his office. "I contacted the command of the Eight Army. They are aware of the situation – apparently your liaison in Cairo made a nuisance of himself. As far as they are concerned the situation is serious. We are going to rush as many troops as we can spare from Somalia and Ethiopia, but that may not be enough."

Churchill stopped pacing and sat at the head of the conference table. "Mr. Mizrahi, we are at a crossroads here. Britain can't be allowed to falter now. The future of the free world is at stake.

"If we fail in North Africa this war will go on for many years." He was vigorously sucking on his cigar, not noticing that he had forgotten to light it.

"Mr. Prime Minister, my government agrees with you. If you have no objections, we will act directly against the Axis forces in North Africa. There are several details we have to agree upon before that's possible."

"So there is a price to pay. And you warned me of the high price Mr. Roosevelt would extract for his help! But no matter, please go ahead."

"Sir, it seems to me that since we are Jewish you are predisposed to misjudge us. The details I am talking about are not a 'price' but rather a means to achieve the maximum gain from this situation." Mizrahi carefully filled and lit his pipe. Churchill suddenly noticed his cigar and lit it.

"There are two separate issues I would like to agree upon," Mizrahi continued. "The first is simple: we need your Eight Army to start advancing now on El-Alamein. They should plan on massing their forces about five miles east of it in two days – November 14. They are to attack on that day early in the morning."

"Wait, wait," Churchill was making negating gestures. "According to the radio messages I've gotten from the staff there, they may be able to have a brigade at best ready for action in that area two days from now. They'll be slaughtered by Rommel."

"No, sir, they will not. You must trust us on this or you will waste an incredible opportunity. Two days from now the Axis forces in North Africa will be down to a fraction of their fighting ability. If you attack when we tell you and follow this plan." Mizrahi laid two typed pages and a map on the table. "You're likely to arrive at the Tunisian border within a week. If you wait and if Rommel is still alive, he will regroup and it will take you a month or more with ten times the casualties. This is the first condition. If you accept it, we can go on to the second."

Churchill smiled. "Mr. Mizrahi, I must apologize. My previous outburst was not called for. Yes, I agree, though sometimes I have a difficult time controlling the generals. Please continue."

"Good. I didn't expect you to oppose a quick victory. Now, the second little detail we need to agree upon is more complicated and involves diplomacy. Here is what we propose…"

***

Major General Horst Egersdorff looked at his watch. It was close to seven in the evening and almost completely dark. He looked one last time at the sky and entered his command tent. If things go well, tomorrow at this time his troops will be beyond El-Alamein, on the main road to Alexandria. Egersdorff was in command of a special force and was ordered by Rommel to advance on Alexandria and from there to proceed to Port Said. He was expected to encounter little resistance with his force of mostly Italian troops. While he was taking the entrance to the Suez Canal, the main force under the personal command of Rommel was to attack Cairo.

Egersdorff told his adjutant to call a meeting of his command staff. He wanted to repeat his instructions and make sure that the Italians understood his plan. He was somewhat dubious of their ability as a military force but trusted his German battalion to stiffen them if necessary.

The meeting started at 7:30 and was disrupted almost immediately by a huge blast and roar. It sounded like a thousand tank engines were running at top power next to the tent. Then the noise receded.

By the time the officers ran out of the tent to take a look, all that was visible were flashes of light some ten miles to the east. Egersdorff estimated that this was where the forward units in El-Alamein were positioned for the night. He didn't have long to wonder what was going on. The terrible roar returned, but this time it was accompanied by explosions of light cannon projectiles and the occasional bomb. The last thing the general saw was a string of explosions running towards him along the ground. Then he was dead – a 20mm cannon projectile will do that to a person, especially if it hits him in the stomach.

In the morning Field Marshal Ervin Rommel surveyed his army. It seemed that everything was quiet and the attackers were gone but so were vital elements of the force he assembled to attack Cairo and Alexandria. The preliminary report indicated that he had no operational tanks or artillery left. Most of his fuel trucks were burning and only a few of the ammunition transports survived. There were significant personnel losses as well. A number of generals died, including Egersdorff who was supposed to lead the attack on Alexandria. Curiously, the losses among the lower ranks were not too bad – he estimated that about sixty to seventy percent survived the air attack. He considered his options and within the hour issued commands. The army was on the move again.

Not having tanks or artillery to speak of, Rommel decided to consolidate his position and dig in. He would wait for supplies to arrive from the west. There were a number of ships in Libyan and French Vichy controlled Tunis ports unloading more tanks, artillery, fuel and ammunition. All was not lost, and he doubted that the British could repeat such an intensive attack anytime soon. If they did, he would be ready – one of his first orders after the barrage was to organize an air defense. Everybody was ordered to shoot at the attacking aircraft, even if they were hard to see in the dark.

By late afternoon, November 13, no reinforcements had arrived and there was no sign of supplies from depots on the road to Benghazi. The field telephone was dead and HQ couldn't raise Benghazi on the radio. Finally, a courier on a motorbike got through to Rommel. "Sir, Colonel Erfurter, the commander of the Benghazi garrison, reports that they've come under intense air attacks. The fuel and ammunition dumps are on fire. The three ships that were unloading in the port at the time were sunk and are now blocking the harbor."

Less than an hour later radio contact was established with Tobruk. The fortress there reported intense bombardment and the sinking of a cargo ship. This was less of a problem than in Benghazi since the port was primitive and more open, so other ships could still unload – if any ships would come from Italy, that is. Tobruk also reported that they thought they saw a burning plane falling and exploding somewhere in the desert to the south of the fortifications. They sent out search parties. The commander of the fortress didn't know the dimensions of the disaster, but understood that capturing the British pilot might shed some light on the surprise attack.

***

Lieutenant Colonel Oren Shaviv trained for the last several months on old Skyhawks. A tedious business, as far as he was concerned. The jets lacked the power of the F-16s or the maneuverability of the Kfir. The Israeli command decided to use the Skyhawks since the country could easily replace the fighter/bomber's wear parts.

At first, Oren was surprised. When red lights and alarms went off in the cockpit of his Skyhawk he thought that the workhorse just died of old age. The plane was almost fifty years old and Oren suspected that all the maintenance in the world couldn't make it new. It took another glance at the instruments and out the left side of the cockpit to discover the problem: he had been hit by a large caliber anti-aircraft explosive shell. This was pure bad luck.

There was a big hole in the left wing with flames licking its edges. The flames looked even more ominous in the dark, but their light let him see that the hole in the wing was too big for the aircraft to survive much longer. He didn't have much time – just enough to head south into the open desert and try to gain some altitude on the way. He would have preferred to bail out over the sea, but he was heading south when he was hit and couldn't turn. Several miles later the wing broke off and Oren ejected.

After landing he buried his parachute and all parts of the ejection seat he could find in a nearby cave. There wasn't much he could do about the aircraft itself. It was probably totally destroyed by the explosion of a bomb he didn't have time to drop, and some of the remaining cannon shells. The fuel it was carrying was burning merrily when it hit the ground. After resting for a little while, he started walking deeper into the desert. There was no way of knowing what the Germans, or Italians, would do. They might decide to look for him; he hoped they would be too busy licking their wounds.

Oren considered two courses of action: going south, as deep as possible into the Libyan Desert, or circling around and trying to get to the Mediterranean. He decided to go south. There was traffic on the road east of Tobruk and circling to the west would mean walking around the city and fortress – many miles of walking close to a populated area with a big Italian/German garrison.

By eleven in the morning Oren was exhausted. Climbing the endless sandy hills was hard. He was carrying about thirty pounds worth of water, emergency rations and arms. In addition to the usual 9mm polymer Jericho pistol he was also armed with a Tavor assault rifle. This was a precaution taken for just the circumstances he found himself in. He needed to stop and rest for a couple of hours – until the hottest part of the day passed. This pause gave him an opportunity to double check his radio and location beacon. Judging by the displays, both were working, but he could get no response to his emergency signal. Finally he wrapped himself in a thin camouflage fabric and lay down on the sand. He chose a position on a down slope of a sandy hill covered with small stones and larger rock outcroppings. Assuming that any search parties were coming from the north, he chose the southern slope, behind a small rock.

The fierce sun notwithstanding, the Lieutenant Colonel fell asleep. An hour and a half later he woke up with a start. He opened his eyes but didn't move – he thought he'd heard a noise and was not going to give his position away until he knew more. He heard something again – it sounded like footsteps crunching on the sand and pebbles just next to his ear. Then he heard muffled speech. It was not really next to his ear – the ground transmitted the crunch and made it sound much closer than it really was.

Oren unwrapped his camouflage blanket, careful not to make any noise. After he was done, he covered himself with it so that just his eyes peeked out. He slowly lifted himself above the rock that was between him and the top of the hill. With only his eyes showing he scanned the scenery. Nothing. Then he heard people talking again. This time he got a better sense of direction: they were men and they were moving along the other side of the hill. He decided to take a look. It took a couple of minutes of slow and careful crawling before he could take a quick peek.

A vehicle was parked at the bottom of the valley between two hills. He thought that it was an Italian Fiat but could not be sure and didn't want to bring out his mini-binoculars – a flash of reflected light could give away his position. Five men were sitting on the ground half way up the side of the hill opposite him. Three wore German uniforms. As far as Oren could tell, one of the Germans was a sergeant, the other two were privates. There were also two soldiers wearing Italian uniforms. Both of them were privates.

***

On the flight to New York Jonathan and Dan were surprised to meet two other Israelis. One was an official from the Absorption Ministry and the other a historian specializing in the Jewish and Zionist history of the first half of the twentieth century.

"Where are you going?" one of the two asked.

"To New York and beyond." Dan responded.

"Okay. Another secret project," the historian said.

"And what are you doing here?" Dan inquired.

"It's our third trip. We're maintaining the contacts between Palestine and the Jewish community in America. These would have been severed when we popped up in this time."

After they returned to their seats Jonathan looked at Dan. "Another government screw-up? Why not use their contacts? We didn't need to bother with Snyder."

"I don't think it was a screw-up," Dan responded. "The Jewish community, I mean the part of the community that is really Jewish and cares about other Jews, has no influence or connection with Roosevelt. They demonstrated and made noise in support of European Jews. All that got them was a notice on the inner page of some newspapers. Not even an interview with the President or anybody from the Administration.

"We did look at possible connections there but discovered very quickly that the only contacts with Roosevelt were through labor leaders and Communists. Snyder was a unique opportunity. We probably could have gotten to him through these two emissaries but it was much handier to speak directly to him in Italy. You think that his visit to the Brindisi facility didn't help us?"

Dan and Jonathan took a taxi from the pier where the flying boat was moored to the Hotel New York. It was close to noon and they expected to be able to wash up and get ready to meet Snyder.

Snyder was waiting for them in the hotel's lobby: "How was your trip? Any problems?"

"No. Thanks for asking. We are fine, any news about our business?"

Snyder pointed to a table and armchairs in the corner. After settling there and getting drinks Snyder said, "I have good news and bad news. Which first?"

"Tell us in chronological order." Dan responded.

"Right. I could not find any approach to the Vice Admiral. It sounds like he is a tough cookie and associates mainly with Navy characters. That's the bad news.

"The good news is that I know a nice woman who used to work for Mr. Roosevelt when he was the governor of New York. She was his Labor Secretary for a while. Now she heads a large union. She's Jewish, but cares nothing about Palestine – her worries are mostly about the labor movement. On the other hand, she cares about Mr. Roosevelt's health and has respect for Jewish doctors.

"To make a long story short: after questioning me for two hours, she agreed to recommend Dr. Brown's services to Mrs. Roosevelt. Eleanor has been looking for a second opinion – she thinks that Admiral McKinley is not the best doctor for her husband.

"Here is the catch though: she will call Mrs. Roosevelt, and maybe the President, only after interviewing you. Our appointment with her is tonight at ten at her office. It's not too far from here and I will take you there. Before I leave, we need to decide whether Dr. Brown is coming by himself or both of you go."

Dan nodded. "That's a good question. My function here is to keep Dr. Brown safe – he's a prominent physician and has knowledge of research done in Germany and other places. He may be in danger if the Nazis become aware of him being here, especially if his mission becomes known to them."

Snyder looked from one man to the other. "I wasn't aware that you were that important, Dr. Brown. If that's the case, by all means let's go together. Of course, you will have to explain the situation to Miss Schiller."

At 10 p.m. sharp they rang the bell at the entrance to a nondescript building in the garment district. The door was opened by a burly man who looked them over and let them enter. The cramped lobby looked old and somewhat dingy. It was lit by a single low-powered bulb which made it look even more worn out that it actually was. There were two other men in the lobby. The doorman motioned for them to lift their arms and patted them down: "Sorry about this, but we have to be careful."

"Yeah," Snyder smiled. "I hear the mob is not too happy with Schiller's policies. They'll get used to it."

The man wasn't amused. "Please follow me."

They went up a creaking elevator that their guide controlled with a manual lever. It stopped on the sixth floor. The man opened the door and led them down a sparsely lit corridor. Close to its end he knocked on a door.

"Come in," a woman's voice shouted.

The first room was obviously a secretary's or receptionist's office. It was empty. The door to the next office was open. A woman in her late forties was seated behind a big desk. She got up to great them. "Hi, Howard, punctual as usual. Pleasure to see you again. Introduce me to your friends."

"This is Dr. Jonathan Brown and Mr. Dan Law." Both shook hands with the woman.

"Sam, thank you. I'll call you when these gentlemen are ready to leave."

Clara Schiller was almost as tall as Jonathan. She looked them over, smiled and pointed to the chairs opposite her desk. "Howard tells me that you are a prominent physician from Palestine. Can you tell me more about yourself?"

Jonathan told her his cover story – basically true, except for the slight modifications necessary to make it fit America in 1941.

"So you can see", he concluded, "how we at Hadassah became a world center for medical knowledge."

"Very interesting. I didn't realize that the little hospital in Jerusalem was so advanced, but it does make sense that with the influx of the best brains from Germany and the rest of Europe you would make progress.

"Mr. Law, what brings you here?"

Dan smiled "Please call me Dan. I am here mostly as a bodyguard for Jonathan. As you know, the German intelligence services are very thorough and probably know of our visit here. They would love to capture him for themselves or kill him to prevent him getting access to the President. I have other functions connected with the Zionist movement, but they are a far second to Jonathan's safety."

Clara Schiller was quiet for a while making notes on a pad in front of her. After she was done she said, "Dr. Brown, what do you expect to be able to do for the President?"

"Before I commit to anything I would need to examine him and run some tests. Only after that will I be able to say with any degree of certainty what I can do."

For a while the room was quiet. Finally Clara Schiller said, "For whatever it's worth, I trust you and will recommend you to Eleanor. Of course, she will want to interview you herself."

"I'll let you know tomorrow. Sam will bring a note from me to your hotel."

***

"Captain, we have a pilot down," the comm man reported to the commander of the missile boat. "He was shot down somewhere near Tobruk."

The captain of the vessel looked at his watch. It was 4:20 a.m., about an hour and a half until sunrise. They were east and north of Tobruk and were scheduled to arrive outside the fortress in an hour.

"Anything from the pilot?" he asked.

"No, sir. Both his beacon and transceiver seem to be either dead or off. I did catch a short burst from the ejection seat transceiver so we know where he ejected."

"Okay. Keep listening. Gil," He turned to his second in command, "Get HQ, tell them what the situation is and ask for instructions. I don't like sending the helicopter out over hostile territory without having the pilot's position."

The HQ responded in a couple of minutes: "The Air Force is looking for him. Standby at the predetermined position. As soon as we know something we will let you know."

At about ten in the morning the missile boat's radar identified two ships approaching their position from the north. One was a merchant vessel, the other a cruiser, both headed straight for the port of Tobruk. Usually Germans didn't escort their cargo ships. They and the Italians had anti-aircraft guns installed on the merchant ships but didn't want to risk their naval vessels. A cruiser could put up some fire but it was likely to be sunk if discovered by the Royal Air Force. On the other hand, if it encountered a Royal Navy ship it would have a fair chance to inflict some damage.

This time it was an Italian cruiser that had the bad luck of approaching Tobruk. The missile boat fired twice. Both anti-ship missiles hit their targets. The two enemy ships disappeared from the radar display about 15 minutes later. The Gabriel sea to sea missile, though old and almost obsolete was extremely effective, especially if the enemy didn't expect it and had no countermeasures.

***

Oren was trying to figure out what to do. He was one against five, but this was not as hopeless as it looked. If he was fast he could shoot all of them within seconds. The question was whether to shoot the radio he saw in the back of the open Fiat. If he did, he was giving the soldiers a chance to do something, but he was also making sure they couldn't contact whoever sent them and call for help. His other problem was shooting people who had done nothing to him and were just sitting there talking and eating. Being a veteran pilot Oren had a lot of combat experience, but never face to face. Now he discovered that it required some determination to kill a person you could see and hear.

In the meantime, he got ready: he carefully moved the Tavor to a ready position in front of him and put a spare magazine by its side. He waited. If the group finished their meal and kept driving along the bottom of the small valley, they would be out of sight in a couple hundred feet. Or they might decide to go back the way they came.

The sergeant got up and walked in Oren's direction. He stopped not more than fifteen feet from Oren next to a sizeable boulder, opened his fly and started pissing. At this moment Oren's radio came on – it was set to vibrate for just such an occasion – the pilot was startled enough to twitch, which dislodged a stone near his foot. The stone rolled down the slope. If the German wasn't so close he probably wouldn't have heard the noise. Even now he didn't seem alarmed. He buttoned up his fly and called to the others. Oren knew no German, but it was clear what the order was: they jumped up and started climbing in his direction.

He shot the four soldiers first – they were farther away and if alerted by gunfire were likely to take cover among the rocks. They were also armed with rifles, which Oren thought were more dangerous than the pistol the sergeant was pulling out of its holster.

The sergeant tried to rush him – it was a short distance. He almost succeeded. When Oren finally hit him, he fell almost on top of the pilot.

After it was over the Lieutenant Colonel shivered for several seconds – the effects of a sudden adrenalin rush. When he felt steady, he inspected his radio and then carefully climbed down to the Fiat. The radio seemed okay but was dead again. Since it had showed signs of life, though at an inopportune moment, Oren decided to open the cover and see what was wrong with it. There was a dent in the battery cover and on closer inspection he saw that the dent was in fact a puncture. The cover and the battery behind it had stopped a fragment of the shell that killed his aircraft. If it hit an inch higher or lower, he would have had to deal with a bleeding wound in his left side. Oren wasn't sure that this wouldn't be preferable to being stranded with a dead radio and an apparently inoperative beacon, even if the radio had come to life for a couple of seconds. There was nothing he could do about it now so he looked at his only alternative.

It took him almost half an hour to figure out the workings of the radio in the Fiat. It wasn't capable of broadcasting in the frequency range of his emergency radio, but he could try to send a message on a short wave frequency that the Air Force was monitoring.

"Zebra, this is Zebra 5. Please respond." He repeated the English message four times before a response came:

"Zebra 5 this is Zebra. Are you safe and can you keep transmitting?"

"I'm fine. Do you want to know where I am?"

"No, don't tell the world where you are. We have you now. Can you stay where you are until dark?"

"I'm not sure. The people that contributed the radio may send somebody to collect it."

"Okay. We'll come for you at 7:15. In the meantime go to map grid 7253. It is not too far. Give us the usual signal when you hear us."

"Good. I'll be waiting for you there."

He shut down the radio, changed it back to the German frequency and started walking. He had ten miles to cover in less than six hours – not as easy as it sounded. The terrain was getting more and more rugged and, though some grasses and dry bushes were growing here and there, it was becoming sandier.

Oren arrived at the rendezvous point with an hour to spare.

The helicopter arrived on time. On the way back they had to fly very high – the skies were again lit up by explosions and heavy anti-aircraft fire. This time the jets attacked from high up, spreading cluster bombs and incendiaries. By four in the morning there were no worthwhile targets left.

***

When Oren got to his base he was met with a barrage of questions, even before his formal debriefing. Apparently he was the only pilot to be shot down in Operation Quicksand.

He was slightly embarrassed, though he knew that it wasn't his fault – just bad luck.

"What happened to the plane?" he asked his commander who debriefed him.

"Believe me," the Colonel answered, "it was much more of a headache than you were. After you called in, it was a simple operation to extricate you. We would have found you anyway – you were clearly visible on satellite images. The plane was another story. We had to send two cargo helicopters and a crew to cut the damn thing up and cart it back home. A real pain. And by the way, you hid the ejection seat real well. If its beacon wasn't running we would have never found it. Why didn't you stay in the cave next to it?"

***

"Oren, I always knew that you were a hothead but endangering your life like that? What if you were killed? My only brother has no common sense at all."

Noam Shaviv paused for breath, "You had no thoughts about Ziva or the boys? You're a squadron commander and not so young. I mean what is a Lieutenant Colonel in his thirties doing flying such a mission. What if the Germans took you prisoner?"

Oren waved his hand at his younger brother, "But nothing happened. I'm here in one piece. So don't get all excited.

"First, you know that I had to fly this mission. What kind of a commander would I be if I only sent others into danger?

"Second, I'm way too young to be flying a desk. This mission wasn't really dangerous. I just had a bit of bad luck. The chances are higher to be killed crossing a street than flying a mission like that.

"And third, look who's talking. I know for a fact that you're always in front of your troops and never pass on a chance to participate in an action."

Noam smiled, "I'm not a Lieutenant Colonel so I'm allowed."

"Sure. And, Noam, when you get to be one you'll start leading from behind. Right?"

The brothers were enjoying their after dinner coffee at Oren's house in Beer Sheba. It was less than a week since Oren came back from his mission. He wasn't too annoyed by his younger brother's rant. In fact he got a much worse talking to from his wife, Ziva, who also mentioned their three sons. He told her the same thing he told Noam, but she didn't accept his explanation and made him promise to avoid volunteering for dangerous missions in the future. Oren wasn't sure whether he could avoid dangerous missions but he was going to try for his marriage's sake.

***

Later the same day a heated argument took place at the Israeli General Staff meeting.

Zvi Kaplan, the chief of Military Intelligence, was finishing his summary: "Both our aerial surveillance and radio intercepts indicate that Rommel's forces suffered a serious setback. He radioed Berlin for urgent reinforcements and complained about the lack of air support. It seems that our air raid last night was quite devastating. Rommel has practically no operational tanks and very little fuel. He is also running low on ammunition. The move towards Cairo and the Suez was canceled and, we think, he is retreating and digging in."

"I recommend another strike tonight," said the Air Force commander. "We can finish them militarily and let the Brits just walk to the Tunisian border."

"Not so fast." responded Yaari. "You can't win a war from the air and even if we could, we need to decide whether we should. There are a number of considerations that go beyond the immediate fate of Rommel and his army. Zvi, please go on."

Zvi Kaplan turned on a projector and brought up a diagram: "You can see from this that the Germans and Italians suffered serious losses in armor, trucks and fuel. Their infantry was also beaten up, but not as badly. This is understandable: the numbers are large and they are dispersed over a significant area.

"If you just count the materiel losses it seems that they should be on the verge of collapse. This is an illusion. The Germans have demonstrated an exceptional ability and willingness to fight. It is evident even now that they are regrouping in an orderly and disciplined fashion and are not about to run."

"This supports my idea of another air strike tonight," insisted the Air Force general. "This is our opportunity to finish them off. We may be able to bring them to the verge of collapse and remove their presence from

North Africa. The British army will have to do its part, but after a third night of bombing it shouldn't be difficult."

Zvi Kaplan was adamant: "I don't agree. Just take a look at our history. The battle for Stalingrad that didn't happen here yet and may never happen is a good demonstration. Even when surrounded and starved, the Germans continued to fight until given the order to surrender. Rommel is a gifted tactician and a good leader of men. His troops trust him and will do whatever he asks of them. He may or may not be a Nazi but he is a typical German officer who will obey orders and do his best to win. He will not surrender or run.

"There is another consideration we must take into account: one of our jets was shot down last night."

"Just bad luck. It happens," interjected the Air Force commander. "We did recover both the pilot and the plane, so no harm was done."

"I agree." Yaari responded, "but we don't know what will happen if we attack tonight. There's no doubt that the Germans and the Italians, will be prepared for an air attack. What if we lose a plane and are unable to recover it?"

The Air Force commander shrugged: "An army that is afraid of losses has already given up its chance to victory."

Yaari was exasperated: "It is not the Army's problem. Don't you see that if the Germans suspect that it wasn't the Royal Air Force that caused last night's damage they will figure out that it must be the Caliph? The consequences will be dire for our people in Europe."

"True," responded the Air Force general, "but you are assuming that they'll figure it out and draw certain conclusions. I think that the risk is miniscule."

"Are you ready to bet the lives of a million people on this?" Yaari asked.

"We can always nuke them again. That will persuade them to be reasonable."

"So you are proposing that we kill some more German civilians and risk the lives of a million Jews for a dubious advantage?" Yaari asked calmly.

"Not really." The Air Force man responded. "It just galls me to miss such an opportunity. You are probably right."

Zvi Kaplan smiled: "You know, I almost agree with you. The chances that something will happen to connect the Caliph to all this are really small. There is another consideration though.

"The Brits got themselves into trouble in the first place because of overconfidence. They may have learned that lesson, but they still have only a foggy idea of how to fight a modern war. If we take the risk of exposure and pound on Rommel some more we will be doing the British Army a great disservice. They'll never learn and will either pay a terrible price when the fight moves to Europe or will require us to do their fighting. With all the respect to the Air Force and the other branches of the IDF" he nodded to the assembled generals, "I can't see us winning the war against Nazi Germany all by ourselves. We probably could leave a number of German cities glowing in the dark but I have no certainty that the crazy Nazis would surrender even then. I also can't see us nuking cities to win this war. With all the talk of civilians being part of the war machine, I can't see our society agreeing to mass murder."

***

The next day, Friday, in the early afternoon, Dan got a call from the reception clerk: "Sir, there is a Mr. Sam Dubliner here asking for you."

Sam handed Dan an envelope and left without saying a word.

The note in the envelope said:

> Dr. Brown, please present yourself at the southern entrance to the White House at 5 p.m. on Wednesday, November 19. Bring your medical bag.
>
> Clara

Snyder called Jonathan's room several minutes later: "Hi, Jonathan. I'd like to invite you and Dan to a meeting of the local Labor Zionist chapter. You know, some food and a schmooze about Palestine. It's not that often that we have visitors from there."

"Let me ask Dan," Jonathan replied. "He just went down to the lobby. I think we have a note from Ms. Schiller. I'll call you back in a moment."

Dan knocked on Jonathan's door a minute later and showed him the note. "We have to leave for Washington now. I'll barely have time to do what I need to do by Wednesday,"

"We're invited to a dinner reception at the local chapter of the Labor Zionists. Shall I call Snyder and apologize?"

Dan made a fast calculation. "Yes. I need to be at the Bethesda Naval hospital tomorrow morning at six. If we leave on the train that leaves at three I'll have enough time to make the arrangements."

The next morning Dan left early arriving at the Bethesda hospital in the uniform of a Navy MP Sergeant – a security officer with Naval Operations. According to his papers he was Sergeant Nathan Johnson, attached to Bethesda security. Nathan Johnson was indeed employed by Naval Operations security but not at Bethesda. A superficial check would show that he existed and conceivably had business there, specifically at the hospital kitchens, having been trained several months earlier in kitchen hygiene supervision.

The Mossad didn't have much data on Vice Admiral McKinley. He was the Chief Surgeon of the Navy and an otolaryngologist. He was also the President's personal physician. Information pointed to the doctor's possible responsibility for the President's poor health. The Admiral resisted any other physician treating Roosevelt. If one offered a second opinion, he did his best to prevent his patient from acting on it. That was the extent of historical data available.

It took Dan all day to inform himself of the Admiral's routine and to develop a plan of action.

The opening he needed was during the Admiral's breakfast. It seemed that McKinley was set in his ways, including in his breakfast and lunch routines. Dinner was less predictable since he often saw the President around that time and usually ate at home.

The next day Dan was at the hospital again. By now his face was familiar to the kitchen personnel and nobody paid attention to the new hygiene inspector. When the Admiral's breakfast of toast, eggs, cornflakes and a pitcher of milk was ready to go up to his office, the new sergeant chose his moment and put a pinch of a white, odorless and tasteless powder over the cornflakes. He didn't spend much time around the kitchen that day and did his best to be inconspicuous. Dan was waiting for news about the Chief Surgeon. There was none that day.

On Sunday he added two pinches to the cornflakes. At noon, when McKinley usually looked in on his patients at the hospital, Dan got the first news: the rounds were canceled. The official line was that the doctor didn't feel well.

On Monday the dose of delayed-release hallucinogen was increased to three pinches. In the early afternoon a rumor spread that the Surgeon General tried, unsuccessfully, to fly off his desk. It apparently annoyed him and he tried to open his office window to fly farther. The window was painted shut and the Admiral called on his secretary to help him open it. The sailor tried to open it, but changed his mind when the Admiral urged him to hurry so he could soar to the clouds as soon as possible. The aide pretended to go for tools and called the resident psychiatrist. The Admiral behaved strangely for a day or so after the last dose was administered. The psychiatric observation would keep him out of the way for several more days.

On Tuesday Dan went to the hospital again to make sure that Dr. McKinley was locked up for a while. There was no breakfast prepared for the Chief that day. The kitchen was notified to stop delivering food to the Vice Admiral's office until further notice.

***

When Jonathan Brown arrived at the south entrance of the White House the weather was lousy: cold, windy and raining. He ran from his taxi to the entrance.

He was taken through a maze of corridors and up and down staircases and soon lost his bearings. Whether this was intentional or not he didn't know, but if he had to retrace his way back to the entrance he was sure he would be hopelessly lost.

The journey ended in a cozy sitting room. It was empty.

Jonathan settled in one of the easy chairs and prepared for a long wait. He was surprised when the door opened a couple of minutes later and Eleanor Roosevelt came in. Jonathan jumped up from his seat.

"Please seat," Mrs. Roosevelt said. "Would you care for something to drink? Tea, coffee?"

"Thank you. Tea please. No sugar and no milk."

"Ah, you are not as British as all that."

"I'm not British at all," Jonathan replied. "I'm American, born and educated and a Palestinian."

"Yes, yes. Clara told me about you. You impressed her, which is not easy. I will not waste our time asking you about your education or trying to verify your credentials. I'm not qualified to do that anyway, but there is a question I have to ask: what is your interest in helping my husband?"

"It's very simple really. You're probably aware of our massive repatriation program. We are offering a refuge to every Jew that wants to escape from Nazi-occupied Europe. This is not a small burden for us and our leadership thought that if we show some good will and offer competent treatment to the leader of the free world, he may be inclined in our favor if we asked for assistance."

Eleanor Roosevelt said nothing for a while. Finally she got up, and Jonathan got up with her. "Dr. Brown, you may have heard that my husband's regular doctor is indisposed. I am inclined, if Mr. Roosevelt agrees, to let you take a look at him. By tomorrow we will have another Navy doctor take a look too and, maybe, the two of you can figure out what to do about his bronchitis. Please wait here. I'll be back." She smiled and left.

The President sat in his wheelchair looking at the miserable weather outside. He was holding a cigarette holder with an unlit cigarette. "Ah, Dr. Brown, welcome to the White House. My wife is very persuasive, so go ahead and take a look and tell me when I can get out of this damn wheel chair."

Apparently Jonathan's face showed the surprise he felt. Roosevelt laughed: "Just a little joke. Don't take it too seriously. But if you can make me walk I will be eternally grateful." He was interrupted by a bout of coughing.

The examination didn't take long. The president was somewhat surprised when Jonathan took a swab from inside his cheek but didn't protest. When his finger was stabbed to draw some blood he asked: "Is that all you are going to take?"

Jonathan smiled: "Mr. President, I'm no vampire. This should be enough to run the tests I have in mind."

"What about the bronchitis? Is there anything you can do about that now?"

"Sir, I would be derelict in my duties if I gave you any medication now. When I swore the Hippocratic Oath I pledged to 'do no harm'. How could I be sure I am doing no harm if I gave you medication before analyzing your blood and making sure what exactly ails you?

"I would like your permission to come tomorrow at the same time. By then I will know more and will be able to discuss with you a treatment plan."

"Okay, okay, you doctors are all the same. I'll see you tomorrow."

Back at the hotel Jonathan analyzed the samples.

"I need your advice," he told Dan.

"I thought that you were the doctor."

"I don't need medical advice. Here's the problem: our patient definitely suffers from Guillain-Barré syndrome. I suspect that there is also congestive heart failure – not acute at his point - but definitely there.

"To make sure that it is heart failure that causes the fluid in his lungs and not bronchitis, I would like to take an ultrasound – nothing better than an image of a beating heart. So how much risk of exposing our secret are we taking in bringing a portable ultrasound scanner to the White House?"

"I thought that you were planning on bringing that strange filtrating device of yours. The ultrasound scanner is about the same size and if you are careful not to show the patient the display I see no problem. Otherwise he may get all excited and have other people come and look. That would not be desirable."

"Mrs. Roosevelt told me about another Navy doctor that is going to be there tomorrow. What about him?"

"Just refuse to do anything while he is there. Demand privacy on the grounds that you have some equipment from Palestine that hasn't yet been patented in the U.S. and you don't want to disclose it to another doctor."

***

"Mr. Ambassador," General Wilson was all smiles, "would you care for tea or something stronger?"

"Well, General, if you think we have grounds for a celebration, let's celebrate."

They toasted each other with glasses of whiskey.

"I apologize for bothering you on a Sunday, but I have the first detailed report from the Eight Army and I wanted to share it with you." Wilson pushed a stack of papers towards Mizrahi.

The report indicated that the British forces in North Africa were slowly moving west. The Eight Army command estimated arrival at the Tunisian border by the end of the next week. The Italians seemed to have collapsed and were surrendering in great numbers.

After Mizrahi finished reading the report, Wilson said: "We need to consider our next steps. The Prime Minister thought about the plan you presented to him at your last meeting. The truth is, he, and I, were skeptical about your, or rather our, ability to carry it out. Now, after our great victory in Egypt and Libya, I believe that we can defeat the Vichy French in Tunisia in short order and go on with the next stage of the plan."

"General, a great victory celebration may be somewhat premature. As far as we can tell the Germans are regrouping and stiffening their resistance. We estimate that it will take the Eight Army at least another couple of months to defeat the German/Italian forces. This is not as optimistic as your estimates, but I recommend that we err on the side of safety.

"I would also like to remind you that our original plan allowed for defeating the French only as a second choice. My government would prefer, as our plan stated, that we do our best to co-opt the French in North Africa. If they decide to abandon the Vichy government, we will at worst neutralize Morocco and Tunis and at best gain an ally. In any case you will not have to spend time and resources fighting and then occupying them.

"We are still conducting our rescue operations in Europe and it seems that the Germans are not aware of our participation in the operations in North Africa. We want to keep it that way as long as possible. This means that the Italian phase of our plan, to which you agreed, will become active only in several months – when we'll be done with evacuating our people. It also gives us ample time to negotiate with the French leadership in Morocco and Algeria. Tunisia is under their control and has no significant forces."

Wilson sipped on his drink and said nothing for several minutes. Since he couldn't out-silence Mizrahi he finally said, "Mr. Mizrahi, I know very well that the Prime Minister agreed to the general outlines of the plan you proposed. I have to admit that at the time the whole affair seemed of secondary importance to resolving the pressing problem in Egypt. Please don't misunderstand me – the plan makes sense.

"We are however extremely uneasy about a big and powerful French fleet sitting in Morocco. What if the Germans take control of the Vichy government and the French attack? We have to be ready for that. This threat is distracting the Royal Navy from other tasks."

"General, I am somewhat surprised," Mizrahi said. "We just demonstrated to you what we can do to our enemies. This applies to the French fleet as well. We will know within minutes if they leave port and an hour later they will be at the bottom of the Mediterranean. There is no need to antagonize them now. With your approval we propose the following course of action:

"In a month or two you send a squadron of Royal Navy to Oran where the Moroccan fleet is moored. Our representative will come with your squadron as a negotiator. Of course, he will officially be a ranking Royal Navy officer.

"We will ask the French to join us, the British, that is, in our fight against the Germans. By then it should be clear to the French that the Nazis and Italians have lost the fight in North Africa. The new situation should make them view this invitation favorably. We also have it on good authority that the French Admiral that commands the Moroccan fleet is leaning towards independence from Vichy and will not need much enticement to do so."

Wilson looked somewhat unhappy. "Mr. Ambassador, you are extracting your pound of flesh for your help. You propose a serious infringement of our independence in making strategic decisions. We are fully capable of negotiating with the French on our own."

Mizrahi got up from his seat and carefully placed his glass on the table. "General Wilson, I wish you would choose your words more carefully. Quoting Shakespeare doesn't make an anti-Semitic reference any more civil or palatable. I doubt that you would respond well to my quoting a number of popular sayings describing the stupidity of John Bull. I suggest that we meet again, maybe tomorrow or next week to discuss this matter. Have a good day."

Wilson was surprised and angry. Mizrahi's response to the common quote from "The Merchant of Venice" seemed excessive. Only after he said to himself, "These people are way too sensitive," did he admit that even he, who considered himself a friend of the Jews, thought of them as "these people". He would not apologize for what he said, but wouldn't repeat the mistake.

***

Jonathan Brown sat next to the President's bed. The blood filter was humming quietly. They were in the fifth day of treatment. He gave Roosevelt medication to improve heart function, which started draining some of the fluid in the President's lungs. This didn't do much to improve the chronic bronchitis that was bothering the man. Now he was on a course of the mildest penicillin-based antibiotic Jonathan could find in his suitcase. It worked like a charm – after two days of treatment Roosevelt was almost free of his cough and was breathing much easier. That was the main reason he agreed to the blood filtration. He almost dismissed Jonathan after the second day, but he felt so much better that it was easy to persuade him to continue the treatment. Another reason for keeping Jonathan was the simple fact that the Presidents regular physician was still under psychiatric observation, though he was about to be released. Roosevelt was also taking medication to suppress the proteins that caused the Guillain-Barré syndrome. The combination seemed to be working, though Jonathan wasn't sure how much the effects of the illness could be reversed after so many years.

Tomorrow would be the last day of the treatment and after that the two Israelis were planning on leaving for home.

The machine beeped and stopped. Jonathan disconnected the tubes, but left the needles in the President's veins for tomorrow's treatment:

"Mr. President, we are done for today. I will be here tomorrow for the last treatment and after that you will be free of the needles.

"How are you feeling?"

"Much better than a week ago, thank you. You did a splendid job."

"Sir, you will have to keep taking the two pills I prescribed. You should not skip even one day – the result may be a complete backslide in your health.

"I will leave a six month's supply and Dr. Burton will supervise you after I go back home.

"Dr. Brown, we didn't really discuss the prognosis of me ever walking again. When do you think I'll be able to get up from this wheelchair?"

Jonathan considered his answer carefully. "I can make no definite promises. You told me yesterday that you no longer have pain when trying to move in your seat. That's a very good sign, but it will take a while to determine how much of the damage done by the disease can be reversed. I believe that you will be able to walk. Probably with a cane and not long distances. You will also require an extensive physical therapy regimen to get to that point.

"One thing I can promise you, Mr. President: if we can't help you, nobody can."

Roosevelt was, with Jonathan's help, transferring from his bed to the wheelchair. "Yes, I realize that inexplicably you Palestinians have developed medical science that even we don't have. I appreciate that your leadership saw fit to offer it to me."

"Ah," Jonathan smiled, "they are politicians, Mr. Presidents, and will expect a quid pro quo. We helped you and, hopefully, you will help us."

"Yes, yes, you said that before. Sorry we didn't discuss it earlier, but I was a bit busy. As you may know, there is a lot of stuff going on in Europe and North Africa.

"In any case, I don't see how I can help. It is not like the President of the U.S. controls the country, or Congress, for that matter."

"Sir, I am only a doctor. These issues have to be discussed with our leadership. My understanding is that they demonstrated their goodwill with the hope that you'll be sympathetic to us when the time comes."

"They definitely have achieved that," Roosevelt smiled. "If somebody asked me a week ago about the situation in Palestine I would have to ask: 'Where's that?' Not anymore."

Jonathan smiled. "Mr. President I know for a fact that you know where Palestine is. Would you be amenable to accepting an emissary from our leadership? This emissary would be able to discuss in more detail what can be done for our mutual benefit."

Roosevelt became serious. "Doctor Brown, this is diplomacy and I will have to defer to the opinion of the State Department and also get the approval of the British Government. After all, Palestine is part of their Mandate. We couldn't receive an official representative of a British colony. Could we?"

"We are not a colony," Jonathan bristled, "Palestine is, like you said, a Mandate which the British are holding on behalf of the League of Nations. But Mr. President, I will let you rest. I'm not a diplomat and won't make the mistake of bothering you with stuff that is outside my area of expertise."

***

Major Ibrahim al Taibeh surprised the Grand Mufti by arriving at his hotel room in Bucharest. His faithful bodyguards were expected to escort and announce every visitor and admit only those who arranged for an audience. Apparently they were so intimidated by the personal emissary of the mighty Caliph that they forgot their duty.

"What a pleasant surprise, Major. How is my cousin, may Allah the merciful smile on him forever?"

"Sir, your cousin is fine and sends his best regards. He sent me here on an urgent mission. As you know, in our time-line Germany lost the war. We thought it was only because of the Jews and so we took care of them. But when we traveled into the future we discovered that the war was still lost, though it took much longer. Look at this."

The Major handed the Mufti three yellowed, old newspaper pages. The date on the first, from the Volkisher Beobachter, was December 11, 1941. There was a big headline - "Germany Declares War on the U.S." - followed by the text of a speech by Hitler. The second page was dated May 7, 1945, and was from a major paper in Frankfurt. The headline said: "Germany Surrenders to the Allies – Herman Göring surrenders to General Eisenhower." The article went on to explain that it was the

American involvement that caused German defeat, which would not have happened except for Hitler's mistake in December of 1941. The third was from the Braunschweiger Tageszeitung and had the same article as the Frankfurt paper.

"I see," the Mufti said after reading both pages carefully. "I can guess what the Caliph needs me to do, but I am not sure Herr Hitler will listen to me."

Moshe shrugged: "There is only so much you can do. I do believe that he will need only a small push in the right direction. Yours may be the decisive argument. The Caliph authorizes you to tell the Fuehrer that you have seen secret information that declaring war on the U.S. will cause great damage to the German war effort. You can tell him that you were shown documents but are not at liberty to discuss them.

"Please also mention to Herr Hitler that he should weigh carefully the benefits of such a declaration against the drawbacks. The Caliph asked me to tell you that you know Hitler better than any of us. Use your knowledge to persuade him but be careful not to antagonize. The Fuehrer should not perceive that you are questioning his judgment. But you know him best and the Caliph trusts you to do the right thing."

Chapter 26

The Leviathan, a Dolphin class submarine, was on its way from the port of Eilat to a classified destination. It left on November 19, 1941. The submarine had been modified: a powerful shortwave radio transmitter was installed in one of its cruise missile silos. The antenna could be extended when the submarine was submerged, so that only a tall, thin structure was above water.

The sub was cruising mostly submerged, using its snorkels to provide air to the crew and its diesel engines. Several radars mounted on top of the snorkels warned when surface vessels and aircraft approached. At those times it dived, so as not to be seen. There was plenty of time to reach its destination cruising at 8 knots, the most economical speed. Since its normal range was about 4500 miles, and the target was about 8000 miles away, a converted cargo ship would serve as a refueling tanker. That ship flew a Swedish flag, relying on the appearance of neutrality to protect it from attack. It was armed with ship-to-ship and anti-aircraft missiles as well as several sets of automatic 40mm cannon concealed in its superstructure, in case the ruse didn't work. They planned to rendezvous at a point northeast of the Christmas Islands, southwest of the coast of Java.

On its arrival in the Philippines the Leviathan came close to the west coast of Luzon, about six miles south of the village of Real. Three men left the submarine in an inflatable boat, which returned to the sub after letting two of them off on shore. They were dressed as U.S. Army sergeants and carried appropriate documents. With their Midwestern American accents, nothing identified them as members of the 13th flotilla of the Israeli navy – its commando unit.

It took the two men almost three days to get to Manila. They rode good facsimiles of standard issue U.S. Army bicycles, which they had brought with them from Israel. The distance from their landing point to their objective was only about 60 miles as the crow flies, but they had to cross rugged terrain using country roads. The two arrived at Nielson Field in Makati City on December 4, 1941.

Their first objective was the base's telephone exchange. It was an old installation, with a manual switchboard tended round the clock by several operators but not guarded. The two commandos infiltrated the base by cutting an opening through the fence on the far side of the airfield, where bushes on both sides made them invisible from the base.

They waited for darkness, and when the lights on the perimeter came on they moved towards the exchange. The commandos walked openly, pretending to belong on the base. They were stopped by a sentry at one of the hangars they passed and released after a perfunctory examination of their papers.

After arriving at the back of the telephone exchange they did what they had trained to do: dug a small hole next to the building wall and inserted a metal box. They connected the wires from the box, one each, to the ten telephone lines entering the building, then covered the box with dirt. The ground was damp and the freshly dug out earth blended in. Any evidence of digging would be completely gone after the first rain, expected that same night. The wires were very thin and easily concealed in cracks between wall boards. After they were done, only a very close examination would reveal their handiwork.

The two did a similar job by the back wall of the base's operations building. This building contained a teletype by which orders were transmitted from headquarters in Manila, less than 10 miles away. It took the two almost half an hour to locate the wires that ran to the teletype, but with the detailed schematics they carried in their heads and a good knowledge of electronics it was finally done.

The two boxes they connected and concealed were similar in design. They contained fairly old technology, miniaturized by the use of computer chips, but otherwise known and used in the 1950s. Each box was capable of intercepting a telephone or teletype call and redirecting it to a miniature radio transmitter powered by the telephone line. It could also do the reverse: initiate a telephone call or a teletype message using the built in radio receiver.

***

On December 8, 1941, at 3:15 a.m. Philippines' time, General Lewis H. Brereton, American Commander of the Far East Air Force, was awakened to take an urgent phone call from General Sutherland, General McArthur's chief of staff.

"General Brereton, I just received word that we are at war with Japan. They've already attacked Pearl Harbor and we expect an imminent attack here. I have new orders for you. You will arm your bomber force as quickly as possible and immediately attack the Japanese airfields in Formosa. Use every bomber at your disposal, not just the B17s. You are also ordered to have all available fighters strafe the airfields immediately after the bombs are dropped. You are ordered to perform as many bombing runs as necessary to destroy your targets. I will confirm this order by teletype. Any questions?"

"No, sir."

Teletype confirmation arrived before Brereton was done giving his orders. The general was elated. He had planned this attack since arriving in the Philippines. He was curious what changed McArthur's mind, but as far as he was concerned, this was a gift horse whose mouth he was not going to examine too closely.

***

The captain of the Leviathan listened in on the conversation between the Mossad agent and General Brereton. "Amazing what you can do with a couple of simple gadgets and some acting. I'm really impressed."

"What do you mean by 'some acting'? It takes talent to be able to impersonate somebody just on the basis of a couple of short telephone conversations. I don't think Brereton had any doubt he was speaking to Sutherland."

"I agree he was convinced, though whether it was your perfect performance or the fact that he wanted to do what you told him to do is a different question," joked the Captain, "I hope this is all the intervention we have to do."

The Leviathan was on its way towards Formosa. Their mission was to monitor the American attack from 200 miles south of the island. If need be, the submarine could intervene to insure enough damage was done, but only if absolutely necessary.

***

General Masaharu Homma, Commanding General of the Japanese 14th Army, was worried. It was early morning and Lieutenant General Hideyoshi Obata had just radioed him from Formosa. His 500 aircraft, both bombers and fighters, were fueled up, armed and ready to take off for Luzon. There was heavy fog which, if it did not disperse soon, would delay the planned air attack. Obata was worried that the Americans would hear about Pearl Harbor and attack Formosa, catching his planes in the worst possible position. Homma told him to just wait. The die was cast and there was not much they could do now.

Homma's worst nightmare came true. General Obata reported that hundreds of U.S. planes were attacking the airfields. They were bombing and strafing. It was a massacre.

The first wave of the American attack was over in about twenty minutes. The Japanese general could see from his command dugout that the situation on this airfield was desperate: planes were burning everywhere, ammunition and bombs exploding. A stray bomb, or maybe it was aimed, who could know, hit a large aviation fuel tank behind the hangars. It was burning merrily, sending smoke and flames high into the morning air. When the second wave of attackers came fifteen minutes later, General Obata jumped out of his reinforced command post and ran to where the action was. He died a hero.

General Homma knew that he would have to be extremely lucky to conquer the Philippines without air superiority. With complete American control of the air, it was unlikely that his forces would survive the first hours of an invasion, even if their transports were not sunk by U.S. aircraft. He radioed the High Command for instructions.

***

"General Wilson, I appreciate you receiving me on such short notice. " Mizrahi sat in the chair Wilson offered him.

"My government thinks that it is time for me to present my credentials to the King. If you see no problem, I would like to do it next week. We would also like to increase our staff and post our own guard in front of our embassy."

"Why wait a week?"

"We need to make some arrangements, including establishing informal contact with the U.S. and the Soviet Union. Can I count on the Prime Minister's introduction to both of them?"

"What do you have in mind?" asked Wilson.

"Maybe he could invite me, the U.S. Ambassador and the Soviet Ambassador, separately, to very private cocktail parties, or a more formal personal introduction. I will accept his judgment on how to do it."

"I suppose he will be agreeable," responded Wilson, "although, as you know, the Soviets are difficult to deal with. In any case, I will present the request to him later today.

"Since you are here, I would like to discuss a number of issues. First let me apologize for the incident at our last meeting. You must understand that I am not an anti-Semite. Some statements are part of the culture and not intended to offend, but I should have shown more sensitivity."

"General, I have to apologize as well. I was a little impatient. I hope we can put this incident behind us."

"Good," Wilson smiled. "I'm glad we're over this unfortunate incident.

"I discussed your proposal regarding French North Africa with the Prime Minster. It's not really an infringement of our strategic sovereignty. Or rather it is, but we are allies and I realize that without your recent help we would have been in a very difficult situation with Rommel. We still have misgivings about negotiating with the French, but we will take the chance and let your officer conduct the negotiations. I hope he will be successful.

"Now, regarding Italy, your proposal is very interesting. If we could knock them out of the Axis it would, at the least, give us a toehold on the Continent. There are risks, especially if the Germans get wind of our activities. They may invade, at Mussolini's 'request' of course, and attack your Brindisi base."

Mizrahi smiled a wolfish smile. "I have no doubt that very soon after we establish formal relations with allied and neutral countries or, more likely, as soon as I present my credentials to the King, the Germans will attack. They may have a nasty surprise. The question is where will the surprise happen and how do we cooperate to make it real nasty."

General Wilson thought for a moment. "Yes, I agree. After your performance against them in North Africa... But this may be different. They will, undoubtedly, devote all the available forces. Italy is close to home. Hitler can't ignore the danger. On the other hand Germany is committed in the East. There is a possibility that if Italy remains non-aggressive he will refrain from interfering."

"Sir, I suggest that we leave the details to our respective military experts. Let me assure you that we will do our best to defeat the Nazis, but it has to be a cooperative effort."

Wilson nodded. "Very well. I agree that we have to establish a joint planning committee.

"The other issue I would like your government to consider is the problems we and the Americans are having with the Japanese. I don't have a clear understanding of your abilities, but it is clear to me that the position in the Far East is precarious. In addition, the American's predicament reflects on their ability to support us through lend-lease. They have already warned us that their first priority will be Japan, since they are not at war with Germany."

"General, I will convey your concerns to my government. In my personal opinion the Soviets are in much greater need of U.S. help. I sincerely hope that President Roosevelt does not cut down on assistance to them. They are on the verge of folding and need only a little push to do so. Hopefully Roosevelt will not push.

"As to the situation in the Far East: In our opinion Japan's attempt to conquer Singapore and some of the other British possessions will fail if you take some necessary steps. Right now, it may be a good idea to transfer more RAF forces to the Far East. A change of command in

Singapore may also be beneficial. It needs a much more aggressive defense. I am saying this based on our history. This is not a guarantee of success but will help enormously.

"With the U.S. controlling the Philippines, the Japanese navy will have problems reinforcing and supplying the troops they have already deployed. You may lose Malaya, but there is not much you can do about it.

"Don't worry too much about the loss of lend-lease assistance. We want the war in Europe to go well, and will assist you against the Germans. I hope that by the end of next week you will be in much better spirits."

Chapter 27

Wolf Frumin was interested in the lecture, or, more precisely, in the lecturer. The Second Lieutenant was maybe twenty years old, and to Wolf she looked beautiful. Maybe not as beautiful as Sheina but still pleasant to look at. He had trouble concentrating on what she was saying. She was pointing with a laser at details on an aerial photograph being projected on the wall:

"Here you can see very clearly the devastation a well-organized attack by a modern air force can cause a ground force, especially one without any air cover.

"But look at this slide," she said as a new slide popped up. "This is the same area two days later. You see the British involved in a shootout with a German unit. Compare this to the previous slide. The Germans have dug in and reinforced their position. There is a very important lesson here: it is impossible to defeat an enemy from the air. The air force may be of tremendous importance, but without infantry and armor there is no victory.

"It will be you…"

Wolf's attention wandered. This was his last day before graduating from the Armor School. He went from a somewhat rebellious eighteen year old with a good education, at least for 1941 Belarus, to a disciplined, though still somewhat argumentative, tank commander – all in six months of intensive training.

It wasn't easy. The first serious battle was with his parents. They refused to sign the necessary forms to allow him to serve in a combat unit. He wasn't a single child but his only sister was lost somewhere in Russia, maybe dead. As far as Israel was concerned Wolf had no siblings and so needed his parents' permission to serve in a combat unit.

Wolf was "rescued" by a neighbor. He was also 18 and planned on enlisting with Wolf. When Wolf told him about his problem, the friend had a suggestion. "Take your parents to the family event the Army is having two weeks before we are due to enlist. They'll show you and your parents what options you have, the equipment you will operate and explain about the career you may expect."

At the event both of Wolf's parents were impressed by the tanks. They saw Wolf's enthusiasm, the large numbers of young people serving in combat units, and were introduced to other parents in the same predicament. They also realized that their son would not be a clerk. He was stubborn and if denied service in a combat unit would ask to be assigned to an armor engineering depot. They asked for clarifications and a young officer explained that Wolf's request would likely be honored, assuming he didn't fail his training. Serving at a depot sounded safe, but Wolf's father had his doubts. He asked for an explanation and was told that the depot wasn't really a depot. It was a mobile engineering unit servicing and repairing armored vehicles in the field. Not at the front line but certainly not very far behind. After this explanation Nachman Frumin figured that tanks looked relatively safe. It was all in G-d's hands anyway. They signed the consent papers.

***

Ze'ev, Linda and Sheina Hirshson picked up the Frumins at eight in the morning. Ze'ev was glad that his Toyota had three rows of seats. Nachman's brothers and their wives also wanted to come. They didn't have space in the car for all the cousins. They had to take a bus to the graduation ceremony held at the Latrun Armor Corps facility, next to the Jerusalem road.

The speeches took at least two hours, after which the graduates of the latest Armor School course were called one by one to the podium to have their new specialist pins and unit insignia attached.

In the early afternoon, after the ceremony was finished, Wolf found his family. Tzila was crying and Nachman looked very proud of his son. Sheina was just smiling, which made Wolf lose a bit of his proud stance and smile back.

The new corporal looked good in his sharply-pressed uniform and black beret. Having fought in the First World War Nachman hoped that his son would never see action, but he was also reassured that if he did have to fight, it would be side by side with other Jews for a good cause.

Wolf had the whole week off and returned home with his parents. He planned on visiting with Sheina in Beer Sheba. She would be the first to know of his plan to apply for officers' school as soon as regulations allowed. He also had plans to apply to college and wanted her opinion on all these complicated designs for his future.

***

Ze'ev and Linda came home late in the evening after the Frumins' party for Wolf. On the way home Ze'ev was thoughtful.

"What's bothering you?" Linda asked after a long while of silence.

"Nothing really."

"Yeah, sure. I know you. What is it?"

"I don't know whether I can tell you. We still do a lot of work on the Merkava tank project and I get to know some classified stuff."

"Yes. So?"

"Well, it's classified."

"And since when did that stop you from telling your wife?"

"Okay. You don't tell anybody though."

Linda nodded, "Did I ever?"

Ze'ev hesitated. "I think that the government is preparing for a big ground battle. I'm not sure where, but from what I hear it's going to be overseas."

"Ephraim is there." Linda sounded unhappy.

"I wouldn't worry too much about him. Generals don't usually fight on the front lines. I'm more worried about Wolf. He was very proud to be assigned to the 7th Armor Brigade. You know their combat traditions."

Linda looked uncertain.

"This is the brigade that did most of the bloody work at the Chinese Farm during the Yom Kippur war. My friend Dan was a platoon commander there – didn't survive the battle."

"Well, they're not going into such a bloody experience any time soon." Linda responded.

"I'm not so sure. The 7th is going to be shipped to Italy in a couple of weeks and not by itself either. Something is brewing there. Makes sense after the job we have done on the Germans in North Africa."

***

The next day Ze'ev was in his Tel-Aviv office. He called Consolidated Research and Development V.P. Omer Toledano.

"I have been to my uncle's graduation ceremony. He is now a tank commander in the 7th." Ze'ev smiled. "It still sounds strange. Anyway, the young man is almost 19 and is going to command the latest model Merkava, which made me think.

"These tanks are powered by a turbine. Why not use similar technology to power your electric car?"

Omer was smiling. "I'm glad you mentioned it. As it happens we came up with a similar idea. Let me give you an orderly update, if you have the time of course. "

"Go ahead, but be brief," Ze'ev chuckled. "I have to leave in about three hours."

"I'll be as concise as possible." Omer got himself a cup of coffee, talking as he did. "First, we hired a number of engineers and a scientist. All newcomers. It's really amazing what these people know. We have several engineers that used to work for Opel, a couple that worked for Daimler and three guys that worked for Citroen. Obviously as soon as the Nazis took control they were dismissed.

"Did you know that both Citroen and Daimler are currently working on turbines? Only as compressors for their regular engines, but these guys have real experience.

"Anyway, we are working on a hybrid of sorts. Use the turbine directly on highways and whenever the slight acceleration lag is not important, and use it to charge a battery in city driving."

"Ah, sounds like a good idea. Keep me up to date on how it's going." Ze'ev took a sip of his coffee. "What was it you said about a scientist?"

"Well, we started funding Arye Kidron's research into this Zero Point Energy thing. I thought that it might be a good idea to have a physicist on staff who knows something about quantum mechanics, so I looked for one. None of the 'modern' ones would consider our offer, but I found a Nobel laureate that would."

"A Nobel laureate? Who are you talking about?"

"Chief, did you hear of Lisa Meisner? She was a department head at the Kaiser Wilhelm Institute. In 1934 her co-researcher received the Nobel Prize in physics for research in radioactivity and its implications on quantum mechanics. She was refused the prize, probably because of being a woman. She did stuff that's really cool that I really don't understand.

"She worked at the Institute until 1938 – being an Austrian protected her from the Nazis, even though all the other Jews were fired or deported, including her colleague Leo Shiller of notable fame. In 1938, after the Anshluss, being Austrian made no difference so she was fired and deported.

"She is our liaison to the Technion ZPE project. Arye admits that she is helping him a lot."

Ze'ev smiled: "So should we expect a magical energy source next month?"

Omer was serious. "I honestly don't know. They are both very optimistic, but Arye always is and I think that Lisa caught the bug from him. I seriously doubt that we'll have a ZPE power source next month. In the meantime they are talking about channeling energy from another universe. This, they claim, is much simpler than a ZPE. It's all Greek to me, but I am doing my best. Hopefully I'll be able to give you a more meaningful report in a couple of weeks."

***

Amos Nir checked his schedule. The Cabinet meeting would begin in an hour. It left him just enough time for his discussion with the Defense Minister and the Chief of General Staff.

"Nitzan, Gad," the Prime Minister settled in his chair, "we need to discuss several things before the Cabinet meeting. I just want to gain a better understanding of the issues.

"First I need an update on the North African situation."

The Defense Minister smiled. "The Germans are indeed in a 'situation'. We are giving the Brits all the information they need to intercept transports going to Rommel. The guy is getting no reinforcements, no fuel and no food.

"Left to their own devices the Royal Navy and Air Force would have missed about 40% or more of the tonnage. They do intercept German communications and decode them with Ultra. Their problem is time: sometimes low priority messages take up to a week to decipher. By then the ship may already be unloading in North Africa. The other difficulty is weather. Even if they know when and from where a ship is leaving it may be impossible for their navy or air force to spot it if the weather doesn't cooperate. The Mediterranean can be treacherous in January and that helps the Germans.

"We have no problems pinpointing the ships for them. The result: zero supplies for Rommel."

"By now he should be starving and out of ammunition," Amos remarked, "so why aren't the Brits on the Tunisian border yet?"

"I have to admit that we all underestimated the German Army," Said Gad Yaari. "They keep fighting against unreasonable odds. The soldiers are well trained and well led. I can't see them surrendering without an explicit order to do so or an extreme situation, like Stalingrad. I also can't see Rommel giving such an order without Hitler's approval.

"The British are advancing at a good pace but it's very far from a German rout. There are no deserters and they are fighting hard."

"You have an estimate of when it will end?"

Yaari looked at Liebler. Obviously the Chief of General Staff and the Defense Minister were not in agreement.

"I think that the Germans will have no choice but surrender way before the Brits chase them to the Tunisian border. By the way, the Italians have no problems abandoning their allies and giving up." The Defense Minister looked at the Chief of general Staff. "Gad thinks otherwise. If I'm right we can expect the Afrika Corps to surrender in less than a month."

"Like Nitzan said, I don't agree. A month is way too optimistic. In my opinion the Germans will go on fighting as long as they have ammo. It will take at least three or four months. Maybe longer.

"If Operation Victor starts before they surrender it will take even longer. The plans the British presented to us call for elements of the Eight Army to be transferred to Italy. This will slow the progress in North Africa."

Nitzan Liebler was shaking his head in disagreement.

Amos asked his next question. "Do we have a coherent operational plan for Victor?"

Liebler replied, "Yes, but we're reworking it thoroughly. I agree with Gad that the Germans demonstrated exceptional fighting abilities. It's one thing to read about it in history books and an entirely different experience seeing their performance live, so to speak.

"Assuming that our soldiers are as good as the Germans, which I think they are, we decided that our modern weapons give us a force multiplier of ten. One of our divisions is worth ten of the German's. This is a bit crude but enough for a general idea. Our computer modeling is much more accurate. For example, we have a much higher advantage in the air and at night.

"We do have a serious weakness, or rather two. The first one is our low tolerance for casualties. If our casualties are a tenth of the German's we'll be in trouble. The other weakness is inherent in the structure of our forces. The IDF is an armed force that really sees offense as the best defense. If we have to defend fixed positions, like the original British plan required, we will have a high attrition rate. This is unacceptable."

Gad Yaari took over: "We are now preparing several versions of Operation Victor. Which one will actually be implemented depends on who the players are.

"In any case we both agree that the forces originally designated for this operation are inadequate. They would do to defend the Brindisi base but have to be at least tripled for this operation to be an unqualified success. Overwhelming force will also reduce our casualties."

Amos nodded: "Okay. That settles some of the issues. I have a more basic question: how long can we sustain a major effort like this?"

"It depends," answered Nitzan and Gad together.

Amos smiled, "It always does. What does this depend on?"

"We're not quite sure what the Germans will throw at us and how intense the fighting will be." Nitzan responded. "We can make assumptions. They will likely attack from two directions. One force will attack from France the other from Austria…"

The discussion went on for a while, until the start of the Cabinet meeting.

Israel was clearly preparing for the largest and longest war in its history. A war against a mortal, uncompromising enemy. An enemy that proved in the past its relentless hatred and did it's very best to exterminate the Jewish people.

There were no doubts in the hearts of the leadership that this struggle has to be joined. The people supported this decision, though, like always in a democracy, there were a number of opposing opinions.

End of Book 1

Made in the USA
Middletown, DE
23 April 2015